Nancy

OUT OF FOCUS

Susan Squire Smith

Do More Pottery

Susan

Susan Squire Smith

Contents

Dedication

To my husband Terry Smith
for all his years of love and support.
You have my heart.

Chapter 1

By Sunday afternoon she knew he was gone.

At first, the hours Anna spent searching for Anton had flown by in a frenzied haze.

Frantic hours were wasted trying to trace his every move, trying to ignore the obvious. Crazy, manic hours were totally consumed in a valiant struggle to protect her heart from certain anguish. In the end however, time slowed and reality could no longer be avoided. The man she loved had suddenly vanished.

Anna had always understood that the world in which he lived was precarious at the best of times, dangerous always. Those with whom he was expected to interact could turn on him at any moment, with disastrous consequences. And though she thought she had come to terms with it, now, she realized she had not. There was no escaping the fact that, as far as she could determine, Anton had simply ceased to exist.

"No," she said forcefully. "Think," she breathed quietly. "You must figure this out."

Much later, after making numerous phone calls came the painful realization that neither his friends nor his colleagues would even acknowledge his absence. It was as if he had casually gone off somewhere and could be expected to reappear at any moment, like nothing unusual had occurred at all. Did they really believe that would happen? No, she finally admitted, they were hiding something.

With no other alternative available she began to rationalize, thinking that perhaps those who knew him best honestly didn't comprehend the situation. That perhaps professing ignorance was their only sanctuary. Or that perhaps because she loved him, she actually was the only one who fully understood the significance of his disappearance.

But did she really understand the situation? Impossible to know. Would she ever? Again, it was impossible to know. She would keep searching.

...Their last Friday together had begun in blistering heat and by one o'clock Saturday morning Cairo remained mired in the grips of hot, dry weather that originated in the endless desert sands to the west.

To compensate for unseasonably warm temperatures most of Ian Stanley's guests had dressed in evening clothes usually reserved for mid-summer occasions. As a result, the spacious chandeliered hallway appeared a sea of white linen dinner jackets sprinkled with an eclectic array of colorful floating silks, chiffons and the sparkle of sequins. On mirror bright silver trays, pale champagne and beautiful, tasty canapés were presented to the guests by an impeccably trained wait staff. Somewhere a chamber orchestra was playing Chopin. Soft strains of their music drifted throughout the rooms.

As usual, the party at the home of the American ambassador showed no signs of coming to an end. It seemed the evening would probably turn into another one of Ian Stanley's famous dusk to dawn affairs.

Anton Kasarov did not arrive until well after midnight, as the party was just getting into full swing. If anyone had bothered to notice, as he wandered unobtrusively through the crowd, they would have seen that the normally unflappable Russian diplomat was visibly upset. His bright blue eyes appeared almost grey under furrowed blond eyebrows. Tall and broad, the handsome Russian stood out in most crowds, but tonight he tried unsuccessfully to remain invisible.

Though he usually found gatherings at the Stanleys' very entertaining, this evening was an exception. He did not want to be here. Tonight's appearance was strictly one of protocol and after having been at the party for almost an hour, Anton was anxious to leave.

It didn't require his diplomatic training, merely instinct, to realize that the persistent tension plaguing him for most of the day had finally managed to tighten every muscle. It showed clearly on his face, in his walk and in the tone of his voice. He felt, in the midst of this spacious opulence, claustrophobic, and longed to return to the freedom of the three small rooms he had, for more than a year, called home. He longed to return to Anna.

For after an unexpected afternoon 'command performance' with Soviet Ambassador Rolenko, he realized his life, their lives together, was about to change. And later after meeting Anna for cocktails and spending the remainder of their day together everything had changed yet again.

Anna DuLac, a French reporter for the International Herald Tribune and Anton Kasarov, Soviet diplomat, had been lovers for almost one year. So, when he called her and suggested they meet for cocktails, she heard the strain in his voice and knew something was up.

Anton arrived early at the Lobby Bar in the Penta Hotel and

was quickly seated. He and Anna often met at the Penta. They both cherished the rare moments when they were able to sit back with a cool drink at their favorite table, in their favorite hotel and for a short time lose their thoughts in the breathtaking view of Cairo at sunset. The distant view of pyramids bathed in an orange glow was not the only reminder that they were both far from home. All around were the sights and sounds even the pungent aromas of vastly different cultures. Through expansive windows they could see busy people on the street below in all manners of dress. And around them in the modern lobby could be heard languages from every part of the world.

As he sipped a glass of the only liquor available, local vodka that would never replace even the least refined Russian distillation, and waited, Anton contemplated the events of the afternoon. Momentarily unable to decide just how much he should disclose to Anna he was comforted by the fact that he had, at least, chosen correctly, to meet her here. He hoped the familiar surroundings might somehow make it easier for him to explain what Rolenko had ordered.

Easier for him, yes, easier for her, probably not. He only knew he wanted to discuss this with her in a place that had filled them both with joyful memories.

"Hello love. Carrying the weight of the world I see."

Anton looked up with a start, surprised to see Anna standing next to his chair.

As usual he was even more enchanted than he had been when they first met. With her petite frame and short dark hair she reminded him of a pixie, a fierce pixie with pale ivory skin and, determined dark eyes. A small scar running through her left eyebrow had been obtained on an assignment and was evidence of just how fierce she could be.

He loved that scar.

"Anna?" He rose and kissed her lightly on the cheek. "Just lost in thought."

For a fleeting moment a slight frown crossed her face. Then, trying her best to cheer him with her genuinely joyful disposition she dropped down into the seat beside him.

"The usual?" he asked.

After the waiter brought her a tall glass of club soda with a generous slice of lime on the side, Anna sat back and took a second look at the man she had tried so hard not to love. There was something about his eyes that triggered concern. A dark cloud shadowed his handsome Arian/Slavic face. Instinctively she reached across the small table and brushed a strand of thick blond hair out of his intense blue eyes.

"Well, are you going to tell me what this mysterious meeting is all about? Remember, I am a very good reporter and I'll know if you are being less than honest with me," Anna teased, in an unsuccessful attempt to lighten his somber mood.

Usually her clever wit and easy manner could be counted on to lift his spirits, but this afternoon he was unable to give himself over to casual conversation.

He knew Anna was perceptive enough to realize that he had something extremely important to discuss.

"All right mon aime," she said, more softly this time. "I'm listening."

He looked at her, hesitated, and finally spoke. "I met with Rolenko this afternoon," he said. "I am being recalled to Moscow … Immediately."

Anna's eyes widened with surprise. They always knew that reassignment could happen at any time, but after a year with no changes they had mistakenly begun to think of his position in Cairo as permanent.

"Why?" she asked, suddenly anxious, the increased pitch of her voice betrayed her true emotions. "Did they give you a reason? I thought you were still involved in oil lease negotiations. I mean," She stammered, "You are needed here. Damn!" Her cheeks flushed, a sure betrayal of her intense concern. She reached across the table and took a large swallow from Anton's glass. The clear liquid burned, she had forgotten to follow it with her soda. Still, it had the desired slightly numbing effect "Now," she resumed. "Tell me."

Suddenly, deciding that it was probably not a good idea to continue the discussion in public, Anton reached for her hand. "Come on, let's get out of here." At well over six feet, when he stood he was an imposing figure and when he took her hand all she could do was follow.

He paid the check, leaving an unusually generous tip. Without bothering to finish their drinks they left.

Once outside Anna suggested a walk. The warm evening air would do them both good. Ignoring the numerous cabs that waited expectantly outside the hotel, they turned down the street and headed toward Anton's apartment. Crowds on the street almost engulfed them, but the hubbub of traffic noise and pedestrians provided them anonymity.

"Anton," Anna asked, much calmer, now that she had had time to absorb the shock. "What reason did they give you for the move?"

He put his arm around her and as they walked with her head resting against his shoulder he told her as much as he thought he could.

"I can't give you all the answers, I can only tell you that the tumultuous changes occurring in Europe, and in my country recently, make it necessary for me to leave. The entire Soviet nation seems on the verge of coming apart. The old line is divided. Gorbachev appears to be losing his grip and those who remain loyal to him are also becoming nervous. They are gathering reinforcements and calling many of us who support Gorbachev and the new order home to Moscow. I think they need to assess their position, determine their strengths…and their weaknesses. If the Soviet Union is to move forward those of us who support the changes must do what we can to make certain that those changes have a chance to work."

Anna understood it all too well. Her own paper had been filled with accounts of the internal problems of the Soviet Union which were being exacerbated by the demands of the American President. She had prayed that here in Cairo they would not be touched by the strife occurring thousands of miles away. Unfortunately the globe had become far too small for distance to be any kind of protection.

Anton continued, "Anna, I must leave immediately. Arrangements have been made for Monday."

Anna flinched, "Anton, No! Monday! Must you leave that soon?" She clung more tightly to him.

"Yes, my love, that soon," he said with a sigh. And Anna this is vital. No one must know that I am returning to Moscow. There are many at home desperate to preserve the old ways. They would go to any lengths to see the country remain as it has for the last forty years.

"Are you speaking of conspiracy?" Anna was stunned.

"I don't know. I hope not, but Rolenko believes we should be prepared for anything. And I must do what I can to help provide a period of stability while the new government strengthens its position. Only Ambassador Rolenko and I know that I am leaving. And now, of course, you. But, Anna," he spoke now almost in a whisper, "if the ambassador suspected that I am discussing my plans with you it would mean my job…or worse. Do you understand?" His throat constricted and his voice deepened as he emphasized the need for complete secrecy. "Do you really understand?"

"Of course I understand," she said softly. "Part of the job description, right?" She tried very hard to make a small joke, but her heart was breaking and she could hardly hold back the tears.

"Anton. Monday only gives us a couple of days together. I don't think I can stand the thought of never seeing you again."

"Never seeing me again?" He was stunned. Had she actually believed...... "Do you think I could let that happen? Anna, listen to me. I love you." The strength with which he said those three words surprised even him. He took her gently but firmly by the shoulders and looked directly into her wide dark eyes. "I love you," he repeated softly.

The only response Anna was capable of at that moment was her own nonverbal declaration of love. Oblivious to her surroundings she put her arms around his chest and squeezed. Suddenly aware of the stares of passing pedestrians she became quite embarrassed, and with flushed cheeks smiled and pulled back.

"Have you thought about what we should do?" she said trying to regain her composure.

Anton contemplated teasing her about her red face, but under the circumstances, thought better of it. Perhaps it is something they would find themselves laughing about in the future. The future, he thought, yes he definitely believed they had a future. He would see to it.

But for now all he said was, "I honestly can't believe that I will be in Moscow for more than a year, maybe even as little as six months. After that, who knows? I may have to find another occupation." It was his attempt at a little humor.

As they continued down the narrow winding streets Anton could feel Anna relax slightly.

"You mean that Moscow is not permanent."

"I doubt it very much, but there may be another problem."

"What could be worse than this?" she asked.

"I don't know what will happen in the next few months, but if Gorbachev loses power those of us who stand with him may no longer be welcomed. At the very least I would probably be without a position...as the Americans put it I would be 'canned'. A capitalistic idea of which I am not particularly fond," he smiled at the irony of it.

Anna found she was actually able to laugh.

"And," Anton continued, "I am hoping that you will still want to be with me when I am finally able to live a normal life again. And...," he added, "If you will wait for me while I am away. Anna," he said very seriously, "What I am really asking is......will you marry me? When this business in Moscow is over...Will you be my wife?"

When he looked at Anna he could see despair had given way to a small smile.

"Anton! Of course I will marry you."

They looked into each other's eyes with deepening love and suddenly realized the enormity of what had just occurred. In the midst of a busy Cairo street they had reshaped their lives and committed themselves to each other forever. A year of separation was going to be hard, no, next to impossible. But at least their lives weren't ending, just being put on hold for a while.

Walking hand in hand they finally arrived at a small, familiar, old world, style apartment building. As they strolled over soft old red patterned carpet through the lobby and up the black, wrought iron staircase toward Anton's apartment their emotions ran high. They knew that their time together was short, that they had to make the best of the few remaining hours. A sense of urgency gripped them both. They knew what they wanted........what they needed.

The door to Anton's flat had barely closed when he swept Anna into his arms and carried her across the floor.

Anna's passion grew uncontrollably and she had the buttons on Anton's shirt completely undone before reaching the bed. Her hands traveled lightly over his smooth chest as she quickly tore off his shirt.

Laying her gently on the blue cotton bedspread Anton skillfully removed Anna's blouse. He cupped her breasts in his large gentle hands and kissed her tenderly on the neck. He then rose and removed his clothing.

Neither Anton nor Anna had ever experienced making love like this. Their need to be one consumed them. Only the pressure of the other's body could keep them each from falling into a million pieces. It was over-whelming. They were trying in one night to fill themselves with enough love to last a lifetime.

Later, an exhausted Anton rolled over and dropped his arm heavily across Anna's naked back. "Darling? Anna?" he whispered.

"Umm," she replied drowsily.

"Why don't I hire a faluka tomorrow and we can spend the weekend leisurely floating down the river. If we leave early enough we can have breakfast on the water."

Anna sat straight up in bed. All of her old enthusiasm had returned. "That is a wonderful idea. I love it. Oh! Anton, why don't we try to find a boat tonight? It's only a little past eleven and an evening on the Nile would be so lovely."

"That sounds wonderful and I wish I could, but you forget. I have that party at Ian Stanley's home this evening and if I don't hurry I will miss it completely."

"Mon Dieu! Must you go tonight of all nights?" Anna was not pleased.

"Ambassador Rolenko was adamant. No one is to guess that I am leaving and that means business as usual. I am expected. Why don't you come with me? You know you are always invited. I am sure that many of your colleagues from the press will be there."

"Ugh No," Anna sighed at the thought of facing all those people. "Not tonight. I'm just not up to it. Anyway I want to get plenty of sleep so that at least one of us will be fresh for an early start tomorrow," she said running her hands through his thick blond hair.

Swinging his legs over the side of the bed, Anton stretched, stood and began walking toward the shower. "Anna, I promise that I will only stay for an hour or so. I'll drop in and make an appearance, say hello to Ian and duck out before anyone can corner me. I'll be back here before you know it and then we will see just how much beauty sleep you get." He gave her a sly wink and stepped under the running water.

As she watched him dress, Anna's heart filled with love. On one hand she was happier than she had ever been, but on the other...... she knew it was going to be a long year.

Mingling with the other guests Anton Kasarov was forced to put aside thoughts of the day. Here, in the American ambassador's home he was no longer a man with a personal logistics problem. He was, instead, a highly regarded member of the Soviet Diplomatic Corps. As soon as he walked through Ian Stanley's front door his thoughts turned from resolving the situation facing him and Anna to a more immediate concern.........business as usual.

He finished his champagne and made his way through the crowd to the American ambassador.

"Ah Anton! My friend. I was worried that you were going to miss my little soiree. It is good to see you." Ian Stanley set his drink down on the tray of a passing waiter and shook the Russian's hand.

"Good evening Ian. I am sorry I didn't see you earlier. I was chatting with your secretary Thompson, very tight-lipped that one. I couldn't get a thing from him."

They both laughed sarcastically, knowing that Thompson was famous for gossiping like an old woman. An unlikely characteristic for a diplomatic employee, but it was purely a facade, a deliberately calculated part of Thompson's persona. Only a selected few in the diplomatic community took anything he said seriously. As a result the secretary was often given assignments of the most secretive nature.

"Did your friend from the 'Tribune' accompany you this evening?" asked Stanley as he reached for a canapé.

"No. Not tonight. She had other commitments," he lied.

"But I see that as usual you have attracted your share of the local paparazzi," he continued. "I imagine that we will be reading about this little get together in the social columns tomorrow morning."

The American smiled. He was well aware that although the affairs, for which he was famous, seemed frivolous to the uninformed, many of the world's most important decisions were made during just such occasions.

Anxious to leave, Anton extended his hand to the ambassador. "Well Ian! I just came over to say good evening and to thank you for the hospitality." For effect he added, "Will I see you next week?"

"Yes. Certainly," said the ambassador. "But you can't leave yet. We have hardly had a chance to chat. Please, join me for a nightcap."

Anton couldn't help but notice the insistence in Stanley's voice and reluctantly agreed. Business as usual, he thought.

"Good! Let's get away from this crowd. I have some fine old cognac in my study.

At four A.M., Anna rolled over in bed expecting to see Anton sleeping soundly beside her. Finding herself still alone she pulled the sheet more tightly around her shoulders and sighed a dreamy sigh. She was disappointed that he had not yet returned, but not concerned. From experience Anna knew how late Ian Stanley's parties could run.

But, when Anton failed to return by eight o'clock Saturday morning, that queasy sick feeling one gets when something has gone terribly wrong, settled in the pit of her stomach and aroused immediate action.

With her voice controlled, showing no signs of anxiety she made a call to the residence of the American ambassador and was assured by a staff member that the festivities had ended shortly after two that morning. She was also told that though Mr. Kasarov had indeed been among the guests, no one was certain exactly what time he left.

After another hour passed with still no word from Anton, Anna placed a call to the Soviet embassy and was told coldly that Comrade Kasarov was out of his office and was not expected to return until Monday. "Liars!" she whispered to herself. "He won't be there Monday either. At best he will be on his way to Moscow."

Frustrated, she slammed down the receiver and tried to think. Could he have been called away secretly in the middle of the night? She doubted it, too dramatic for the Soviets. And she trusted Anton; he would have found some way of letting her know what was happening.

"Damn it!" This time she was startled to find that she was actually shouting at her reflection in the bathroom mirror.

"Think, be logical, treat this like research, you can find him. He will probably show up later with some perfectly reasonable explanation for driving you crazy."

After only a few more moments of self-motivation Anna began contacting her most trusted friends. Unlike Anton's agency acquaintances, they were all concerned and supportive and she knew she could count on their help as well as their discretion.

Aware that some of her colleagues considered her affair with Anton as "fraternizing with the enemy," she avoided anyone she thought would harangue her with a childish "I told you so". She did not have time to explain to those idiots that her feelings for Anton were in no way "political".

Fearing she might miss a crucial phone call, Anna rejected the answering machine and remained in Anton's apartment all day Saturday. Making the most of those long hours, she spoke to everyone she knew in Cairo.

She talked to several people she knew would have been among Ian Stanley's guests. She also called the police and learned that they would not get involved until instructed to do so by the Soviet embassy. In the long run that proved to be her greatest disappointment. For without any assistance from the local police she was totally incapable of breaking through the Soviet's wall of silence.

And, of course, the Soviets volunteered absolutely no information. As far as they were concerned Anton may never have existed at all. Even those embassy colleagues she knew he considered personal friends offered no assistance.

Finally, as a last resort, left with nowhere else to turn, she contacted, she bribed, her most trusted underground resources. In the end, all her efforts were of no avail.

By early Sunday afternoon Anna was totally exhausted, and

overwhelmed by a desire for sleep. Completely defeated and alone she lay down on the bed she and Anton had so often shared and quietly wept. Until, finally, the world around her disappeared.

Although it wouldn't be official for some time to come, Anna knew then that Anton Kasarov, her beloved Anton had quite suddenly... vanished.

That same day in Afghanistan the car belonging to Serge Petro-vitch was discovered abandoned along the side of a deserted mountain road.

In Tel Aviv the wife of Pieter Roscoff waited anxiously for the phone to ring.

And off the coast of the Greek island of Kithnos a fishing boat that had been chartered by Misha Gorky and Nicholas Davidov was found empty and adrift.

Chapter 2

Bags in hand, Genie Lawrence literally ran up four flights of stairs to the small stylish apartment she and Richard shared on West 73rd St.

Anyone who knew her could tell by the contents of the bags that she was in a terrific mood. Two very expensive steaks, napoleons from Jacque's, Richard's favorite bakery, and all the ingredients for a wonderful Caesar salad were in one bag. Candles, flowers and a bottle of Pouilly Fusse were in the other.

Today had been the last day of the semester and she intended to celebrate ten glorious weeks of freedom by preparing a fabulously romantic dinner for two.

Breathing heavily, Genie placed one bag on the floor and balanced the other on her hip. "Damn," she muttered as she fumbled to unlock both the latch and the dead-bolt. The dead-bolt was a pain in the neck, as far as she was concerned, but an absolute necessity, installed by Richard, after the building's second break-in.

Closing the door behind her, Genie walked through their brightly sunlit living room, the one large room in the flat, to a tiny alcove that the landlord insisted on calling a kitchen.

Depositing both bags on the only available counter space she thought back to the day, two months ago, when she made what she considered a 'life altering' decision and moved in with Richard.

At that time she was certain she would never be able to manage 'cooking in a closet' and envisioned a life of fast food, "take out" and a generous sampling of New York's numerous restaurants, but with a bit of organization she had grown accustomed to the cramped quarters and now actually thought of it as convenient.

Taking great care Genie filled a beautiful Irish crystal vase with dozens of Shasta daisies. She placed the vase on a small glass top dining table positioned under a montage of Richard's black and white photographs hanging on the wall at the far end of the living room.

Richard had lived in the apartment for years and simply took for granted the fact that the living room faced the street. Gen, on the other hand, counted it a blessing for it, at least, received a considerable amount of daylight. Their bedroom too had several large windows along the outer wall and although it faced a narrow alley, it too, was bright and cheery most of the time.

Of course, facing 73rd street did have its drawbacks. For one thing the noise from traffic could be unbearable at times. Richard was used to it, Genie was adjusting. And the kitchen, bathroom and second bedroom, which Richard used as his darkroom, were on the interior of the building and were dismal with no windows at all. Genie had some ideas, though, and was going to use this summer to brighten and lighten as much as she could.

The unmistakable sound of her grandmother's antique Seth Thomas mantle clock suddenly striking one chime caught Genie mid-daydream. It was already 4:30. "Damn," she said annoyed at her mindless drifting, she was determined to make everything perfect. "He'll be home in an hour."

In the bedroom, she hurriedly pulled off her pink oxford cloth shirt and tossed it into the wicker hamper. This was the room with which she was most dissatisfied. A combination of both their tastes, it was obvious that Richard's heavy mahogany furniture and her favorite rattan rocker were not suited to each other. "Oh well, Miz. Scarlet!" she mused, "Tomorrow is another day."

Having planned this evening for days, Genie knew exactly what she was going to wear and reached into the back of the closet for a strapless silk sundress that she had been saving for a special occasion. The vibrant teal silk was the same shade as her eyes and looked perfect with her shoulder length, somewhat curly, definitely unruly, strawberry gold hair and her fair, slightly freckled complexion.

The dress had a mid-calf length full skirt which she loved. It gave her "hips" and helped add curves to an almost boyish figure. She knew she would never have her older sister Marion's luscious figure, her long legs or the "good hair" but she did have the eyes. From her grandfather she had inherited startling blue/green eyes, and she did whatever she could to help them stand out. Staring into the bathroom mirror she added mascara and sighed. Genie knew that no one would call her beautiful, her cheeks were just a tad too full, and she didn't have Marion's height, but her nose was straight, well-proportioned for her face and, of course, there were those eyes.

Everyone had always thought of her as fairly pretty or cute. Whatever that meant? She would always be the Lawrence sister with the infectious smile and vivacious personality. She felt fortunate that people usually liked her. They found her interesting and fun to be with and instinctively, they knew she could be trusted. At thirty-five, Genie had, long ago, accepted her flaws and focused on the positives. The one thing she could not do, however, was to think of herself as cute. "Too old for cute," she murmured to the mirror.

Quickly slipping into the dress she discovered to her delight that she felt exceptionally elegant, really quite sexy. Imagining the effect this dress would have on the already overactive hormones of her adolescent male charges at Washington Irving Academy, she couldn't help eyeing herself in the mirror one last time. "If they could see me now," she hummed. A slight self-satisfied smile brightened her face. She hoped it would have the same effect on Richard.

Garlic, parmesan cheese, an egg, dry mustard and olive oil appeared on the kitchen counter. "Damn! Where are the anchovies?"

While Genie searched for the missing ingredient she recalled the first time she and Richard had shared a Caesar salad.

"Could it really have been eight months ago?" she reminisced.

She had been living in a high rise apartment in Fort Lee, New Jersey and commuting to her teaching job in Manhattan.

"Thank God for Judy and Ira," she thought as she remembered how totally depressed she had been about her upcoming thirty-fifth birthday.

Turning thirty hadn't bothered Genie in the least, but for some ridiculous reason the idea of thirty-five was driving her crazy. It was a personal milestone of the worst kind. The biological clock was winding down and she seriously wondered if a 'career' would be enough. Since there had been no important man in her life since that near disaster with Stan a few years earlier, she had even begun to contemplate the option of becoming a single parent. On the verge of total misery her best friends, Judy and Ira Fishman, saved her sanity by throwing a huge surprise party and not inviting anyone under thirty-five.

Ira, a writer for the New York Times, had invited a friend, one of the staff photographers, and convinced him to take some pictures of the bash.

And so, Genie Lawrence met Richard McBride. When she walked into what she had been led to believe was going to be an intimate dinner for four...she had managed to cajole one of her fellow teaching buddies to accompany her, she was blinded by a dozen flashes popping in her face. Staring through the sea of blue dots dancing before her eyes, she was immediately attracted to the stranger with the unkempt sandy grey hair, slightly scruffy beard and charmingly mischievous smile.

Blinking at Richard, Genie could not believe that she was face to face with someone who so immediately captured her attention. "He looks like a bit of a rogue," she whispered to Judy. "This is going to be an interesting evening."

It was apparent that Richard was equally intrigued and seeing the looks that passed between Richard and Genie, Genie's date knew when to fade into the crowd.

"And to think," He said to Ira. "You practically had to drag me here."

Judy and Ira were not at all surprised when Richard and Genie left the party together. They had, in fact, been trying to get the two together for months.

After they managed to slip out of the party, Richard suggested that they go into Manhattan for a nightcap. Instead of drinks, however, they found themselves sharing a Caesar salad at a small west-side cafe not far from his apartment.

Six months later Genie moved out of the high-rise in New Jersey and into Richard's brownstone flat in New York.

"Hard to believe," she sighed, a Cheshire cat smile appearing on her face.

The sound of the key turning the dead-bolt brought Genie back to the present. Somehow in the midst of her reverie she had managed to pull dinner together...including the salad.

"Richard," she called, and quickly untied the linen towel she had wrapped around her waist.

"Hi, Gen!" Richard closed the door and dropped his camera equipment into a peach Queen Ann chair in the living room.

Genie entered the room, his martini in hand, and suddenly nightmarish visions of turning into June Cleaver spurred an overwhelming urge to slug down the martini herself, slap him on the fanny and drag him to the most expensive restaurant in town.

It was a fleeting moment. A weird sort of TV induced déjà vu, of seeing herself trapped between then and now. It was gone in a flash. Genie saw no contradiction in being a feminine feminist, and was actually able to laugh at herself when she realized that she had almost elected to wear a necklace frighteningly similar to June's ever present pearls.

Any lingering effects of her 50's flashback disappeared the moment she noticed the way Richard was looking at her...all he could do was whistle. It was exactly the reaction she had hoped for.

"Hello sweetheart. Here you go." She handed him the drink. "Very dry."

"You look spectacular," he said, placing his glass on a small table next to the peach chair. He then took Genie into his arms and kissed her gently on the neck.

"Umm! That does feel good," she whispered. "What exactly do you have in mind?"

"Come with me woman and I'll show you." Richard, in his best mock caveman routine, smiled slyly and started for the bedroom.

"Later for you buster," Genie teased. "Right now I would like you to join me at a most elegant restaurant for a very romantic dinner. Grab that martini and we will have cocktails before the main course."

Genie led him to their pale aqua brocade couch. They sat facing a large white marble fireplace that spanned the distance between two sets of leaded glass windows covering most of the living room wall. She had filled the hearth with an array of green and flowering plants that would stay there until they lit their first fire in the fall.

"This really is a nice idea Gen. What's the occasion?"

"Richard!" she scolded. "How could you forget? Today is freedom day. You know…no more pencils, no more books, etc., etc."

"That's right!" he exclaimed. "We need a toast." He stood and with glass in hand made an exaggerated bow before his 'lady'. "To all those poor, little bastards who will have to do without you for two whole months."

"Two months and two weeks," Genie corrected.

They finished their cocktails and Genie led Richard to the 'restaurant'. She had set the table with her only two settings of 'good china', a delicate peach and black "Art Nouveau" pattern by "Fitz and Floyd". The crystal vase she used for the flowers belonged to Richard. Left to him by his mother, it was a cherished possession. There were also eighteen inch tapers on the table, which Genie lit even though summer sun was still streaming through sheer white curtains.

Richard opened the wine and Genie served the salad, steaks with morel sauce and piping hot rolls.

"Remember the first time we had Caesar salad Gen?"

She smiled and looked across the table into his warm hazel eyes. She loved his eyes. And she had to admit, she loved his body too. At five foot ten, he was four inches taller than Genie and with his strong build could easily carry her into the bedroom on a whim.

At times like these she loved him to distraction. She knew he was occasionally less than perfect. There were times when he failed to come home because he was 'on assignment', times when she was left alone to wonder just how well he got to know his 'assignments' and other times when his photography seemed to consume him.

But when they shared moments like this she could forgive anything. Well almost anything, she thought.

"Hello! Gen? Where are you?" Richard tapped her on the hand trying to get her attention.

"Oh! I'm sorry sweetheart," Genie said realizing how her mind had wandered and thinking she'd been doing a lot of 'wandering' lately. "How could I forget the most important salad of my life?" she said, rejoining the world.

After dinner Genie served the Napoleons with cafe au lait.

"You've been to Jacques bakery. You really have gone all out," Richard said as they again relaxed by the fireplace, this time with dessert, coffee and Johnny Mathis.

By 9:00 o'clock in the evening, on almost the longest day of the year, sunlight was finally beginning to fail and the glow from the candles flickered throughout the room.

"Gen, have you given any thought about what you are going to do this summer?" Richard asked.

"Well you know that I want to finish redecorating the apartment, but other than that...no...not really. Why?"

"I was hoping you could help me catalogue my prints."

Although photo journalism was his profession, Richard's real passion was art.

His photographic pieces were predominantly black and white, because of, or to be more exact, in homage to Ansell Adams. Just beginning to gain a reputation for creative lens technique, he participated in numerous local shows.

"I could really use some help updating my portfolio, especially, if I ever hope to get into the galleries on a permanent basis. What do you think?" he asked, lightly stroking the back of her left arm.

Genie was very proud of Richard's photography, and was, in fact, the subject of some of his best work. "I would love to help you

sweetheart. You know with some effort we might just be able......
........."

They sat quietly for a while chatting, making plans and enjoy-ing the evening. Darkness was falling when Richard put his arm around Genie and kissed her softly on the lips. His beard was soft against her cheek and she felt her body respond to his kiss. I'm pretty lucky, she thought, Richard may not realize it yet but he really does love me. She pulled him closer.

"Genevieve Lawrence, you are lovely," he whispered. "I need you in my life." He pushed her gently down onto the couch. Running his hands over her bare shoulders he found the zipper at the back of her sundress and slid it to its base. The aqua fabric rustled softly as he slipped the dress down over her hips and off onto the floor. Genie was eager for him now and quivered to Richard's touch. Strong hands removed the sheer lace lingerie that did little to mask the soft hidden areas of her supple body. He could not resist touching her and began by sliding his hands down over her hips, massaging the tops of her thighs.

For her part, Genie did not even try to control her need. She tore away his half unbuttoned shirt and then tackled the brown leather belt she had given him for his birthday. Wrapping her legs around him she unbuttoned and unzipped everything she could until they were both lying naked on the couch.

Much later, their bodies shining with perspiration, they found themselves uncomfortably laying together on the carpet. Untan-gling herself, Genie stood first and gave Richard a hand. They staggered drowsily into the bedroom.

At 5:00 AM the telephone rang. Sounding like an alarm, it awakened both Richard and Genie from deep sleep. Genie rolled over and turned on the bedside lamp, Richard lifted the receiver.

"Ahem! Ah! Hello?" he said groggily. Not hearing an answer he tried again. "Hello! Hello! Who is this?"

"Yes, this is Richard McBride. Go ahead." Richard looked over to Genie and rolling his eyes indicated his confusion about the call.

As the conversation progressed, however, she could tell that something was terribly wrong.

"Yes. No. I haven't spoken to him since Christmas." Richard's eyes widened. "Oh, damn no! When? How is Molly? May I speak to her? All right. Of course. Tell her I'll be there," Richard reached for a pencil and began jotting down dates and times on the back of an old envelope. "Give me that again. Thanks. Thank you for calling and give Molly and the boys my love." Richard returned the receiver to its cradle and sat on the edge of the bed staring at the envelope in his hand.

Knowing something awful had just happened, Genie waited.

"That was David Barrow. He is Molly Sims' brother. Did I ever tell you about Roger and Molly?" Richard asked in a distracted monotone voice.

Genie nodded, but Richard didn't really seem to notice as he told her the story she had heard many times before...

Roger Sims and Richard McBride had both been photo journalists in Vietnam. It was near the end of the war and Richard was young and on his first assignment free-lancing for a number of reporters. Roger was working for the 'London Times'. They spent several months together in the jungles of Southeast Asia and became fast friends. The fact that Richard's mother had been a "war bride" from England enhanced the feeling of kinship he felt for Roger.

After his stint in Vietnam he went to London and spent some time with his friend and his friend's new bride, Molly. He had, in fact, visited several times since then and had been there for the birth of Roger's first son John Richard.

Although it had been three or four years since the two had seen each other they always kept in touch by letter and phone. Richard considered Roger Sims his best friend.

"Roger was killed in an automobile accident." Richard spoke with the emotionless tone of someone in shock.

"Sweetheart! No! When did it happen?" Genie was herself stunned by the news and saddened by the pain she saw in Richard's eyes.

He looked up, "Last night. I am not sure exactly what time. I guess it had been raining pretty heavily and his car skidded off the road and over an embankment. Damn stupid way to die!" He pounded his fist against the nightstand.

Genie brought him a snifter of brandy and sat with him while he cried for, and talked about his friend.

"Gen, I told David that I would be there for the funeral. I really want to be there for Molly and the boys......and for Roger. They are having the service on Saturday and I am going to try and catch a flight out Thursday or Friday. The soonest I can book."

"OK, sure," Genie agreed. "But, do you think that you can arrange to leave that quickly?"

"Yes, I can clear things up at the paper. I would like to leave now...today, but there are a few lose ends that just have to be tied up before I go...and something else," he said still a bit dazed. They sat together on the bed watching the daylight break through the curtains; Richard reached for Genie's hand. "...Will you come with me Gen?"

Genie had never met the Sims and was surprised by the request. "Do you think that would be appropriate? I mean wouldn't it be uncomfortable for the family?"

"I promise, I'll handle it sensitively. I want Molly and the boys to love you as much as I do. And," he added. "I could really use...I need you there."

Looking into Richard's eyes was all it took, Genie readily agreed to the trip.

After several minutes of silence Richard finally spoke. "Gen, what would you think about staying in England for a week or so after the funeral?" he asked.

"I don't know?" she was unprepared and found it a little hard to keep up with the turn of events. "Is that what you really want?"

"I think it might do a lot of good. I'd like to spend some time with Roger's boys, and to be near Molly if she needs me." For a moment he again lapsed into silence then added almost conspiratorially. "There is someplace that I would like to take you. It's very special to me."

Genie was surprised. Richard had never been quite so mysterious. Maybe Roger's death brought undeniable evidence of his own mortality. Instinctively understanding that even his experience in Vietnam hadn't prepared him for the loss of his closest friend, she slid a comforting arm around his shoulder.

Endless moments of silence were finally broken when Genie could stand it no longer and had to give in to curiosity. As well as concern for Richard she was fascinated by the idea of a 'special place'.

"I didn't realize you were so familiar with England," she began cautiously. "I thought that you had only stayed in London. Where is it...this special place?" she continued almost in a whisper.

"Remember when I told you about my Mother, and how she came here as a war bride from England?" Richard began, Genie nodded. "When she died my father took her back to England to be buried in her home town of Dickson Abbot. I was too young to understand at the time, but apparently that's where they fell in love and it's a place that meant a lot to both of them. My dad would have been buried there too if his body hadn't been lost in that damn boating accident."

"And Dickson Abbot is where you want to go?"

Richard only nodded, but Genie was amazed. He had never spoken much about his past. She realized from what he was saying now that he thought he had told her a lot more about his family than he actually had. All she had known before this morning was that his parents had died and that he had no brothers or sisters. Now, as he spoke, his family was taking on character, becoming real to her. For some reason it seemed to add depth to Richard as well.

She thought she was beginning to understand him a little better, to understand why he felt that nothing could be counted on to last, why he seemed afraid of the commitment of marriage. Perhaps, Genie mused, he has somehow convinced himself that security and love would ultimately be torn apart by tragedy as his family had been. She could only hope that her support, her continued presence in his life would be enough to sustain him while he wrestled with the difficult days ahead.

Genie was wrong. She had not read Richard as accurately as she thought. The emotion she had seen was very real. He was genuinely distressed over the death of his friend and deeply concerned for Roger's family, but Richard did not feel 'touched' by tragedy. His mother had died when he was very young, but he and his father had shared a good relationship that lasted well into adulthood. His father's death a few years ago had left him shaken, but still he did not for one moment consider himself a tragic figure. Richard's avoidance of marital commitment was purely selfish. As much as he loved Genie, he simply wasn't ready for the responsibility of family...at least not yet. When he was ready he imagined it would be with Genie at his side, but it was no deep emotional scar that kept him from marriage. Rather it was a bit of emotional cowardice, immaturity and a grain of selfishness that delayed commitment.

The grief for his friend cut deeply, the pain was real, but he knew he could handle it. He could be strong for himself and for a family he loved in England.

"Have you ever been to Dickson Abbot?" Genie continued.

"Only once. It's on Dartmoor. I went there while I was staying with Roger and Molly. I took a couple of days and visited the area. It really is beautiful and I think you will love it. We could have a relaxing few days. And anyway," he continued brightening a bit. "I know that you will be nuts about my aunt Sarah."

Genie was astonished. "Aunt Sarah?" she exclaimed. "I didn't know you had any family Richard, let alone an aunt in England."

"It's really not a deep dark secret Gen. It just never came up. The only time we correspond is on holidays and birthdays. Special occasions, you know. I haven't seen her for years, but I know that she would be very pleased if we spent some time with her. Every card she sends contains an invitation. What do you think?"

Overwhelmed by the events of the last few hours Genie needed some time to take it all in. Her mind began to race. She couldn't imagine how she would ever get ready for a week or two in England in one day. But fully comprehending the emotional implications of this trip she was determined to do her best.

At 8:00 AM Friday morning the 747 carrying Genie Lawrence and Richard McBride touched down at London's Heathrow airport.

Chapter 3

"The Eagle has the chicks?"

"All five are in the nest."

"Safe?"

"All are well."

After completing the confirming telephone call General Armstrong Walker, an imposing man in a uniform wallpapered with ribbons of every stripe and medals that gleamed under fluorescent lights, placed the receiver of the scrambler phone back onto its cradle. The large underground room echoed with the sound of his cane tapping on the hardwood floor as he slowly walked to the far end of the oversized oak conference table. He seated himself so as to have an unobstructed view of the wall sized global map and turned to face the only other person in the room.

"Show me," he barked.

The other man, small, balding, unimposing, dressed in a perfectly tailored dark grey suit was already seated at the opposite end of the table. He pushed a button on a lighted display panel recessed in the table top. Immediately the section of the world map containing the Middle East became illuminated.

"They are located here, here and here General. Each one thinks he is alone."

"Good! Let's keep it that way for the time being. Has there been any speculation by our Red friends?"

"No General. They haven't even admitted that their men are

missing. And they won't until they are certain that there have been no defections."

"And what about the problem that developed at the Ambassador's party?" Thinking back to the time he had recently spent in Egypt the General once again began to pace while he waited for an answer.

The man in the grey suit opened the confidential report he had received by courier that morning. "The problem has been eliminated," he began. "Unfortunately, there seems to be some evidence missing."

The General ran his hand through his full head of steel grey hair. Cold, stormy grey eyes, stared intently at the map. He turned to face the other. "What?" he said in a voice barely audible. "What exactly do you mean evidence is missing? Didn't I tell you to take care of all the details?"

"I have my best man working on it," the other answered. He was not as confident as he appeared. Though he knew the abilities of his accomplice and had every reason to believe that all would go according to plan, a nagging doubt born of instinct and experience continued to plague him. "I can assure you that nothing will go wrong. Every detail will be taken care of."

The General was livid. This operation was going to be his coup. It would place him where he knew he belonged. He would be the next Chairman of the Joint Chiefs of Staff. They wouldn't pass him over...not this time. Once again he would show them how to carry out a covert operation. After all, hadn't he been doing just that all these years.

His performance in Korean combat had been brilliant so when it became evident that the U.S. would not escape the conflict in Vietnam he was sent to the Far East as an 'advisor'.

While serving in that position during the sixties and early seventies the General executed numerous "Black" operations and was beginning to gain a reputation for his ability to "get things done" with absolute secrecy.

More recently, with the increase in world terrorism, he had been given carte blanche to enact covert operations anywhere terrorist activities threatened world security.

Immune from scrutiny by Congress or any investigative committee, he and his special forces had been given access to all U.S. intelligence agencies and he had used these resources extensively.

But his career hadn't gone as he imagined. The influence was there, he certainly had power, but it was all clandestine. For all his efforts, his abiding loyalty, he never received just recognition and he knew that, unless he took matters into his own hands, he never would.

And, of course, his government, his compatriots had underestimated him, never anticipated the lengths to which he would go to attain the affirmation he knew he deserved. His plan had taken many months to devise and required great skill to pull it all together. He was not about to let one piece of misplaced information leak out and ruin it now. Oh no! This operation was going to work. It had to work. He would show them all just how to handle an enemy. He would get that long deserved appointment.

The General glared at the small man seated at the end of the table, and found it hard to believe his reputation. Found it hard to believe that this nondescript, almost effeminate looking man was feared by all who knew him. He wasn't the least afraid of this little mouse. He had hired him and he expected results. "You listen to me," he said in his most threatening tone. "I want you personally to find that evidence and bring it back to me. If there is anything incriminating I want to see it for myself, I want to destroy it myself."

The man nodded, a sarcastic smile crossing his face, but the General was too enraged to notice.

"If you fail in this I can guaranty that you will be replaced," the General hissed.

The man smiled again. The stakes in this game were, as always, very high indeed. The General had promised him ten million dollars upon completion of the "ultimate trade". He wanted that ten million and understood all too well the General's driving ambition. He knew what the old man wanted and knew he would go to any lengths to get it. There was never any doubt that the General could have him replaced in the ultimate "six feet deep" sense of the word.

Of course that possibility didn't scare him; he had dealt with fanatics before. No, this operation was a challenge. He could pull it off and he didn't want the General to cause any problems by acting too quickly. Something had to be done to calm the old bastard. He'd charm him a little and get him off his back. "General," he said. "I understand your concerns, and for that reason I will go to London myself and alleviate any complications. If there really is any incriminating evidence I will place it in your hands personally." He wondered if the General realized he was being patronized.

The briefing continued. "And what about our man in Cairo?" asked the General.

"He is getting edgy. He might talk if the operation isn't completed soon."

"I thought you had convinced him to go along with our plans. He doesn't want that nasty little rumor about his wife exposed, does he? It would not do his career any good," the General continued.

"He is having second thoughts about his part in our action." the man in the grey suit admitted. His nervous habit of fondling a slender sterling silver pen, rolling it between his fingers, toying with the cap was the only sign of his discomfort.

"We can't go ahead with the final phase until all the loose ends are tied up. No leaks and no evidence. Do you understand?"

"Of course, General. As I said, I'll take care of it."

"Immediately?" The General was now leaning heavily on his cane.

"Immediately," the man replied.

The General turned abruptly and limped out of the room. The cavernous space echoed with a slow tapping sound as he left.

The small man picked up the telephone and dialed the airport. He booked a first class flight using the name Finch. It wasn't his real name, of course. Only his deceased mother knew that one. But it was the name he was using for this operation. It was the name on all his current documents. He had everything he needed to go from Washington to London and then on to Cairo.

Chapter 4

An hour after landing at Heathrow airport Genie was still trying to get through customs. There had been a particularly long queue and to add to the frustration she had been unlucky enough to have been picked for a spot check of her luggage. Richard, who had no trouble at all, had gone on ahead to secure a taxi.

He stood waiting by the TWA information center fidgeting nonstop with the strap on one of his many camera bags, a sure sign that he was becoming anxious. "Where is she?"

"Richard McBride?"

He was startled by the sound of his name and as he looked up was surprised to see a short, dark haired man in a Burberry raincoat approaching with his hand outstretched. "Yes?" Richard answered, somewhat confused.

"I thought so," said the man smiling. "I am David Barrow, Molly's brother."

"Oh yes. Hello. I wasn't expecting you," Richard said, shaking the man's hand.

"Molly sent me. She thought it would be easier if I met you. She is very pleased that you are able to be here. And frankly, so am I. She has taken this awfully hard and I think it will be good for her to see old friends. This is such a terrible business."

"I am anxious to see her too. Roger's death came as quite as blow. Just awful."

David Barrow shook his head in agreement and reached for

Richard's luggage. "I have my car. If this is everything we can get out of this madhouse."

"David just a moment please." Richard felt a bit hesitant as he began to mention Genie. For the first time he wondered if it had, indeed, been wise for her to come along. "I hope you and Molly won't mind, but I've brought a friend with me. Actually," he stumbled, feeling childishly embarrassed. "She is more than a friend. We have been living together for some months now."

"Oh! I see. It's like that is it?" said David with a grin. "No, of course not. I am sure my sister will be happy that you have found yourself a 'friend'. She and Roger often wondered if you were ever going to settle down. Where is she then?" he asked as his eyes surveyed the terminal.

"Having a bit of trouble with customs, I'm afraid. Security seems particularly tight this morning."

Genie appeared suddenly, looking thoroughly disgusted. "Richard, you would not believe what I just went through. Do you know they opened all my bags? They went through every item of clothing," she said in exasperation. "You would think I was a drug running mercenary or something. I have to pick my bags up over at that counter," she continued, catching her breath and pointing across the terminal.

As she turned to head back toward customs she was suddenly aware of the man standing next to Richard. He looked very British and, for some reason, a bit shy, reserved perhaps.

"Hello," he said finally speaking up. "I am David, Molly's brother, and I am terribly sorry that you have had such an unpleasant and inconvenient introduction to British hospitality. I do hope that we can make it up to you."

She shook David's hand as Richard recovered her luggage and in less than an hour David's car was on Park Lane pulling up in front of Grosvenor House hotel.

Later that day a small, balding man in a dark grey suit stepped of another TWA flight and carried two tattered bags to the same customs counter at which Genie had had so much difficulty. He was confident that the weapon he carried would, as always, go undetected. Mindlessly he fingered the sterling silver pen in his breast pocket. A superb writing instrument, he had only to push the white star on the elegant custom designed Mont Blanc pen once and from beneath the gold nib would appear a slender scalpel-like blade.

He had designed the weapon himself and used it often. In the circles within which he travelled it had become his trademark.

Like most of the many business people and tourists who pass through Heathrow daily, he had, as anticipated, no trouble with customs. He then hailed one of the large, black, spotlessly clean cabs, for which London is famous, and headed toward London's West End.

Emerging from the cab in front of the Covent Garden Opera House, he walked across the street to the Lion's Head pub.

Once inside he chose a secluded corner booth, ordered a pint of ale and waited.

A short time later a tall, pasty looking man wearing a nondescript raincoat and a bowler sat down beside him.

"Do you have a package for me?" Finch asked, noting how his contact shifted nervously in his seat.

"I don't have it with me." The man in the bowler could feel perspiration begin to slide down his back. "I...I know where it is. I should be able to pick it up tomorrow."

"You idiot! You assured me that you had taken care of the problem."

"Th...Th...the problem," the contact stammered, "has been eliminated. An unfortunate vehicle accident. No witnesses, no questions. The evidence he obtained, however, was not with him. I am confident that it is still at his home."

"That should be easy enough. I will get it myself. I can't believe you are having this much difficulty."

"It isn't quite as easy as it looks. W…We have to be certain that there are no copies, and we have to take care of anyone who may have seen it." The man in the bowler sighed heavily. He always stuttered when he was anxious or believed he had lost control of a situation. That was definitely the case now. He had to calm down. He could not let this man see how tense he really was. "Listen, I will be invited to the house tomorrow after the Sims' funeral, and I'll be able to get the package then. I shall also be able to ascertain exactly who has seen it and whether or not there are any copies to worry about." He was feeling a bit more confident. "Meet me here tomorrow at three and you will have what you want."

"And if you find that someone, his wife perhaps, or one of the children, has seen the evidence?" Finch questioned.

"You can take care of that," said the tall man nervously. His momentary confidence had quickly evaporated. "I've done mo… more than my share already. Just pay me for my work and let me get back to my life. This has all gotten out of hand and far too complicated for my tastes."

"As you suggested. We will meet here tomorrow afternoon, and you will have the package. I am warning you I want everything…… originals, copies and the names of anyone you even remotely suspect may have seen them. Do you think you can do that?" he asked, sarcastically.

Without another word the contact quickly left. Removing a meticulously folded white handkerchief from his breast pocket he wiped his receding brow then sat back and finished his ale. He watched the other shuffle out of the pub. "Thank God I won't have to deal with him much longer," he thought.

Unpacking is such a chore, thought Genie as she hung her clothes in an antique armoire. Relieved by a knock on the door indicating that room service had finally arrived, she quickly dispensed with her last wrinkled garment and closed the cabinet. Richard was right; having a light lunch in their suite was a perfect idea. It gave them both a chance to unwind after the long flight. It would be quite some time before she overcame the disorientation of jet lag.

Later, after they had their fill of fruit, cheese, French bread and white wine, Genie and Richard strolled through a light drizzle across Hyde Park to Roger and Molly's house on Hampton Gardens. Most of the terraced houses in this part of Kensington were being renovated and the Sims' home was no exception. The exterior sparkled with a freshly applied coat of white paint, and when they stepped inside they noticed, as well, the smell of fresh interior paint, and had learned from Molly's brother that a great deal of work had recently been completed.

Roger and Molly had obviously been spending a good deal of time and effort creating a comfortable secure home for themselves and the boys. The original parquet floors had been stripped and refinished. A butler's pantry had been converted to a breakfast room and the once nonfunctional fireplace had been reopened. The most constructive change, however, could not be seen. The old coal heating system had been converted to cleaner gas central heating. Even the unusual decor, a combination of English antiques and modern oriental pieces, seemed perfect in the sunny rooms and Genie felt immediately at ease. The atmosphere was tasteful, but not pretentious and she could tell that Roger and Molly were less conscious of style than they were of comfort.

Molly, a short, motherly woman with dark hair and large sad green eyes, greeted Richard with a kiss and a long hard hug. "Richard, I am so glad you've come." She smiled as she wiped tears from her eyes.

"I couldn't stay away. I loved him too you know."

After some long comforting moments Richard introduced Genie.

"I am so sorry about everything," she said. "I hope you don't mind that I am here with Richard? I can only imagine how difficult this time is for you." Genie tried to express her genuine concern, but felt a bit uneasy about intruding during such a private moment.

Molly assured her that she was welcome, and then turned again to Richard for support.

"Uncle Richard!" shouted a tall, dark haired boy who came bounding through the front door.

"Hi there Johnny," said Richard, grabbing him and giving the nine year old a squeeze.

"Gosh I am glad you are here. How long can you stay?" he went on breathlessly.

"A few days, I'm not sure yet. Say, where's Tony?"

"He is still out in the park. I saw you walking up the steps."

At that instant the younger boy, shorter, stockier and with lighter hair came charging into the room. "Hello," he said a bit shyly. Only three the last time he had seen his Uncle Richard, he wasn't exactly sure how to act.

Richard walked over and picked the boy up into his arms. "Ho! You have grown up, haven't you? I won't be able to do this much longer," he said giving the boy a hug, and setting him back down. "Are you sure you're the same little guy who lived here three years ago?"

Tony smiled. He was thoroughly enjoying the acclaim of his rarely recognized maturity. "Hello!" he said brightly, turning to Genie with his hand extended in greeting.

"You get right to the point don't you hot shot?" Richard said, chuckling. He introduced Genie to the boys. She was enchanted by their exuberance and open, friendly demeanor. It didn't take much convincing for her to accompany them across the street to the small private park designed exclusively for the residents of Hampton Gardens.

As Genie left the house with the boys, she was confident she had judged correctly that Molly and Richard needed some time alone.

Sitting together in the living room Richard and Molly had a chance to share their feelings. "How are you really doing Molly?" Richard began.

Molly sighed, "I don't know what to tell you Richard. I'll be alright I guess, but now… it happened so quickly and it was so unexpected," she hesitated. "I begged him not to go out that night. It was storming frightfully, but you know Roger, he had something he just had to do. I don't know, it was important at the time, but now I can't even remember what it was." Molly paced the library a bit, then continued. "When he hadn't gotten home by eleven thirty I was worried, and then there was a knock at the door. That knock is something I will never forget. Somehow I knew what it was. Isn't that crazy? I mean I've never believed in precognition, but somehow I just knew. Inspector Whiting was very apologetic when he told me about the accident and he assured me that everything possible was being done, but there wasn't really any need for much of an investigation. The whole damn thing was straight forward enough. His car skidded around a curve and went over an embankment." She began to cry softly. "Oh, Richard! I miss him so much."

"I miss him too, Molly," he said trying to comfort her. "I'll stay as long as you need me," he offered. "How are the boys doing?"

"They seem to be holding up quite well," she said. "I don't think the impact of what happened has hit home. Especially for Tony, I really believe that he expects his father to come walking through the door. I know John is being strong for my sake. He has already started acting like the man of the house. Do you know the boys haven't had one spat since the night of the accident?" Molly continued. "Richard," she said taking his hand. "Will you talk to them for me? I know that they are both keeping a stiff upper lip for my sake. Maybe you can find out how they are coping. You know…things they might not tell their Mom."

"Of course I will. I'll make a point of it, tomorrow after the funeral."

Molly walked over to a long black lacquered cabinet. Opening the left door she removed a bottle and a beautifully cut crystal glass and poured herself a scotch, neat.

"I feel like a drink. How about you?" she offered.

"Whiskey, water, if you have it?"

While pouring Richard's drink Molly realized she was quite curious about his "friend".

"Tell me about Genie. She seems awfully nice. It's about time you found yourself a girl."

Richard was surprised to find he was blushing, something he hadn't done since adolescence. He smiled, regained his composure and told her all about Genie and about their life in New York. "She really is a wonderful woman."

"I don't doubt it at all…the way you have been carrying on."

Molly gave him a sly smile and by the time the boys dragged Genie through the back door an hour later, Richard and Molly were both feeling better.

"Hi there, you two," she said. "Those boys of yours are just packed full of energy. I am totally exhausted."

Molly offered Genie a drink, which she gratefully accepted.

As she dropped wearily into an overstuffed chair she could sense that the atmosphere in the room had lightened a bit and was glad that Richard and Molly had had some time to themselves.

Later, they walked back across the park. Richard draped his

arm over Genie's shoulder. "I think Molly is going to be OK," he said.

"What about you?" Genie whispered.

"I'm alright," he said "I think I'll be back to my usual self after a few days on Dartmoor. Wait until you see it." The excitement rose in his voice. "I guaranty you will fall in love.

While Genie dressed for dinner Richard made reservations for the rest of their stay. He also placed a call to his aunt. Needless to say she was completely shocked to hear from him so unexpectedly and equally surprised that he was in England. As he expected she was thrilled that he planned to visit. "And with a young lady as well," she said, and Richard could tell she was smiling.

"We will see you in three or four days, Aunt Sarah," he said. "And by the way, I've made reservations for us at that nice little Inn by the river. Is it still as I remember?"

"You mean 'the Grange'? Yes it is still as lovely as ever, but I do wish you two would consider staying here with me," she complained.

"Don't worry, you will see enough of us to last years," he teased. "Take care of yourself, and we will see you soon."

Wearing a taupe silk suit that she knew Richard liked, Genie poured them each a Perrier from the small but well stocked mini-bar in their suite.

Her most cheerful smile in place, she handed Richard his glass. "How is your aunt?" she questioned.

"She is anxious to see us. Especially you," he laughed.

"You know she just wants to give me the once over. She wants to make sure that I am worthy of her handsome, talented nephew," she teased. "She is looking out for your interests," Genie said with exaggerated sarcasm.

Leaving the hotel they appeared as simply two lovers without a care in the world. Richard had been able to put the sad events of

SUSAN SQUIRE SMITH

the day out of his mind for a while. He found himself really enjoying the evening.

Genie's enthusiasm for the London's West End was contagious. The crowds lining up for the theaters created an air of excitement while the shopping along Oxford and Regent Streets almost put New York to shame. The aroma of fine Italian cooking engulfed them just before they reached Julio's. The small Italian restaurant on Neal St. was a favorite of local musicians. As Richard and Genie entered the lobby someone was playing a piano in the dining room. The maitre d' showed them to an intimate table on the second floor. The atmosphere perfectly suited their mood. It was romantic and mildly festive.

After a delicious meal of scaloppini, wine and Zabaglione Richard and Genie sat quietly sipping their coffee.

"What are you thinking about Richard?"

Staring into the candle light he hesitated. "Gen, I feel so close to you right now. I don't know what I would do if I lost you. Can two people be too close? Thinking about Roger and Molly scares the hell out of me. They were so committed to each other. I don't know if I could handle what Molly is going through. I know I'm rambling...but..."

Knowing what he was struggling to say Genie cut him off midsentence. "You mean," she said. "You love me, but you aren't sure if we should get married. That maybe, if we do get married, we would be even closer than we are right now. And that is what really scares you... And," she added. "You don't know if you are ready to give up your rambling ways...right?"

He smiled self-consciously and nodded, still staring into the candlelight. Genie reached across the table and took his hand. "Sweetheart, I think I understand what you are going through and I love you too, very much. But you know we never talked about marriage before and I don't think we have to talk about it now. For the time being it is enough that we love each other."

Richard looked directly into her bright, aqua eyes. "Gen you are spectacular. No wonder I love you so much."

"I know, I'm a gem," she said, "Let's just get through tomorrow and go on down to Dartmoor. We need to leave the world behind for a while. This trip will be wonderful for both of us."

Returning to their suite they enjoyed a leisurely nightcap then slipped out of their clothes and into the king sized bed. After a long loving night of caring, passionate pleasure they awoke nearly as tired as they had been the previous evening.

Chapter 5

It was a dismal morning. Warm rain splattered off the glistening black umbrellas of silent mourners. At the graveside an Anglican Vicar, solemn black robes edged in thick red mud, moved slowly around the casket giving a blessing.

Several yards away, partially hidden by an ancient grave stone, Finch stood watching the ceremony. Although there were a great many people at the funeral, he was intent on memorizing only the faces of those closest to the deceased.

He heard the quiet sobs of the man's wife and saw the pain in the face of his friend. He would remember them. He noticed too, the red haired woman. She stood close at hand but appeared to be less emotionally involved. With an appreciative glance he calculated that he would remember her as well.

Among the faces in the crowd he saw his contact. For an instant the bowler donned head turned to face him, and then, just as quickly, turned back to the ceremony. They would meet later.

He left.

Surrounded by family and friends, Molly was holding up well. The house was filled with a variety of foods and beautiful spring flowers thoughtfully provided by friends and neighbors.

As well-wishers came and went Genie found herself playing hostess. Keeping busy made her a little less uncomfortable. She was feeling a bit harried, but relished the distraction until, intent on carrying a steaming hot casserole from the kitchen to the dining room, she inadvertently careened into a tall gentleman just removing his old beige raincoat and rain spattered black bowler. Surprising them both she splashed droplets of casserole gravy over his shirt.

"Oh damn! I am sorry," she gasped quickly placing the hot dish on a nearby table. "Here let me clean that up for you. I've really made a mess."

"That's qu…quite alright," he said in a soft voice that belied his somewhat stern appearance, "I should have been… m…more careful, while on duty anyway."

"On duty?" questioned Genie as she mopped his shirt with several cloth napkins.

"Yes. Let me introduce myself," he said politely extending his right hand. "I am Inspector Whiting. I am afraid I was in charge of the investigation of Mr. Sims' death. Such a shame."

"Nice to meet you," she said. "I am Genie Lawrence. I am sort of a friend of a friend," she added evasively not wanting to go in to all the details. "Did you say investigation? I thought it was an accident."

"Yes," he stammered. "You are absolutely right. It was a most unfortunate accident. Exactly as my investigation has proven," he added.

"Well I think it was very thoughtful of you to attend the service." She continued to mop his shirt. "There, I think that's gotten most of it. I hope you will forgive me I'm afraid you are still pretty damp."

"Th…Think nothing of it," said the tall man mumbling as he rejoined the crowd.

"Genie?"

Still distracted, Molly's call from across the room took Genie somewhat by surprise.

"Have you seen Richard?"

"No I'm sorry. I haven't. Can I help?"

"I would like to speak to him for a few minutes. Do you think you could find him and ask him to meet me in the library?"

Opening the door to the boy's room Genie peeked inside. "I thought I might find you in here," she smiled at Richard. "How are you boys doing?"

"We're fine now Miss. Come in if you like," said Tony, still not exactly certain how to address her.

"I would love to, but right now I need your Uncle Richard. Do you two think you could spare him for a little while?"

"I guess," mumbled John. "Will you come back later Uncle Richard?"

"Sure thing kiddo, in a flash."

"What is it Gen? Is something wrong?"

"No. I don't think so. Molly wants to see you in the library."

The library had been Roger's domain. It was filled with his photographs and equipment. A large ebony desk dominated one end of the dark cozy room.

Through the half opened door Richard could see Molly leaning against the desk. He knocked. "Come on in Richard," she said. "Genie is welcome also if you like."

Richard nodded to Genie, who was standing hesitantly in the doorway.

"It's probably not surprising that I feel closer to Roger here than in any other room in the house."

"I can understand that," said Richard as his eyes took in all the evidence of Roger's presence. "These photographs are awfully good. I'm guessing they were all taken for his paper."

"Most were. He was an excellent photo-journalist if I do say so myself." A sigh escaped her lips, but she quickly recovered.

"He certainly was," agreed Richard thumbing through one of the many albums stacked on book shelves.

"Richard," Molly continued. "The reason I asked you here is to give you this." She handed him a thick manila envelope that had been addressed to his New York apartment.

"I know Roger was anxious for you to have it."

"Do you know what it is?" he asked turning it over in his hands.

"No. Not really, but I suspect, from the way it is packaged, that it contains photographs. Anyway I wanted to make sure that you got it."

"Thank you." Richard began to open the package but for some reason hesitated and, tucking it under his arm, said, "Do you mind if I look at these later? I have been having quite a discussion with those boys of yours."

Although extremely interested in the contents of the mysterious envelope, Molly was pleased to see Richard spending this time with John and Tony. She didn't want anything to jeopardize that. Her curiosity could certainly wait.

At three o'clock Finch entered the Lions Head pub. He ordered a pint of Old John Courage and seated himself in a booth that would afford the required privacy. He didn't have long to wait before his contact made an appearance.

"Do you have the package?"

"No," said Whiting. A tall man, he appeared a beanstalk to the much shorter Finch. Removing his raincoat he slid awkwardly into the booth brushing at his still damp shirt.

"What do you mean no?" he hissed.

"I mean that I wasn't able to get my hands on it. What do you think I m…mean?"

"Where is it?" he said nervously fingering a sterling silver pen.

"She gave it to that American friend of hers. But don't worry I can assure you that she doesn't know what it contains."

"How can you be certain?"

"I overheard them talking. She doesn't know anything."

"You truly are an idiot. Does this friend of hers know what he has?"

"I doubt it," he said, a nervous tic just beginning under his left eye. He wiped his profusely sweating palms on the legs of his pants. "He wasn't expecting it. He didn't even open it while I was there."

"What about the girlfriend?"

"She is of no concern," said Whiting, tapping afoot and fidgeting anxiously in his seat.

"Where is the package now?"

Whiting wrote the American's name, hotel and room number on a page from his notebook, tore it out and handed it to Finch. He wanted to leave as quickly as possible.

"I am going to get that package," Finch seethed. "And I want you available to create any cover-up that I may need. Do you think you can do that?"

"What are you going to do? I don't want to get involved in any more messes."

"Don't you worry about what I do? I am going to get that evidence and I am going to get rid of anyone who has seen it. I expect you to make sure that I don't get caught." He continued, "If our American friend is a lucky man he hasn't opened that envelope yet. If he isn't. Then I'll take care of it, and all you have to do is keep things clean. Understand?"

Whiting sighed audibly.

"If you can't handle it...you can be replaced." A vicious smile crossed his face.

He understood completely. He was in this 'project' far deeper than he had ever anticipated, and if he was going to live to enjoy old age he knew he had to see it through.

On the large double bed in their hotel suite Richard lay quietly listening to Genie's slow rhythmic breathing. It was useless. He was far too restless to sleep. They had both agreed that a quick nap before dinner would be just the thing to relieve the stress brought on by the funeral and all the activity that followed. But the harder he tried to unwind, the more fitful he became.

Now, lying flat on his back beside the peacefully sleeping Genie, Richard realized that his only accomplishment had been memorizing the unusual oriental pattern of the ceiling tiles. The intricate design of chrysanthemums and dragons above his head duplicated that of the rug beneath the bed. Nice touch, he thought. His artistic eye appreciated the detail.

It wasn't only the funeral that was causing his restlessness; curiosity had finally gotten the better of him. Stretching, he rose carefully, so as not to awaken Genie. This seemed like the perfect opportunity to open that package he had received from Molly. Tiptoeing into the sitting room Richard gently closed the door. He poured himself a rather large whiskey, and with a sigh seated himself at an antique Victorian desk. The manila envelope, emblazoned with his New York address was there, on the desk, where he had dropped it earlier.

With the aid of a letter opener Richard easily unsealed one end of the package and removed its contents. As he had suspected the envelope contained several 8" x 10" black and white photographs.

"Well, Roger! Where were you when you took these?" he

mumbled to himself as he quickly looked through the pictures. "Certainly not in merry old England, that's for sure."

Taped to the back of one of the photographs was a note from his late friend:

> Richard old man,
> I need your investigative expertise
> on this...etc...etc.........

It was an enigmatic message that served to further peak his interest. Richard picked up the photos again and reexamined them; this time with considerably more care. He looked at the shots over and over. He wasn't certain how long he had been staring at them before he suddenly began to realize their significance.

"Damn, Roger! What did you get yourself into?"

Most of the photographs were typical journalistic fare, but some had obviously been taken clandestinely. It was these that most concerned him. Certain areas had been circled. They were grainy, and would have to be enlarged, perhaps even enhanced, to get a clearer picture, but by using a magnifying glass that he always carried among his numerous items of photo equipment, Richard was able to see enough detail to tell that these photos were hot... very hot.

As he studied the pictures perspiration began to collect under his arms and roll down his back. Mounting apprehension forced him to get up and pace the room. Richard realized he had to have a clear head and dumped the last of his whiskey down the sink. He refilled the glass with plain soda. Thankfully Genie was still asleep in the other room. He needed time to himself.

Getting back to the photos, Richard noted that within the circled areas there were some familiar faces. He recognized the man in the uniform and, of course, the ambassador, but the other

...he just couldn't be sure. The only thing, of which he was now certain, was that Roger's death had been no accident.

Someone knew about these photographs and wanted them, would kill for them, had killed for them. He also knew that until he had the proper equipment to get to the bottom of this he would have to keep them in a safe place.

He ached to be back in his darkroom right now. So anxious was he to get started he actually contemplated canceling the remainder of their trip. If he thought he could explain his sudden decision to return home, without Genie, or for that matter Molly, becoming overly suspicious he probably would have caught a plane that evening. Better not, he thought, and began to realize that many of the answers he was looking for would likely be found right here in London.

He dismissed, as too dangerous, the idea of telling Molly about Roger's package, but planned to begin his research by talking to the investigating officer...an Inspector Whiting, Genie had said. He would do it as soon as possible.

As he gathered the black and white glossies together and returned them to the manila envelope Richard hit upon an idea. "Brilliant," he whispered to himself. Smiling, he quickly finished his soda, dressed and slipped into his raincoat. He wrote Genie a note explaining that he had gone out for a walk and not to worry, he would be back in plenty of time for dinner.

"......be back soon......Love R."

He tucked the package under his arm and slipped out the door.

At the front desk Richard was grateful to find that they were able to furnish him with an envelope large enough to hold his package. He dropped the manila envelope into the new one, wrote some instructions in the corner and handed it, with a 5 pound note, to the concierge.

Satisfied that the photographs were, for the time being, safely stashed away, Richard left the hotel. A good brisk walk was exactly what he needed to collect his thoughts. As he headed through Grosvenor Gate toward Hyde Park he began to experience that feeling of exhilaration he always felt when he knew he was on the brink of a hot story. He tingled with excitement and anticipation.

It had been years since he experienced the thrill of living on the edge. And now, suddenly, here it was again.

Richard thought of Roger and knew that he had cause to be wary, but he wasn't. He was more alive than he had been in ages.

"This is Pulitzer material McBride," he said to himself and broke into a slight jog as he entered the park.

Failing to notice that a man in a dark grey suit had been following him since he left the hotel was his first mistake. And now as Richard slowed his pace to a casual walk he made his second mistake.

Instead of taking the left path which led across open rolling park-land, he chose the right. The walkway meandered through groves of trees and flowering Rhododendron toward a sparkling lily pond. At six o'clock on a drizzly Saturday evening it was dark, dismal and deserted.

Following him, Finch was elated. Catching McBride like this was a bit of luck. Instinctively, he removed the sterling silver weapon from his pocket and clicked the button.

Instantly the blade appeared. He could see that McBride was in good physical shape, so he would have to be fast. He was ready. It only took him a moment to catch up to his prey.

The blow to the side of his head surprised and disoriented Richard, but it didn't leave him unconscious. Stumbling, he was pulled off the path and behind a hedge row. Through the ringing in his ears he could vaguely hear a voice asking questions......

uttering threats. As his head cleared and awareness returned Richard realized the danger. He saw the blade and knew instantly that the man who held it wouldn't hesitate to use it.

"OK McBride, where is it?" demanded the short balding man.

"What are you talking about? Where is what?" gasped Richard, struggling in vain against his attacker.

The blade flashed before his eyes and came to rest against his neck. Feeling the cold steel on his throat Richard abruptly ceased his useless effort.

"Don't play games. All I want is the package and you and your lady won't be bothered again."

"Leave her out of this she doesn't know a thing about those pho......"

The man's eyes flashed and Richard knew he had said too much. He would have to do some fast talking to get out of this.

"Look, I destroyed them," his voice shook. "I didn't want to get involved. It was Sims' problem not mine."

"I doubt that very much." The man's grip on Richard tightened. "Let's take a little walk back the hotel and see if we just can't find that package you say you conveniently destroyed."

It was then that Richard made his final, fatal mistake.

As the two men turned to walk back toward the hotel Richard sensed Finch loosen his grip slightly. He used the opportunity to break away, but as he sprinted toward the path he realized he had underestimated the speed and agility of his pursuer. He was caught before he cleared the bushes.

The skirmish that ensued was short, but violent. And in the end Richard didn't even feel the razor sharp blade as it slipped between his ribs.

Chapter 6

The sudden ringing of the telephone startled Molly out of a fitful sleep. Opening one eye she looked at the clock and was amazed to see that it was not yet midnight. She could have sworn she had been asleep for hours, yet, according to the clock it had been only 45 minutes.

Lifting the receiver she thought she recognized the American accent.

"Molly?"

"Yes, Genie is that you?" Molly was confused. Why on earth would Richard's girlfriend call at a time like this?

And Genie hated to bother her. She had debated for an hour about making the call, but finally her concern for Richard overrode 'good manners' and she called the only person she could think of who might know where he was. "Yes. I am so sorry to bother you, but by any chance is Richard there?"

Genie tried as best she could to sound unconcerned, only curious, but was betrayed by the quivering in her voice.

"No, I am sorry he's not. Is he supposed to be?" Molly was half awake and somewhat bewildered. Had she forgotten something? It had been an abominable day and she had retreated to her room as soon as the last guest left. For hours she had tossed and turned in a vain effort to escape the day, but she had been unable even to close her eyes until a short time ago. Now this. What could Genie possibly want? Was Richard supposed to be here? She shook her head trying to clear away the cob webs. Trying to comprehend what was happening she repeated, "Is he supposed to be here? You thought Richard would be here."

Genie detested this. She didn't want to intrude but Richard had been gone for hours and she was beginning to get a little frantic. "I was hoping he might be," she said taking a deep breath and trying to remain calm. "After we left your house we came back here and took a nap. At least I took a nap. When I woke up around six, Richard was gone. He left a note and said that he needed some fresh air and was going to take a walk. I just assumed that he had stopped by to see how you were doing. Anyway," she knew she was blithering, but couldn't help herself, "that was hours ago and he hasn't called so I thought.........Well... It isn't like him to disappear like this....But I guess if you haven't seen him..."

This wasn't New York. She had no idea where he might be, no idea where to look.

Molly was baffled, but not really worried, "I wouldn't be too upset about Richard yet," she tried to be consoling. In an odd way it was a relief to have something else to think about. "He is quite sensible you know. He probably needed a little time to himself. My guess is that he went to a pub and simply doesn't realize what time it is. I can see it now. He has gotten himself sloshed and can't remember which hotel he is staying in," she said trying to convince herself, as well as Genie, that it was indeed what had happened. "If he isn't back soon call me again and we will go out and have a look ourselves."

"Thanks, I'm sorry I bothered you. You're probably right. I'm sure he will show up shortly," Genie said, endeavoring to believe her own words.

Replacing the receiver, she began pacing the room. Her nerves were on edge. She knew Molly meant well, but there was an uneasy feeling that she couldn't seem to shake. "I hope you are right," she whispered to herself.

Now, as she paced back and forth, the room seemed alive. The faucet dripped, the heater hissed, the floorboards squeaked, she had never been so alone. She always prided herself on being independent and self-sufficient, yet now she felt completely helpless. Thank God for Molly, she thought.

An hour later the two women were driving around the streets of London. Most of the pubs had closed so it was a long shot, but neither of them had been able to think of a better idea.

Dark streets glistened with heavy mist and at two o'clock in the morning were nearly deserted.

"I know this is a stupid question, but are you sure Richard never mentioned any other friends he might meet?" Molly was reaching for straws. This midnight street search had been her idea and, other than giving them both something concrete to do, it obviously wasn't working.

"No not to me," said a disheartened Genie. "He isn't the type to keep secrets." Genie stared out the window into the darkness. She turned to Molly, "I can't even see straight anymore," she confessed.

"I know how you feel," Molly answered. "We're both exhausted. Why don't we go back to the hotel and wait? Richard will probably already be there, more worried than we are and convinced that we are both nuts."

But, when the two women returned to the hotel there were no messages, and there was no Richard.

Exhausted, they literally dropped onto the large double bed. Molly slept, Genie did not. And as the early morning sun shone through curtained windows it brought with it the realization that

Richard was not merely late, but missing. It was time to ask for help.

Anxious to get back to the children she had unceremoniously delivered to her neighbor at one o'clock in the morning; Molly left Genie alone in the suite. Before leaving she promised to get in touch with Inspector Whiting as soon as possible. She also promised that she would be back as soon as she could manage it.

With Molly gone Genie suddenly realized how drained she was. Her nervous energy depleted, she lay down back down on the bed and fell into a deep sleep.

It was late, after nine in the morning when Genie rolled over and looked at the clock. Oh no! She thought, I shouldn't have slept this long. Sitting up she picked up the phone and dialed the front desk. "This is Ms. Lawrence, room 317. Have there been any messages for me?" she asked. The negative reply was a mixed blessing. Richard hadn't called, but had she really expected him to? On the other hand she apparently hadn't slept through anything urgent.

Struggling out of her clothes she dragged herself to the bathroom. The hot shower tingled against her skin, cleared her head. A plan, she thought, I've got to have a plan. As she rinsed the soap from her body she formulated some ideas.

She would stay in the hotel room, unless absolutely necessary, in case..."Oh please let it happen"...Richard tried to contact her. "And I'll call every hospital in London." She didn't realize she had spoken out loud. "And I've got to get in touch with that Inspector Whiting myself." Instinctively she knew that keeping busy was the best way to maintain her sanity.

Aunt Sarah could wait. There was no sense in worrying her unnecessarily, she thought.

Genie had just slipped into her most comfortable old jeans when there was a knock on the door. "Am I glad to see you," she said when she opened it and found Molly standing there with Inspector Whiting. "Come in please." She grabbed Molly's arm. "Hello Inspector," she added breathlessly.

"Any word? asked Molly.

"No nothing," she said trying not to reveal her anxiety.

"I've brought Inspector Whiting with me. He knows as much as we do and he wants to ask you some questions."

"Of course, anything that might help."

The three of them spent the next hour covering all possibilities. There were the usual questions about possible enemies, arguments and the like. The Inspector was very thorough, but not very encouraging. He had his own ideas as to what happened to McBride, but until they were confirmed he would play the role of the diligent police officer. "I wish that I could give you b...b better news, Miss Lawrence, but at this point there isn't much to go on. I do think that you ought to call his aunt. She may know something. We can't afford to overlook any details."

It wasn't what Genie wanted to hear. She dreaded making that call reluctantly admitting she had put it off for as long as possible.

The Inspector closed his notebook. "I can promise you that we will do everything we can do to find Mr. McBride," he said. "And p...please call me as soon as you speak with his aunt." Inspector Whiting then left, closing the door behind him leaving the two women alone in the room.

"Is there anything I can do for you Genie?"

"No, not really. I'm grateful that you are here though. I know what a strain this must be for you."

Suddenly famished, Genie ordered room service for both of them and they spent the rest of the day calling hospitals, hotels, pubs, airports, any place they thought Richard might have gone.

At five thirty Molly absolutely had to get back to the boys. "I know you want to stay here," she said. "But please do come over to the house if you feel you need to get out for a while. And call me later...Promise." She gave Genie a hug as she left.

As afternoon became evening Genie found herself sitting in a darkened room. She hadn't been aware of the passing time and finally steeled herself for that phone call to Richard's aunt. It absolutely couldn't be put off any longer. "Here goes," she sighed.

Switching on the lights she dialed the number and tried to think of the right words to say. After what seemed like an eternity the phone was answered by a woman with a strong British accent. "Hello," said Genie tentatively and she proceeded to explain to Sarah Newell exactly what had happened.

Surprisingly, Aunt Sarah was a rock. She didn't become hysterical or lose control. She simply wanted to know all the facts and she convinced Genie that she would be as helpful as possible. "We will get through this, dear. Don't you worry. I expect to see you both down here in no time. Everything will be just fine."

Chapter 7

Everything was not fine. At eleven that evening Genie, exhausted and drawn, answered a heavy knock on her door. Inspector Whiting and a local police officer were standing, uneasily, in the hallway.

"Inspector, come in, please," she said nervously. Seeing them there she sensed what they were going to tell her. She prayed she was wrong. "Should I sit down?"

"Miss Lawrence," said the Inspector, failing to answer her question. "Officer Michaels here is with the local precinct. He has s…s…something that he would like to show you."

The officer reached into a plastic bag and pulled out a gold watch. "Do you recognize this miss?" he asked too softly.

Genie took the all too familiar watch in her hands and turned it over slowly until the inscription on the back was visible. "Richard, all my love. Gen." simple words of love, positive proof of ownership.

"Yes," she said in an inaudible whisper. "Yes I do."

"You are absolutely certain, Miss Lawrence," said the Inspector.

Genie lowered her head and nodded.

"If that is the case Miss, then I am afraid that we have some b… bad news for you," he said wishing more than ever that his nervousness wasn't so easily betrayed by his ungodly stutter. Would he forever be plagued?

His next words were like a knife. She knew they were coming

and could do nothing to prepare herself. The only sound she heard seemed to be coming from a great distance and as the room faded around her she whispered one word *Richard*......

In the blackness of the night she could almost grasp the viscous fog swirling about her feet. A constant drizzle fell, but somehow she seemed immune to the damp. She wasn't sure where she was or quite how she had gotten there, but in the distance she thought she heard the sound of a train whistle.

As she walked along the endless platform she concentrated on amber light shining in the distance. Through the ever thickening haze it shone like a beacon, drawing her in. Instinctively she knew that when she reached it she would be completely enveloped in its warm glow. She knew too that when she reached the light she would find Richard.

Quietly she turned...straining to listen. She thought she heard him. She stood absolutely still not even daring to breathe. It was very faint, like the final ring of an echo. Yes, it was definitely Richard and he was calling her name.

Her pulse quickened and she began again.

Richard's voice grew louder and soon she was able to see his face through the fog. He was standing on the deck of the last car of the train she had heard. He was holding on to the rail and his face was aglow.

She called to him and he waved. He was smiling and motioning for her to get aboard. She tried to run to him but her feet were lead. It took all her strength, but she finally reached him. She held out her hand, touched his fingers and......he was gone.

The train was now even further down the track and she looked for him once again.

"Richard," she called. "Richard, get off. I can't reach you."

"I can't Gen. I can't leave the train. I love you."

Richard stood by the rail and waved.

"Richard! Please I don't understand." Tears streamed down her face as she watched him fade into fog and amber light.

"Richard!"

.........."Richard!" Genie was startled by the sound of her own voice. And as a steady downpour battered against the windowpanes, she awoke disoriented, groggy and with a terrible headache.

Where was she? She recognized Molly's face, but why was she looking so concerned? "Richard?" she said trying to sit up in the unfamiliar bed. "Molly!......Richard?..." Her memory was muddled. She wasn't sure what was real and what had been a dream. She thought she remembered something about Richard and a train. Had he gone someplace on a train?

"Shhh Genie. Just lie back and try to sleep. You will feel better later" Molly said, speaking from experience. "You're at my house. Rest a little longer and then we will talk."

Genie obediently lay back against the pillows. She was very confused. But with sudden brutal clarity the veil lifted. The dream was gone and the nightmare of reality came flooding back. She remembered the Inspector, the policeman and "Oh God! Richard."

Tears began streaming down her face. Throwing off the quilt, she swung her feet to the floor. The tears became uncontrollable sobs and she found herself crying onto the shoulder of a man she didn't recognize. She didn't care. All she wanted was to cry and cry until the hurting stopped. But the crying made her head ache even more and she finally had to stop. Two pills and a glass of water appeared from out of nowhere. She swallowed them gratefully and waited for relief. It came quickly in the form of deep dreamless sleep.

When Genie woke again it was almost dark. Molly was sitting in a chair near the bed and there was a hot pot of strong tea nearby.

"Molly?" Genie said questioningly. She propped herself into a sitting position.

"Well! Welcome back," Molly answered.

"I feel like I've been living a nightmare. But it is all true, Richard I mean, isn't it?" Genie said with a catch in her very dry throat.

"I am afraid it is," Molly said as she poured her a cup of tea.

Genie could see that Molly's own eyes were red and swollen. "How could this happen?" she mumbled, not really expecting an answer.

Molly just shook her head.

After a few moments of absolute silence she reacted to the darkness, "What time is it? Perhaps I should ask, what day is it. I guess I'm pretty confused."

"Monday, almost six o'clock. You have been sleeping, more or less, for most of the day."

"I can't believe it. Everything is so fuzzy. I remember Inspector Whiting being here, no, no I mean at the hotel… and, oh damn; I remember crying like a baby on someone's shoulder."

"Alex Templeton. He is a good friend and neighbor and, luckily for us, a doctor." Molly walked around the bed and fluffed Genie's pillow. She was fussing like a mother hen.

"He gave you a sedative which really put you under," she continued. "I am afraid your lack of appetite and stress caused it to hit you a little harder than expected. Though, Alex seemed to think that the extra sleep would be good for you in the long run."

"Was I that bad? I must have put you through hell. I really am sorry," said Genie concerned. "Hell! I don't even remember how I got here."

"Inspector Whiting called me," Molly said, and she reminded Genie of all that had happened.

"He said that you were very shaky when you answered the door and that you collapsed when he...when...Richard... Well, he knows I am the only friend you have in London so he called me and I called Alex. I know you don't remember much, but we brought you back to the house. I grabbed a few of your things. I want you to stay here with us. Open invitation. Call this home for as long as you like.

Sitting on the bed the two women hugged forming a bond, sharing their pain.

"I think I can remember most of it now," said Genie unable to shake a feeling of awkward embarrassment at her own lack of control.

Molly understood, but didn't say anything.

"I remember," she repeated, "but the details are lost. I feel lost."

"There is one more thing Genie. And this is going to be difficult. The Inspector needs you to identify Richard's body.

Shocked, Genie moaned, "No! I don't think...do I really have to."

"Apparently they can't start the investigation until he is officially identified."

"An investigation?" Her eyes widened. "What...Why? I don't even know what happened. I guess I just assumed that there was an accident. How stupid of me. Molly, what...?"

Molly suddenly realized that Genie collapsed before Inspector Whiting had been able to explain the whole story. She hoped she was up to hearing the details.

"Genie," Molly took hold of the young woman's hand. "Richard was murdered," she said speaking as softly as she could.

Genie's eyes opened wide in disbelief. "What?" she gasped. "You mean mugged?"

"No!" Molly continued. "I mean murdered."

"Impossible. No! Richard didn't have any enemies. A bit of journalistic competition, you understand, but no real enemies. Especially here. Honestly, I'm fairly certain that he didn't even know anyone in London, other than you and Roger that is." She sat in stunned silence. What she was hearing was crazy. It had to be a mistake. It didn't make any sense. Why would anyone want to murder Richard?

"Can you tell me anymore? Please I want to know everything. I have to know it all."

"Apparently a man was walking his dog in Hyde Park and heard a commotion. He came across Richard's...um...body...near some bushes. When the police arrived they found that he had been stabbed. It looked like there had been a terrible fight because he was bruised and his clothes had been torn. Unfortunately, there doesn't seem to be any evidence of his attacker." Molly held her breath waiting for Genie's reaction.

"Well maybe it was a mugger then," said Genie after a prolonged silence.

"No, I am afraid not. Nothing was taken. It took a little while, but the police found Richard's wallet in bushes near the scene of the struggle."

"Damn," she screamed, at no one in particular, and hugged her arms tightly. "Do you think...could you possibly...will you come with me tomorrow...to see Richard?" She hated to ask Molly to go with her but it was one task she knew couldn't handle alone.

"Certainly, we can go there together," said Molly a bit hesitantly.

"No never mind," said Genie noticing Molly's reluctance. "It's really too much to ask. I'm sure Inspector Whiting will make someone available..."

"Oh honestly!" Molly berated herself. "What am I thinking? Of course I'll go with you. And after we've finished there we will check you out of the hotel. As I said earlier I want you to stay with me."

Genie was relieved. She had forgotten that most of her things were still at the hotel. Her things and Richard's. She sighed resting her head on folded arms. She was going to need all of her strength to get through the next few days.

Chapter 8

Tuesday morning was warm and sunny. But the beautiful early summer day did nothing to ease the chill. Despite the cup of strong, hot coffee Genie cradled in her hands, it caused a shiver and goose bumps ran up her arms. Thinking about yet another phone call she would have to place to Richard's aunt only added to her distress.

As she sat in Molly's bright little breakfast room, trying to gather her thoughts there was a rapping on the back door. "Ah ha," said the man she recognized, with some embarrassment, as 'the shoulder'. "I see you are feeling a little better."

"Yes. Thank you. A little. You are Dr. Templeton, aren't you?" Genie asked, blushing.

"Alex, please. Anyone who cries on my shoulder is definitely allowed to call me Alex."

"I am so sorry," she said. "Thank you for everything."

"Honestly now, how are you feeling? Is there anything I can do?"

"No, you have already been very considerate."

Now that she had a chance to meet him without the fog of drugs and tears, Genie was surprised at how tall Alex appeared. He actually had to duck a bit when coming through Molly's door. Without really thinking about it, she also noticed his soft blue/grey eyes and very dark hair that was graying slightly at the temples. What she was aware of was his gentle demeanor, and it struck her that he probably had a good bedside manner.

SUSAN SQUIRE SMITH

Obviously comfortable in the Sims' home, Alex poured himself a mug of coffee and easily fell into the chair next to Genie.

"I know how bleak everything must seem to you now, but give it some time."

Without thinking, but with instinctive compassion, he covered her hand with his.

Genie felt too sad to immediately pull away. His kindness was welcome. With comfort and support she might, possibly, live through this nightmare after all.

"Good morning Alex," said Molly as she filled a tea ball with 'Earl Grey' tea leaves. "It is nice of you to stop by. We had quite a night last night. You were wonderful to help."

"Had to check on my patient you know."

"Do you think you are prepared for today," she asked, turning to Genie. Then directing her attention to Alex she told him about identifying Richard's body.

"I think I will be OK, but I'll tell you it's not the strong coffee that is making me shake like this."

Alex looked concerned. He knew from experience that the city morgue was, at best, a difficult place to be. It could, in fact, be terrifying. "Let me come with you," he offered. "I have had some experience with matters of this sort and I know it will not be easy. You can even take advantage of my shoulder again if you have the urge." He gave her a warm reassuring smile.

Genie experienced a stab of guilt but was genuinely thankful for the offer and felt somewhat reassured knowing that Alex and Molly would be with her.

Hours later, leaving the examining room in the morgue, she was more than grateful that Alex and Molly had come along. Never in her wildest dreams could she have imagined how deeply seeing Richard...like...that... would affect her. Though a stark white sheet covered his body, his face was bathed in harsh florescent light. It was surreal.

Get up! Get up! Get up! She silently screamed. She knew she shouldn't be angry at him, but she was. It was unreasonable. Logically, she understood that, but emotionally...she would have to deal with it. She would have to come to terms with seeing him laid out on that cold steel slab because it was definitely something she would never forget.

Walking down the corridor she began to shake uncontrollably. They sat her in the nearest chair, and Alex got her a glass of water. "Here," he said in a soft, but very firm voice. "Take this." He handed her a small yellow pill.

"What is this?" she asked.

"Just something to relax you a little. Don't worry it isn't very strong."

Always wary of pills, she declined.

"Well at least take some deep breaths," suggested Alex.

After a few moments Genie was back in control.

"What about a bit of lunch?" Alex asked both women as the three of them emerged from a cab in front of Grosvenor House.

Molly and Genie both looked horrified. "Now?" they questioned, unified in their astonishment.

Genie's stomach was in knots. "Alex, maybe you could have something and then meet me in the lobby later," she offered.

Alex realized his mistake. "You're right...food...stupid suggestion."

"Genie, why don't we pack up your clothes, check you out of the hotel and then grab something to take home?" said Molly, "Our appetites might return later."

"That sounds like a smart idea. I think once I get today behind me, I'll be in better shape."

The elevator finally reached the third floor. Though very hesitant about the prospect of dealing with Richard's belongings, Genie was relieved that she would soon be leaving the hotel.

Alex and Molly were one step behind her when she opened the door to the suite and let out a loud gasp. "Jesus Christ!" she shouted as she stepped into the room and into a total mess. "Look at this," she said in amazement as the other two entered the shambles.

"It looks like you've been robbed," Molly said catching her breath.

"Damn! Damn! Damn!" exclaimed Genie. "What the hell else can happen?" She was furious and slammed shut the door of the disheveled armoire.

"Let me look around some Jennifer," offered Alex.

She turned toward him, mouth half opened, as if to say something but changed her mind and focused on the destruction.

"What is it?

"No, nothing, don't worry. I haven't gone over the edge," she said seeing the puzzled look on his face. "It's just that everyone makes the same mistake...about my name I mean.

For some strange reason, in the midst of all this...chaos...well it was just so mundane, so ordinary, it struck me as, oh, I don't know really... Who knows maybe I have gone over the edge." Genie knew she was sounding muddled, but sighed and didn't care.

Dumbfounded, Alex couldn't help but smile. "Well, Miss Lawrence, my mistake, what exactly is your name?"

"Genevieve, Genie is short for Genevieve."

"Ahh, got it." Alex smiled.

With that cleared up, they surveyed the disorder. Reality had to be dealt with...immediately.

"I'll call the manager," Molly said as she picked up the receiver and dialed the desk. "Why don't you look through it all and see what is missing."

"I can't understand it," Alex stated. "The door was locked when we arrived and I checked the window. It hasn't been touched. I don't think it's been opened since Victoria. Whoever broke in here must have had a key."

"Do you think it...maybe the police when they were investigating?" asked Molly, of no one in particular.

Minutes later the hotel manager, closely followed by the house detective, arrived on the scene. He was shaken. He knew what had happened to Mr. McBride. "Where will this all end?" he mumbled.

The house detective, Mr. Tilly, also aware of the McBride investigation immediately called Inspector Whiting. He waited to ask questions until the Inspector arrived.

Meanwhile, Genie went through her belongings and Richard's. Surprisingly, nothing appeared to be missing. Even Richard's expensive camera equipment was intact.

"Are you positive that everything is here?" asked the Inspector who had arrived during her search.

"Yes, I am sure of it. Our traveler's checks, my jewelry, even the cash. It's all here."

After he arrived, Whiting and Mr. Tilly went over the room detail by detail. "I am going to seal the room until I can get a team from our lab up here," said Inspector Whiting surprised that he hadn't yet started to stutter. It was a good sign. He was in control.

"I suspect, as I am sure you must, that this probably has a great deal to do with Mr. McBride's murder."

Genie, Molly and Alex had all privately come to the same conclusion.

"Inspector, may I take my clothes and my personal items with me tonight?" asked Genie. "I shall be staying with the Sims for a while."

"Yes, I think that is a good idea Miss Lawrence, but please leave all of Mr. McBride's belongings as they are."

Genie gathered it all together while Alex and Molly tried to calm the distraught manager.

"Inspector," called Genie, catching him as he was dialing the police lab. "Something is missing. At least I think it is. I don't see it around."

"It is?" he said. "What's that?"

"Well it may not mean anything, but there was a package. You remember Molly," she said turning to her friend, "the package that you gave Richard after Roger's funeral." Was that only three days ago? she thought. "I can't find it anywhere?"

"Do you kn…kn…know what was in the package?" Now he was nervous, very nervous.

"No, I am afraid I don't. I don't think Richard ever opened it. At least I didn't see him open it."

"You gave this package to Mr. McBride, Mrs. Sims?"

"Yes Inspector I did. Actually it was from my late husband, and other than guessing that it probably contained photographs, I haven't any better idea than Gen…Miss Lawrence does about its contents."

"All right, thank you," he said and turned to finish his call.

Busy collecting the items Genie would need while she stayed with the Sims; the three of them did not give any thought to the decidedly deep frown permanently affixed to Whiting's face while he continued his inspection of the room.

It was getting dark when an incredibly fatigued Inspector Whiting let himself into the council house he rented in the area of Muswell Hill.

Never married, he had lived there alone for over twenty years, and the eclectic assortment of furniture reflected a distinct lack of interest in his home.

It was on his way to the kitchen when he first noticed a figure in the shadows. Finch was there, waiting in the darkened living room.

"How did you get in?" Whiting exclaimed with surprise.

"Do you really think that is a problem?" Finch sneered.

Opening himself a much needed pint of ale, Whiting joined the intruder in the shadows. He didn't bother to turn on the lights. The darkness seemed, somehow, more appropriate.

"Well I am glad that everything is over," he said.

"Nothing is OVER!" growled the intruder.

"What do you m... mean? McBride is dead and you have the package. What else do you want?"

"I do not, do you hear me, do not have the package."

"But I saw your handiwork in the hotel room. Didn't you take it?" This was incredulous.

"The package was not in the room. If it had been there I would have found it."

Inspector Whiting sighed heavily, he wanted this to be over with. He wanted this man out of his house......out of his life. And, Jesus, he wanted to sleep. When this mess was finished he would sleep for a week.

He told his unwelcome visitor everything he knew...everything he had learned from the girl friend.

"She said that she didn't know what was in the p...package. I believe her. And the Sims woman doesn't know about the evidence either. I don't know what happened to it. I honestly thought you

had taken it." He finished his ale and quivered, almost imperceptibly, while he waited for Finch to respond.

"Then we must continue the game. I know that McBride saw
the pictures. I got that much out of him before his untimely
demise, but that is all he revealed. I think we are going to have to
keep a close eye on that girl friend of his."

"But I told you she d...doesn't know anything. I am convinced
of that," he said frantically.

"Then we will have to play a waiting game. She is our only
link," he hesitated. "I am going out of town for a time. While I am
away stick to her like glue. And when I return you WILL have
results for me. Won't you my friend?"

The inspector nodded. A knife blade glinted ominously in the
moonlight, and a cold shiver run up his spine.

Without another word the intruder silently departed. When he
was gone Inspector Whiting turned on every light in the house.
Breathing deeply, he sat with a thud on an old green divan. . He
was scared. For a few pieces of silver he had sold his soul to the
devil and he wondered, now, if there was any way to buy it back. In
his heart he didn't think so.

After spending the entire afternoon and early evening with the
hotel manager and the police Alex, Molly and Genie were finally
able to check Genie out of Grosvenor House.

It was somewhat past dusk, not quite dark when they were
greeted at the door of the Sims' home by Molly's two very somber
boys. Molly could only begin to guess how the tragedies of the past
few days had affected them. She also knew that they must be
starving so while she fixed a large plate of sandwiches for everyone
she made a mental note to ask Alex to recommend a good child
psychologist. They had seemed to cope quite normally with the

death of their father, but add this second blow…well it was just too much for them to deal with. It was too much for anyone to deal with. She only hoped she could keep it together herself.

"That was so difficult," Genie said after finally making the inevitable call to Richard's aunt. "Richard was Sarah's only family."

Alex was devouring a sandwich and Molly was having tea when Genie finally completed the unavoidable phone call.

"I am sure that it must have been difficult for both of you," said Alex, noticing the tear stains streaking her lovely face.

"How about a cup of tea and something to eat?" he suggested.

"Just tea I think." She was not yet able to face food.

"Sarah and I have made some plans. Molly, I hope that you approve. We have decided that Richard should be buried on Dartmoor, with his Mother."

"I think that's a lovely idea." Molly responded quietly, and with difficulty contained her own rollercoaster of emotional reaction to the day. "Have you made any arrangements?"

"We have planned a small ceremony for Saturday. That should give the police department enough time to arrange…" she hesitated, "…to move Richard to Dartmoor."

"Oh Lord!" sighed Molly. "Saturday! Do you realize that Saturday will be exactly one week since we…since Roger's…"

Her head rested momentarily in her hands. Again the enormity of the events of the past week threatened to overwhelm her. Then raising her tea absently to her lips she stood and stared at a collection of Roger's photographs. She began to tremble. "I can't believe it. Who could have guessed……?" A tear ran down her cheek and she did not bother to wipe it away.

Genie walked across the room and put an arm around her. "This has been, to cite an old quote, 'the worst of times', Molly, but we're here for each other, we can support each other no matter what the future holds. We have to get through this and make it better. Think of the boys and you know we just have to."

Later, that moment would be difficult to explain. Though they had bonded through grief, each woman, in her own way, knew their friendship would grow stronger as time eased their pain.

After a short while, Genie continued, "I am going to hire a car tomorrow and drive down to Dickson Abbot. I will be staying at 'The Grange'."

"I've heard of it," said Molly, "I think Richard stayed there the last time he visited his aunt."

Genie warmed her hands on the cup. "Yes, I believe he did. He was very enthusiastic about it. We were going to have a nice relaxing vaca……" It was hard to continue. Tears threatened to choke her words. But they were tears of anger, not sorrow. "Who could do something like that to Richard? And why?" she said heatedly. "I promise you two I am going to find out what the hell happened." They could see she was fuming.

"Gen," remarked Alex, who had picked up the diminutive Richard had been fond of using. "You know that we will support you, but don't you think you should leave the investigating up to the police?"

"Oh, I will. But I want to stay here, in London while they work. I would feel like I deserted Richard if I don't see this thing to its conclusion."

"You do realize, Genie, that they may never solve Richard's murder?"

"I know that Molly. I'll be reasonable. I can't stay forever, but I want to be of as much help as I can. It's the least I can do for him."

Only after promising to give Genie some pointers on how to drive on 'the wrong side of the road', was Alex allowed to leave.

As the two women sat together in the quiet library Molly finally broached a subject that had been bothering her most of the evening.

"Genie, I don't know how to tell you this, but I am not going to be able to join you on Dartmoor for the funeral. I simply can't leave the boys again. They are still trying to be brave, but this has been terribly difficult for them and I don't want them to be alone just yet. I hope you understand."

Genie was disappointed. She had come to rely on her new friend, perhaps too much, but she did understand. She realized it was the only decision Molly could make. "Don't worry," she said gently. "Please, don't feel guilty. I know that this has been hard on the boys. Richard's death coming so close to their father's must have been quite a shock for them. It definitely is one of life's lousiest coincidences."

The evening drew on and the two women, each lost in her own private reverie, took comfort in the other's silent presence. It was well after midnight before they bid each other goodnight.

Chapter 9

Driving down A303 was certainly a lot easier than negotiating the traffic and winding one way streets of London.

Poor Alex, thought Genie, he had been so patient with her. He wasn't the least bit perturbed...actually had the nerve to tease her...when she bounced, rather unskillfully, around a few left hand turns. Puzzled that the left side of the tiny car suddenly seemed enormous, she wished there had been time for just one more lesson. But there hadn't so it would be 'on the job training' from now on.

Though the English countryside in June was absolutely breathtaking, Genie was only vaguely aware of it as she sped down the highway toward Exeter. More important things occupied her mind......... The cable she sent to Judy and Ira was explicit, but concise. Knowing how upset they would be she had added that a letter, with more details, would soon follow. She prayed that Ira would receive the cable before the wire services delivered the news of Richard's death to the paper...and she decided not to call her parents, just yet. They would be frantic and on the next plane to London. She loved them dearly, but couldn't handle that right now... "I just hope I haven't forgotten anything," she sighed, and added a mental note to call Molly in the morning.

Stress was beginning to take its toll. All major muscle groups were screaming for relief and her hands were white knuckled from the vise-like grip she had on the steering wheel. This is not good, she thought, shaking one hand, then the other, twisting her head and neck and squirming to relieve aching back muscles.

And she had not been paying much attention to her surroundings for she suddenly realized that most of the other cars on the road were passing her at quite a pace. So much for my 55 mph programming, she mused and pressed a little harder on the accelerator.

If anyone had pointed out the grey sedan that had been following her for the last several miles she would have dismissed their observation as coincidence. She would have found it impossible to believe that its only occupant, Inspector Whiting, had, per instructions, been watching her every move......the driving lesson, the trip to the bank, the cables sent, and the service stop. He was 'sticking to her like glue'. Where she went, he would go. What she knew, he would know. She could not have guessed that his life depended on it.

Passing through Exeter, the last large city before Dartmoor, brought tremendous relief. With only 10 or 15 more miles to go, she knew she would reach Dickson Abbot before dark.

After several hours behind the wheel she was now quite confident in her ability to cope with the road and confident also that she had attended to every possible detail. For the first time in what felt like years...Genie allowed herself to relax.

Her thoughts drifting back to childhood tales of the bleak moors, she was pleasantly surprised by the splendor of the countryside. Lush green forests had rapidly given way to rolling hills. Covered in rose and violet heather, the moor was far more beautiful than she had imagined.

Eyes glued to the hillside, Genie failed to notice a large boulder in the road ahead. In a heartbeat she became aware of the situation, braked and swerved moments before impact, just in time to save herself from serious injury or at the very least an unwanted repair bill. Breathing heavily, she brought the car to a screeching halt on the shoulder of the road. To her absolute astonishment the 'boulder' got up and lazily ambled down the road. The large black-faced sheep returned to the burrow it had managed to dig for itself in the high roadside embankment. "I'll be damned," she said after realizing that this bizarre practice of burrowing had been carried out by most of the moor's ovine inhabitants.

After the sheep incident her encounter with the Dartmoor ponies should almost have been expected. But who in their right mind would believe that free range ponies would have such an affinity for tourists. Small, sturdy animals, with incredibly shaggy coats, they roamed the fields at will. When she stopped to check her road-map she found that the aggressively friendly creatures did not hesitate to stick their head through any open window. It was certainly disconcerting, but she couldn't help laughing at the ridiculousness of the situation.

"Thank you," she said quite loudly to the resident wildlife. "You sure know how to make a person feel welcome."

Genie's own personal black cloud was beginning to lift and she was actually glad she had made the long drive. At least until she finally met her match.

About to negotiate a very pretty, but very narrow little bridge she found her way blocked by the reddest, the most unkempt looking, definitely the strangest cow she had ever seen. "Is everything around here shaggy?" she shouted in frustration, as she contemplated her next move. The cow was not about to give an inch and there was no way for Genie to go around her.

Without warning a friendly face in an old black Daimler came to her rescue. "May I be of some assistance?" said the elderly woman behind the wheel. Genie, who had gotten out of her car to survey the possibilities, turned in astonishment. "Aunt Sarah?

Pardon me, I mean Mrs. Newell?" Had she actually recognized the voice?

"Yes, I am Sarah Newell," the soft, yet distinguished voice continued. "Have I made your acquaintance?"

"Only by telephone, I'm afraid. I am Genie......Genevieve Lawrence." She walked over to the Daimler.

"Why Genie, my dear. Come here." And when the older woman stepped out of her car there was a tearful embrace.

A quarter mile back on a low hill the Inspector watched the encounter through heavy binoculars. He noted the license plate of the Daimler. At this distance he couldn't make out the face of the older woman, but he was certain it was McBride's aunt. He returned to the sedan and jotted her name next to the number. "It will be easy enough to check," he mumbled.

Not wanting his presence known he remained there, by the side of the road, until the two women had enough time to move the stubborn beast.

"Old Nan has a mind of her own," Sarah Newell said with a grin. "But a few honks on the horn and a gentle nudge should get her on her way."

The deed done Genie followed Sarah into town.

Situated on the banks of the Bovey River, Dickson Abbot was a small country town whose only income, other than farming, came from the few tourists who stopped there on their way to the coast.

The one main street boasted a grocer, a combination post office and gift store, a garage and two pubs. The few side streets accommodated a small number of shops and the homes of the town's residents, many of whom still lived in traditional thatched

SUSAN SQUIRE SMITH

cottages. The quaint, well kept, little village reminded Genie of postcards she had seen picturing rural England.

Following the Daimler past the town's ancient church, Genie could see 'The Grange'. Located at the far end of the tiny hamlet, the centuries old building was separated from the rest of the town by a long winding driveway and a lush grove of white birch trees. The clear waters of the Bovey River, really no more than a wide stream, babbled past the building and there was a foot bridge which led to garden like walks on the other side of the stream.

The town had gotten its name from an 8th century monastery. Over the years 'The Grange', as it had come to be called, had undergone many changes. Originally used as a retreat for a reclusive order of monks during the 11th and 12th centuries it had eventually been given over to an order of friars famous for distilling their own spirits. It was rumored that several bottles of their special cognac were still hidden somewhere in a secret cavern beneath the structure. Years later during World War II 'The Grange', then owned by a colonel and his wife, had harbored children evacuated from war torn London, and finally, in the early sixties a local family took over the deteriorating building. After extensive renovation it was reopened as a country inn.

With Richard's aunt by her side Genie checked in at the front desk. The manager, who was also the bellman and sometimes bartender, greeted her profusely. "Hello miss," he began. "We've been expecting you. So sorry to 'ear about Mr. Richard. Sarah told us all about it. We'll all try to make things as comfortable as possible. I 'ave a lovely room just waiting for you."

Genie was a bit taken back by all the attention. She should have realized that in a town this size, her arrival wouldn't go unnoticed. Shrugging to Aunt Sarah, who had been smiling quietly through-out the exchange, she proceeded to follow Mr. Wilkes up a broad staircase. At the top of the stairs they turned to the left and quickly covered the few yards to her room, the room she and Richard should have been sharing.

Stepping into the small, bright corner room was like stepping back in time. The large cherry, four poster bed, with its fluffy down quilt, took up most of the floor space. The furniture was a mixture of styles, all, if not actually antiques, were very old sturdy English country pieces. Pretty, multi colored, flowered chintz curtains were drawn back, letting in what little daylight was left. French doors, obviously an afterthought, led to a tiny balcony. Genie opened the doors and walked out onto the porch. Taking a deep breath she found herself looking over the river to the woods beyond the footbridge. It brought tears to her eyes to think that she should be enjoying all this with Richard.

"Now, now dear," said Aunt Sarah. "I know what you are thinking. But it will do no good to brood. We will mourn Richard together, but brooding will not help. What you need is a home cooked meal and a hot cup of tea, and I know where you can get both."

Parked in the church yard across from the entrance to the inn, Inspector Whiting watched as the two women, in Sarah's Daimler, drove back down the road. He then pulled up in front of the hotel, parked his sedan as discreetly as possible and walked into the lobby. At the front desk he requested a room on the second floor with a balcony that overlooked the river. As he had hoped, he was given the room next to Genie Lawrence. Unlike Genie, however, he paid no attention to the view. He waited in his room for darkness to fall. The anonymity of night would allow him the flexibility he needed to survey the town.

An hour later, unnoticed, he leaned against a low, stone wall and studied the home of Sarah Newell.

"Doesn't it leak?" asked Genie as she entered the picturesque cottage. Until today she had no idea that thatched roofs were still in use.

"Of course not, dear. Actually, the roof gets thatched every few years," Sara explained. "This house has been in my family for generations. It has undergone some changes over the years, but the living area is substantially the same as it was a century ago."

The cottage with its white stucco walls and wide oak floor-boards was spacious. On the other hand, low ceilings made it very cozy. At first glance "quaint" was how Genie would have described it. That changed when she noticed that it had all of the modern conveniences. Aunt Sarah was definitely a modern woman in both her thinking and her appliances. To ward off the evening chill a fire crackled in the oversized hearth and Genie, feeling very much at home, sat herself in a nearby chair while Sarah prepared a sumptuous dinner of potatoes, green-beans and lamb with mint sauce. Genie tried not to think of her 'friends' on the road.

At the end of the meal Sarah surprised her by offering a wide variety of after dinner drinks. She selected a Grand Marnier which Sarah served in a lovely crystal glass. With a start Genie noticed that the pattern of the glass was the same as that of the vase that had belonged to Richard's mother. "Richard has…had a piece of crystal that matches this glass."

"Oh yes, the vase. This crystal, like the house, has been in the family for years. It came from Ireland originally. With some long lost ancestor, I suppose. When Richard's mother and I were children these pieces were only used on special occasions, but I think they are too lovely to keep stored away so I use them often." Seeing the look of longing on Genie's face Sarah continued, "I hope you will keep the vase. I would like to think of it as a tie between us."

"Thank you, what a thoughtful idea. I will cherish it always." Genie wiped a small tear from her eye.

For the rest of the evening the women talked about Richard. They laughed and cried. Sarah shared family stories with Genie and Genie shared New York stories with her. By the time Sarah dropped her off at the inn Genie knew that she would learn to live with Richard's death......but not with his murder.

Chapter 10

Thursday morning Genie slept late, she had no idea what time she had gotten back to the inn, she didn't care. Sarah was going to Exeter and she planned on spending the entire day exploring Dickson Abbot and taking a stroll through the inn's lovely gardens. This was the first time she had been truly alone since touching down at Heathrow. A good day for reflection, she mused while uncharacteristically rolling over, allowing for just a few more minutes sleep.

She woke again at ten o'clock. It was definitely time to get up. The small bathroom was equipped with a tub and a rubber hose contraption that she had to attach to the faucet to create a make shift shower. When she had finally figured out a workable solution she was disappointed to find that, unlike larger hotels, the hot water did not go on forever. Jumping out of the cold tub Genie wrapped herself in one of the large fluffy towels provided by the inn. Still undressed she sat on the bed, and picking up the ancient receiver dialed the front desk. "How do I call London?" she inquired of Mr. Wilkes.

"Give me the number miss and I'll get it for you."

She gave him Molly's number and waited while he made the connection.

Molly was relieved to hear that Genie had made the trip safely. She was also pleased that she and Richard's aunt were getting along so well, and laughed when told of how they had met.

"I am afraid that nothing else is new here Genie, I haven't

heard anything from Inspector Whiting. There is one thing though...the coroner has made arrangements to have Richard at the church in Dickson Abbot tomorrow evening. I hope that will be alright with you?"

"Yes, that will be fine. Thank you for taking care of it for me. The service is scheduled for Saturday morning. I am not sure how soon I will leave, after that, but I will let you know."

Still sitting in the towel Genie called the front desk again and ordered room service. Determined not to stay cooped up in her hotel room she decided to take advantage of the balcony and have breakfast in the summer sun while she planned the rest of the day.

By the time room service arrived with hot tea, crumpets and a large platter of egg and bacon Genie had changed into the crisp white sundress and sandals she hoped would be perfect for a day of walking.

Walking..., she thought, walking will help. No matter how she tried, it was impossible to ignore her sadness. This complete sense of loss was an alien experience, but everyone always said keep busy so she figured that getting dressed, having breakfast, just occupying time was essential. "Genevieve Lawrence, you will get through this."

In the next room Inspector Whiting was also having breakfast. He hated being stuck in his room like this, but couldn't take the chance of being discovered. He hoped she would leave soon so that he could at last get away from these four walls. He was actually looking forward to following her around all day. "She sure is a pretty one," he said with just a hint of longing in his voice.

As she had planned, Genie spent the day wandering through town. She browsed through the post office/gift shop and was surprised at the number of homemade handicrafts for sale. It seemed that everyone in town had contributed something to the shop's inventory.

Stepping up to the window in the post office area of the shop Genie purchased several stamps and used one of them to send a letter to her parents.

Finally able to write it this morning she had managed to chronicle the events and was now confident that she was emotionally capable of handling a phone call to her family. She would, in fact, be sure to do it before their letter arrived.

She had also written to Judy and Ira. It was a long letter explaining as much as she could about all that had happened, and also asking them to please look after the apartment until she returned. She enclosed, in the package, apartment keys and a check to cover rent and utilities for the rest of the summer.

Taking care of these details caused her to truly focus on the significance of Richard's death. She was alone. In one short moment there was suddenly no one 'significant' in her life. No one with whom she could share this lovely little town; no one to share her sadness, her anger; no one to share a cool shower on a hot summer day; no one to share the rent; no one to share her love... ...no one to share her life.

"Ugh!" She needed the fresh air again. Hastily slipping the remaining stamps into her purse she stepped out into bright daylight.

From behind a car parked across the road Whiting watched as Genie left the store. He had briefly surveyed her room earlier, but not wanting to alarm her, hadn't given it a thorough search. Instinctively he knew that the damned package wasn't there anyway. He could only hope that she would lead him to it, but so far he had no luck. Hell! At this point she wasn't even thinking about it. He was beginning to think the trip worthless, to think he would never find that missing evidence.

"Damn! I am a dead man," he mumbled and hurried to follow her as she continued toward the far end of town.

Casually strolling through the village Genie occasionally had the oddest sensation that she was being watched. A couple of times she actually found herself turning to see if anyone was behind her, but of course no one was there.

"Face it girl!" she said more loudly than she meant to, causing a few curious looks. "You are really losing it. And talking to yourself too. Great, just great!" She admonished herself for being paranoid, but couldn't quite shake off those peculiar feelings.

Despite her momentary discomfort the rest of the day seemed to go by quickly and when she finally met Aunt Sarah at 'the Grange' for dinner she was exhausted.

On Friday she and Sarah explored the area together. Sarah regaled her with more family stories and legends of the moors as they picked heather and walked along the river.

Late in the afternoon they went to the church and spoke with the vicar. He assured them that everything was well planned and that they had nothing to worry about. At his suggestion they went directly to Sarah's house, put their feet up and tried to relax. There was nothing more they could do for Richard until tomorrow.

Chapter 11

It was a bright and all too cheerful morning. Genie dressed for the funeral wishing, unaccountably, for rain. It didn't seem right, somehow, to be burying Richard when the world looked so fresh, so new. She would have felt better if the weather today had been really God awful.

The knock on the door made her jump. "Come on in Sarah," she called; slightly surprised that Richard's aunt had arrived so early.

When the door opened she gasped in stunned embarrassment. "Alex! What are you doing here?" Only half dressed she fumbled with unopened buttons on her blouse.

"Sorry," he said, his own discomfort causing an endearing and somewhat stupid smile to cross his face. "I...uh...I thought that perhaps you could use some company. You know a little moral support."

"That's ni...very kind," she stumbled through her words while slipping into her skirt, "...of you. And yes, I suppose I...we could." Regaining her composure she added a wide black belt to her black and teal linen suit.

"It was actually Molly's idea," he added. "She is hard to refuse when she gets an idea."

In spite of the occasion Alex thought she looked lovely. Her hair was pulled away from her face and twisted intricately about the back of her head. A few wispy golden red tendrils had escaped and curled defiantly down the nape of her neck.

His awkward smile softened as he looked at Genie, confident that he, or rather Molly, had made the right decision.

"Do you think we have time for breakfast?" Having been on the road since before dawn, he was very hungry.

"I am sure we do," said Genie "Would you mind if we invited Sarah? She has been wonderful to me. I think you will find her fascinating. She really is quite a character."

Alex readily agreed to the idea and as the two of them rode toward Sarah's home Genie told him all about the drive through the moors and about Richard's amazing aunt. By the time they arrived at the cottage Alex sensed that he also knew Aunt Sarah quite well.

He was not disappointed, Sarah Newell was everything Genie had said she would be, warm, supportive, caring and more than a little bit eccentric in the large, flowered hat that she had chosen for the ceremony.

Although Alex invited the women out for breakfast Sarah insisted on fixing it herself. She served it on the patio in her beautiful little 'English garden' overlooking a small fish pond.

The small funeral was held in a church that had been built in the eleven hundreds. The ancient stone building was dark and cool with pews that had worn into irregular seating over centuries of use. Central to the altar, was an eight foot long permanent stone crypt with a sculpture of its 12th century occupants, a knight and his lady, on the lid.

Candles gave a warm glow to the interior and the vicar appeared to know just the right words for the occasion.

The service was not long. After the funeral Alex, Genie and Sarah returned to Sarah's cottage. Several of her oldest friends dropped by to pay their condolences and to meet Genie. Although most of them didn't know Richard they were all very fond of Sarah and shared in her loss.

Both women were comforted by Alex's presence. Sarah instinctively saw him as a kind and caring man. He had provided strength during the ceremony, and now, as the day progressed, he wasn't letting either of them become morose. When their spirits began to lag he would cheer them up with his quick wit and dumb jokes.

By five the last of the company had gone. Sarah set the table on the patio with tiny cakes and strawberries with clotted cream. It was a treat that Genie had never before tasted. "This is wonderful," she said sampling the rich cream. The three of them sat together quietly in Sarah's garden enjoying tea and cakes and conversation. By evening Sarah, Alex and Genie, who only a week ago had been strangers, were chatting like old friends? Shared grief eased a bit as the day came to a close.

"Thank you for being here, Alex. You made everything a lot easier. You will never know how grateful I am that you showed up this morning," said Genie opening the door to her hotel room. "Would you like to come in? I have a lovely balcony that is going to waste. In fact why don't I call room service and have them bring us a nightcap."

"That sounds perfect. It has been a long day." he said, his body reminding him that he had been up since three.

Upon entering the room Genie suddenly stopped, and with a puzzled expression, looked around. .

"What's the trouble?" Alex asked concerned.

"I don't know exactly. It seems different......It is different. Alex I think that someone has been in here. "

"It was most likely the maid." Alex wasn't an alarmist. "Let me have a look," he said entering behind her. "Everything seems to be in place Gen." He saw no obvious disorder.

"You're right I am probably being paranoid, but I could swear I hung my robe on the hook," she said lifting it from the chair.

Circling the room she tried to put her finger on any concrete evidence of intrusion. "Alex, I know I'm right. Look at this......" She was about to mention that the French doors were ajar when she heard Alex swear. From the little she knew she thought it very unlike him.

"Bloody hell," he said. "Gen, I think you're right. Unless, of course, you usually live in this sort of disarray."

Turning away from the doors, Genie saw Alex standing in front of the large walnut wardrobe. Now, with its doors open, she could see that her clothes were completely disheveled.

"Terrific," she sighed. "Just terrific." Apparently they had surprised the intruder before he had time to put her things back in order. "What the hell is going on? First Richard, then Grosvenor House, now here. If someone is trying to scare the hell out of me they are beginning to succeed."

"Gen," said Alex, seriously contemplating the situation. "Is anything missing?" He was ready to bet his life that everything was there.

"No," she responded dejectedly. "This is just like the last time. Why?"

"Listen to me," he said earnestly. "Obviously someone is following you......I am certain of it. Whoever it is must think you know something, or believe Richard knew something or more to the point had something of importance... They are willing to kill for it... have killed for it."

As he paced the floor he thought of the envelope Roger left for Richard and was positive it would prove to be the missing link.

"My guess is that we're both thinking the same thing."

"The package," they said in unison.

"Inspector Whiting has all of Richard's things under lock and key. And you know there was no envelope. So I have no idea why anyone would follow me here."

"Well, since nothing is missing we can presume that they didn't find what they were looking for. Which means," he paused.

"What? What are you thinking," Genie asked, with concern.

"It means, I am afraid, that whomever it is, is probably still around. Come on," he ordered suddenly. "Get your things together. You are getting out of here...Now." He was concerned for her safety.

Genie was a bit stunned when he began gathering her clothes. "Alex, wait a minute. Shouldn't we contact the police or something?"

"We will. And you should tell that inspector... what's his name? Whiting? But right now I think we ought to get you away from here."

Instinctively Genie knew that Alex was right, so, without stopping to worry about where they would go at this time of night, she finished packing her things.

Seeing the look of discomfort on her face, Alex tried to put her at ease. "Stick with me kid," he said. "I know any number of ways to rescue ladies in distress." He put an arm around her to assure her that said everything was going to be alright. Of course he wasn't quite sure he believed it himself.

Mr. Wilkes was quite distressed when Genie checked out. "Is there anything wrong?" he asked.

They had decided not to tell him of the incident in the room. Perhaps they were being a bit too suspicious, but at this point they wanted a little time to think things through.

"No, no. Everything was lovely," she lied. "I will be leaving for London in the morning and I have decided to spend the evening with Mrs. Newell."

It was an understandable decision that Mr. Wilkes readily accepted.

Actually, the decision to stay with Sarah was no lie. While Genie packed her belongings Alex had called Sarah and explained the situation. As he expected, she insisted that the two of them stay with her for the night. She had even offered to return Genie's rental car to the 'Hertz' agency in Exeter. It was an offer Genie couldn't refuse.

As Genie was leaving the lobby Mr. Wilkes called her name. "Miss Lawrence," he said, hastily coming out from behind the counter. "Pardon me, but I almost forgot to give you your mail."

"Mail?" she questioned incredulously.

"Yes miss. This came for you in the afternoon post," he said handing her a large white envelope.

The handwriting of the address was all too familiar. A wave of emotion, and things fell into place. Tucking the package under her arm, she rushed out to meet Alex in the parking lot.

Whiting had almost been discovered twice. The first time in her room, but he escaped by ducking out onto her balcony. Then as he stood frozen in the shadows Genie had noticed the slightly opened doors. If the doctor had not called her name he would surely have been discovered on the porch.

His decision to remain hidden outside her room, instead of chancing the three foot jump to his own balcony had, in the long run, proven more beneficial than the fruitless room search. He had been able to listen to their hastily conceived plans.

Taking advantage of the information, he hastily secluded himself in a darkened corner of the inn lobby and watched while Genie Lawrence checked out.

Now, as he sat and reviewed what he had just witnessed he

understood why that bloody package, that damnable evidence, had been so elusive.

McBride was a clever bugger after all, he thought, chuckling to himself. He must have mailed it here, in the Lawrence woman's name, shortly before that madman murdered him. Well, finally it had been located, he had located it and now all he had to do was wait for the perfect opportunity and the photographs would be his. He figured that in time she would probably bring the envelope to him, but God knows how many people would have seen the photographs by then.

No, he couldn't wait. He couldn't risk the life of anyone else. He was absolutely certain that little weasel he had gotten involved with would expect him to "take care of" anyone who viewed the "evidence" and he just couldn't do that anymore. No, Whiting couldn't wait for Genie Lawrence to bring the photographs to him; he had to get them......now.

Gulping down the last of his brandy, he left the inn and, leaving his car in the parking, lot hurriedly walked the short distance to Sarah Newell's house.

Genie popped nimbly into the low seat of the dark green Jaguar. Alex nodded at the envelope tucked under her arm.

"It's from Richard," she responded to his questioning glance, and sensed his discomfort. "You think this is it, don't you Alex?"

"Don't you?" he said.

She nodded.

"Gen, do you know what it is?"

She turned the package over and over. "I have a good idea. Let's wait until we get to Sarah's, though, before I open it."

They turned the corner. Sarah Newell stood waving at them

from her open front door. "Come in here you two," she called as they got out of the car. "Tell me what this is all about."

Genie was reluctant to have Sarah become any more involved in this than she had too so, while she did explain about the break in, she did not mention the package, which was now neatly tucked into her carry-all.

She and Alex finally convinced Sarah that the police were on top of it......a slight exaggeration for her benefit as they hadn't contacted the local police and wouldn't contact Whiting, in London, until tomorrow. They managed to convince her that everything that could be done was being done.

Sarah had gone back to bed and Genie sat in a chair by the glowing hearth sipping from a mug of hot tea. She was staring at the package Alex had retrieved from her bag. "I am positive this is the envelope that Molly gave him. He must have mailed it here before he was......murdered."

Alex noticed the tears that welled in her eyes. "The one you thought had been stolen from your room at the hotel?"

Genie nodded. "Well, there is only one way to find out." Anxiously, she tore open the package and pulled out the original manila envelope that had Richard's name and New York address printed in black marker. With only slight hesitation she nervously opened that one too.

It wasn't what she expected. Actually, she hadn't known what to expect, but this......well...she couldn't contain her disappointment. "Damn it," she swore, accidentally knocking the envelope to the floor. "These certainly don't look like a reason for murder."

Alex picked up the package and sorted through the contents.

"Alex, they're only pictures of some damn party. I really hoped..."

Scanning the dozen or so 8"x10" black and white photos, Alex had to agree. They certainly didn't seem to be worth a man's life.

But while sliding them back into the manila envelope he noticed the letter. Taped to the back of the last photograph was the note from Roger:

> Richard old man…
> I need your investigative expertise on this.
> Take a look at these snaps and tell me if you
> see what I see. I have circled some areas of
> interest. Call me with your conclusions.
> We will need to talk.
> Roger
>
> P.S. Better keep this under your hat
> until we decide how to proceed.
> Thanks!

After reading the letter Genie and Alex carefully reexamined all the photographs. They noticed that on several of them Roger had, indeed, circled certain areas.

"What does it look like to you Gen?"

"A party," she said sarcastically. Though she now realized that these pictures were significant, that they were the key, she did not know how or why. Holding them under the light she tried to discern what was contained within the inscribed areas. "I can't tell much of anything. The circled areas are much too small to be clear. God this is frustrating."

It was well after midnight when they at last admitted to themselves that they were getting nowhere. They needed their sleep. The investigation would have to wait until Genie was, as per recent plans, remotely tucked away at Alex's mother's home in St. Albans. For if she actually was in danger she couldn't take the chance of staying anywhere near Molly and her boys.

Alex put his arm around Genie and gave her a reassuring hug. "Get some rest. We have a long drive ahead of us tomorrow," he said. "Don't worry we'll get to the bottom of this."

Genie closed the door to the bedroom hoping he was right.

Alex turned out the lights and settled himself on the couch.

Chapter 12

By the time Finch had checked into his hotel room he was perspiring profusely. He had always been told that dry heat was easier to tolerate, but obviously his body hadn't adjusted. It was probably over one hundred degrees in the sun. All he had done since landing was drink gallons of water and sweat.

"Damn this heat!" he swore, his treasured silver pen slipping between damp fingers, dropped to the floor. He quickly retrieved the weapon and examined it. Finding that it was undamaged he carefully placed it on top of the dresser. He couldn't wait to change his clothes and quickly stripped himself of the "trademark" dark grey suit he had worn on the plane.

Twenty minutes later he emerged from a long cold shower feeling refreshed and anxious to "get on with it." For a few seconds he sat, naked, on the edge of the bed, with the air conditioner on hi-max, wallowing in the cool breeze that emanated from the noisy unit. Reluctantly, he reached over and turned the knob to low. He picked up the telephone and dialed the unlisted number.

"Thompson, this is Finch. Is the ambassador in? Good. I will be there in exactly one half hour. I have a message for him from our mutual friend in Washington. Oh! Thompson, don't tell him I am coming. I want it to be a little surprise."

Without waiting for a reply he abruptly replaced the receiver. Now, more appropriately dressed in linen slacks and a safari shirt he casually slipped the silver pen into a breast pocket and left the room.

Busy streets shimmered under a scorching desert sun. Finch couldn't believe it; the city was inundated with tourists. Finally able to hail a cab, an ancient Mercedes, he directed it to a street near the address across town. He walked the last quarter mile to Ian Stanley's residence. On the second ring Thompson answered the door.

"Good day Mr. Finch."

"Hello Thompson, is he still in?"

"Yes, upstairs."

"Alright." Finch turned to Thompson. "I want you to leave. Spend the rest of the day with friends. Be seen around town; don't come back here until morning."

Thompson responded without question and as his car turned out of the driveway onto the street Finch silently climbed the stairs.

Through the open door to the bedroom suite he could see that the ambassador was preparing for a bath. He slipped through the door without a sound.

"Mr. Finch." The ambassador said startled by the unexpected visitor. "What the hell are you doing here?" He grabbed a towel and tied it snugly around his waist.

Finch sneered at the overweight, middle aged body with mild contempt. "I have a message from the general. He is afraid, Ian, that you are beginning to regret your decision to work with us."

"My decision... Ha! You mean your decision...or was it his decision...that I work with you...don't you?" Ian Stanley hissed.

"Semantics," Finch said as he slowly worked his way around the spacious room. He looked out a window to the quiet courtyard below. He looked into the bathroom and adjacent dressing room and into the closets.

The ambassador grabbed his arm. "What exactly do you think you are doing? Just say what you have to say and get out of here."

Finch easily removed Stanley's hand. A sinister grin crossed his face. "I have come to tell you that we are concerned about you. We know how worried you have been about your participation in our little venture. We want to put you at ease."

Ian Stanley's eyes widened as Finch deftly removed the pen from his pocket. With a silent click the four inch, needle like blade appeared.

"Now wait a minute," the ambassador stammered while backing across the room. "There is no need for violence. I'm not going to say anything."

"I know you're not," Finch said still grinning as he approached Stanley.

"You can't do this," shouted the ambassador. "Thompson! Thompson!"

"I'm afraid he can't hear you. In fact I believe he's gone...out."

"Listen to me. Please!" Stanley was sweating and breathing heavily. Terror crept into his eyes. "You will never get away with killing me. You know that." The Ambassador inched slowly toward the wall button that would alert his guards.

But Finch stalked his prey like a cat. He walked around Ian Stanley in ever decreasing circles, backing him further and further into a corner.

"But I am not going to kill you," he sneered.

The ambassador sighed with relief.

"No, actually, you are going to kill yourself."

Ian Stanley's muscles tightened involuntarily. "You are crazy," he said, barely able to make the words audible.

In the next instant Finch sprang on Stanley and held him in a locking grip. The ambassador struggled, but was no match for his small, powerful attacker.

Finch was careful not to use his knife for the moment. He had needed it for the threat, but not for the attack. After a short struggle he easily pinned the out of condition ambassador to the floor and, grabbing a pillow, covered his face until the struggling ceased.

He dragged the unconscious man into the bathroom. It wasn't exactly how he had planned it, but the naked ambassador and the bathtub full of hot water was more than he could have hoped for. He lifted the unconscious man from the floor and dropped him to a sitting position in the tub.

Aroused by sudden contact with the water the ambassador flail-ed his arms and attempted to fling himself at Finch.

Finch's shirt and slacks were quickly soaked with the hot scented water, but the ambassador's attack came too late. Finch worked swiftly, easily overcoming the disoriented man. The time was right. With two quick strokes of his knife he deeply slashed the ambassador's wrists.

Holding the man's arms under the water the blood flowed swiftly. Elated he continued to hold Stanley with a firm hand and wallowed in the arousal he experienced as he watched the man's life blood turn the tub to crimson.

"How inconsiderate of you not to leave a note old boy," Finch said as he rummaged through the ambassador's bathroom and, soon finding exactly what he needed, dropped a razor blade into the tub. He easily cleared up all signs of the struggle, then wiped off his weapon and put it back into his pocket. There was one problem. His shirt was stained in spots with pink watery blood. He quickly grabbed one of Stanley's shirts and threw it on over his bloody clothes. It was large and sloppy...not great, but it would do.

Everything in order, he had just started down the winding stairway when the sound of a car on the gravel driveway stopped him in his tracks. Keeping an eye on the front door Finch backed up the staircase and returned to the bedroom. He heard the front door close.

"Ian," the woman's voice was slurred. "Ian? Darling? Where are you?" The sing song voice of Katherine Stanley revealed her proclivity for afternoon martinis.

Arrogantly, Finch sauntered to an open window. He had surveyed the situation earlier and knew it would be an easy climb. With little difficulty he exited through the window and dropped silently from a convenient tree to the courtyard below. He made his way through bushes at the rear of the house and had only gone a short distance when the sound of the woman's scream pierced the air.

Finch took his time getting back to the hotel. The dry heat quickly evaporated the damp evidence of his encounter with Ian Stanley.

After such a stimulating afternoon he felt in need of female companionship and spent the next few hours on one of Cairo's more infamous side streets sating his obscure desires. No one there questioned his peculiar choice of attire.

Later, lying on the bed in his hotel room he waited for the prearranged call. With typical military precision the phone rang at the appointed time. Finch answered with one word. "Done."

"Anything else to report?" asked the general.

"Are we on the scrambler?" he asked.

The general answered affirmatively.

"The missing evidence is still giving us trouble. We had to take out the American. My man in London is on it and I can assure you that we will have everything soon."

The general was not satisfied. "I am going ahead with the negotiations," he said. "Eagle will make contact with the Kremlin in two days. Arrangements will be made for the switch."

Finch was uncomfortable. The general was giving Eagle too much responsibility.

"I'll show them all," the general continued. "When I walk into Washington with those missing Americans the President will give me anything I want." He was beginning to rant. Finch brought him back to reality.

"General. Wait for a few days before you give Eagle the go ahead. Let me get those photographs or this whole thing could blow up in our faces." He was thinking of the money he would lose if this crazy old bastard did something stupid.

"No," said the general. "We must move now." His rising voice was beginning to crack.

"Listen!" Finch literally screamed into the phone. "Do you want to end up on the President's staff or in jail? Just keep everything under wraps until I get back to London and terminate the situation.

Intimidated by the thought of incarceration instead of laurels the general listened to reason. "Alright Finch, you'll have your time, but make it fast. The Eagle won't wait forever. If he doesn't get to act soon he'll start shooting those Soviet bastards purely for the hell of it."

The conversation was over. As crazy as the general was Finch knew that on this one point he was right. The Eagle was most untrustworthy. Bloodthirsty and unstable, the operation......the kill...... was more important than the payoff.

Although anxious to return to London, Finch decided to remain in Cairo through Sunday. He wanted to hear, first hand, the reaction to Ian Stanley's 'unfortunate suicide'. Once again he picked up the telephone. This time he dialed room service and ordered himself a lavish dinner. He replaced the receiver and with an expression of self-satisfaction slowly crossing his face lay back down on the bed and took a well-deserved nap.

Chapter 13

The drive to the rolling hills north of St. Albans took several hours. After the first anxious moments, leaving at dawn, to avoid being followed, Alex and Genie were able to settle into a more comfortable routine. They passed the time getting to know a little about each other.

Alex entertained Genie with stories, both humorous and heart rending, of the twelve years he had spent in Africa. She knew he had been a doctor since the seventies and wondered why his pediatric practice was only a few years old. Now, listening to him recount the early years, years spent treating children in under-developed nations, she understood.

He told her a little about his present practice and his special interest in treating child and adolescent burn victims. His compassion for severely burned children appeared to go beyond the normal desire to heal. It was truly a passion.

Genie had met very few people who seemed so dedicated to a cause. She listened, and watched his eyes sparkle as he continued to talk. "It is such a challenge, Gen. Burns are bloody awful to deal with under the best of circumstances, and the children, if they survive, are left with both emotional and physical scars. They often need years of continuing care."

As Alex discussed his practice with Genie, he was uncomfortably aware that he felt a growing wish for her approval and support. For him, it was an unusual reaction, and without even realizing it he glanced at her briefly with a quizzical expression. It was gone almost as quickly as it appeared. He would simply put it out of his mind.

Genie listened carefully and realized she was becoming increasingly fond of the warm and talented Dr. Templeton. She was pleased they had become friends. Richard would have liked him she thought with a sigh, and wondered how long it would be before she stopped comparing everyone to Richard. How long she would continue to need his posthumous approval?

Watching Alex out of the corner of her eye she noticed a puzzled expression come over his face. It was there for only an instant, gone before she could question him about it. She wondered what thoughts had caused that curious look.

For a while after that, there was complete silence until Alex abruptly brought up the subject of the photographs. "Well I guess it's time to talk about it." He got right to the point. "What do you think of those pictures Gen?"

Genie reached behind the seat into her bag. "I have been going over and over them and I don't recognize anyone. I am certain they weren't taken in England though. The environment is all wrong. Look," she pointed to an area behind a large house. "There are definitely palm trees in the background. And something else, Alex, the clothes are…well…I don't know…international. It looks like a gathering of the jet set. The best thing we can do is have the circled areas enlarged. Until we can see them more clearly we aren't going to get anywhere."

Alex looked pensively for a moment. "Gen, we should talk to Molly. She will probably know where Roger was when he took these shots."

"I know you're right, but I really hate to get her more involved. It could be dangerous for her and………." Genie continued to talk, but it soon became apparent to her that Alex had stopped listening. "Alex? Alex, what do you think?…Alex?"

She was right. For the past few moments he hadn't heard a word she said. His attention had been fixed on the road and the rear-view mirror. "Oh, sorry. I'm afraid I haven't been listening. I think that someone has been following us."

Genie turned and glanced out the rear window. "Which car?"

"The grey sedan."

"I see him. Alex, you know that car looks like one that was parked near mine at the Grange. You're sure he has been following us?"

"There is one way to find out," he said. He pressed his foot on the accelerator and the car lurched ahead. They were driving more than 100 kilometers an hour and the grey sedan followed suit.

Genie looked back. "He is still behind us."

"That does it. Buckle up. I am going to lose him."

She couldn't help but smile. Alex actually had a grin on his face.

"I think you like this cloak and dagger business Dr. Templeton. I only hope you are good at it." Genie gripped the dash board and held her breath while Alex pushed the accelerator to the floor.

Until this point, Inspector Whiting had been having no trouble keeping track of the doctor's green Jaguar. He had, in fact, spent most of the long trip cursing himself for his inability to get hold of the photographs the previous evening at the Newell woman's home. "Lucky for the old dame they didn't show them to her," he said to himself. It would be hard enough to deal with the woman and the doctor, without getting some old biddy involved. "Bloody hell! This is getting to be some damn mess."

So far both cars had been driving at a leisurely pace, but as the car he followed abruptly accelerated Whiting knew that he had been spotted.

"B...Bloody hell," he swore again and raced to catch the speeding vehicle. He prayed that he had not been recognized.

The Jaguar continued to accelerate and he realized that it was hopeless. There was no way that his sluggish old sedan could keep pace with the sleek sports car. By the time they turned off onto the road to St. Albans he knew he had lost it. He turned around on the M1 and headed back into London. With a little research he knew he could figure out where they were going, and if he was lucky Miss Lawrence would call him about her amazing discovery of the photographs. Whiting could only hope that the woman realized how dangerous the pictures were and was smart enough to keep them to herself. "And of course the doctor," he laughed sarcastically and slammed his hand against the steering wheel.

It was late afternoon when Alex and Genie rumbled up the long beige, brick driveway to 'Channing House'. They drove around a circular that enclosed a flowering garden and left to the rear of the home. Genie turned to Alex in amazement. "This is your Mother's country house?" She gasped as the expanse of the estate came into view. "Why didn't you warn me?"

"I was afraid you might be after me for my money." He winked as he teased her.

The massive granite building stood proudly on immaculately tended grounds. It was surrounded by ancient imposing oaks and neatly trimmed boxwood hedge rows.

"It is absolutely lovely, but it is so lar...imposing. Does your mother live here alone?"

"No," he explained. "My sister, Jackie, has been living here since she and good old Peter were divorced. And there is a small staff to look after the house and grounds."

Genie was enthralled by the extensive gardens and intricate

miniature maze that had come into view, and she listened attentively while Alex related some of the family history.

"We only live in the east wing. Like many families we still have the titles and the land, but not the fortunes, so we turned much of our home into a museum."

"A museum?" She was intrigued. "What do you mean?"

"We invite tourists to visit the home and grounds from May through October. The money is used to pay the taxes and for maintenance."

"It sounds like a wonderful way to share all this beauty. But doesn't it bother your family to have strangers going through your home?"

"Not really," Alex explained. "The east wing and the grounds behind it are very private. While you are here you will find that you hardly notice the visitors. And most of them respect the fact that we are trying to preserve a bit of English history. Actually, I believe mother likes all the activity. Well," he continued. "That's enough for now. I am beginning to sound like a professional tour guide. Let's go inside and get you settled." He got out of the car and grabbed her bags. Jokingly he added, "If you have a pound note mother will give you the grand tour tomorrow."

Stepping through a large oak door Alex carried their bags into the entrance hall of the east wing. He was greeted by one of the staff. "Good afternoon Dr. Welcome home. We haven't seen you for several weeks."

"Thank you Hollings," he said and handed the ancient retainer only the lightest bags. "This is Miss Lawrence. She will be staying with us for a time. See her things are put in the yellow guest room."

"Yes sir." Hollings bowed slightly as he left. Alex chuckled at the gesture. "We tell him constantly that he doesn't have to do that, but he has been bowing since he worked for my grandfather. I think it's genetic."

At the rear of the home, the spacious hallway was unexpectedly bright and cheerful. The floor, tiled in a large black and white checkerboard pattern, and the walls, papered in white rice cloth, created a distinctively modern appearance. Several large green plants gave the space, warmth and elegant comfort.

They walked through a hallway to the front living area.

"Ah Mother, there you are." Alex called to the small delicate woman descending a wide oak staircase.

Dressed in a pale pink linen suit that enhanced her naturally stark, white hair and soft rosy complexion she smiled brightly at Alex.

Genie's anxiety waned as she saw that Mrs. Templeton had the same gentle eyes as her son. Instead of offering a hand, the older woman gave Genie a warm hug. "Welcome to 'Channing House' my dear."

"Thank you Mrs. Templeton," she said. "Thank you for having me in your home."

"Please, call me Ruth. We are not very formal around here. I am truly afraid our ancestors would turn over in their graves if they were to listen in on many of our conversations. Isn't that so Alex?"

"It is all you're doing mother. I am perfectly willing to be a stuffy old country doctor, but you would have nothing to do with me. Would you, love?" He gave her a small kiss on the cheek.

"I think that maybe you two could use some tea," Ruth offered. "I was just having a cup out on the patio. Why don't you join me?"

"You are right about needing some refreshment Mother, but I have something a bit cooler and a bit stronger in mind. Gen, how would you like a tall gin and tonic?"

"That sounds wonderful." Genie followed Ruth onto the patio that overlooked a private rose garden. Alex had been right. The grounds behind this wing of the home were completely secluded.

A few minutes later Alex joined them. He was carrying two ice cold drinks, one of which Genie readily accepted. Sitting in the quiet garden she could almost forget the insanity that had become her life. As she sipped her drink she listened intently while Alex described, for his mother, a carefully edited version of the events of the past two weeks. He told her, of course, about Richard's murder, but not about the photographs, nor the hotel break-ins, nor the fact that they had been followed. He also left out the fact that they were trying to solve this thing themselves. And, of course he didn't tell her how he was beginning to feel about Genie. That he hadn't even admitted to himself...yet.

"You poor dear. You have had quite a time of it. Well, I want you to stay right here until everything is resolved. Are the police working on the case?"

"Yes," said Genie, finally finding her voice again. "There is an Inspector Whiting involved. I am certain that he will come up with something soon."

"And what about my son? I hope he has been lending you his support. You know ever since he was a little boy he has loved mysteries."

"Now Mother, don't bore Gen with tales of my sordid youth," said Alex. He quickly tried to steer the conversation in another direction. "Where is Jackie this evening?"

"She is out with Constance. They went into London to the theater. They went to see some show about roller skating, or maybe it was trains, I'm really not certain." Ruth's puzzled expression revealed that she wasn't really sure what her daughter was up too.

"Starlight Express, Mother. It is quite something. I will take you to see it myself. You will love it." A slight frown crossed his face. "Do you think that Jackie will be home this evening? I would like to introduce her to Genie."

"I really can't say. You know Constance. She can talk your

sister into almost anything. Truly, Constance can talk anyone into almost anything," Ruth exclaimed, with a knowing wink to her son.

"I know," said Alex in a tone that caused Genie to wonder about his relationship with his sister's friend.

"Well now Mother," he said, again changing the subject. "Why don't I take you and Gen out for dinner?"

"As long as you promise to make it an early evening. From what I've heard so far I think Genie can probably use a good night's sleep." Ruth could see how quiet Genie had become.

Genie agreed. She was hungry... but for the most part she was simply exhausted.

Chapter 14

Slowly, Genie opened her eyes. Sunlight streamed through sheer yellow curtains and danced across the delicately flowered down quilt. Seeing the room for the first time in daylight she was grateful that Alex had suggested she sleep here instead of in the larger, but darker, guest room across the hall.

The yellow and white flowered wall covering matched the quilt and reminded her of the room she had as a little girl. Even the way the canopy tented the bed brought back fond memories of childhood. Lazily, rolling over she realized she felt better than she had in days.

After a shower she dressed in white linen slacks and a lavender silk shirt. Pulling her growing red hair back away from her face she twisted it into a unique, slightly skewed, knot of her own creation, and noted that she would soon have to find a good stylist. It was becoming much too unruly.

By the time she walked down the long winding staircase it was almost noon. Alex would be in London with his patients by now, she thought. She discovered, much to her own surprise, that she missed his company.

"Hello! You must be Genie," said a pretty young woman with Alex's curly dark hair and infectious smile. "I'm Jackie, Alex's sister." She reached out to shake Genie's hand and Genie immediately understood why Alex was so passionate about his work. Jackie's right arm, from the wrist to just below the elbow, was badly scarred. From their appearance it was obvious that the scars were the result of an old incident, probably a fire.

"You're just in time for lunch." Jackie offered brightly.

"I am sorry I slept so late," Genie apologized. "I hope I haven't inconvenienced anyone."

"Nonsense, from what Mother has told us you have really been through it. I'm surprised that you didn't sleep for a week."

The two women went out onto the patio where Ruth and Constance were enjoying freshly squeezed lemonade.

"My dear, please join us," Ruth patted the chair next to hers. Her hand jingled with an assortment of copper and gold cloisonné bracelets. Momentarily, a luncheon of tomato bisque and shrimp salad with croissants was served by a nervous young girl in a stark grey dress and frilly white apron.

Genie was introduced to Constance.

"Well I think it is all absolutely frightful darlings. You are so fortunate that Alex came to your rescue," remarked Constance.

As the conversation continued it became quite apparent that the tall, cool looking blond was not nearly as concerned for Genie's welfare as she was about her relationship with Alex.

It was obvious that Constance and Alex had once been an "item". From her tone Genie surmised that Constance thought they still were. Well, maybe they still are, she thought. It unnerved her that she suddenly experienced a twinge of jealousy. She was suddenly very curious about Alex's relationship with Jackie's sophisticated friend.

After lunch Genie found some privacy in a small, very masculine, den and phoned Molly. Reluctantly she told Molly about the incident at the Grange and about locating the missing photographs. As she predicted Molly insisted on seeing them.

"I am planning to see Inspector Whiting tomorrow. Hopefully the photographs will give him the lead he needs to find Richard's...

killer." She still had a hard time saying those words. "I'll stop by your house after I see him."

Genie hung up the phone hoping she had done the right thing. What else I could do, she thought. Molly is the only one who knows where Roger was when he took those......

A sudden knock on the door startled her.

"Excuse me."

She turned and saw Ruth standing in the doorway.

"Certainly, come in," said Genie as Ruth entered the room.

"I thought that you might enjoy seeing the rest of the house. We have some interesting bits of history tucked away here.

"That would be wonderful." Genie was genuinely glad for the chance to wander through the rest of the wonderful old home, and decided to put off a call to Aunt Sarah until the evening.

"You must be very proud of Channing House," she said.

"I hate to admit it," Ruth conspired. "But I am. Don't tell Alex, though. He will think I've gone soft."

Ruth took Genie's arm and the two women strolled down the corridor toward the great hall.

When they returned to the east wing it was almost four, tea time, a custom Genie had come to look forward to. They were joined in the Library by Jackie and Constance. Exhausted from an afternoon of tennis Jackie dropped unceremoniously into a 14th century chair of unknown origin. "So Mum showed you the relics did she? Personally I think we should chuck it all and move to Kensington or Mayfair," Jackie teased.

"Do you play?" Constance asked Genie nodding to the racket leaning against her chair.

"Yes, actually, I do Constance. Perhaps we can play a set or two." For some reason Constance brought out a streak of competitiveness in Genie that she thought was as far behind her as were her days on the high school tennis team.

"How about doubles when Alex returns?" suggested Jackie enthusiastically.

"Wonderful. I'll wager Alex and I beat the sox off you two," bragged Constance immediately deciding teams.

Fortunately for Genie the discussion was interrupted before it became strained.

"Excuse me Madame, but Dr. Templeton is calling. He would like to speak to Miss Lawrence."

"Thank you, Hollings," said Genie, grateful for the escape. As she rose to answer the telephone she was sure that she was the only one who noticed the "if looks could kill," stare from Constance.

"Gen?"

"Yes, Alex, hi."

"How is your day? Is Mother taking good care of you?"

"She is wonderful. She gave me the grand tour. Now we're all having tea."

"All?"

"Jackie, Constance, your Mother and I."

"Constance? Is she still there?" Alex didn't sound pleased.

"I believe she is staying for a few days. As a matter of fact you're in for doubles when you get here. Constance has lined you to play against Jackie and me."

"Wonderful," he said sarcastically.

"Oh, Alex she's alright. I believe she has a case on you though." She regretted the words as soon as she said them.

"That's old news. Don't let her get to you."

What does he mean by that, she thought, and kicked herself for trying to second guess? She changed the subject. "I called Molly. As you can imagine she is really anxious to see the photographs. I am planning to see her tomorrow after I stop by the police station and speak to Inspector Whiting. Hopefully he has come up with something since last week."

"I should think he will have something by now. If not, the photographs ought to help. And I'll feel much better when he knows about the Grange. I want him to assign someone to protect you. Gen, tell Mother that I will be there in an hour and don't forget to put on your tennies."

She was just hanging up the phone when Constance "popped in" to remind her that her tea was getting cold.

Chapter 15

Tuesday morning Inspector Whiting nervously paced the floor of his small office. Daylight shone through the room's only window illuminating one corner of his cluttered desk.

As he suspected it had been a simple task to discover where Templeton had taken the Lawrence woman. Channing House was a well-known estate and as soon as he had identified that the doctor was one of "those" Templetons he knew he had found them.

Whiting had hoped that Miss Lawrence would contact him with the news of her latest misadventure or bring him the photographs on her own. He had waited all day Monday for her to make the first move, but his patience had proven fruitless and now that Finch was due to arrive he knew that he would have to take some action. He wanted to be able to place those pictures into Finch's hands. If that "crazy bastard" felt it necessary to "deal" with anyone else, he thought with a sigh of Genie Lawrence......such a shame......he could do it himself. Whiting wanted out.

Grabbing the keys to one of the squad cars he rushed out the door, into the morning mist. It was time to go to Channing House himself.

"I wish every day could be as relaxing as yesterday," Genie said as she and Alex sped down the M1 toward London Tuesday morning.

"Just leave yourself in my hands m' lady and I'll see that your wish is granted."

"All I have to do is snap my fingers, is that right?"

"Absolutely."

"I'll remember that. Alex..." A look of concern suddenly crossed Genie's face. "Do you think the Inspector has any answers for us yet?"

"I doubt it. But he doesn't have all the facts either, does he? Listen, when you show him the photographs, don't let him talk you out of them. Remember we still need to make copies and enlarge-ents."

"Don't you think he will find it awfully strange if I don't hand them over? Perhaps I shouldn't even mention them until we show them to Molly and have the copies made."

"You are right that he might think it suspicious, but we're here now so see what he has to say. And then go with your own instinct. You really are beginning to think like a detective, aren't you?'

"I guess that's true enough," she said breathing deeply and turning her head so that Alex couldn't see her eyes tear and redden. Genie knew Alex's remark was meant to be lighthearted, but she felt a deep need to see this thing through for Richard. It was the last thing that she would ever be able to do for him. She couldn't let it just drop; let him become just another statistic. And for her own sake she had to know... why the hell this had happened.

Alex reached over and took her hand. It was a compassionate act, nothing more he reasoned, just that. But in a small corner of his mind he wondered if anything more was going on.

He had a good idea what was going through Genie's mind and he also wanted Richard's murder solved, but perhaps for more selfish reasons. He knew she would not be able to find some peace until the question of McBride's murder was resolved. He still couldn't admit to himself that his feelings had gone beyond mere concern.

"Now remember," he said as he dropped her in front of the

station house. "I'll pick you up in 45 minutes, but don't hurry if that's not enough time I'll wait right here."

Genie waved as Alex eased his way into the congested London traffic and headed toward the hospital.

The hospital visit had taken longer than expected, and it was a full hour later when he pulled back in front of the large grey stone Police Station. Not seeing Genie he prepared to park, but before he had even come to a complete stop the passenger door flew open and she jumped in, ashen faced and shaking.

"God, Gen! What is the matter? You look like you've seen a ghost."

"Let's get out of here," she whispered. "Something very strange is going on. Let me catch my breath a sec. I'll tell you on the way to Molly's."

"OK," he said after they had rounded a couple of corners. "What is it?"

She could hear the concern in his voice. "It was Inspector Whiting."

"Inspector Whiting?"

"It was Inspector Whiting," she repeated. "Who followed us from Dickson Abbot. And not only that." She was talking so rapidly that she could hardly catch her breath. "He knows that I am staying at Channing House."

"Gen, calm down. Take a deep breath and tell me what this is all about."

When I went inside, into the station house," she recounted, still speaking quickly, "I asked at the desk for Inspector Whiting. The officer on duty told me that he had gone out and wasn't expected to return for a couple of hours. I started to leave a message, but... when the officer heard my name he said that the Inspector had gone out to Channing House to see me. At first I wasn't too concerned. In fact, I was annoyed with myself for having just missed him. It didn't occur to me that neither you nor I had told him I was no longer staying with Molly. And then when I saw the car......" Genie finally managed to complete her thought and was calming down, but Alex's heart was racing.

"Wait a minute. What about a car Gen?" Alex interrupted, anxious to know the whole story.

"The car, the grey car that followed us Sunday," she continued. "When I left the building I knew you wouldn't be back for a while so I took a walk around the block. In the back of the station there is a parking lot and there it was......the grey sedan."

"Are you certain it was the same one?"

"Of course. See...... The license," she said waving a slip of paper. "You can imagine my surprise. I went back to the desk and asked the sergeant if he knew who it belonged to. He just laughed about it being an old clunker and told me it belonged to Inspector Whiting. I tried not to act surprised and told the officer that I would speak to the Inspector later in the day. Then I came out to wait for you."

Alex squeezed Genie's hand. "Whew," he whistled. "This is definitely not what I expected."

Alex's green Jaguar turned onto Hampton Gardens and he parked in front of his own house, just three doors down from the Sims.

"Why don't you come in for a few minutes? We need to think this over before we talk to Molly and I could use a good strong cup of tea. How about you?"

Genie agreed. Lately, she had consumed more tea than she could ever remember. Tea under stress was becoming a habit. Tea at the drop of a hat was becoming a habit.

She had no idea why Whiting had been following her, but instinctively she knew it wasn't good.

Alex's townhouse... she could immediately tell it was owned by a man. It exuded the same feeling that Richard's apartment had, before she moved in. Perhaps it was the dark woods and heavy furniture, very tasteful and very masculine. Though quite different, there were enough similarities to bring a lump to her throat.

Enough, she thought, deep breath and focus on how dissimilar they really are.

As she looked around she found it hard to believe that Alex's home and Molly's were basically identical. Decorating trumps floor plan, she mused.

From the living area through to the kitchen Genie felt that Alex's home conveyed the same comforting warmth as did he himself. It even smelled like him...she couldn't put her finger on it exactly. Maybe old wood and musk, whatever, it was very pleasant though a little disquieting.

"So," said Alex as the two of them sat sipping freshly brewed Darjeeling at a small, round oak table in his kitchen. "Whiting followed you to the Grange. We can bet that he was the one who broke into your room. He wants those photographs very badly...... but why? How does he even know about them?"

"The hotel... Remember," Genie stated. "We told him that we thought the missing package contained pictures."

"True," Alex recalled. "But that small piece of information certainly wouldn't cause him to chase you all over England... unless, of course, he has known about them all along? And if he has..."

Their eyes met and locked. The possibility that Whiting was somehow connected to Richard's murder struck them both simultaneously.

"No. I just can't believe that," said Genie. "Perhaps it isn't the package he is after at all. Perhaps he followed me because, for some reason, he suspects me of Richard's murder."

Alex had to agree that it was a possibility. "You could be right," he admitted, "but I can't imagine anyone thinking you capable of murder."

Alex continued, "Of course, if he is after those pictures, why follow you? I mean, he must have guessed that you would show them to him when and if you found them." A glimmer of an idea shone in his face.

"And," he said after a few moments of contemplation, "if it is the photos he wants we will just have to give them to him."

"What?" Genie was astounded.

"After we make all the copies we need," added Alex. "Roger has... Damn! had...an excellent darkroom."

"I see. Then I give the Inspector the whole package...photos, negatives, the letter and all. Right?"

"Right, except for the letter and the photo...the one it was taped to. I think we should hold that one back. At this point I am not willing to trust him, and perhaps without that piece of the puzzle we will have a bit of an edge. We can certainly use one... because right now we don't know what the bloody hell is going on. Fortunately we Brits love a mystery," he mocked a satire of Alfred Hitchcock.

"Do you think he will leave me alone once he has the pictures?"

"I don't know. I hope so. At least we might have some idea of what he is thinking. If he followed you to Dartmoor because he thinks you are a suspect, he will probably continue to hound you with questions. But," Alex added emphasis to the remainder of his thoughts, "...if he himself is actually involved...if he knows that you know nothing about Richard's death... Then receiving the photographs should be enough. He should leave you alone. As long as you can convince him that you don't know anything about them. If he suspects that you have seen them or that you believe something peculiar is going on you could be in serious peril."

"Oh! Lord, Alex," sighed Genie. "I don't know if I can face him again."

"You have to Gen. You can do it. After all you want to get to the bottom of this. I know you do."

"You're right," she said regaining some enthusiasm. "I just didn't anticipate that the police might not be on our side that I wouldn't have anyone to turn to."

"Well now I am hurt," he mocked. "You do have me in your corner, you know. I was beginning to think my detecting skills were quite remarkable."

"Sorry, I didn't mean…it's just…Oh! Hell you know what I'm trying to say."

He winked, she nodded in return.

"So, are you up to it?"

It only took Genie a moment to respond. "Of course. The more I think about it the more enraged I become." She looked at him with fire in her aqua eyes. "I want to know everything. I want Richard's killers caught."

"Alright," he said excitedly, her determination was infectious, "In my opinion, for now at least, the best thing you can do is play the innocent. You know…'oh! Mr. Inspector, guess what happened to fall into my hands? I mean there I was down in Dartmoor and well…here, it's all yours'," he said mustering an absolutely dreadful feminine voice.

Rinsing her mug out under the tap Genie couldn't help but laugh. Alex had an amusing charm that she found very reassuring, as they walked up the street to Molly's house.

"I'm not too surprised," said Molly pacing the library after hearing the news concerning Whiting. "Yesterday, after you called I started thinking about all that has happened and there are just too many coincidences. I know I haven't mentioned this before, but I always suspected that Roger also may have been murdered. When the Inspector was so definite about it being 'an accident,' I dismissed my feelings and convinced myself that I was being an hysterical widow. Then when Richard died I tried not to believe their deaths were in any way related, but it kept nagging at me. You understand." She turned toward Alex and Genie who nodded their heads in agreement. "And now that Whiting is up to... God only knows what...I am more convinced than ever that Roger's 'accident' was no accident."

Genie handed her the manila envelope. "These are the only link we have Molly. See what you think."

Molly studied the photographs carefully. Genie's heart sank when a frown crossed the woman's face and she shook her head from left to right. "It's odd," she said. "He usually showed me all of his work, but I have never seen any of these before."

Then abruptly she stopped. "My God, Alex. Do you know who this is?" Molly was suddenly very excited, both Alex and Genie jumped to their feet and rushed over to get a better look. "Hold on a moment," she said and she dashed into the living room. She returned quickly carrying Sunday's paper. "Look at this. Isn't this the same man?" She held one of the photographs up next to the picture in the Times. It was easy to see the resemblance. The smiling face in the obituary section of the paper was much clearer, but it was definitely the same man.

"Ian Stanley, the American Ambassador to Egypt, died in his home in Cairo Friday afternoon. The cause of death has not yet been revealed, although there is strong evidence that his death may have been a suicide," read Alex aloud.

"Roger's last assignment was in Cairo," said Molly quietly. "That must be where these shots were taken." She was carefully reexamining the other glossies, and beginning to realize exactly how dangerous things could get.

"Do you recognize anyone else?" Genie asked.

"No, sorry I don't."

"What about that man in the uniform?" Alex pointed out.

Again she shook her head in the negative. "You know what I do have though?" Her eyes widened, and she pulled out a drawer in her husband's large mahogany desk. "Here, take a look at this. I received a short note of condolence from a French journalist and see?" Molly pointed to the stamp. "It's postmarked Cairo. I didn't think much about it. Roger had friends all over the world, but if she was in Cairo...well, perhaps she knows some of the same people. She might even have been at that party."

"We should send her enlargements of the people in the photographs; she might be able to recognize some of them," Alex mused. He was thinking out loud.

"No," said Genie, suddenly bright eyed. "I'll do better than that." Excitedly she announced, "I'll take them to her."

"What? You can't do that." Alex was stunned. "It is far too dangerous. That area of the world is in an uproar. Do you know anything about Egypt?" He was genuinely concerned that she might actually carry out this crazy idea.

"What? Egypt...no...Not really. But I have to go, Alex. Cairo is a large city. Tourists go there all the time. I will be perfectly alright and I must talk to her." Then turning to Molly she asked, "Do you think she is still there?"

"I have no idea Genie, but really you mustn't..." She was cut off mid-sentence.

"Molly, this is important to me. I have a very strong feeling that this..." she read the signature on the note, "this Anna DuLac might be able to help . Everyone connected with these pictures has died," she continued. "Roger, Richard...... the Ambassador. What if I am next, or you, or Alex?"

"That's exactly my point Gen," implored Alex. "You can't go

traipsing around the Middle East, on a wild goose chase, by your-self. You don't even know if she is still there."

Genie conceded he had a point. There was no reason to go all the way to Egypt if the woman couldn't be found. "Alright," she finally acquiesced. "I'll try to contact her first and I won't go unless I find her."

"Let's continue this discussion after you talk to her," said Alex begrudgingly. "In the meantime, Molly, I would like to use Roger's darkroom to make copies and enlargements. Can you give me a hand?"

"Of course," Molly answered then turned. "Genie, as long as you are determined to do this you might as well have this. Maybe it will help." Molly retrieved a small brown book from one of the library shelves. "This was Roger's. He kept all of his business numbers in it.

Genie took the address book and gave Molly a squeeze. "Thanks, I knew you would understand.

While Molly and Alex were busy in the darkroom Genie began flipping through the pages of Roger's book. Listed under D was the name she was looking for: DuLac, Anna, c/o Herald Tribune, Paris (Cairo). Well, she thought, it's a start.

Chapter 16

At the prearranged time the two men met, once again, in a room in a modest boarding house on King Street in Georgetown. It had been rented under the name of Johnson and they had met this way four times in the past two weeks. Of course, neither man was named Johnson.

"So, you finally admit then that your men are missing," said the American General. His steel grey eyes flashed as he spoke.

"It is a difficult problem, one that my government has been unable to resolve for themselves." After twenty years in the United States, the Russian's accent was almost indiscernible. "But why should you want to help us. You are an American patriot, are you not?" the stocky Russian sneered.

The general rose from the old slat backed chair and paced the room. His cane tapped dully on the threadbare carpet as he walked. "I have my reasons. Good reasons, just and moral reasons, yes, you could even say patriotic reasons. I can save this country. And when our President realizes what I have accomplished……Well!…He will take notice. Everyone will take notice."

The Russian was somewhat amused by the ranting of this crazy old general. He had heard them before. He was used to them. But if there was any hope at all of retrieving their operatives he knew he had to hear him out……at least for now.

"As I said," the Russian intelligence officer repeated, "what makes you think you can help us find our people?"

"I have certain......information. Vital information that will be very useful to you...to your government."

"And you are willing to share this with us?" There was cold blooded sarcasm in the Russian's tone. "For...shall we say......a price? Is that correct?"

"Yes. Of course......for a price," said the general.

How will we get this information?" the Russian continued.

"One of your people in Moscow will soon be hearing from a friend. A friend with the name of a bird," mused the General. "If it can be arranged for this "bird" to speak to the proper authorities and be assured of your government's assistance......well...then you will receive what you are seeking."

"Again I ask, at what price?"

"At what price? Why, cooperation, of course. That is the only price I ask. Simple, neighborly cooperation."

The Russian couldn't help shaking his head. Was it he who was crazy or was the general raving again? Whatever! He would play along.

"And the code name?" the Russian asked.

"Eagle," said the General so proudly that the Russian was certain the man had come up with the name himself. How patriotic.

London   *Tuesday, July 3, 1990*

On the road from St. Albans back to London, Whiting was more annoyed than ever at having missed Genie. He kicked himself for not waiting just a little longer. He should have realized that she would get in touch with him. He should have been more patient. Now after wasting the whole morning chasing out to Channing House, he could only pray that she would be at the Sims home when he arrived.

At least he wasn't driving his old sedan; the police car he was using would shorten his drive time considerably. He stepped on the gas and quickly passed the other cars on the motorway.

"She is still there," said Genie excitedly when Alex and Molly finally emerged from Roger's darkroom. "She is still in Cairo."

Alex was less than thrilled with the news. He knew that it would probably be impossible to stop Genie from going to Egypt now that she had tracked down Anna DuLac.

"What did she say when you called?" asked Molly. "Did she mention Roger?"

"I didn't exactly speak to her directly…"

"Oh, great."

"Now, Alex, just listen. She was following up on a story, but one of her colleagues gave me her address and telephone number. And I promise that I will speak with her personally before I go anywhere. But listen, this is interesting." Genie nervously paced the room. "Apparently she was supposed to go to that party, but didn't, and that same night her boyfriend, who, by the way, did attend the party, disappeared…with absolutely no explanation. I didn't get the whole story. The person I spoke with had a very strong accent and I could hardly understand him. He did assure me that he would have her call…. oh, Molly!" she said, "I left your name and number. I thought that if she recognized the name she would be more likely to return the call. I hope you don't mind."

Minutes later, to no one's surprise, the doorbell rang. Although they had been anticipating his arrival, Alex and Genie were, none the less, quite uneasy at the sound of Inspector Whiting's voice in the living room.

Alex thought Genie looked a little pale and squeezed her hand for reassurance. "This will be a piece of cake," he whispered to her as they joined Molly by the front door and greeted the disheveled constable.

"Ah, Miss Lawrence," Whiting said. "How are you doing today?" He reached over and shook her hand with what almost seemed like genuine concern.

"I am quite well, thank you. My friends have been a great help to me."

"Yes, I am sure they have. I've come to speak to you about the disposition of Mr. McBride's things. I do wish I had better news for you about the investigation, but I am afraid we have come to a dead end." She had better mention the photographs soon, he thought, or I'll run out of excuses to be here.

Listening to him rattle on about Richard's belongings Genie understood all too well that the Inspector did not think her a suspect. It was ridiculously ironic that she had actually prayed she would be considered a murderer, that the only way she could trust this man were if he thought her capable of killing her lover. Her heart was beating wildly but she realized it was now or never. She had to begin the charade. "Well perhaps..." she breathed heavily, a deep calming breath, "perhaps I can help you. Do you remember that as we looked through Richard's things I suggested that a package may be missing?"

"Yes, as a m...m...matter of fact I do." That damn stuttering, he cursed to himself. He too took a deep breath and waited for her to continue.

"Well it seems I've found it after all. Apparently Richard mailed it to our hotel in Dartmoor. It was a curious thing for him to do... don't you think?" she asked innocently. "Anyway," she began again, "let me get it for you."

When she returned Genie was carrying a neatly sealed manila envelope. "I hope this will help," she said handing him the package. "Will you tell me what is in it when you are done?"

"You mean you haven't opened…?"

"No. I thought that you…the police should be the ones to open the package," she tried to act as naively as a child. It was a role she found extremely distasteful.

Whiting didn't buy it, but he was more than willing to play along. At least he could honestly tell Finch that as far as he knew the Lawrence woman didn't know what was in the package. He, himself, hadn't actually ever seen these photographs, but, whatever they were, they couldn't be worth getting involved in another murder.

"What do you think?" Genie asked when Whiting had finally left.

"I don't know," said Alex. "He didn't ask very many questions. It was a little too easy."

"I suppose you are right. Let's just cross our fingers and pray that he has what he was looking for and that he will leave it at that."

There wasn't anything more any of them could do just then so with a quick goodbye to both women, Alex left for his office.

Genie was grateful for an opportunity to spend time with Molly. It passed all too quickly, however, and before she realized it, Molly's boys came bounding in from cricket practice. It was good to see them. They reminded her of her own students. It had been such a short time since the end of the school year, yet it seemed like an eternity. Her whole life had changed. She wondered if she would ever be able to pick up the pieces.

Chapter 17

Whiting sat at his desk. An old, snake-necked reading lamp provided the only light in the otherwise dark office. With his door closed he was completely cut off from the unceasing activity of the station house. Before him the manila envelope lay unopened. He stared at it wishing for "X-ray" eyes, for although he was aching with curiosity he knew instinctively that the package was better left intact.

As if on cue Whiting's door opened and the small familiar figure silently slipped in. He seated himself in a chair across from the nervous Inspector.

"So," he said staring directly into Whiting's eyes, "I see you have finally retrieved the package." He picked it up and examined it. "What's this?" he said noting that it was still sealed. "Not even a little curious?"

"Curious, of course. St...st...Stupid, no," said Whiting. He could feel the perspiration already beginning to run down his back.

Finch removed his trusted silver pen from an inside jacket pocket. He flicked a finger and its long razor like blade appeared more quickly than the eye could perceive. With expert precision he deftly slit open the envelope.

The ease with which Finch handled the blade did nothing to restore Whiting's confidence and he shifted slightly in his chair.

The mousy little man emptied the contents of the envelope onto the inspector's desk.

In complete silence he examined the photographs one by one.

To Whiting, the wait seemed eternal. He sat motionless while Finch surveyed the cache. "Is this everything?" he said, finally breaking the silence. "This is all she gave you?" His voice grew loud with anger. Instinctively Finch knew something was missing.

"Yes. She gave them to me voluntarily. The package was just as you found it. Why?"

Finch ignored the question.

"Are you certain this was all?" he barked then added, "Do you think she has seen these?"

"She said she hadn't opened it, but that is hard to believe."

"You're right it is hard to believe," Finch broke in.

Whiting wasn't sure what Finch was getting at so he continued. "Even if she had seen them would she be able to...you know...p... put any pieces together?"

"Where is she now?" Finch said still ignoring Whiting's questions?

"I presume she is at Channing House. Do you know it?" Finally reviewing the pictures for himself he looked across the desk and saw menace in Finch's eyes. "It appears," he continued, "that she has b...b...become quite friendly with a doctor Alex Templeton. She has been staying at his mother's home just north of St. Albans."

Leaving the pictures scattered on his desk, Whiting rose uneasily from his seat. He stood and stared out of the small sooty window, his back turned to his visitor. Anything was better than looking into those ferret like eyes. "Listen, Finch," he said cautiously reemphasizing what he had said earlier. "I don't know if she saw those photos or not, and anyway, I seriously doubt that they would mean anything to her. Hell! Even I don't know the whole story."

"Be thankful that you don't," Finch hissed. "I'll find out exactly how much she knows and deal with it. Just be ready to back me up if I need you. Am I making myself clear?" Finch too had risen. He was now standing only inches from Whiting's ear. "I want you to leave everything up to me," he whispered malevolently. "As far as you are concerned, the McBride investigation and your contact with those involved is over...Until, of course, I need you."

Whiting nodded his head and continued to gaze through the grimy glass. When at last he turned to respond the room was empty. He stood there quietly for a few minutes and said a silent prayer for Genie Lawrence. Then, as was his habit, he put on his coat first, and then his hat, picked up a twenty year old umbrella that had never been unfurled, turned off the light and walked out the door.

Although it was nearly midnight when Alex and Genie returned to Channing House they found both Jackie and Constance still awake. They were in the drawing room engaged in what sounded like a lively conversation.

"Good evening, ladies," said Alex. He walked over to the couch and kissed his sister on the top of the head. "May we join you?"

"Of course you can big brother. As a matter of fact you can pour me a brandy. How about you Genie?"

"That sounds wonderful. It has been quite a day."

"Oh!" said Constance curiously. "How so?"

"I am afraid the police are ending their investigation. They insist that there is nothing more they can do. At this point it seems that Richard's murder may go unsolved."

That, at least, was true. Inspector Whiting had said as much earlier that evening. It was all she was going to tell the family. As far as they would know, the investigation was over and she was simply going to stay in England for a time while she decided what to do next.

"You poor dear," Constance continued solicitously. "What are you going to do now?"

"Ruth has graciously offered to let me stay here while I make some decisions. I have to admit that I am not looking forward to facing our empty apartment." She deliberately avoided any mention of Anna DuLac or Cairo.

"Yes, I can see where that would be difficult. You and Mr. McBride were living together, weren't you?"

Genie wondered if anyone but she noted the sarcasm. She also wondered if anyone but she noticed that when Alex handed Constance a snifter of brandy she released his hand reluctantly.

Beginning to feel a bit uncomfortable with the direction this conversation was taking, she silently blessed Alex when he stepped in and changed the subject.

"So what were you two arguing about earlier?"

"The usual," pouted Constance. "I have been trying to convince your sister to come and work for me in the gallery. I could really use the help."

It was a familiar discussion. Constance owned a successful gallery in the Mayfair section of London and had, for months, been trying to persuade Jackie to help her with the business. But since her divorce from Peter, Jackie had been unusually reclusive.

Although she put on a good show around family and friends, Alex knew how deeply the separation had affected his sister. He knew her confident demeanor was often only skin deep.

"Well, Constance," said Jackie, impulsively standing, "you may regret you ever brought the subject up, because I have decided to accept your offer."

Alex and Constance were at once surprised and pleased.

"No more living the life of a dilettante. Beginning on Monday it's back to being a working girl." Jackie grinned and raised her glass as if to toast.

"Wonderful," Alex said hugging his sister. "I must say it is about time," he teased.

Constance was ecstatic. Certainly she was grateful to see her best friend finally making an effort to rejoin the real world, but more importantly she was convinced that this business arrangement with Jackie would bring her closer to Alex. More than anything she wanted to have Alex again.

Constance Corwin, called C.C. as a child, had been in love with Alex since the first day they met. At that time, however, she had been a shy teenager while he was a young doctor going off to Africa.

It wasn't until he returned home for an extended holiday, four years later, that their relationship had a chance to develop.

Alex's arrival home that December in 1978 was meant as a Christmas surprise for his mother. But it was he who received the surprise. After making it quietly up the stairs to his bedroom, he slipped silently through the door and dropped exhausted onto his bed. To his surprise, it was already occupied by his sister's, now very grown up, best friend. The lanky young girl had become a sophisticated blond beauty who, upon seeing Alex next to her in bed, did not let him leave. It was the beginning of a stormy relationship that had run hot and cold throughout the years.

When Alex was in England they were usually together, but when he was gone Constance occupied herself with an endless string of men.

Eventually Alex returned to London to stay. He established a small practice and affiliated himself with London's Children's hospital.

Everyone, especially Constance, thought that the two of them would finally make it legal. Alex too thought that he and Constance would marry, but after a year of steady companionship, he found he was as unable and unwilling to accept her lifestyle as she was to accept his. He soon realized that the relationship they had developed over the years had depended upon their separations. They were together during his "African years" when he was home on holiday. During that time they partied with friends, went to concerts and the theater, and generally spent their time in pursuit of a good time. Unfortunately, when he returned to England permanently, Constance expected that kind of life to continue... and for a while it had.

But Alex was ready to settle down, and as much as he cared for Constance, the word love never really entered the picture. He couldn't imagine that she would be happy with a quiet, "normal" existence. Hoping that she would realize this on her own, he made the mistake of trying to break things off slowly.

Sensing the coming split only made Constance more persistent, until eventually, Alex was forced to make the decisive move. The end came one evening in her gallery after the opening of a new show. It was a scene of crying and recriminations that left them both bitter for some time to come.

That had been two years ago. They now had a tenuous friendship based upon the fact that, unbeknownst to Alex, Constance was determined to get him back.

Constance sat warming brandy in her hands. She was not at all pleased with the relationship she could see developing between Alex and this Genie Lawrence. And although she was positive that nothing serious had happened......yet, it was too soon after the boyfriend's death...she knew that this woman could be a threat. She was going to have to find some way to eliminate the competition. She will just have to be persuaded to return to the States, Constance thought as she sipped the last of her drink.

Chapter 18

Late the next morning Genie borrowed Ruth's car and drove into London. She was completely taken aback by the amount of traffic encountered as she entered town. "I suppose it isn't any worse than Manhattan," she grumbled checking her rear view mirror. She always hated driving in the city and as she maneuvered her way through congested traffic on narrow winding streets, tension knotted the muscles at the base of her neck giving her a "god awful" headache. Finally, breathing a sigh of relief at having done no damage to Ruth's Rover, she rounded the corner onto Hampton Gardens.

Genie pulled up past Alex's town-house and parked in front of the Sim's house. She noticed, somewhat disappointedly, that Alex's car was not there. "He must be at the hospital...or maybe his office," she sighed as she ran up the steps to Molly's front door.

When Molly opened the door Genie immediately sensed that Molly was having a bad day. "Why don't you let me treat you to lunch," she suggested. Happy to get out of the house, Molly readily accepted. "I have an idea," Genie continued, "How about showing me Harrods's? But first," she added with a pleading sigh and a hand at her temple "Do you have any aspirin?"

Sometime later, after Genie had purchased a pair of linen slacks, two short sleeve cotton shirts, a lightweight cotton jacket and a pair of comfortable sandals, Molly confronted her. "Genie, the truth. All those clothes! You really are planning on Cairo aren't you?"

Standing next to a long glass counter top covered with what appeared to be hundreds of cosmetic samples, Genie stared absently at one shiny black jar filled with questionable green goo. Without thinking she rubbed a dab of it onto the back of her hand. "Molly," she spoke quietly, "I have to. If I have any success in contacting Anna DuLac I'll have to leave as soon as possible. And Molly listen! I am going to need your help. Please." Genie implored and prayed her new friend would understand. Much to her relief she found that she understood perfectly.

"Well, to be honest. As much as I am concerned about this trip...and I really believe that it could be dangerous...I have to admit that I was hoping you would decide to go. I know I am being selfish, but Roger's so called, accident has been haunting me. I need answers almost as badly as you do Genie. God! You know, if it weren't for the children, I actually believe I would go there with you."

Genie was relieved to find she had an ally. For some reason the last time she brought up the subject of Cairo, Alex had become extremely distressed. He was now dead set against even the suggestion that she might venture to Egypt. It made things very touchy, so over lunch in the restaurant in Harrods department store Genie and Molly devised a plan. Genie would tell everyone that she was going to spend a few days with Richard's aunt. She was certain Aunt Sarah would agree to keep her secret. Molly would take her to the airport and cover for her if things got sticky. It seemed simple enough. Genie was sure that she could be there and back in three days......four at the most.

Later that afternoon in the living room of Molly's town-house the two women continued to plan the surreptitious adventure.

Everything, of course, depended upon being able to contact Mademoiselle DuLac, and this time when the call was placed it was successful.

When the connection was finally completed the phone was answered in French by a woman with a delicate voice. "Bon Jour," returned Genie using the only French she could remember. "My name is Genevieve Lawrence and I would like to speak with Anna DuLac."

"Yes, this is she." Even with the considerable static, Genie could tell that Anna spoke almost perfect English. Thank God, she thought, relieved that there would be no language barrier. "Mademoiselle DuLac," she began again. "My name is Genie Lawrence and I would like to speak to you about the death of Roger Sims."

As Genie related the entire sequence of events, beginning with Roger's death and continuing through to the discovery of the photographs, she could tell, by the tone of the reporter's responses, that she was becoming thoroughly engrossed in the situation. It was evident that she was as anxious to see the photographs as Genie was to show them to her. "It is very possible, Miss Lawrence, that I may know some of the people in those pictures. And I think you are wise to bring them to Cairo personally. When you have made arrangements for a flight call me. I will have someone meet you at the airport and I will arrange for a location where we may meet... ah...discreetly. You understand?"

"I understand perfectly," said Genie. "And I will call you again very soon. Thank you." When Genie replaced the receiver there was elation in her tone. "Did you hear that?" she asked turning to Molly.

"Yes, most of it. You are really going then?"

"Yes!" she exclaimed, and gave Molly a big hug.

"Oh lord! I have got to get going. I want to stop at the travel agency in St. Albans and arrange for a flight. And I want to be back at Channing House before Alex arrives." Genie grabbed her packages and nearly flew out the door.

By the time Alex returned to Channing House that evening Genie's plans were set. She had booked a flight on British Airways for 3:40 Friday afternoon with a return trip scheduled to arrive back in London late Tuesday evening. It was perfect scheduling, and as far as anyone but Molly would know, she would be spending a long weekend with Aunt Sarah.

Genie had just finished tucking her new clothes, tickets, passport and visa safely into the bottom drawer of the dresser in the guest bedroom when there was a knock on the half opened door. Looking up she was surprised to see Constance leaning against the door jamb. How long has she been standing there? Genie wondered, and she made a mental note to change the location of the tickets as soon as she had a chance. For now she simply stood and invited her uninvited guest into the room.

As Constance walked through the door Genie could see that she was surveying every inch of the room. Constance had a knack for making her feel uneasy. I am just being paranoid, she thought. That's what comes from keeping secrets. Genie was determined not to let Constance get the better of her.

"Constance, I didn't realize you were still at Channing House. I thought you had gone back to London."

"Actually, darling," Constance always managed to sound condescending, "I had planned to leave this morning, but now that Jackie has finally made up her mind to come and work with me at the gallery we decided that I should stick around for a few days and, well, you understand, work out all the details."

Genie didn't have to guess whose idea that had been.

Constance prattled on, "Anyway, I will probably stay until Monday so we absolutely must play another set."

"Perhaps we can do doubles again," Genie said evasively. She didn't want Constance to know, just yet, that she wouldn't be there for the weekend. She could just imagine the pleasure she would get out of that bit of news.

"As I was coming upstairs I thought I heard Alex's car. I imagine we will be having supper shortly. Will you be joining us?'

"Of course," said Genie, as off handedly as possible. "Shall we go?" She maneuvered Constance out of the room and together they walked down the long winding staircase. When she saw Alex smiling up at her from the foot of the stairs Genie felt a knot in the pit of her stomach. She didn't want to believe that it was there because she was pleased to see him. She preferred to believe that it was purely a result of the deception she was about to begin. She hated having to lie, even when there seemed to be no other option.

In the middle of dinner, not long after Genie revealed her "weekend plans" to everyone, Constance excused herself. Between the soup and the main course, she left the table and ran gingerly upstairs crossing her fingers that she would have enough time.

"Maybe I should have waited until dessert," she thought. But it was too late to change her plans now, and anyway this was the only time she could count on no interruptions. "What the hell," she mumbled, "nothing ventured nothing gained...boy is that cliché," she chuckled and quietly opened the door to Genie's bedroom.

She went directly to the drawer she had seen Genie closing earlier. She pulled it out as far as it would go, without crashing to the floor, and immediately began searching the contents. Constance wasn't sure exactly what she was looking for, but instinct told her something was "afoot"... she would know it when she found it. As soon as she spotted the tickets and visa she knew she had struck gold. "So, Richard's Aunt Sarah lives in Cairo now does she." Constance smiled slyly remembering the fabrication Genie had told them all of her planned weekend visit. "That little sneak I wonder what she is up too?"

Placing the items back where she found them, Constance

closed the drawer. She was about to leave the room when she noticed several scraps of paper in the wastepaper basket by the dresser. Instinctively she reached into the wicker receptacle and retrieved the crumpled bits. "Oh! This is too perfect," she mumbled and tucked a memo on which Genie had jotted airline flight numbers and times, into her pocket.

With a Cheshire cat smile on her face she walked across the hall to one of the many bathrooms. She flushed the toilet, ran the tap and then returned to the dinner table.

Later that evening when they were finally alone in the drawing room Alex tried valiantly to get Genie to change her mind. "Are you sure you don't want me to drive you down to Dartmoor?" he asked, for what seemed to Genie like the hundredth time. He hoped she would relent, but she seemed to have her heart set on visiting Aunt Sarah on her own.

"Honestly Alex, ordinarily I would love to have you with me, but not this time. I really need to be by myself. I hope you understand." She said it with difficulty and almost let the secret slip...Alex could be very persuasive. "The drive will do me good," she explained. "And a weekend with Sarah will give me the time I need to put things into perspective." Genie hoped she sounded convincing. She really wanted to tell Alex the truth. But she knew he would rather tie her up or lock her away than let her go to Cairo on her own. Of course, he wouldn't really force her hand. He wasn't a chauvinist; thank God, just a bit too protective. But she didn't want to argue and she didn't want him to worry. She didn't want anyone to know about this trip until it was over. After all, she would be back in London on Tuesday...Wednesday, at the latest.

Chapter 19

Finch had been standing in the drizzling rain for fifteen minutes on Friday afternoon waiting for the three o'clock tour of Channing House to begin.

Now, as his group stood admiring the hand painted oriental silk wall covering in the "Chinese" room, he searched for an unobtrusive exit. He had to find a way into the living quarters or this whole ridiculous tour would be a waste of valuable time. Looking around it was evident that there would be no quiet slip from this room. He was becoming anxious. There was only one more area on the tour and as the group pushed slowly through a long dark hallway toward the kitchen facilities, he could feel a tingling sensation down the middle of his back.

Finch held back and positioned himself at the rear of the group.

Not finding any direct route from the public areas to the living quarters he decided on a second, riskier plan. As everyone else left the building through the kitchen door, he quietly sequestered himself in a small utilities closet he noticed, almost completely hidden, under a set of unused kitchen stairs. It was a cramped hiding place, but he did not think he would be there long. He had only to wait until the last person exited the building, and the guides had time to check for stragglers. He would give it twenty minutes at most.

In the darkness he reviewed his plans. He knew the Lawrence woman was staying at Channing House and he had no doubts about his ability to "convince" her to give him her copies of the photographs. No matter what that idiot Whiting had said, he just knew she had made copies.

After that, well......he hoped he could make it look as if she had just suddenly decided to leave...without a trace, of course. "But that may prove a bit difficult," he whispered to himself. Cloistered there in the gloom he began to have some doubts. He wasn't sure he would have enough time to make anyone believe that the woman had simply taken off. "Hell!" he finally concluded. "The London Bobbies will just have to add another unsolved murder to their books." Another body more or less...It really didn't matter to him.

He briefly contemplated dealing with the doctor in the same manner, but dismissed that as an unnecessary risk. He had to consider the fact that the death of a prominent physician would generate an investigation that even Whiting could not control.

As his eyes adjusted to the enclosure he found that he could actually see fairly well in the small shadowed room. Enough light filtered through loose door boards so that he could see most everything around him. Finch reached into his pocket and pulled out his wallet. He reexamined a bogus "New York Times" identification card. It had been manufactured hurriedly, but he was convinced that the false identification would pass all but the closest inspection. He only hoped it would be enough to convince Ms. Genevieve Lawrence that he was a friend and colleague of her "dearly departed".

Enough time had passed. Finch quietly opened the door and looked about for any sign of activity. Everything was still. He scurried through the ancient kitchen and out into the kitchen garden. The empty garden, although well-manicured, had seemingly not been used for years. It was completely surrounded by a six foot hedge row. To his left was a break in the shrubbery, the only exit, which led through more gardens and around to the front of the estate.

He knew that path would get him nowhere. On his right, however, where the hedge met the building, there was a small gap. With only slight difficulty he was able to inch his way through the opening.

After brushing off a number of dead leaves and twigs that had managed to adhere to his generic "tourist clothing", grey linen blazer, black slacks, camera, Finch looked up and found himself standing in a mirror image of the kitchen garden from which he had just escaped. This one, however, was obviously well used. There were several varieties of herbs and plants growing both in the ground and in pots. There was also a small table with four chairs that were, apparently, often occupied.

He guessed, correctly, that the dual kitchens and gardens had, generations earlier, been one large working area and had been divided when the family moved into their separate living quarters.

Finch peered through French doors that led into the private kitchen and could sense no activity. Although the doors were locked it took only minor manipulation with a credit card to get into the house. His footsteps echoed slightly as he proceeded, with practiced stealth, across the spacious room. Still, there was no other noise. He was alone. He knew the old lady was with her treasured tourists and he had made sure that the doctor was at his office, but where were the others, the sister and especially Genie Lawrence? He would look further and, if necessary, find a place to hide until "she" returned. Perhaps the wine cellar would do. Most of these old homes had quite extensive storage areas.

Before bothering to hide in some out of the way corner Finch had to be certain that Genie was, indeed, not at home. Upon deciding that an inspection of the upper floors was in order, he found his way through a long corridor, obviously a servant's hallway, to a room which, to him, resembled a museum or gallery.

There were a number of suits of armor standing like statues along one wall. The opposite wall was almost entirely glass and looked out onto extensive private gardens. Among several pieces of sculpture also occupying the area was a Henry Moore that Finch knew would bring a fabulous price if sold to a discriminating collector...but he didn't have time for that now, he had a much more urgent matter to attend to.

In one corner stood what Finch thought the most intriguing of all the artifacts. There, almost hidden in the shadows was a beautiful six foot tall, intricately carved, ivory bird cage. It absolutely fascinated him. He became so absorbed by the thousands of tiny details etched into every area of the cage that he failed to notice footsteps approach from behind.

"I beg your pardon," said the sultry female voice.

Finch froze.

"Excuse me, but may I ask what you are doing here?"

Finch slowly turned around. He found himself facing an extraordinarily beautiful, tall young blond woman. He relaxed a bit. "Yes, hello...ah... Perhaps you can help me. I seem to have gotten separated from my group, the three o'clock tour."

"Separated. I see," Constance continued, not believing him for a minute. "But how did you find your way to this part of the house?" she asked skeptically. "Perhaps I should call a guard?"

At the mention of the guard Finch's hand automatically began to reach for the security of his blade. He caught himself and decided to try to play the scene to a less violent, more advantageous conclusion...if possible.

"Yes, perhaps you should. I really don't know exactly how I arrived here. I was in the old kitchen and there was a stairway and a hallway, and before I knew it I was here. Please forgive me. I didn't mean to intrude," he said in his humblest voice. "If you will just show me the way out…"

Maybe he is telling the truth, thought Constance, but she wished she could search his pockets. "All right then. If you will come with me I will show you to the public areas."

"Thank you. You are very kind."

They were back in the kitchen when Finch played a hunch. "By the way," he began, "I was hoping that while here, I might run into someone. Her name is Genevieve Lawrence. She was very close to a colleague of mine. Mutual friends told me that she has been staying with the Templeton family since the poor boy's untimely death. Do you happen to know her?"

"Miss Lawrence? Yes, I know her. You are right. She has been staying here for a few days. Tell me, Mr.…ah…"

"Talbot, John Talbot." Finch quickly took out the "Times" identification and handed it to Constance.

"Yes, Mr. Talbot, how is it that you know Genie?" Constance was still wary of the stranger. She instinctively distrusted him. A weasel, she thought.

"Actually, I don't know her, personally, that is. I was quite close to Mr. McBride. We were colleagues for many years. I was hoping to extend her my sympathies."

This could be interesting, thought Constance, as an idea began to turn over in her mind. Perhaps…why not…it might prove to be very interesting indeed.

"I am sorry, Mr. Talbot, but you have just missed her."

"Oh, that is a shame. Will she be back soon? I could leave her a note and maybe see her another day."

"Actually, she has gone on a bit of a trip," Constance continued "I am afraid she will be away for several days."

Damn! thought Finch. He could hardly control his anger.

"A trip, how nice for her," he said smoothly. "Would it be too forward of me ask where she has gone?" He was finding it difficult to hide the growing anxiety. Tell me, his mind screamed, tell me where the bitch has gone.

Finally, thought Constance. I thought he would never ask.

"She left for Cairo earlier this afternoon. Odd! It is so hot there at this time of year. But who knows why people do what they do?" she said wistfully. Although trying to sound nonchalant, Constance was thrilled. Between this weirdo and the bits of paper she had picked up in the guest room she was certain she could arrange for word of Genie's clandestine trip to reach Alex...with, of course, no connection to herself. In her mind she could just picture the pique Alex would be in.

"Cairo," he said with a composure that belied the intensity of his anger. "That is interesting. Tell me do you know where she is staying? I may be able to put her in touch with friends."

"Oh no, sorry," said Constance, suddenly having been snapped out of her daydream and back into the conversation. "I honestly don't. I wish I could be of more help, but she didn't tell me any of her plans."

After what she considered a discreet pause, Constance made what she hoped sounded like an off handed suggestion. "You know, Mr. Talbot... now that I think about it. You might talk to Dr. Templeton. They are quite good friends. He may know where she is staying," Constance schemed.

"Yes. Perhaps," he said distractedly. He had other things on his mind and other ways of finding the information he needed. He had no desire to get tied up with these people...although he had to admit that the blond was another story...damn...he could really... But there was no time. That Lawrence woman was on to something. He had to eliminate her...immediately. Shit, he swore to himself, I should have just stayed in Cairo. He could not believe that he had to get himself on the first plane back to Egypt.

Chapter 20

Oblivious to the constant droning of jet engines, Genie reclined the back of her seat in an unsuccessful attempt to find a comfortable position. She couldn't seem to unwind, and wished now, as she awkwardly crossed her legs, that she had requested an aisle seat. Resigning to the fact that it was going to be an uncomfortable trip she made up her mind to ignore what she could and take advantage of the cramped window seat to get her bearings. However, when she gazed through the small double paned glass she could see only darkening blue sky and, below, pink billowing clouds. Restful, but not a clue as to where she was.

Leaning her head back against the seat she closed her eyes. Had this been the right decision? She couldn't imagine discovering anything in Cairo that would help her understand Richard's death. Only a few hours ago it seemed like her only option. Now, a thousand miles from everywhere, she wasn't so sure.

"Maybe I should have confided in Alex after all," she thought. "Who knows? When I'm settled into the hotel I'll call Molly and have her tell him...tell him what...where I am...what I am doing, hell I'm not even sure of that." She was beginning to have strong doubts about the whole trip. "Bad attitude," she chided herself and brought her seat back to the upright position.

After ordering black coffee from the stewardess she opened her large canvas duffel and pulled out the manila envelope. Looking at the photographs she tried to make some sense of them, but became more convinced than ever that she didn't know what she thought she was doing.

"Well, it's too late to turn back now," she sighed as she sipped the hot black liquid and again reviewed the increasingly familiar faces. She was certain that, by now, she would recognize any one of them in a crowd.

London

Finch stormed into his hotel room. He was seething with anger and frustration. The next flight to Cairo wouldn't be leaving Heathrow Airport until almost four o'clock the following afternoon and he had barely managed to get on that. Pacing nervously, he tried to figure out how everything had gotten so 'fucking out of control'. "Well, it won't be out of control for long," he hissed and pulled out the one bag he would need for the trip. With renewed anger, Finch violently tossed the case across the room.

He poured himself a large whiskey, no ice, and downed almost half the glass in one swallow. Immediately feeling better, calmer, more self-assured, more in control, he picked up the phone and dialed.

"Yes, it's me......Just shut up and listen. We have a problem. The girl has gone to Cairo.........No. I am going to take care of it. I want you to keep an eye on the doctor and the Sims broad. Put a bug on their phones. The Sims' phone and the doctor's......both of his, you idiot. His townhouse and his office. And don't forget the Channing estate. You got that? Immediately. I want it done tonight.........I don't care how difficult it is...Do it......I'll be staying at the usual place, but don't call me. I will get in touch with you as soon as I check in. I expect results. Find out where she is staying. I don't want to waste my time checking every hotel in the city...

you understand? You don't really mean that, do you," he said coldly. "It is a bit late to back out now......don't you think?" Finch's voice carried an emphatically sinister warning. "Good. I knew I could count on you." Finch replaced the receiver.

At the other end of the line Inspector Whiting clenched the phone in one trembling hand. His other knotted into a fist which he brought down hard against his desk.

Cairo

It was 9:25 in the evening when British Airways flight 156 touched down at Cairo International Airport. After passing through customs, Genie stood with her bags just outside the terminal doors. Becoming aware of the dry desert heat, she hadn't expected it to be quite so hot this late in the evening. Nonetheless, it was surprisingly tolerable. Not as bad as New York during the "dog days" of summer, she thought while resetting her watch.

Her driver arrived within minutes looking just as Genie had expected; short and dark with a full, black mustache that somehow didn't quite suit his face. She was further assured that he was the man for whom she had been waiting by his western attire. He was wearing exactly what she anticipated...what she had been told to look for...a white shirt, a Mets baseball cap, and American Levis. Seeing him jump out of the car she experienced a strange sense of déjà vu. "I could be grabbing a cab at LaGuardia."

"Miss Lawrence?" he asked shyly.

"Yes," Genie replied with some caution.

"My name is Bill," he said in a thick accent that Genie couldn't quite place. "I have come to take you to your hotel."

His name, she knew, was not "Bill", but upon hearing the code, that Anna had devised, Genie felt safe handing him her luggage. He reached for the bags and put them into the trunk of an old, almost dilapidated tan Volvo.

"Miss Lawrence," said "Bill", "Mslle. DuLac has arranged a room for you at the Ramses Hilton. I hope that is satisfactory."

Genie looked at "Bill" in astonishment. Now that they were both safely sequestered in the old car his enunciation completely changed. He spoke to her in excellent English with only a slight French accent.

"Yes, of course, that will be fine," she replied in answer to his comment about the hotel, "but you are not Egyptian are you?"

"No, I am not. I work on the paper with Anna and I, too, was a friend of Roger Sims."

"Do you really believe that all this cloak and dagger routine is necessary?" asked Genie.

"Anna said that you were being followed in England and there is no reason to believe that whoever it is won't come after you here. It is best to play it safe."

"But I do know who was following me, a police inspector named Whiting. And I doubt that he would come all the way to Cairo. In any case, only Molly...Roger's wife...knows that I am here, and she wouldn't say a thing, especially to the Inspector."

"And do you think that he is acting alone?" "Bill" asked pointedly.

"No, I suppose not. I hadn't given that possibility enough consideration. You know, I didn't tell anyone but Roger's wife that I was coming to Cairo because I didn't want them to worry need-lessly. Now I am glad I didn't tell them because they might actually have something to worry about," Genie remarked sarcastically and wished she were back at Channing House sitting safely next to Alex.

Alone in the back seat of the car, Genie sat quietly and stared out through a cracked window. The route Bill had chosen to take through the dark, dusty back streets of the city seemed oppressively foreboding. She was relieved when they pulled up in front of the brightly lit, modern hotel.

"Bill" stepped out of the ancient sedan and retrieved Genie's luggage from the trunk. She was pleasantly surprised to see that the mustache was gone, so too was the Mets cap. To complete the transition from "Bill", a driver of some question, to Phillipe Martin, reporter, a beige linen blazer had been added to his attire.

Phillipe let a porter take Genie's bags into the lobby while he accompanied her to the reservation desk. He spoke up before she had a chance to say anything.

"I believe you have a reservation for Mslle. DuLac," he said to Genie's astonishment. It only took a moment for the clerk to confirm that Mslle. would be staying in room 1022.

"How do you wish to pay for that, Mslle?" he asked, addressing Genie.

She reached into her bag, but again Phillipe spoke up. "Please charge that to me," he said handing the man a gold American Express card.

The desk clerk took the card, processed the necessary paper-work, and shortly handed both the card and the room key to Phillipe.

They were halfway across the lobby, following the porter to the elevator, when Genie grabbed Phillipe's elbow. "Exactly what was that all about?" she questioned, a bit loudly.

"Shhh," he warned. "Wait until we get to your room. I will explain it all then."

"Well!" said Genie a short time later.

"Just a moment please." Phillipe put his finger to his mouth to indicate the need for silence while he checked the room for listening devices and the phone for any "unusual electronic equipment". "It seems quite safe," he finally proclaimed.

"All right. Tell me. What exactly is going on?"

"As I said in the car, it is very possible that you are being followed. We just want to make it difficult for anyone to find you."

"But, honestly, I can pay for my own room." Genie was highly annoyed.

"I am sure you can, Miss Lawrence. Anna and I didn't mean to imply anything...as you say...derogatory...but we thought it would be a bit safer if you didn't use your own name or credit card for the time being. Tomorrow, after you have spoken to Anna, we may find that all these precautions have been a colossal waste of time, but please, for this evening at least, let us be cautious."

"Yes, of course, I understand. With everything that has happened...did Anna tell you?"

"Yes, she did," Phillipe answered somberly. He couldn't think of anything more to say.

"Well, I guess I'm going to have to get used to looking over my shoulder all the time. At least until I...or should I say we...sort out this mess." Suddenly exhausted, Genie sat on the edge of one of the two queen size beds in the large comfortable room.

"Perhaps you should get some rest now," he said, sensing her weariness. "I will pick you up tomorrow at ten. Anna has arranged a secluded location for your meeting. She is looking forward to seeing you."

"Thank you, Phillipe. You have been very kind. You're right. I am exhausted. All I want is a good night's sleep."

"Remember," he said as he left her room, "put the chain on the door and don't open it for anyone. Oh, and here. This is my phone number and this one is Anna's. Call us if you need anything."

"Thank you, I will," she said closing the door.

Alone at last, Genie kicked off her shoes and unbuttoned her blouse. "It will be wonderful to get out of these things," she said aloud while pulling at a stubborn zipper in her denim skirt. It was nearly 11:30 and she had not yet telephoned Molly. "I'd better do that right now before she begins to worry." Why, on earth, was she talking to herself?

Sitting in her slip, cross legged on the bed, she reached for the receiver. "Yes, operator, this is Ms. Law......Mslle. DuLac in room 1022. I would like to place an overseas call please." She gave the operator the number and in only a few minutes Genie heard the ringing of the Sims' phone.

"Hello," Molly answered anxiously. She had picked up on the first ring.

"Hi! Molly. It's Genie."

"Genie, thank God," Molly shouted with relief. "How was your trip? Is everything alright?"

"I just wanted to let you know that I am staying at the Hilton. And yes everything is fine. No need for anyone else to know I'm here...at least not yet."

"Don't worry, much as I would like to tell 'a certain party', mum's the word. But I must tell you that all this makes me frightfully nervous, and listen, before you ring off I think you ought to know," Molly continued breathlessly, "that Inspector Whiting stopped by this evening. He specifically asked about you. He asked again if you had seen Roger's photos."

"What did you tell him?"

"What do you think? I lied, though I am not very good at it. I told him that neither you nor I had seen the pictures. I doubt he believed me, of course, he seemed oddly nervous. And the curious thing is that he almost seemed relieved at my lie."

"I'm convinced you did the right thing. Molly, listen to me."

Genie's insistence strained her voice. "Don't tell anyone...I mean absolutely no one about those pictures. You must promise me that...ok?"

"Alright," said Molly. She was alarmed by the tone in the woman's voice. "I promise."

Genie continued, "Have you spoken to Alex?"

"Yes, and before you ask he hasn't got a clue, but he is definitely out of sorts. He called Aunt Sarah and was more than disappointed when she told him that you had 'stepped out'."

"Thank goodness for Sarah," said Genie with relief. "I'll call him as soon as I have a chance. Well, I'd better not talk for too long. I'm meeting Anna tomorrow morning...I'll call you again when I have some news. Thanks for everything...... Give my love to the boys."

Genie hung up the phone and lay back. It had been an exhausting day. All she wanted now was a nice hot shower.

She stepped out of her slip and tossed it and her bra and pants onto a chair. Grabbing a light cotton caftan she dragged herself into the bathroom.

The warm water felt wonderful. It tingled against her skin massaging all her aching muscles. Fragrant lather cascaded over her body. Her thoughts drifted......floated. With some surprise she suddenly found herself remembering...reliving... the last shower she had taken with Richard. It was in the wonderfully old ornate bathroom in their hotel room in London. She had gone in first, thinking that he was still asleep, but when she turned around to grab the soap he had been there like a ghost smiling at her through the steam. It was wonderful to remember...she could again feel his hands sliding down her back, over her stomach to the inside of her thighs. Eyes closed, she imagined him in front of her, holding her firmly in his large hands. With a shudder she remembered how they had made love under the running water.

Gasping she breathed in droplets of water and coughed. The spell was broken. Would she ever have that again? Tears ran down her face. Genie turned the tap to cold. She let the icy water wash away the soap......wash away the memory.

Chapter 21

Alexandria, Va.   *Friday, July 6, 1990*

Dove grey light filtered through leaded glass windows announcing the dawn.

The old man rested one elbow on the well-worn back of an old, brown, leather wing chair and leaned heavily against it. Like so many times before, he swelled with pride as he surveyed this very private domain.

The library of his Alexandria home was a monument, an altar, really, at which he worshipped the past, worshipped his long history as a warrior.

Among the many books and papers arranged in orderly fashion on the library shelves were hundreds of trinkets and souvenirs of times gone by. There were souvenirs of his career, a helmet, an ancient Japanese dagger, a bayonet, scores of medals...and there were relics from the careers of others, bullets fired during the Civil War, the scrap of a letter written by General Washington and a pair of epaulettes from the uniform of Napoleon.

On the mantle, above a red brick fireplace, stood dozens of photographs. Faces of the people who mattered most in his life stared at him from across the room.

There were, of course, pictures of his family and friends. There were also pictures of his heroes. Men like McArthur, Eisenhower, Kennedy and Rommel held a special fascination for him. He admired them all and was proud to have met each of them, with the exception of the last, during his lifetime. Among this honored group stood a photograph of Corporal Robert Ernest Smith. It was the young face of Bobby Smith, a smiling boyish 19 year old, that now had him transfixed. As he stared into impish eyes, memories of a day in 1943 flooded back............

On a godforsaken Pacific island, in the midst of a heated battle, Bobby Smith jumped out from behind the protection of the only cover around, and sacrificed his life to save that of his buddy, his pal, his very best friend...to save the life of another scared young soldier...to save the life of a man who was now a tired old General.

On that day in hell Corporal Bobby E. Smith became his own personal hero, a man he would love forever.........

Now, after almost 50 years, he would repay his debt. For it wasn't purely coincidence that the plan the General had so carefully devised to bring him the public acclaim he deserved involved the Americans who had for so long been held hostage in the Middle East. His glorious mission would repay a life for a life, for he knew that Robert E. Smith Jr. was among those missing, and he was determined to see this man, the son of his long lost companion, returned to his family and his country.

Without the use of his cane the General walked, hesitantly, across the room, to a treasured watercolor, a Maine seascape by Andrew Wyeth. He swung the hinged frame away from the wall to reveal his private safe. Not the family safe where important documents and his wife's jewelry were secured, but a personal hiding place in which he kept his deepest secrets. The papers he had locked behind three inches of steel were explosive. They had the power to change history. The papers, so carefully guarded, outlined in detail the plan he had set into motion months earlier.

From the safe, he removed a detailed map of the Middle East.

Pushing paperwork aside he laid it out on top of his large walnut desk. He studied the map intently. There was a remote area in Syria about 75 miles from Beirut that he had circled in red. He knew that was where the Eagle held his "chicks". With his finger he traced a line across the map to another spot just outside the Lebanese capital. Tapping his finger absentmindedly, he knew instinctively that this was where the Americans would be found. With a pen he drew stars and stripes over the area. He scribbled a hammer and sickle over the Eagle's location and with a sigh refolded the map and replaced it into the safe. It was all beginning to come together. If only he would hear from that weasel Finch everything would be perfect. Well, he couldn't worry about that now. He had to shower and dress for his appointment in George-town. He was confident that all would go as planned. He would be back home in plenty of time to spend the afternoon with his family. Yes! Things were going well. When he finally left his sanctuary his mood was equaled only by bright morning sun that had begun to shine through heavily leaded windows.

Georgetown

Twenty miles away in Georgetown, the same morning light found its way into a dingy room in an old boarding house.

For the Russian, the surroundings were becoming much too familiar. He sat impatiently drumming his fingers on the grey Formica table top and waited...but not for long. The general was, if nothing else, prompt.

"General, thank you for joining me," said the burly Russian. "I know it is hard for you to get away."

"Anything for you, my friend," replied the General as the two shook hands. "Our business is much too important to delay."

"But as I remember today is your birthday. Won't you be missed?"

"We have time. My children have planned a small celebration for later. I don't wish to disappoint them. I am confident we can come to an understanding long before then...aren't you?"

"Perhaps. But I am not as......ah...optimistic as you seem to be." He hesitated and then got to the point.

"Your 'Eagle' works very quickly. He has already contacted certain friends in Moscow." The Russian's heavy brows knotted into a brooding frown giving him the preposterous expression of a disgruntled bulldog. "You know, of course, that what you ask is impossible."

The General sat quietly while his companion continued.

"There is no way my government will become embroiled in a situation such as the one you propose."

So it begins, he thought. As I suspected, he is here to negotiate. "My friend," the General began. "I know it's a difficult situation. Both of our countries have people missing. American families have been waiting for years while fathers and sons sit and rot in hovels in West Beirut. It is a situation that can no longer be tolerated." The General paused, then continued in a much softer, calmer tone. "I personally would like to see all our countrymen returned safely to their homes and families. Don't you agree?"

"Most certainly, I agree with you......my government agrees with you...to a point. But the solution you envision...that is the problem."

As he walked slowly back and forth across the small room, the General realized, with regret, that it would, after all, be a long afternoon. The Russian, also prepared for a long day, pulled a flask of Vodka from his pocket.

"Come," he offered... "Sit and have a drink with me while we work out our little differences."

The afternoon wore on and both men wearied of the endless, fruitless arguing.

"Look," said the General finally reaching his limit. "Your men are safe...for the time being. But there may soon come a time when their situation will...change. With the information I have I can assure you that they may be returned safely to your country. But, damn it! If you don't help me secure our people...then...well then...your operatives just might find themselves in the hands of our CIA. Does your government really want to take that chance?"

Having played his trump he was breathing heavily, there was tightness across his chest that caused him to break out into a cold sweat.

"My government does not yield to threats. Of course, we are concerned for the safety of our people, but we will not be black-mailed, not by another government nor, as I suspect is the case here, by one individual."

"It's a simple matter really," said the General trying desperately to regain his composure. "A trade... your people for ours."

"But we do not have your people. As you said, they have been missing for years. If your government can't get them out, how do you think we can? How could we possibly......"

The General's eyes widened at the words he had just heard. At last, he thought......the breakthrough. "The foxy old bastard has stopped saying NO! And has begun to ask HOW?...I've got him."

He leaned over to his Russian friend and calmly handed him a folder...handed him the plan.

Incandescent blue, red and gold fireworks, in chorus with rockets, waterfalls and cannons, exploded above his head. As part of the post 4th of July celebration the local orchestra was playing Aaron Copeland's "Theme for the Common Man." It was glorious. The

General genuinely loved Independence Day. His family knew him well. There wasn't a better way to complete his birthday celebration than to be right here, lying back on the park's cool green grass, surrounded by loved ones, enjoying festivities sparked by the recent holiday.

"This is what it is all about......freedom, pride in your country." He felt omnipotent. What he had accomplished today would put the crowning glory on his life's work. What he had done today would save lives and return to his country the dignity she deserved. The wheels were in motion and soon...very soon his country would be as proud of him as he was of her.

But somewhere, barely at the edge of conscious thought, was the tiniest nagging doubt. Why hadn't he heard from Finch? He resented having to wait until Finch assured him that everything was clear before going ahead with the plan. Today had worked out so perfectly. Never mind, it didn't matter. He would contact Finch in the morning. He wouldn't let anything spoil this moment.

Surrounded by friends and family, the General clasped his hands behind his head, lay back staring into the night sky, and drank in the magnificent display above.

Chapter 22

The warm sunny morning was no match for Alex's foul temper. "Women," he mumbled with exasperation as he lifted his hand to knock on Molly's door. "Oh! hello there, Tony," he said in surprise when the door jerked open, seemingly of its own accord, revealing an equally astonished boy.

"Off for cricket, are you?" He nodded to the youngster who stood, bat in hand, poised to dash down the front stairs.

"...Lo, Dr. Templeton, Mum is in the kitchen," Tony quickly replied, then flew through the door and raced down the street.

Molly heard the exchange and by the time Alex entered the kitchen had poured two cups of tea. "Tea?" she asked, handing him a cup without waiting for his reply. He gratefully accepted and seated himself at her table. Molly could see Alex was troubled. His face was clouded in brooding contemplation.

"Where is she, Molly?" he asked staring into the dark amber liquid.

"Genie? I believe she is still at Sarah's," Molly said fumbling with the cream. A terrible liar, she was certain that Alex could see guilt plainly written on her face.

"Forget it. She telephoned me earlier this morning," he said. "She tried to convince me that everything was terrific, that she was having a lovely visit with Sarah...... It was a complete fabrication."

"What makes you think that?"

"Take a look at this." Alex tossed a crumpled piece of paper in Molly's direction. "I found this on the dresser in the guest room this morning. Flights to Dartmoor, I presume." His frustration masked itself in sarcasm, and he flung the crumpled London-Cairo flight schedule across the table. "And that call this morning... The connection was terrible. When I offered to return her call she refused. In fact she was evasive about receiving any calls at all and equally evasive about her return. Bloody hell, Molly! She avoided specific questions of any sort. Oh! And when I asked to speak to Sarah she became flustered and then said...if you can believe this for convenience......that Sarah had gone into town. All in all, Mrs. Sims, it was a very disconcerting conversation," he said looking her straight in the eyes. "And I have the distinct feeling that you, my friend, can clear it up."

"Alex," Molly pleaded in confession, "I promised her that I wouldn't say anything. Please don't ask me to break a trust."

Molly could feel his frustration turning to anger.

"You know this is something she has to do on her own," she continued. "I think she needs to feel that she has some control, that she is accomplishing something...anything. So much has happened and there haven't been any answers. Believe me, I understand what she is going through. She feels she owes it to Richard to find answers, any answers."

"And you wouldn't mind it either," he said pointedly, "if she found the answers...would you?"

Molly didn't answer him. What could she say? He was absolutely correct.

"Damn it! Didn't she think she could trust me to understand? My God! Molly, I am her friend. She didn't have to lie, or make up some asinine story."

"Alex, listen." Molly hoped she could make him understand. "I know she considered telling you what her plans were, but she knew you would try to stop her. Right? She was afraid that your reaction would be...well...just like this. In any case, it was a decision she had to make quickly. She'll be back in a few days and I know she will tell you everything then. Please be patient."

"Can you at least tell me where she is staying?" he said quietly.

Molly didn't answer.

"Molly, I am concerned about her." Alex began pacing the kitchen like a caged bear. "And I'm angry. Why in hell couldn't she confide in me?"

He must care a great deal for her, to be this angry, this frustrated, Molly thought. She wondered if he had any idea what he was feeling.

"Men!"...she mumbled in exasperation.

"Alright, alright...I won't ask you any more questions, but please, do me a favor and let me know if you talk to her. And for God's sake tell her to be careful." Still fuming he slammed the kitchen door and stormed out of the house.

An hour later Alex's green Jaguar pulled up behind Channing House. He drove beyond the main residence and parked the car in front of the stables. A long hard ride on Dante, a wonderful chestnut stallion he had owned, and quite frankly loved, was definitely in order. A few hours with his handsome friend would help him work out his anger and disappointment. "Women," he mumbled again, but didn't stop to consider why he was so furious.

"Hello there, old friend," he said stroking the horse's strong neck. "How about a nice long jaunt?"

"Alex?"

"Constance!" He looked up startled at the sound of her voice. What are you doing here?" He was surprised and somewhat annoyed to find his solitude disturbed...especially by Constance.

"Come now, darling, there is no need to be rude. Jackie invited me to go riding, but she has been held up so I thought I would take advantage of the invitation and meet her later. Why don't we ride together?"

"Not today, Constance. I am in no mood."

"Oh, come on, don't be such an old bear. It will be fun...like old times." She was smiling slightly. She had an idea that certain casually though perfectly planted bits of a flight schedule were causing his pique and she was quite pleased with herself.

"That's what I'm afraid of," he said, already beginning to relent. Constance could be a pain in the ass but she could also be amusing. He needed to be amused.

Chapter 23

Hanging up the phone was a relief. The early morning call to Alex had been more of a strain on her than she imagined. It was obvious to Genie, that Alex was not fooled by her supposed visit to Sarah. Although he did not come right out and accuse her of lying, she could hear the accusation in his voice and knew by his questions that he didn't believe a word she said. Well, there was nothing she could do about it now. She would try to call and explain everything later. But now, she had other things on her mind.

Unable to sleep, Genie had risen early and still had almost an hour to wait before her meeting with Anna.

From the large windows in her room she looked out over the city. This was certainly a city where the ancient world met and worked in harmony with a modern metropolis. From her tenth floor perch she could see towering skyscrapers, bustling traffic, and across the Nile, the gleaming new Cairo Opera House. Farther off in the distance she could see the ancient Citadel and directly below, across the Sharla el Tahrir square, the Cairo Museum, keeper of some of the world's most treasured antiquities. Could she make time for a visit? She had a pleasant suspicion that Richard would chastise her from the beyond if she did not. "Go there," she heard him say.

The city enchanted her, and for a brief moment Genie could almost forget what brought her to the shores of the Nile. Her reverie was short lived, however. The reality of what she was about to do surfaced with startling clarity at the sound of gunfire. She jumped. No, not a gunshot, she realized. She wouldn't have heard that, just a crash in the hallway. "Brother," she sighed. "I'm becoming as nervous as a cat. Where's James Bond when you really need him?"

She checked the time. It had passed quickly. Hurriedly stuffing the tail of her white cotton blouse into linen slacks, she rushed out the door.

As instructed, Genie left the hotel through the lobby at the back. She was almost tempted to stop at a coffee kiosk displaying chocolates and French pastries, located near the rear entrance. But, not wanting to chance missing Anna, she hurried past them to the street. Once outside she immediately reached for her dark glasses. The sun was blazing, the dry heat stifling.

From across the square the Cairo Museum again beckoned. She regretted that, right now, she would not have time to wander through its cool corridors. Perhaps later, she mused, though she realized it was highly unlikely.

Within minutes, the familiar tan Volvo pulled up in front of her and came to a noisy stop. She had expected Philippe but he was not behind the wheel. It was instead driven by a petite, dark haired young woman. "Mslle. DuLac?" the woman called. Genie nodded in acknowledgement of the pseudonym.

"I, too, am Mslle. DuLac." Anna smiled and flashed her press identification. She indicated that Genie should get into the car.

"Anna, it's good to meet you at last," Genie said as the old car lurched forward.

"Yes, for me also," replied Anna. "Hang on, this old wreck has been acting up and I am afraid it may be a bit bumpy."

The dusty ride through narrow winding streets seemed to take forever, but they had actually been driving for only twenty minutes when Anna pulled the car into a narrow alley between two buildings. She parked the car as close to one wall as possible and squeezed her through the slightly opened door.

"Come on. We are going for a little walk."

After a short distance, the two women found themselves in the midst of the bustling Khan El-Khalili Bazaar. Genie was fascinated by the sights and sounds coming from the crowded shops and stalls. The pungent mixture of aromas, cinnamon, musk, roses and others she would never recognize, combined to make her head swim. Covered stalls with men, women and children shouting their wares were selling everything, from beautiful hand woven carpets to fine silks and live chickens. It all converged into a claustrophobic sea. Genie had difficulty taking it all in. Anna led her into a small shop that she could tell, from the corroded sign hanging above the entrance, specialized in the trading of coins and jewelry. "Good morning, Aji," said Anna. Genie could see that she slipped something, presumably cash, into his palm. "When Mr. Martin arrives, please send him upstairs."

"Of course, mademoiselle," replied the slight, dark skinned shopkeeper. He bowed almost imperceptibly in her direction.

The lack of direct sunlight made it eerily dark for mid-morning as Anna and Genie went through the shop and up a narrow flight of wooden stairs. On the second floor a battered sky-blue door opened into a small dusty room. It was only slightly brighter in the room than on the stairway and not terribly clean. Newspapers strewn on the floor were covered in part by a threadbare oriental rug. Four folding chairs and a table, a narrow bed, and a chest with a hot plate sitting on top completed the furnishings. The air was heavy with the aroma of strong coffee and cardamom.

Genie was hesitant when Anna offered her a cup of black liquid.

"Come in and make yourself comfortable. This room is used by

Aji's son. Fortunately he is out of town so we will be quite safe here. We will be able to talk without fear of being discovered."

"I have to admit, Anna," said Genie, cup in hand, "that I am still uncomfortable with this secrecy, but under the circumstances I guess you're right to be cautious." Genie sipped the strong brew, wishing she could add a little sugar.

Anna smiled. "It is my own concoction," she said. "A cross between the deadly Egyptian stuff and plain old coffee. I can add a little water if you like."

"Maybe just a little," said Genie, then after a moment began, "I don't really know where to start except to show you these." She reached into her duffel bag and retrieved the envelope. "These are pictures Roger took when he was last here...in April, I think. As I told you over the phone, they seem to be of a party at the home of the American ambassador. You remember...the man who committed suicide, Ian Stanley. Molly and I are convinced that these photographs are connected to Roger's "accident" and to Richard's murder."

Genie slid the 8 x 10 glossies out of the envelope and laid them on the table. Even though there was no shade covering the bare bulb in an overhead socket, the lighting was poor. Together the two women dragged the old table across the floor and placed it in front of the room's only window.

"Better?" asked Anna.

"Better," she replied.

"Anna, I know that someone......and this is really strange......A British Police Inspector, an Inspector Whiting...has tried at least twice to get these pictures."

Anna, brows knotted in thought, had been listening carefully to Genie and looking at the first few pictures.

"These are definitely pictures of one of Ian's famous parties. I recognize many of the guests, but I don't remember... Wait! You said April. No! No, no."

Anna had to bite her lip to keep from screaming.

"What? What is it?"

Anna took another photo from Genie and read the note on the back. She had almost finished when her eyes dropped to the grainy area of the photo that Roger had circled in pen.

Genie watched in amazement as Anna became as rigid as a statue. All the blood drained out of her face and her hands began to shake. "Mon Dieu," she exclaimed. "Mon Dieu," she said again and nearly collapsed from her chair.

"Anna! What, what is it?"

"It's Anton. Genie, it's Anton," she whispered. "He has been missing for months......yet he is here in this photograph. Look."

"Anton?" questioned Genie.

"I must explain," she said quietly. "He is Russian. You should know that. A diplomat. But beautiful, you understand. Not like most of them. Very kind, very open-minded. We have been together for almost a year......we love each other." Anna sighed deeply, then continued to tell Genie about the incident that occurred in April.

"I have tried so hard to find out what happened...but nothing. Now you show me these. I don't know what to think."

"Show me again, Anna? Which one is he?" She crossed her legs under the old table.

"Look...here he is. These men, they are helping him...or pushing him...I don't know... into that car."

"Are you certain, Anna? It is such a bad picture."

"Positive...I know him......you understand."

Genie nodded. "And the other two, can you recognize them?"

"Not the man in the uniform, but the other...it is definitely Ian Stanley."

"I can't believe it...what in God's name is going on?" Genie questioned. It was all too incomprehensible to be true.

"I can't believe this myself. But it is true......here is the proof." Anna waved the photographs. "These must have been taken at that last party. I told you it was the last night Anton and I were together. We were making plans...plans for our future." She laughed sarcastically. "When Anton left for Ian's party he promised he was only going to make an appearance...then he would return......but, of course, he didn't. He never returned." Anna sat quietly staring at the last picture taken of her missing lover.

"Do you think any of the other guests know what happened that night?"

"No...I don't think so, at least no one is saying. I have spoken to many of them since Anton's disappearance and I am quite certain that no one was aware of anything unusual happening that night. There is one thing, however. There are rumors, very credible rumors, that Anton is not the only one missing."

"You mean other guests have......"

"No, no, not that. It seems that several other Soviet diplomats are also missing. No official report has been made; everything has been handled very secretly. But I have been told that Anton was not the only 'Comrade' to inexplicably vanish."

"A plot," said Genie aghast, "......some sort of conspiracy?" She felt a sudden chill.

Anna stared at Genie with dark questioning eyes as they read each other's thoughts. "Something Roger stumbled onto," they mumbled almost in unison.

'Something he shared with Richard," Genie added.

"Should I conclude that we have our work cut out for us?"

"Oui," agreed Anna. "We certainly do."

"And the first thing I must do," Anna began moments later, pointing to the man in uniform, "is to find out who he is. Perhaps you should call Roger's wife and try to get as much information as you can from her. Even the most insignificant details might help.... What do you think?"

"I think the reporter in you just kicked into gear," she smiled.

"You are right. It feels wonderful to have a direction, to be able to do something constructive again."

"I understand," said Genie wistfully.

Anna was the first to hear footsteps on the stairs. She motioned to Genie. "I don't want him to know about Anton just yet."

"Please, trust me," Anna pleaded. She gathered up the two pictures that clearly showed Anton and put them into her bag. "I must choose the right time to tell him what we have found."

"Well, what have we here?" Phillipe said, astonished to see the two women embracing.

"Phillipe, I am so glad you are here," said Anna standing. "We have been going over and over these photographs and I am quite convinced that they were indeed taken at Ian Stanley's last party. Come, have a look."

Phillipe agreed with their conclusion. "Yes, here in the back you can see the Wilsons and that twit Thompson."

Anna pointed to the man in uniform. "Do you recognize him?" she asked trying not to sound to insistent.

"No, I don't. Is it important?"

"I don't know...I just have a feeling," she hedged. "Phillipe," Anna continued. "I am going to take these photographs to the office and try to identify some of the guests. Will you please drive Genie to the hotel?"

"Certainly, Anna, but wouldn't you like me to go with you too? I could help."

Genie noticed a look and wondered if he wished for more than a working relationship with Anna.

"No, merci, no. I can handle it but Genie needs to get back to the hotel. She has an important call to make, and I think," said Anna, suddenly coming to a conclusion, "that she should check out of the Hilton and come to stay with me. What do you think?" Turning to Genie she continued, "It would make it much easier for us to collaborate...No?" She didn't mention that she was becoming more and more concerned for the American woman's safety.

After a few moments thought Genie answered, "No, Anna. I don't believe that would be a good idea."

"Oh!" The French woman was surprised.

"Think about it," she said. "If someone is following me I wouldn't want them to know that you're involved. It would be much safer if they aren't chasing both of us."

"I see what you mean. Alright," Anna reluctantly agreed. "But be careful."

"Don't worry, I will be. In fact I think it might be a good idea for me to change hotels," she said. "What do you think?"

Without much more discussion, they agreed on a plan. It was decided that Phillipe would take Genie back to the hotel so she could pack and check out. They would all meet later at Anna's apartment.

Within the hour, Genie had left the Hilton. Bags hastily tossed into the old car, she and Phillipe wound their way through crowded streets toward another smaller, quieter hotel that they hoped would provide discreet refuge.

Chapter 24

Three hundred miles southwest of Cairo, in a cramped room in a dilapidated building in the isolated desert community of Jal Abba, the Eagle waited. A large man of unknown origin, his dark skin glistened with sweat. This whole operation was taking far longer than he had been promised. He had completed his part. Negotiations with Moscow were finalized, at least a far as he was concerned. In his impatience he spat on the sand covered floor and vowed that Finch would pay dearly for his extra services.

In three adjacent rooms in the ancient mud and straw structure, his band of renegades guarded the prisoners. Not that these hostages were going anywhere. The remote oasis was fifty miles from absolutely anything. Anyone foolish enough to try to escape would be dead in less than a day, dehydrated and burned to the core by unrelenting sun and heat of the eternal desert. And no help could be expected from Jal Abba's few permanent inhabitants. Unlikely allies for anyone attempting such an adventure, they were mostly an unsavory lot of thieves, murderers and drug dealers who had fled into this cruel terrain in hopes of escaping certain capital punishment. The Eagle and his company fit right in.

In the largest of the three rooms Anton sat as he had for days, his eyes tightly blindfolded, chains shackling a wrist and ankle, with his back against the rough mud wall. He could hear harsh breathing and occasional moans from his colleagues, and silently said an old, long forgotten, Russian prayer that his captors would soon bring water for their relief.

Listening carefully he guessed that there were at least two others in the room with him and wondered what had become of the rest of the men who had been with the group in the beginning. He suspected they were near, but because of their recent move to this new location, he couldn't be sure. He could only hope that they were all still alive. He could only hope that they were in better shape than he was.

To keep his mind occupied, to keep it off the filth, the smell of unwashed bodies and urine, hunger, pain and the constant, nagging, debilitating thirst, to keep himself from going completely mad, Anton replayed in his mind the circumstances of his capture. Over and over and over it repeated unrelentingly until nothing seemed real. It reached a point where he almost believed it had happened, not to him at all, but to some lackluster character in a grade B movie. A movie that had been created out of chaos, with a muddled beginning, an unfathomable plot and no end in sight.

In his mind's eye he could still see the beautifully dressed women in blue sequins and ivory chiffon, wearing diamonds that sparkled in the candle light. Had he actually been one of the nattily attired men circulating cheerfully throughout Ian Stanley's spacious home? He could hear the soft jazz,…no, no…it had been Chopin, that's right, chamber music. It floated through the air and disappeared on the warm evening breeze. He remembered vividly how anxious he had been to return to Anna. Where was she now? he wondered. What was she doing? If only she had come to the party with me, perhaps then…but life is full of "if only". Hell, it might have been worse…if that is possible.

Anton's thoughts began to wander. He found it hard to concentrate on the facts. He remembered clearly that Ian had practically begged him to join him for a drink alone in his study. Though, now, he wasn't certain they had been alone, for it was then that things began to get fuzzy. He reasoned that the brandy had been drugged and that in itself was an incredibly irrational act for an American ambassador. He had a vague recollection of a long automobile ride, but by then he had been blindfolded and disoriented by the drug. And then blackness.

He recalled waking later to find himself tightly bound and lying on a stone floor. To his amazement he was not alone. Four other men, similarly bound, were lying or sitting in the tiny room. What amazed him even further was that these men were not strangers. He knew them all, not well, but they had been colleagues. They were all members of the Soviet diplomatic service. It puzzled him then and still did, for it was, of course, no coincidence that they were all together.

He had seen at the first glance of his captors that they were members of the Shi'ite Muslim fundamentalist group called Hezbollah. This made no sense at all. It was, for lack of a better description, backward. The Americans, certainly not the Soviets, had a long standing feud with these madmen, fueled primarily by the fact that they were holding American hostages in Lebanon. So what were they doing working with the American ambassador? It made no sense. And why would they want him and his comrades? To his knowledge they would have no reason to hold Soviet prisoners.

To add to his confusion Anton had no idea where he was. Had he somehow been sent to Beirut? The others in the group were of no help. They too had been spirited away under drugs and in shackles. The one difference in their circumstances was that only Anton realized the involvement of anyone other than the Hezbollah. He wondered how soon that would become a fatal difference.

Before this most recent move the men, resigned to their circumstances, had tried to make the best of them. When they were alone, without guards in the room, they had been allowed to remove their blindfolds and occasionally their wrist bindings.

Their feet remained tethered. They were able to get up and move around a bit and tried their best to get some exercise, shuffling several times around the room.

Meal time had become the most critical period of the day. Though the food itself was just barely edible, usually consisting of Arabic bread, strong cheese, some sort of nondescript broth, and black coffee or tea, it was enough to keep a man alive. And more importantly, it was the only time when the men were allowed to speak. The psychological boost each man received from the simple act of conversation was immeasurable.

But something had changed. The mood of his captors had become sullen, more hostile. He sensed a growing impatience which led him to believe that he and the others had been held captive far longer than expected. He prayed their impatience wouldn't cause them to do anything rash... He also prayed for a miracle and reflected with wry humor that for a Soviet he had been doing a great deal of praying recently.

Propped against the rough mud wall of his prison, Anton thought about the days that had turned into weeks and now, it seemed, to months. He tried, in vain, to push from his mind the similarity between his capture and the fate of the American hostages. Was anyone out there trying to secure his release or the release of his comrades or would they too be held captive for years?

Would this go on forever?

Just outside the small mud hut the Eagle paced. He had had enough of waiting. If Finch wasn't going to take action he was. Calling two of his men he ordered them to provision the jeep. He intended to find out exactly what was going on, and the best place to do that was in Cairo.

Chapter 25

The moment he entered the familiar hotel room, Finch unceremoniously dropped the dark grey jacket he had been carrying since arriving at Cairo airport to the floor. With one foot he shoved his brown, leather travelling case roughly into the room's small closet.

"Damn," he swore breathlessly after the four flight climb to his room. "I can't believe I'm in this shit hole again!"

An old double bed screeched in protest when he collapsed heavily onto its threadbare spread. He kicked off tight black wingtips, ripped away his tie, tossing it across the room, and lay back against the imitation wicker headboard. With growing anger he pondered the circumstances that forced his return to Cairo.

The antagonism he felt toward the general for putting him in a position of having to rush this operation; that he felt toward an incompetent Whiting for botching his end of things and an unreasonable hostility toward McBride had all, coalesced over the past few days into overwhelming rage.

Somewhere deep within his malicious mind he began to focus his anger upon the one person left whom he believed could possibly determine the success or failure of his mission. In Finch's agitated state of mind the only person standing in the way of complete success was Genie Lawrence.

Her meddlesome interference had cost him precious time, had caused unnecessary difficulties. Though he had no absolute proof, instinct convinced him that she had what he wanted. She would die because of it.

He banged his fist hard against the wall. He was angry and frustrated. This time the target of his rage was a woman. In most cases, when he felt this kind of unresolved fury, it was because of the circumstances of his "profession," usually directed at another man. In any event, it really didn't matter whether the object of his antagonism was male or female, the result was the same. Though he would never permit himself to believe it...Finch's anger always generated intense sexual arousal. He didn't even realize the connection. He just knew that the more he hated a man, the more he wanted to kill him in the most obscenely torturous means imaginable. And the more he hated a woman...the more he wanted to take her body and use it in any number of sadistically sexual ways.

Lying there on the bed he gleefully envisioned all the things he would do to "that American bitch" before he killed her. In his mind he could hear screams of terror as he tied her to his bed. Oh! The games he would play with her naked body. Before he was through with the slut she would be begging for him. She would want it alright.

Finch felt himself growing hard. He would have her anyway he wanted her and then he would leave his mark. When her body was finally discovered...would the authorities be able to determine exactly how those special slash marks, the ones his fine weapon would draw across the soft white skin of her abdomen, were actually created? "I will have her." Finch gasped, shuddered and experienced release. Warm fluid ran over his thighs and between his legs.

Much later, refreshed after a long cold shower, he picked up the telephone and placed a call.

"Whiting?" he barked into the mouthpiece. "Where is she?"

He wrote Whiting's response, Genie's Hilton room number

and the name Anna DuLac on a notepad, and without saying another word, abruptly slammed the receiver onto its cradle.

From the brown leather bag Finch removed a caftan that could easily have been worn by a typical Egyptian shopkeeper or street merchant. He slipped it over his head, smoothing the wrinkles as it dropped to his feet. He then pulled out bronzing gel and applied it liberally to his face, neck and hands. Next, he carefully adhered a full, dark brown mustache to his upper lip. Opening a small plastic case he gingerly lifted out two dark brown, almost black, contact lenses. After spraying his sparse hair with dark brown aerosol hair color the disguise was complete.

Blinking a few times to insure the lenses were a comfortable fit, he stepped back and appraised the image staring at him from the glass. The change in his appearance was dramatic. No one would guess he was not a swarthy Egyptian laborer.

Finch went nowhere without his silver weapon. It was securely tucked into the top pocket of a shirt worn beneath his robes. "Time," he whispered. He grabbed a pair of dark glasses and left the room.

Snuggling back against the well-worn vinyl seat of the ancient green taxi, Genie tried to make herself comfortable for the nine mile ride to Giza. Drifting back to the morning's telephone conversation with Anna her brow involuntarily knotted. She realized with dismay that Anna would be furious with this spontaneous decision to tour the pyramids. She had all but promised her that she would stick close to the hotel. But, hell! There wasn't a damn thing she could do anyway, at least not until Anna had completed researching the photos, and that alone would take the better part of the day.

It was obvious by now that it would not be easy for her to track down all the names of the guests Roger had captured on film. The plans they had made to meet at Anna's apartment last evening had fallen apart. From their phone call it was apparent that Anna had gotten nowhere yesterday and was back at it again today. Not being able to help was extremely frustrating.

She just had to get out. The small old hotel Phillipe had found for her was quaint, but certainly not luxurious. She was going stir crazy.

By the time Finch found himself walking through the modern spacious lobby of the Hilton hotel it was already late in the afternoon. Carrying a large bundle of lilies he bowed his head slightly and humbly approached the concierge. "Ahem!" He coughed.

"Yes, may I assist you?"

"Ah! Yes, yes." Never being good with accents or dialects Finch simply tried to speak as indistinctly as possible while still getting his point across. "I, ah, lovely flowers for Mme. Lawrence. Room please?"

"You are delivering flowers to a Miss Lawrence?"

Finch nodded.

"One moment. Let me just check her room." The concierge dialed the front desk then responded, "I'm sorry there is no one by the name of Lawrence staying here at the present time."

Finch was unconcerned and pressed on. "Ah! Friend, she stay with friend name Mslle. DuLac. Room please?"

"Well, why didn't you say so? I swear...you delivery people. Just one moment." Annoyed at the seeming incompetence of the man, the concierge again dialed the desk. "No. Thank you." He turned to Finch. "I am afraid you have missed Miss DuLac. It seems she checked out of the hotel last night."

"What?" Finch almost lost control, but checked himself long

enough to try to get additional information. "Please, you know where lady is?" He could feel the muscles in his arms tighten and involuntarily he began to crush the delicate flowers.

"Sorry, she left no forwarding address. Now look," said the concierge in exasperation, "you're dropping those petals all over the floor. I really think you must leave."

Angrily Finch threw the remaining flowers to the floor leaving the baffled hotel employee to clean up the mess.

Standing outside the Hilton Finch took in a deep breath. He was about to grab a taxi to his hotel when he changed his mind and went back inside the Hilton. At a public telephone he opened the directory and looked up the name Anna DuLac.

A short time later in the lobby of a modern multistoried apartment building, Finch surveyed a bank of mailboxes until he found the one he was looking for......Anna DuLac 15C. Getting through the security door proved ridiculously easy. He simply waited for someone to exit the building and then feigned loss of his key so they would let him enter. He was within the tenants' lobby in ten minutes. Once inside, Finch rode the elevator to the fourteenth floor and made his exit. There appeared to be four apartments on each floor, two on either side of a long hallway. At one end of the hallway this floor had its own small waiting area with a couch, two chairs, a coffee table and a variety of assorted plants. If the floor above followed the same plan it would provide a perfect vantage point from which he could watch the DuLac apartment without seeming suspicious.

He found the exit stairs and quietly made his way to the floor above. The door opened with a slight squeak, but as there was no one in the hallway it was of no concern. Was she home? Was the Lawrence woman with her? He didn't know, but he was about to find out.

While in the main lobby, Finch had memorized the name

Mahib, the name of the occupant of 16C, the apartment directly above the DuLac apartment. He would simply knock on Anna's door and ask for them...an easy mistake, he had gotten off on the wrong floor, etc...etc.

As Finch approached Anna's apartment he heard the elevator whoosh open. He held his breath until an elderly European couple entered apartment 15A and closed their door behind them.

Finally he pressed the buzzer. No answer... He knocked...still nothing. Convinced that no one was home, he walked to the waiting area and sequestered himself behind a large acacia. Without being easily seen himself, he had a clear view of 15C.

As she neared Giza, Genie began to have second thoughts about her excursion into the past. What if Anna was right? What if she was being followed? Without thinking she instinctively turned and stared out the rear window of the rumbling old taxi. Nothing. No, she knew she was being ridiculous, but she couldn't seem to shake a sudden feeling of discomfort.

"Driver," she said suddenly, "please turn around. I would like to go back to Cairo." She felt foolish, but just couldn't bring herself to continue.

"Miss?" the driver asked incredulously. "You wish to return to the city?"

"Yes, please. I just. I ah! I am not feeling too well," she lied, embarrassed by her own paranoia. "It must be this heat," she continued. "I'm afraid I am not used to it. You understand."

"Certainly, miss, we go now," he said quickly, not wanting to jeopardize his good fortune at this quick run. He would get twice the fare and still have time for another trip.

During the entire ride back to Cairo Genie found herself staring out the taxi windows. She wasn't certain what she was looking for, who she was looking for; she simply couldn't escape the feeling that she was being watched.

At the edge of the city Genie handed the driver a slip of paper with Anna's address. "Please drop me off here," she requested and in a few moments the driver pulled up in front of a tall modern apartment building.

By the time Genie climbed out of the taxi it was early evening. Though she hadn't bothered to call ahead, she was certain that if Anna wasn't at home now she soon would be. She would wait.

Genie gave her name to the doorman who rang her through the security door. She quickly walked across the hall to the bank of elevators.

On the fifteenth floor Finch heard the elevator whine as it began its ascent. He had been keeping an eye on it for at least an hour and was, by now, very familiar with the sound.

It rose slowly and finally came to a stop. Hoping it would, at last, be the DuLac woman Finch leaned back further behind a large plant and hid his face with a magazine.

The lone ride up seemed to take forever. Finally, she stepped out of the elevator and into the deathly silence of a long dark hallway. Eerie, she thought taking a deep breath. Looking over her shoulder she hurriedly knocked on Anna's door. No one answered. "Damn," she whispered and rang the doorbell several times in frustration. Alone in the unfamiliar hallway Genie again fought a bout with anxiety. Slight tension tightened the muscles in her shoulders and back. Nerves on edge she stared up and down the hall. She saw no one. "This is really nuts," she whispered. "There is absolutely no one here."

A slight flash to her left made her jump, but to her relief she realized that the automatic lights had come on in a small lobby at the end of the corridor. She decided to sit there and wait until Anna and Phillipe returned. "At least I can stay for a little while," she mumbled, and noticed how loudly her footsteps echoed as she walked toward the far end of the hall.

Finch recognized the red hair immediately. When she crossed the hall to 15C he quickly ducked further back into the lobby. He was sure she hadn't seen him. This was more than he could have hoped for. What luck. His eyes gleamed and his fingers instinctively reached for the slight protrusion caused by the weapon in his shirt pocket. His mind raced. How would he handle it? This was one scenario he hadn't envisioned and he wasn't about to let the moment slip by. Of course he couldn't do it here. He didn't want to do it here. He wanted this one to last. Somehow he had to get her back to his place. Then...then he would have his fun.

For a moment he feared the realization that no one was home would send her immediately back to the main floor. He rose from his chair prepared to catch up to her before the elevator returned. But then he heard it...the slow rhythmic pace of her footsteps. She was walking directly toward him.

He removed the knife from his pocket. With a flick of his finger the long slender blade sprang free. He positioned himself so that he could grab her the moment she walked through the wide, doorless entrance. Soon it would all be over. He would have her.

Genie walked down the corridor with deliberation and realized she was actually anxious to get out of the dreary hall and into the warm inviting light of the waiting area. With a sigh of relief she reached the lobby.

"Genie?" Phillipe's voice echoed her name.

Just into the lobby she turned and saw him waving to her from the elevator. Anna was already opening her front door and waved also. In her haste to get back to the apartment Genie noted with surprise that she was not alone. "Excuse me," she said, almost bumping into a dark, wild eyed man who seemed to have appeared from nowhere. He was so close to her that he was blocking her way. She actually felt him grab her arm. "Excuse me," she said again, trying to get past him.

Phillipe was halfway down the hall when Finch decided to let her pass. It was a spontaneous decision. He had been so close to her he could smell her perfume. He had actually touched her, almost grabbed her arm. He could have killed her easily. Not as much fun but it would have done the job so...why hadn't he? Certainly the two witnesses had made things a bit more difficult, but he knew he could have slipped the slender knife lethally into her side and still managed get away. What instinct had prevented him from ending it there?

As he watched her hurry back up the darkened hallway he silently cursed himself for the momentary hesitation. With no one in sight he pounded his fist heavily against the wall.

Later that evening, standing in the shadows of the building Finch waited.

This time he would follow her to her hotel.

Having made the decision Finch rationalized his actions.

"Hell! She didn't have those damn photographs on her anyway," he swore. "I have got to have them. And now I have to find out how much those other two know. It was really lucky I didn't off the bitch when I had the chance," he continued to mumble to himself. "I've got to...um! persuade... her to tell me everything. And she'll fucking well tell me the names of absolutely everyone who knows what's going on...you just bet she will." He smiled slightly, and with vacant eyes stared at the flickering street lamp. The slender silver blade danced easily between his fingers, coldly glistening in reflected lamplight.

Chapter 26

It hadn't made much sense, starting a fire in July, but Alex didn't care about the sense of it. Somehow it seemed absolutely essential, so he stirred the dying embers with a poker and dropped another log on the hot coals. Sparks flew about like fireflies on a June evening. Most escaped up the chimney, a few managed to drift lazily beyond the screen only to flicker and die as soon as they encountered cooler air beyond the hearth.

He loved the quiet old library. Of the many rooms in his family's home this was his favorite. The dark mahogany panels and soft leather chairs, which age and use had turned the color of good port wine, provided cozy warmth that always managed to give him comfort. Sinking deeply into his favorite chair he slowly sipped a snifter of brandy and thought of Genie.

He was worried about her. He knew he shouldn't have expected her to call today. He understood what she was trying to accomplish, but it didn't make him feel any more at ease with the situation. And it certainly didn't help that he couldn't explain his feelings toward her. When she left without confiding in him, he was furious. Now that he hadn't heard from her he was concerned. Admit it, he thought, very concerned. How would he react when she returned? He simply couldn't be sure.........And of course there was Constance.

As if on cue, his solitude was broken. "Hello, darling," the familiar female voice purred. Constance walked over and gave him a kiss on his forehead. "You are being quite reclusive this evening.

God, it is absolutely stifling in here. Why don't you come and join the rest of us in the living room?"

"Perhaps in a while," he said without looking up.

"You are a stubborn old mule," she said and leaning over the arm of the chair gave him an affectionate hug.

"Not now," he said more abruptly than he meant to and tried to put her off.

"My goodness, darling, what is it?" She was startled by the rejection. "We had such a lovely time yesterday. I thought..."

"I know," he said, fumbling like a teenager for just the right words. "It was almost like old times, wasn't it?"

"Almost!" she said, her voice rising. "I thought it was EXACT-LY like old times."

He could see anger flashing behind her wide blue eyes. "Constance, come here. Sit down. I think you know what I mean. We have both changed...moved on, so to speak. There will always be affection between us..." Oh, damn. How could he explain this? How could he make her understand what had happened yesterday. He wasn't sure he understood it himself.

......He had been unreasonably angry when he discovered Genie gone. A brisk ride on Dante was exactly what he needed. When Constance had shown up in the stables at the same time he had been surprised, but put up only token resistance to her offer to ride along. "Like the good old days," she had said. And to his relief it had been. They rode for hours over fields and through familiar woods. It was a ride they had taken many times before and he had actually begun to imagine it was years earlier.

They talked about old friends and laughed at some of the crazy things they had done together. Alex was actually enjoying himself.

How could he have forgotten how much fun Constance could be? He had definitely begun to feel better.

"Alex, look," she had said. "Isn't that the old gamekeeper's cottage we used to stop at? Come on let's have a look."

Like an idiot, when she took off at a gallop without waiting for an answer, he had followed close behind.

"Boy, look at this place. What a mess."

"It was always a mess." He recalled he said that clearly. "Don't you remember?"

"I suppose you're right. Though in my mind it always seemed more a fairy castle or perhaps 'Toad Hall'."

Wrapped in the past he had been overwhelmed with youthful longings and when she turned to him, her eyes too sparkling with memories, he was lost.

"Remember, Alex, the first time we found this place?"

"How could I forget?" Standing in the disheveled old cottage the years dropped away like so many dying petals. He was overcome by a strange lingering déjà vu. When he looked at Constance busily brushing debris off an ancient divan he felt a yearning for her he presumed long since dead. Was this truly a magical cottage where yesterdays could, at the wink of an eye, take the place of today? He didn't know. He only knew that standing there, in that dimly lit mote-filled cottage, he had an inexplicable urge to hold her.

The soft lilt of her voice drew him across the room.

"Constance," he said softly.

She turned to him provocatively, and he couldn't have guessed the joyous triumph she experienced when she read the longing in his eyes.

"Yes, Alex," she said and fell easily into his arms.

Her hair smelled of fresh herbs and flowers. The instant he kissed her lips he felt the old passions rising between them.

They undressed each other slowly. She wanted this moment to last. He didn't want to break the spell. Their hands caressed the familiar curves of each other's body, touching, kissing all the tender sensuous spots they had known so many years ago.

Alex spread his coat over the old divan and rolled his sweater into a pillow. With inviting arms outstretched, Constance lowered herself onto the makeshift bed.

She could not believe she was here again with Alex. It was exactly what she wanted and she always got what she wanted. His body on top of her, inside her, it was wonderful. It was driving her wild. She craved him like a drug. Her body responded without thought. She arched involuntarily to his touch. She couldn't get enough of him. He almost couldn't do enough to satisfy her and she clasped him to her with all her strength.

With two separate driving forces their bodies moved as one......he looking for familiar passion to ease his frustrations, she looking to recapture the past and build from it a future. Two entirely different desires brought them to this point. And for a time they reveled in the pleasures of each other's body.

"Alex, please. Oh please." she moaned breathlessly.

He had been holding back. Trying to give Constance as much enjoyment as she was giving him, he had been waiting for her signal. Now his body burst with relief.

She could not believe how satisfied she felt. None of her other lovers had ever been able to compare to Alex. His timing was impeccable. A rare talent she had been unable to find in other men.

Constance was determined then to have Alex forever.

When finally they walked through the door and rejoined the world, Alex knew that the brief spell of the past was broken.

Damn! He swore silently. What have I done?

For some reason, neither of them had the urge to linger. They had simply gotten dressed quietly and closed the door behind them.

Constance too was unusually silent. In fact, as they rode back toward the stables they hardly spoke a word to each other.

Alex now felt extremely awkward. He was afraid he knew what Constance was thinking, and it was his fault. He had led her on, led her to believe that they could go back, that they could erase the years. But in his heart he knew it was impossible. He knew he couldn't return to the past. He only hoped he would find a way to put the afternoon into perspective for Constance.

First, of course, he would also have to put it into perspective for himself.

"Affection between us?" The harsh words startled him into the present. "Is that what you call it? Affection? Bloody Hell! Alex, I am in love with you. I have always been in love with you. You know that."

He sat with his head in his hands. This wasn't going well.

Chapter 27

"You saw him, right? What a creepy character." Once within the safe haven of Anna's apartment Genie felt inexplicable relief. "You don't know him, do you?" she asked.

"No, I have never seen him. Et vous, Phillipe?"

"No, but he seems to have gone for now," said Phillipe standing half in and half out of the doorway. "Did he bother you?"

"No, no. I am just a bit edgy…brings out my suspicious nature, I guess. Never mind, I'm letting my imagination get the better of me." Without hesitation she added, "So, you two, tell me…what you have found?"

Anna smiled conspiratorially and dumped her satchel onto the dining room table. Dozens of photographs and enlargements spilled out across the glass top. The three of them gathered around while Anna explained what had been discovered.

"See here," Anna began by showing Genie comparisons between Roger's originals and the enhanced copies she had processed. "This clearly shows Anton's face. He looks…ah distressed…yes?" She struggled for the English she hoped would accurately express her perceptions. "And here in this one," she continued. "These are all people I know quite well. I will speak with them as soon as I can. They may be able to help us."

While Anna excitedly shuffled through the mass of pictures and paperwork jumbled together on the table Genie noticed that Phillipe seemed withdrawn, he was particularly quiet. Curiously she wondered exactly what had gone on between them. Anna finally showed Phillipe the photographs that included the face of her missing lover. It appeared that Phillipe was torn between his feelings for Anna and the possibility that he may actually help her find love in another man's arms. Was Phillipe a good and honorable man? Genie could only hope he was because she had come too far to allow his feelings, no matter how strong, to interfere with her goal and Anna's search.

"Voila! Here it is." Anna pulled something from the bottom of the stack. "This is what I was looking for." Anna placed the photo of the uniformed officer in front of Genie and next to it she placed a small newspaper article about a General Armstrong Walker. His picture was in the upper left corner. "They are one in the same... no?"

Genie looked closely at the two faces. "They are one in the same...yes?" she agreed. "But an American General.? What would Anton be doing with an American General?"

"Actually," Anna replied, "I am not at all surprised. He knew many people and Ian's parties attracted much attention."

"So you are not concerned?"

"About the fact that he knew the American...No. But this picture," she mindlessly tapped on one particular photo with her finger. "It concerns me. Look at it......Ian Stanley and this General Walker may have been the last ones to see Anton." Her voice saddened. She became almost inaudible. "And Ian is dead... and Roger is dead."

"And Richard," Genie quietly added.

"Oui, and your Richard."

"But the General, he is very much alive, added Phillipe, encouragingly.

"Yes," said Anna, "he is."

For the next few moments the silence in the apartment was

absolute. Phillipe was the first to speak. "Anna, I know what you are thinking," he could read her perfectly, "and I am against it."

Eyes widening, Genie turned to Anna.

"I am going to Washington," Anna answered the unasked question.

"Honestly Anna," Phillipe broke in. "You mustn't. It is far too dangerous.

The discussion between Anna and Phillipe that followed became quite heated. Through it all Genie sat on the sidelines, biting her tongue, trying avoiding voicing her opinion. Though she could hardly understand the furious French that flew between them, it was all too obvious that Phillipe was more than simply concerned for Anna's safety. For a moment the feelings he had tried so hard to contain surfaced. She sensed that Phillipe was desperately afraid Anna might actually accomplish the task. She might find Anton again.

Fortunately for her, the brief argument between Anna and Phillipe proved one important point. Phillipe was basically a decent man. Though at this moment fear for her safety made him angry with her decision he would not try to stop her from confronting the American General.

He just doesn't want Anton back in her life, Genie thought. I'm sure he realizes he wouldn't stand a chance with Anna if Anton were suddenly resurrected from the dead.

"Mon dieu, you are an exasperating woman," Phillipe grumbled. He grabbed his jacket and left in a huff.

"He was really angry."

"Do not worry. He will calm himself. Believe me I understand Phillipe. I know he has certain feelings toward me, but what he doesn't seem to realize is that I will never be free...Um! Emotionally free...Am I explaining it correctly?" she looked at Genie, who nodded in acknowledgement, and continued. "Emotionally ready to begin any new relationship until I know what happened to Anton. I still pray every night that he is alive. I must do everything I can to find him. And if he is not," she spoke softly, almost unable to say the words. "Well then I must know that too."

They were caught up in the same game. The American teacher and the French reporter shared the same feelings, had the same need. Genie too, though she knew Richard was dead, needed to close a chapter in her life. If she were ever to move ahead she needed answers. Intuitively she realized that they were on the right path and that despite Phillipe's objections...and, for that matter, Alex's...the only thing they could do was go forward.

In the street below he waited, but his prey never emerged. When the lights in the apartment finally went out Finch concluded that she was spending the night with the DuLac woman. No matter. He would return to his post in the early morning. It wouldn't be long now before he would have her.

Monday July 9th

Genie tried in vain to ignore the morning as it crept quietly through the curtains allowing her not even a few more minutes of sleep. As one bright ray of sunlight danced across her face she rolled over and cautiously opened one eye. For a brief moment she was confused, not sure exactly where she was. The disorientation of yet another strange room quickly passed, however, and she wearily slid out of bed and wrapped herself in Anna's borrowed robe.

"Bon Jour," Anna greeted. "You look like you are still half asleep."

Genie stretched and shook her head both in affirmation of Anna's observation and in an attempt to get rid of the cobwebs.

"I must have been really exhausted last night. I've been running on nervous energy for so long now that it finally caught up with me. This coffee should do it," Genie said taking a steaming mug from Anna. "Thanks."

It was well after 1:00 pm when, at last, Genie rushed out of the building. If she were going to catch the 3:30 flight to London as planned she would have to hurry. She still had to get to the hotel, pack and check out before she could be on her way. Luckily the doorman had a taxi waiting.

Traffic, unfortunately, was horrendous. The cab inched its way along the congested street. Resigned to the fact that there was nothing she could do she settled back and took in the hustle and bustle of the city. Playing tourist, she convinced herself, would make the interminable ride bearable.

The mind games seemed to be working...until she spotted him. Doing a double take she turned to get a better look and swore she recognized the same wild eyed man she had run into in the apartment lobby last evening. "It can't be," she mumbled but as she stared out the window to the corner across the street their eyes locked. "It is him," she said in shock causing the driver to turn around.

"Miss?"

"Oh nothing," she anxiously replied. "I...um...Never mind. Just try to hurry please. I must catch a plane."

"Yes miss," he responded and stepped a bit harder on the accelerator.

After the drivers interruption Genie turned around again to take yet another look at the mysterious man, but of course he was gone. Faded into the crowd. "Damn." The whole incident made her very uneasy, but at least traffic seemed to have let up a little and the driver was indeed hurrying to the hotel.

Finch couldn't believe he had missed her, but when she went past him in the cab he realized his mistake. Immediately he found an unoccupied taxi and commanded the driver to follow Genie. The ride was agonizingly slow. If only he knew where she was headed he could probably get there more quickly on foot.

Suddenly his cab came to a grinding halt. "Move it you bastard," Finch shouted, but the distressed driver, who spoke very little English, simply raised his hands in dismay and pointed to the red light. "An extra twenty if you go through it," he hissed.

"But sir, the light?" the driver cried.

"Fifty," Finch yelled. "Now go."

The cab proceeded cautiously through the light. But the taxi with Genie Lawrence was nowhere in sight. He had lost her again.

"God damn it," he swore. Then looking around he had an idea. He recognized this part of the city. A couple of blocks away there was a street with three small old hotels. He had a hunch, leaned forward and gave the driver directions.

Genie packed furiously. If she missed the 3:30 plane she would have to stay here at least until tomorrow, maybe Wednesday and she didn't want to remain in Cairo any longer than she had too. Especially now. Especially since she was positive that man was following her.

Fortunately she hadn't unpacked much. It didn't take her long to collect everything and dump it into her bags. She did take the time to change her clothes. Having been in the same things for two days she simply couldn't stand them any longer.

Out of her bag she pulled her favorite denim skirt and a crisp white linen blouse, a bit wrinkled, but clean. She changed her sandals in favor of socks and Reeboks and tied her hair back with a yellow ribbon. "Ready," she said to herself and looked around the room one more time.

Finch had checked both the King Farouk and El Calan hotels with no success. Now as he entered the busy lobby of the old Colonial Desert, a relic from a past era, he became elated. Across the room he could just barely see the familiar red hair of Genie Lawrence. His enthusiasm soon waned, however, when he realized she was checking out. In an effort to gain more information he carefully made his way around the room to the house phone near the front desk. He lifted the receiver and feigning a call strained to listen. Though the conversation she had with the clerk was incomplete he distinctly heard her mention British Airways.

This time he would not miss. Finch hurriedly left the small old hotel determined to reach the airport well ahead of his unsuspecting victim.

Carrying her canvas duffel, Genie followed the bellhop to the front door. "Phillipe!" she said in astonishment after almost bumping into Anna's equally surprised friend. "What are you doing here?"

"Genie! I came to speak with you. But what is this? Are you leaving?"

"Yes. Anna and I discussed it last night. We agreed that the best thing I can do right now is to take copies of the photos back to London and show them to Molly... Roger's wife. There really isn't much more I can do here. Anyway I'm afraid I am in quite a hurry. I wish I had time to talk but......" she continued to speak while rushing out to the street where she gave the bag boy a tip.

"If you would like," Phillipe said following her out of the building, "I have my car. Let me drive you to the airport. We can talk on the way."

Genie readily agreed, thankful that she wouldn't be obligated to ride in another dilapidated old junker.

"Anna gave me copies of the enlargements," she said patting her duffel. "Hopefully Molly will be able to come up with some ideas. And there is something else......" She was about to tell Phillipe about spotting that man again when he interrupted her.

"Genie," he began, and from the distraction in his voice she was sure he had been only half listening to her. "...I am really worried about her. She is determined to go to Washington...I know her... once her mind is made up...I was hoping you could speak to her."

"Phillipe, honestly I don't think you need to worry. You really must let her do this you know...If you ever want her to let Anton go." She couldn't help feeling sorry for him.

"I understand...It's just...well, when you speak to her tell her to be careful. I am afraid if I mention it again......Ah...Here we are." Phillipe turned the car into the short term parking lot near the international flights entrance.

"Don't worry you will make it," he assured her as they dashed through the doors and raced to the ticket counter.

From where he waited at the far end of the concourse, Finch could see both the door and the ticket counter. She better be here soon, he thought, or she will miss her plane. Maybe his luck would hold. Maybe she would miss it. Then maybe...... Just before his mindless thoughts turned into full-fledged fantasies he saw her. With only a few minutes to spare she came running through the sliding glass doors.

"Shit." He swore loudly enough to cause stares. She was not

alone. He strode purposefully toward them. He would kill them both. That's all. He would do the guy first and in the confusion get her too. He was about ten yards away when the crowd closed in. Looking around, he realized his chances were slipping away. He would never be able to pull it off with this many people jostling about.

Seething at his misfortune, Finch surreptitiously placed his weapon back in his pocket. He kept his eyes fixated on Genie.

Finch had become a man possessed. She was his obsession. Lately, when he dreamt of what he would do to Genie Lawrence he only vaguely remembered the photographs, or the General's plan, or her part in it, or his. And if it weren't for the money the General had promised, money he desperately needed, he would have completely dismissed the old man and his crazy plan. If it weren't for the money...time wouldn't matter. He could take as much of it as he liked. If it weren't for the money he would actually enjoy playing cat and mouse with this broad all over the god damned globe...knowing that in the end, of course, she would be his. "You will be mine," he mumbled and stared intently as she rushed toward the gate.

Ticket in hand Genie dropped her canvas bag onto the security conveyer. She retrieved her bag and turned to say goodbye to Phillipe. But Phillipe was already halfway up the hallway. And in Phillipe's place...he stood...the wild eyed man in the long caftan... stood there leering at her.

Frantically she tried to get Phillipe's attention, but he was too far away. By the time she found a security guard...the man was gone.... Or was he ever there...had she imagined him? "No... He was there," she scolded herself. "You did see him."

As she stepped onto the plane a cold shiver ran up her spine.

Chapter 28

Though he busied himself with hospital rounds, plunged headlong into research he had begun months earlier, and pored over old medical journals, Alex could not get Constance out of his mind. Guilt. There was no way around it. Saturday had been a mistake. He wasn't sure what payment Constance would exact, but he knew there would be some price to pay for his momentary lapse into past passions.

He spent most of Sunday trying to talk to her, made what he thought a reasonable effort to straighten things out, but she simply wouldn't be dissuaded. Constance insisted that their relationship could get back on track if only he would give it a chance.

He explained to her in every way he knew how, that he was sorry, that he would always care for her as a friend, would always be concerned for her welfare. *Concerned for her welfare*...that had really infuriated her.

Alex kicked himself for being such a jerk, but what could he do? He just didn't feel "that way," about her. He knew that Constance wasn't simply being obtuse. She was a smart woman and used to getting her own way, and when that didn't happen she became particularly stubborn.

It was no good. He couldn't concentrate. Tossing a two month old copy of "The New England Journal of Medicine," onto his desk, he grabbed his coat and car keys and left the, now empty, office to his nurse and her assistant. "Good night ladies," he said absentmindedly and walked out without closing the door, leaving the two women to look at each other and shrug at his "most unusual" behavior.

Still fuming, he didn't realize that he was actually stomping around his townhouse. He pulled out a frozen dinner and slammed the microwave door with a little extra force. "She even accused me of being in love with Genie Lawrence," he complained to the walls. Why he and Genie hardly knew each other. They were friends, yes, but he certainly wasn't in love with her...was he? No... He wasn't in love with her, he was almost positive about that......almost. He smiled at the thought of it. It was a crazy notion.

And what about Genie anyway? Why hadn't he heard from her? Not a word since the phone call. Of course... the phone call, that was it. He had been too rough on her.

Amazing, he couldn't seem to deal with women at all anymore. He felt like a bloody teenager.

Constance had a problem. Saturday had been wonderful. It had gone exactly as she planned. Granted, it was a hastily conceived plan. But as soon as she had seen Alex drive up to the stables she knew she had to take control of the opportunity. Constance was very good at turning chance events to her advantage. No, Saturday had been perfect...Sunday had been the problem. Alex spent literally hours trying to tell her that he wasn't in love with her.

"Nonsense!" she said. He just doesn't realize it yet. His mind, though he refuses to admit it, is too clouded with that pain in the ass... Ms. Genevieve Lawrence. "Well I can take care of that."

"What are you talking about?" Jackie demanded in exasperation at her friend's mindless muttering.

"Oh nothing... Here, give me a hand with this." She was struggling with a very large Miro lithograph that had just come into the gallery for a new showing. Although she and Alex's sister had been best friends for years she wasn't certain it was quite the right time to enlist Jackie's help.

Jackie knew something was up. "So what is going on in that devious mind of yours Constance? I know you and Alex went riding Saturday. Tell me. Are you two an item again?"

"Don't be silly love," she replied, her effort to be coy a miserable failure. "But what would you think? I mean…um…what if Alex and I were to get close again. How would you feel?"

"Hey don't put me into the middle of this. I've been there before remember. You're my best friend C.C., I love you dearly and of course I adore Alex, but to be honest I was surprised the first time you two got together. You are so different. I mean honestly Constance…can you really see yourself as the wife of a staid old country doctor. Face it," she added a little sarcastically. "You are both wonderful, but think…are you wonderful together?"

Constance feigned shocked. "I can't believe what I'm hearing. You know how much I've always loved your brother. And believe me…he isn't quite the stuffed shirt you think." She recollected some of the wild situations she had gotten them into in the past and smiled.

Jackie saw the Cheshire cat appear. "What are you smiling about?" she chuckled.

Constance's smile spread brightening her whole face. "Oh nothing let's just say that Alex needs me…to…ah…release his inhibitions."

Constance's sudden candor surprised Jackie and brought both women to the brink of laughter causing them to almost drop the Miro.

"Jackie?" Constance began after they had regained their composure. She decided that, after all, now was as good a time as any and carefully broached the subject, "What about Genie?"

"Genie? What about her?"

"Don't play games with me. You know what I mean. What about Genie and Alex?"

Jackie avoided Constance's eyes wondering if she should tell her what she really suspected. No, there was no use upsetting her with speculation. She decided to be vague.

"I don't know Constance. Alex hasn't said anything. He wasn't exactly pleased with her when she took off this weekend. I wouldn't worry about her. After all she just lost one boyfriend. I really don't think she is ready for another...do you?"

Jackie had a point. The woman did seem terribly griefstricken at the sudden loss of her friend. But there was something Jackie wasn't telling her...something in her demeanor that caused concern. For the first time Constance realized that she might have a fight on her hands. It might be a bit harder to get Alex back than she originally imagined.

The sudden blaring noise shocked Alex into wakefulness. For a brief moment his left arm flared about in a vain attempt to silence the alarm. As his head cleared he realized that it was not the alarm at all, but the telephone that had brought him back to consciousness. It took him another moment to comprehend that it was not 8:30 in the morning but only 8:30 pm.

"Uhm...Yes...Hello." He tried to clear the frog in his throat.

"Alex? Hi. It's Molly. Are you alright. You sound awful."

"Molly," Alex cleared his throat. "Oh sure I'm fine," he said brushing his hand through his rumpled hair. "I was dead to the world though. The phone gave me quite a start. What can I do for you?"

"I just received a call from Genie. She is at the airport. I thought that perhaps you might like to fetch her."

Alex was not at all certain that would be a good idea.

"I don't know Molly. The last time we spoke...well things were a bit strained."

"I know. That is why I am suggesting it. The hour ride back to Channing House would give you two some time to……"

Alex interrupted. "You're right. It's a great idea."

Molly wasn't surprised at his enthusiasm. She gave him the time, flight and gate numbers and made him promise to call when they got back to his mother's home.

Genie remained near the gate and waited for Molly. She watched while harried passengers, excited children, airport employees all hurried past. She heard announcements for outgoing and incoming flights, and the clacking of luggage carriers. She smelled the aromas of coffee and cinnamon coming from a nearby café. All this, she did, while unconsciously looking for a wild eyed stranger.

Gripping her canvas tote bag tightly enough to turn knuckles white, with eyes trained on arriving passengers she didn't notice Alex until he was standing beside her. His voice made her jump and turn defensively.

"Genie?"

"Oh! Alex you scared the shi... You really gave me a start," she said breathlessly. "What are you doing here? Where is Molly?" She knew she was rambling but was so surprised to see him she flushed with embarrassment. And the lies she had told...it was obvious that she had been found out and she wasn't sure how to handle it. But, before she had time to pull her thoughts together Alex astonished her. He began to apologize to her.

"Listen," he stumbled. "I acted like an idiot on the telephone this weekend. You had every right to go wherever you wish without any questions from me. I hope you will forgive me."

Genie was a bit dumbfounded. She had been ready with any

number of excuses as to why she had lied and now felt oddly disappointed that they were all unnecessary.

"Alex," she stumbled. "When did you realize? About Cairo I mean."

"Oh almost from the beginning," he smiled. "You are not a very convincing liar. And those flight time notes you jotted down… well…"

"I suppose I'm not, but at least now," she said voicing as much annoyance as she could under the circumstances, "you will realize that I am perfectly capable of taking care of myself. You see standing before you a fully adult female…in one complete piece."

The bravado she mustered at that moment was not just for Alex's benefit, but for her own. She still could not shake her peculiar sense of apprehension.

It had begun at the Cairo airport when she caught sight, once again, of that elusive stranger. Wariness had settled in the back of her mind barely at the edge of conscious thought, but near enough to the surface to erode small bits and pieces of her self-confidence.

On the surface, the trip to Channing House seemed pleasant enough. Alex and Genie appeared to be back at square one, chatting amiably, both apologizing for any misunderstandings about Cairo. In fact, Alex began to share Genie's enthusiasm about the results of the trip and agreed with her that the next logical step would be to work carefully with Molly and try to derive as much information as possible from the photos. He even agreed that Anna's decision to go to Washington was completely logical, though he didn't mention that he was glad it was Anna, not Genie making the trip.

But, despite all their friendly banter there was tension in the air, a slightly disquieting feeling, mild discomfort, an uneasiness that comes from secrets.

Neither Genie nor Alex was prepared to be completely open. Certainly Alex had no intention of telling Genie about the mess he had gotten himself into with Constance. He had to straighten that out himself.

In large part that meant he would finally have to admit to himself that what Genevieve Lawrence thought of him mattered. Admit that he cared. He could only hope that Constance wouldn't blurt out something too revealing before he had the courage, or could find just the right moment, to explain everything to Genie.

And, of course, on second thought, he realized that he had better act quickly. Knowing Constance as he did, he understood all too well that he couldn't count on her discretion. She had, in fact, already proven that she was out to stake her claim.

A deep frown furrowed Alex's brow but Genie was too caught up in her own thoughts to notice how pensive he had become. She too had a secret she was not yet ready to share. How could she tell him that she was again being followed? That wherever she went lately a mysterious, menacing stranger appeared. The more she thought about it the crazier it seemed. Whiting had been one thing, he was obvious and they knew exactly what he was after, but this man in Cairo, it didn't make sense; at least not yet. And perhaps she was wrong, just imagining the whole thing. Had the stress of the situation actually made her more apprehensive than she needed to be, or should she trust her instincts?

Whatever her decision, she wouldn't let anyone know what had happened. Not until she could figure it out herself or not, at least, until she had some proof.

Chapter 29

Across the street, somewhat hidden by an overgrown lilac bush Anna stood watching the General's house…waiting. If he followed the same schedule as the previous day he would soon leave for some unknown destination…a lunch or perhaps business meeting … that would occupy most of his afternoon.

Behind her Henry Goodman anxiously paced the sidewalk. Henry was a thief, or if you believed him a retired thief. He liked to refer to himself as a cat burglar. Authorities labeled him a petty criminal and the word "petty" had always annoyed him. There had never been anything petty about his work.

He had spent a total of fifteen years in various prisons for his crimes, but considering the length of his career, Henry was almost sixty-two, and the amount of money he had accumulated, it seemed a small price to pay. This job, for which he was being paid less cash than usual, was more or less a favor.

He owed a debt to someone who owed a debt to someone and so on and so forth until he found himself hanging around this tony neighborhood, waiting to break in to a prime location. Doing the odd favor was sometimes necessary, but he was really annoyed by the fact that, as part of this deal, he agreed that he wouldn't heist a thing.

Anna had hired Henry. He came highly recommended, as the best person to get her into the General's house. She realized the risk, but was so certain the General had at least some of the answers she needed that she was willing to take it. She just wanted to get in and look around and was becoming as agitated as Henry seemed to be at the endless waiting.

Time passed slowly, it was almost three when Anna finally gave up.

"What do you think Henri, shall we leave?" she said expressing obvious distress.

"It's up to you miss. You're the boss, but, well, if I were you I'd stick around a little longer." Henry, a small, compact man with grey frizz for hair, felt a protective fondness for the petite young French woman. He wanted to do a good job. He hated to see her disappointed.

"No, I am afraid today is not our day," she said and began to walk back toward the rental car she had cautiously parked on an adjacent block.

"Miss." She heard Henry suddenly whisper. "Ain't that him there? The General, ain't that him comin down the stairs?"

Anna turned around. "Yes Henri, I believe you are right. What do you think? Do we have time?"

"Well he's takin his car, he's got his briefcase, and my guess is we'll have at least an hour or so. Hell, I can get you into that place in no time."

It only took Anna a second to make up her mind. "Let's do it," she said decisively.

After a quick survey of the exterior, Henry selected his point of entry, a small, first floor, bathroom window at the back of the house.

The home was equipped with an alarm system that, if tripped, alerted a security station. However, the system posed little problem for Henry who knew from experience that in most cases not all the windows were hardwired.

The window he had selected appeared to be painted shut and he guessed correctly that it was not connected.

As time was of the essence, he quickly gave up useless efforts to jimmy the window and simply broke the glass. He pulled away the broken shards and climbed gingerly through the opening.

"Go around to the side door miss, I'll let you in." Out of habit he whispered though there was no one anywhere in the yard to hear him.

Leaving the powder room Henry cautiously looked for signs of an internal sensor alarm and found four areas blocked by an infrared beam system. Sensors were situated so that beams crossed the front door, the back and side doors and also across the bottom of the main stairway. Fortunately the detectors were placed about four feet from the floor...must have a big dog, Henry thought... and were easy to duck under.

Scared to death that someone would see her, Anna waited anxiously outside. It took only three minutes for Henry to get from the bathroom, crawl beneath the beam blocking his way and reach the mudroom door. To Anna it seemed an eternity.

She was about to scurry through the doorway, when to Anna's surprise, Henry caught her arm. In the midst of her protest Henry cautioned "There's an alarm." He said it quickly, pointing to a wall plate flashing a small red light. "If you walk through it, it'll go off. Here," he said pushing lightly on her shoulders, "scrunch down."

Anna followed his instructions glad she had dressed in jeans and running shoes. On hands and knees she pushed a canvas bag ahead of herself, across the tile floor, then crawled through.

Although it was a bit cumbersome, her bag contained all the things she considered essential for "breaking and entering" and she wasn't about to leave it behind.

After checking into her hotel room Wednesday afternoon Anna had gone out and purchased the bag as well as latex gloves, several throw-away cameras and the brightest penlight she could find. The cameras and flashlight she dropped into the bag along with her tape recorder, the gloves, and a Swiss army knife...not much of a weapon, but handy none the less. She also made sure she had paper, pen and of course an extra pair of glasses as she would be dead on the ground if she happened to lose a lens. Finally, hoping she would be able to recognize some faces, maybe even put names to them, she stuffed a side pocket with the photographs.

"This way," Henry said grabbing the bag for her. Though the house was obviously empty, he was still whispering.

They climbed four stairs to a large modern kitchen. A forest green Aga stove, stainless steel appliances and a large hanging display of highly polished cookware, were good indications that either the General, or his wife loved to cook. Stealthily proceeding through a butler's pantry and back hallway, they reached the main part of the house. It wasn't long before they knew exactly where to begin their search.

To the left of the large oak front door, across the entrance hallway from a spacious formal living room was the "General's room." It was so obviously his domain that the two intruders did not even consider beginning their search anywhere else.

Anna pulled out her camera and snapped a few shots of the room. Later she would use these to recapture the character of the man.

There were numerous photographs around the room and Anna recognized many famous faces smiling back at her through glass and frames. However, only Ambassador Stanley and his wife were to be found in both sets of pictures, hers and the General's.

"So much for that idea," she mumbled and rested the heavy bag on the seat of a well-worn wing chair while she continued to poke through numerous papers and correspondence found on his desk.

"Here miss," Henry called excitedly. "Take a look at this."

It hadn't taken him long to discover the safe behind the Wyeth seascape.

"Can you open it?"

"Of course," he answered a little hurt that she doubted his expertise. "No problem. These little wall safes are just fine for protection against fire and stuff, but hell, I can open this baby in a jiffy."

"Well," Anna urged, realizing that, she too was whispering.

"There you go," he said proudly when no more than five minutes later the door swung open.

Anna was impressed. She carefully pulled several documents from the safe, leaving what looked to be a large amount of cash, under Henry's eager gaze.

"You remember our deal Henri. No souvenirs," she reminded.

Days were passing quickly. The General could feel his plan beginning to come together. After what seemed like endless negotiations, the Russian faction had clandestinely agreed to participate. In fact, the General was almost positive that his Soviet compatriot hoped to gain the same personal acclaim for returning his country's missing comrades, as he knew he would receive when he triumphantly returned the American hostages to the homeland.

Deeply engrossed in the excitement of his own thoughts, the General inadvertently drove through a red light, nearly hitting a pedestrian in the crosswalk.

The loud blaring of surrounding car horns broke through his reverie and when he comprehended what had almost happened he began to shake. "Shit!" He couldn't afford to have anything go wrong now.

Half a mile ahead was the entrance to a newly renovated Georgian Colonial style strip mall. He cautiously pulled his car into the parking lot and took a moment to regain his composure.

Definitely not as young as he used to be, his reflexes were slower and his recovery times just a bit longer. He hated the changes the years were making. They were worse than the limp, that he had come by honestly. His combat wound, though at times painful, could at least be viewed with pride, but age…there was no honor in growing old.

"Damn!" he swore again and pounded his fist against the steering wheel. Where is that madman Finch, he thought. Why haven't I heard from him? He almost regretted the decision he had made to hire him, but the General needed Finch's 'services' and so far they had been worth the money. The greatest concern the General had was that Finch was not a team player. Once he was given an assignment Finch completed it when and how he liked and rarely bothered to make contact until the deed was done. The General was not used to dealing with men he could not control. Finch was something of a wild card and needless to say he didn't like it.

He didn't know how much more time he could give Finch before he would be forced to go ahead without him. Everything was going extremely well, moving along on schedule so he knew that it wouldn't be long.

Now that they had agreed to involve themselves with his scheme, the Russians were becoming impatient. They had already begun recruiting a select group of "volunteers" to play the role of generic Middle Eastern radicals, and they had used their considerable influence to determine the exact location of the Americans. If things didn't happen quickly there was an almost certain probability that, once again, the Americans would be moved. And the chances that the "volunteers" would discover their real mission were too depressing to calculate.

No... He couldn't let his years of planning come to nothing. Not when he was so close. It had become his life...he wouldn't let it collapse now.

If he had to go ahead without Finch's assurance that all the loose ends were tied up, he would. He would take the chance. He and the Eagle would handle this without Finch if they had too. And he would be successful. Everything was too well planned to fail.

So what if there were a few photos out there somewhere. Finch had faxed copies to him and he didn't think they would be too damaging. Of course, Finch insisted there were others, but when and if they ever surfaced he would handle it.

That nosey British photographer, what was his name...Sims, for all his sneaking around, couldn't possibly have taken any pictures that would be interpreted as incriminating. After all I was only with Ian and that young Soviet for a moment or two, he thought. Finch was being too cautious. "That bastard seems to have forgotten exactly who the hell is in charge here" the General shouted angrily, steel grey eyes flashing fire. He would give Finch a few more days...the weekend, he could stall the Soviets that long... and then...well then the hell with everything, he would bring the Americans home and assure himself of the rewards he deserved.

With some dismay the General noted that bright afternoon sunlight had taken on the golden glow of an early summer evening. How long had he been sitting here? His watch indicated that more than an hour had flown by. He could only be thankful that his bank stayed open late on Thursday evenings and that his wife was visiting the children. Lately, he noticed, she worried far too much about him, would probably have been out, looking for him herself by now, had she been at home.

He sighed audibly, a slight smile softened stone like features. Despite all her fussing he adored the small, graying, ever cheerful woman he had been married to all these years. He still saw in her the young, beautiful, brown-eyed blond he had married almost fifty years earlier. She was the only person who had ever intimidated him and he was certainly glad she would miss this little episode.

After starting the engine of his immaculately bright black Town Car, he opened the windows for air and continued to the bank.

Channing House

The fuzzy yellow ball hurtled toward her.

Three days had come and gone, with no word from Anna. To add to Genie's frustration, Inspector Whiting, it appeared, had dropped off the face of the earth. At least he was making a concerted effort to avoid her calls. Nothing was happening.

Thwack... She slammed it back across the net, no thought simply instinct, for all she could think about were those damn pictures.

...All day Tuesday and Wednesday she and Molly had poured over photographs. Molly had taken time to practically ransack Roger's office in an effort to locate even a single additional clue, but they hadn't gotten anywhere. With all their digging "what they knew" remained about the same......During April when Roger was in Cairo he attended a party at Ian Stanley's home and inadvertently snapped photos of the American Ambassador and a General Armstrong Walker "assisting someone into a limousine. That someone turned out to be Anna's lover and now he was missing...

and Roger was dead…an accident? Richard was dead…a mugging? Ian Stanley was dead…a suicide? And a police Inspector was covering up facts. And though she hadn't told anyone, Genie was positive she was being followed…or at least had been followed in Cairo.

The key, she knew, would be found in the photographs. They had to be staring right at it. They just couldn't see it.

…Whumph! The ball flew past her, an easy shot she shouldn't have missed. Much to Jackie's advantage, Genie was finding it impossible to concentrate on the game.

And Alex. Things hadn't been the same between them since she returned. Before she left Genie sensed that Alex was developing feelings for her. A woman knows those things, usually before the man. At the time her mind had been so clouded with anger and grief over losing Richard that she dismissed it as simple kindness, a developing friendship.

Now, she was confused. She sensed him backing off and it bothered her. But why? She couldn't quite get a grip on her own feelings. She certainly wasn't ready for another relationship. So why did it matter? Why should she care if he avoided her? Was it simply the attention she missed, the consideration, the companionship he offered. No, she had to admit it was more and yet she couldn't reconcile her guilt at being inexplicably drawn to another man so soon after Richard's death.

"What kind of a woman am I anyway?" she muttered and slammed a serve solidly over the net.

London

The 5 year old girl in his office had been lucky. The burns covering her chest, neck and upper arms looked far worse than they actually were. As she grew, she would need more surgeries, but ultimately they would heal with almost no scarring.

The tiny dark eyed child winced as Alex gently removed a pressure bandage to examine her arm. She reminded him of his sister. Jackie had been the same age as this little girl when a similar accident had almost taken her life.

It had been almost thirty years since he found his sister, screaming, arm in flames, still holding on to pieces of a smashed oil lantern. He had never been a believer in destiny, but there was nothing else, other than providence, that could have directed him, that day, to the small hideaway secluded behind an abandoned building near the stables.

Fortune led him to his sister in time to save her life, but not before irreparable damage had been done to her arm.

Fate had not only saved his sister, but unbeknownst to him at the time, had given him direction. Direction that, after many years led him to this office and the positive prognosis he could now offer the parents of his young patient.

If only the rest of his life were going as well as his practice, he thought as he reviewed several files in the now empty office. Professionally, he felt almost charmed; all his current patients were doing extremely well. Tissues were healing rapidly, infections were at a minimum and he hadn't seen a life threatening or seriously disfiguring new case in weeks.

It was simply everything else that was falling apart.

Much to his dismay he found himself increasingly drawn to Genie Lawrence and the more drawn to her he became, the more he tended to pull himself away. At least for now. Things were in too much of a mess and he was convinced that pursuing any romantic notions he might have at this time would only make things much more complicated.

This nasty business they had gotten tangled in was becoming

unbelievably confusing. And, to make things even more difficult, progress had come to a screeching halt. For now, it appeared, the investigation was out of their hands.

All things considered he came to the conclusion that, for the time being, the only relationship he could allow himself to have with Genie was that of a friend. The question he avoided asking himself was…could he do it?

And of course, to make life even more interesting, there was Constance. Fortunately, she had been out of town for the last two days, but she was due back momentarily and he wasn't looking forward to facing her. He had to convince her that they simply did not have a future together. He couldn't deny the strong physical attraction between them. That had always been there and probably always would be. But, other than sex, they didn't have anything in common. He could see it. Why couldn't she?

"Damn!" he sputtered in frustration. Tearing off his white lab coat, he grabbed a ratty old blue nylon tote, stuffed with miscellaneous sports gear, from the closet. "I need a swim."

Realizing with some surprise that he was the only one left on the floor, he turned out the lights to his office and the examining rooms and locked the doors, before driving across town to his club.

The Ritz Hotel. Luxury. That's what he deserved and that's what he had. Finch sank stocking feet into the lush blue pile of the bedroom carpeting. He was sick of the dives he had been staying in. This was much more to his liking. Walking slowly around the room he surveyed his new surroundings.

Massive oak bed, self-service bar with fridge and snacks, real antique furniture and a modern bath with steam chamber and telephone, it all suited him perfectly, and with the money he would soon be getting from the General he would be able to live like this indefinitely. Completely self-satisfied, he smiled and poured himself a drink.

Even missing that bitch in Cairo didn't bother him as much in a place like this. He'd get her, and soon, he knew that and the thought excited him. Just sitting here in the Ritz hotel he didn't have a care in the world. He had everything under control. The whole mess would be over next week. The General would have the missing evidence...he could go ahead with his plans whenever the hell he wanted...he would have his money...and, of course, delicious memories of a luscious redhead.

Reaching for the phone, Finch decided he would call the General and tell him so.

Chapter 30

The sudden, loud, ringing startled Anna, causing her to jump. Papers flew to the floor.

"Take it easy," Henry said with a smile. "It's just the phone."

"Oui," she replied breathing a sigh of relief. "I don't suppose we should ans…"

"Don't even think about it."

"No. You're right. I do wish it would stop."

No sooner had she prayed for silence, than the ringing ceased and a machine greeting clicked on. Anna's curiosity would not be satisfied though, the caller hung up abruptly, as soon as the greeting began.

Shrugging their shoulders they resumed the search.

Several of the papers Anna had pulled from the safe were maps which she now took the time to unfold. As soon as they spread out before her on the walnut desk top, she became intrigued. If it had not been for the unusual doodles of American and Soviet symbols she may have dismissed the Middle Eastern maps without much thought, but the symbols caught her attention and she began to study them with more care.

From her own research, she knew the location near Beirut was one area considered a possible holding place for American hostages, but the other area, the one in Syria with the hammer and sickle drawn over it baffled her.

Leaving the maps momentarily, she looked through the remaining papers, but found nothing of interest until she came to a large blue envelope. Carefully she unwound the string securing the flap and pulled out the contents.

Rifling through the papers, she soon realized what she had found and the implications of the documents so astounded her that her legs actually became weak. Papers still in hand, she more fell than sat into a hard-backed walnut swivel chair.

Mouth agape, she turned thinking to say...well! She didn't know what exactly... to Henry. For one of the few times in her life, she was completely speechless.

Henry didn't know what to make of her strange behavior. "Why miss?" he said baffled. "Are you alright?" He was at a loss as to how to help her.

"Oui, Henri. Just give me a minute," she said breathlessly. "I...I have it...I believe I have found what I was looking for..." Her voice softened and she spoke almost as if talking to herself, "and... More...really...much, much more." Shaking her head slowly, she again began to read through the papers trying to comprehend as much as she could in a short period of time.

"Well then," Henry said impatiently. "We better get outta here."

"No!" Anna almost shouted. "Not yet," she said more calmly. "I must get pictures." While she spoke she was rummaging through her bag for another camera.

They had been in the house for well over an hour and Henry was beginning to get nervous. He had second sight about these things and knew instinctively that they had overstayed their welcome.

"OK, I know it's your party, but let's hurry. I'm getting that itchy feelin."

"Here," she said all but ignoring his warning. "Help me set these up." She was spreading the papers out all over the desk. Shoving the rest of the stack into Henry's hands she began taking shots. "As soon as I snap a picture pick it up and lay out another one. And don't worry so much. I promise you we will be finished in ten minutes."

It took longer. The maps were too large to get in one shot and there were many more documents than she had realized.

Halfway through the second group of pictures Henry jerked up his head. "He's back," he said authoritatively and began collecting everything...

Anna hadn't heard a thing but took his word for it and shoved the mess together as quickly as possible.

"Here, here," she whispered and pushed the hastily closed blue envelope into the safe. "Wait a minute, the maps." But Henry had already closed the heavy door.

"Give me those," he said grabbing them from her hand he stuffed them in the bag. "Now let's hit it."

With Henry in the lead they swiftly crept past the entrance to the living room, down the hallway toward the side door. Through living room and dining room windows they could see that the General was not going to enter by way of the front door, but was instead coming up the path and around to the same side entrance they had used.

They quickly detoured to the bathroom realizing they would have to climb out through the broken window Henry had used to enter the house. Henry wasn't at all sure they could do that before the old man reached the door.

"Thank god for the cane," Henry whispered. "Gives us a couple more seconds."

But Anna wasn't listening.

"Merde!" He heard her say and was dumbfounded to see her rushing back to the library.

"What the hell are you doing?"

"My bag. I forgot the god damn bag."

In her haste Anna had taken off with the camera still clutched in her hand but had left the bag in plain sight on the seat of the wing chair.

"Forget it. Get back here," Henry whispered.

"No." Anna was determined. "You go. Get out of here."

Henry stopped and turned to follow her.

"No. I mean it. GET OUT." With that she snuck back into the library.

Henry was halfway out the window when the General turned the doorknob. A warning alarm blared, but was quickly silenced when the General punched in his security code. By the time the internal alarm was turned off Henry's feet had touched ground and he was sprinting across the yard. The General had not yet noticed a thing.

As soon as she reached the library Anna grabbed her bag and crouched behind a huge overstuffed leather couch. On second glance she could see that the room was a mess. They hadn't done much of a job putting things back in order. Maybe, with luck, he wouldn't come in here until she had a chance to sneak out. Now that the alarm was off, she might be able to get out through the front door.

Certain her heavy breathing could be heard throughout the quiet house, she tried to hold her breath as she sat without moving a muscle waiting......

By the time he returned from the bank, the General had all but forgotten the incident on Broad Street. He was feeling better. Confident that everything was under control and confident about the mission he was about to command, he wasn't about to let one minor mishap...hell nothing had even happened...spoil the excitement.

Late afternoon sun had begun to cast long shadows as he made his way through familiar old rooms to the library. He couldn't be certain how the ritual evolved; it had simply become his habit to stop there first. Mail was dropped on the desk, magazines read, bills paid, calls made...anything that he and his wife had, over the years, come to consider his responsibility was handled in this room. He sometimes joked that he should be stuffed like Trigger and left sitting in his wing chair to keep vigil over the place, when he was gone. It was a joke that didn't go over too well with his wife, though his son shared his humor at the notion.

Dusk had barely begun to wrap fingers around the day when the General entered his domain. His eyes weren't what they used to be and he reached across his desk to turn on a reading lamp. The dark green shade cast an eerie spectrum through the room. The General did not move.

Someone was there. Even before he noticed the disheveled state of his desk, or the papers that had fallen to the floor he sensed it. Slowly...very slowly he stood straight up, turned and carefully walked over to the glass covered bookcase spanning one wall. Not wanting to alarm the intruder, he opened the cabinet door as if to remove one of the many leather bound volumes within. Instead, he reached in and wrapped his right hand around a 9MM Browning hand gun secreted behind a first edition Mark Twain on the middle shelf. The cool steel against his palm gave him a feeling of security. As he turned, his finger released the safety and he was ready to face anything...anyone.

Anna remained squeezed behind the couch peeking at him as he took something from the cabinet. When she spotted the gun her heart went to her throat. Perspiration began beading on her forehead and running down her back.

Cautiously, the General walked behind his desk, sat himself in the heavy walnut chair and faced the room.

"Show yourself," he said with calm deliberation. "I know you are in here."

Anna didn't know what to do. Should she stay hidden and take the chance that he was guessing or should she show herself and hope for the best?

The General's next move, however, canceled all her options.

With a horrendous crashing noise the world around her exploded. No more than six inches in front of her face a huge hole appeared in the couch. Stuffing flew everywhere as a second hole splintered the baseboard near her right foot. The General had blasted a shot through his own furniture, barely missing Anna and ruining a good portion of molding and floorboard....Hands trembling, she cautiously stood up.

London   *Thursday July 12th 10:00 PM*

"God Damn that crazy old bastard. Just when I'm gonna give him some good news, he takes a walk," Finch, careful to never leave taped messages, slammed the phone onto the receiver just as the General's answering machine began its recorded greeting. He could never have guessed that, had he been careless enough to leave a message, it would have been overheard by a very eager French reporter.

"The hell with him." He was about to begin his final lethal game of cat and mouse. Nothing...no one was going to interrupt his fun until the game was won.

Picking up a Channing House brochure, he circled the best times to enter the home. He had done the tour once and didn't want to look suspicious but believed confronting the Lawrence woman on familiar ground would be the easiest way to gain her confidence.

He pulled out the "New York Times" credentials he had used the last time he "toured" Channing House. Remembering the gorgeous blond he had run into brought a smile to his face. "Such a shame," he muttered, "but I'm going to have to avoid that one. At least for now..." Finch's mind always examined possibilities.

His greatest concern was recognition. Would Genie Lawrence make the connection between American journalists, a friend of McBride's, no less...and the dark skinned Egyptian who had followed her around Cairo?

Reviewing his movements around the ancient city he doubted it. She had only seen him briefly and his disguise, if he did say so himself, had been very convincing.

So...when would be the most opportune time for this little reunion, he pondered as he read through the pamphlets he had picked up on his previous visit.

The weekend was out, too many people around...the place was closed Monday, that left Tuesday...Tuesday it would be. There were four days until then. Four days in which to plan...to get things ready for his lovely guest. Finch would let the General stew in his own juice till then. In fact, it would do the General good to be out of touch. Let him know who's really in charge.

But, in actuality, could he wait four days? Not if he just sat around doing nothing. He would keep himself occupied.

There had been other times like this, occasions when nervous energy seemed to take over, when his body screamed for activity. Finch had never even tried to understand the psychology behind his actions. He would never have the insight to grasp that his deeply rooted hostility toward all women, especially the "Lawrence bitch", morphed into rage and intense sexual desire. It had become a desire that almost overwhelmed him every time he thought of her.

Over the next few days he would watch her, follow her, and monitor all her moves. "Who knows," he muttered, "what opportunities may arise? I might not have to wait until Tuesday after all."

Alexandria, Va.

Dropping her bag, Anna raised her hands slowly and peered out from behind the ruined couch. It was evident to her that this man was crazy. But just how crazy? Would she soon know? Did she really want to find out?

The General was completely surprised when a petite, young woman with dark, frightened eyes appeared from behind the shattered divan.

"Who the hell are you?" were his first words. "I could have killed you!" He was immediately taken by the fragile beauty of the small dark haired woman. She was obviously no threat and he was almost as afraid of the possibility that he might have killed her as she was.

Anna tried to regain her composure. She wasn't certain how much to reveal. If she confronted him, would he kill her? If she left it alone, would she ever know the truth? Could she live with herself if she didn't at least try to stop this man?

"General Walker," she began hesitantly, "my name is Anna DuLac. I have some pictures that I would like to show you…"

Chapter 31

"......and I must tell you General that I have read the documents."

For an instant the old man's head turned ever so slightly toward the safe. Cautiously, Anna continued talking while one by one the ashen faced General slowly reviewed the incriminating 8 x 10 inch black and white glossies. "Your plan...it is incroyable. I must compliment you on the conception of such an elaborate operation," she said hoping some small flattery would soften his subdued rage and ultimately lead her to the information she desperately needed. For although she had indeed read the papers, she had only a vague idea where the Russian diplomats were being held. Nor was there yet absolute confirmation that Anton was actually among the captives. Her attempt failed. The flattery had no effect.

Color returned to his cheeks, cold steel grey eyes cut deeply, but she stood her ground, hoping he could not see how badly she was shaking, and braced for further attacks.

"And do you think you can stop me...with these," he shouted slamming the photographs down in a scattered heap on the desk. Pointing the pistol directly at her head he stepped out from behind the massive piece of furniture and stood facing her. I could kill you here where you stand and no one would ever know. Or I could arrange an accident, somewhere miles from here. No one would ever make the connection."

"You are mistaken...," she was barely able to get the words out. "I didn't break...come here by myself. I had help."

"Nice try," he said sarcastically, his bad leg forcing him to lean heavily, almost sitting, against his desk.

"I assure you, I am telling the truth. I am no thief. I could never have entered your home...opened your safe without assistance."

Unfortunately, the General believed her. She certainly didn't appear to be a common burglar. He looked carefully around the room and out into the hall for signs of her accomplice.

"He is gone," she said watching him. "He escaped through the bathroom window as you were coming in the side door. But he will know..." She was becoming a bit more confident. "He too read the documents," she lied. "And you see, if anything happens...if I disappear..."

A few moments of absolute silence passed between them until, quite suddenly, the implications of what had happened caused the General to be struck with a wave of nausea. He felt extremely ill. Could this young French woman actually cause his downfall? No, he wouldn't let that happen. Hands shaking, he kept the gun pointed in her direction, maneuvered to the safe and awkwardly managed to open the door, removing the blue envelope.

"Stay where you are," he cautioned in a voice that belied any sign of weakness. "Everything is here," he said after examining the contents. "Even if he does know about this, he has no proof. No one would believe such an outrageous tale."

Especially from a convicted felon Anna thought, thankful the General couldn't read her mind.

"General," she said softly. "The photographs...his word alone may not be conclusive, but there are other pictures, of those papers," she lied.

While examining his options, the General gathered the photos and placed them with the blue envelope, back into the safe.

Anna looked directly into the grey eyes and no longer saw them as threatening. They had, instead, the look of a man who was beginning to understand defeat. Without uttering a word she slowly shook her head from left to right.

He knew exactly what she was saying. With one small, ordinary gesture she was telling him his life was falling apart. All the plans he had made, the years of strategy, not to mention the money spent…it was all crumbling. How could this have happened? How could he have let it happen?

He lowered the gun and turned away. He knew he wouldn't kill her now. What would be the point? His life was over… he would soon be disgraced; his family humiliated…why take another life?

Anna knew she was watching the man self-destruct before her eyes; she wasn't certain how to react. She had what every journalist dreams of…THE STORY. The pictures coupled with the documents she had photographed would win her a Pulitzer, of that she was almost positive, but she still didn't have the answer she had come for. She still did not know where, or if, she would find Anton.

Desperation caused her to go a step further. "General, I have a question," she began.

But he didn't care. He only wanted to be left alone, about that he was vehement. "Get out!" he screamed and once again turned and pointed the gun in her direction. "Get out before I change my mind."

His glazed eyes were more menacing than the gun and Anna forced herself to carefully slip the strap of her bag over her shoulder. Keeping her eyes fixed upon the General, she cautiously backed out of the library.

Once in the hallway, out of his line of vision she leaned heavily against the wall and took a deep breath. She was frightened, but also furious with herself for getting so close yet just missing the information she really wanted. "How could I have been so stupid?" she chastised herself.

After taking a few more moments to collect herself she realized her dilemma. What should she do with the information she did possess? Write her story? Yes, of course she would do that. But should she also go to the American authorities...the CIA, the FBI, the military...who? There was a man in the other room whose life she was about to destroy, and she wasn't even certain how to go about it.

Anna had one hand on the brightly polished brass doorknob when the idea came to her...a flash, inspiration, she wasn't sure what to call it, but in an instant she knew what she was going to do.

She turned around and went back into the lion's den.

London

Alex approached his townhouse with curiosity rather than caution. Light shining through the curtained window alerted him to the fact that someone was there. He presumed it to be either his sister or perhaps even his mother...though he doubted his mother would drive into town at this late hour.

After very brief consideration, he dismissed, as unlikely, the possibility of harmful intent. Most criminals do not leave all the lights on he reasoned, though he did enter the front door a bit more gingerly than usual.

Perhaps what he found waiting should have frightened him, but instead he was simply annoyed?

"Constance!" he was at once surprised and displeased. "How did you...?"

"My key darling. Did you forget? You gave it to me years ago."

He had forgotten. During the midst of their affair he had, after many requests, given her a key simply to keep the peace. Like an idiot he had never bothered to retrieve it or change the lock. Or maybe it was deliberate, maybe some part of him always wanted to keep the door open. At any rate, it had never been a problem before. Now, he was paying the price. He had stirred things up again to the point where she obviously felt free to use the key.

"What are you doing here?" He hadn't meant the question to sound quite so accusatory, but he wasn't feeling very hospitable.

"Why darling is that any way to act? I just got back into town and I missed you. Come on now, didn't you miss me even a tiny bit?"

Alex didn't recognize this side of Constance. If this coy, little girl routine was for his benefit it wasn't working.

With arms outstretched, she approached him and gave him an all-encompassing hug and long lavish kiss.

Alex tried to disentangle himself from her with as much grace as he could muster, but finally had to simply push her away.

"We have discussed this to death Constance. Weren't you listening? It isn't going to work, not this time."

"But why not? We are perfect together. When we are 'together' that is." Summoning her most seductive smile, she looked deeply into his eyes. "You can't have forgotten already?"

That look of hers always made him a little weak. He took a deep breath and stepped back a pace. "You're right. I can't deny it. The sex between us is wonderful."

Seeing triumph momentarily shine in her eyes he hurried to continue. "But there has to be more...for both of us. And there isn't...at least not for me." He absolutely couldn't make it any clearer, but like most men up to their necks in guilt he tried. "Damn! Constance this has all been said again and again. You know very well that our lifestyles, well...they are like oil and water...they..."

Cut off mid whine, without getting a chance to say another word he slumped into his favorite old leather chair.

"What on earth do you mean our lifestyles don't go together? That really is one of the more stupid things I've ever heard you say." Her voice raised several octaves as her anger gained speed. Taking on the characteristics of a bull in heat she began pacing the room, talking to him, or rather at him, almost on the run. "I don't know exactly what has gotten into you Alex Templeton, but I've spent a good portion of my life loving you and as recently as last Saturday I believed that love was returned."

"Constance I........"

But she wasn't about to let him get a word in...At least not yet.

"Oh! I know we've had our share of falling out. No relationship is ever perfect, but we are older now and we share a history. And, Alex, the other day...it was very special to me. Wasn't it special for you?" She was going for it all, laying on as much guilt as she could squeeze out of their recent brief interlude. Constance knew she was on the brink of pushing things a bit too far, but what the hell. She didn't have anything to lose.

Alex sat stunned. He watched in awe as Constance rampaged around the room. He had witnessed her performances before, but had never been privy to one embellished with quite so much drama.

For one brief moment he felt the urge to tame that fiery temper. But that is how he had gotten into this mess in the first place so, with considerable restraint he simply sat and watched, praying she didn't realize the effect she could still have on his hormones.

Sometimes she made him feel like a schoolboy.

Then quite suddenly, almost mid-sentence, she stopped pacing, turned and stared down into his eyes. With a wry edge to her voice that Alex, for some reason found very disquieting, she put words to the opinion she had held for quite some time.

"It's not just us, is it Alex?" wanting him to believe this was a new revelation to her she spoke almost softly. "The reason you and I don't have a future is because you are in love with someone else."

"Constance, honestly there isn't anyone else," Alex protested though he suspected she was right.

"Don't lie to me and don't lie to yourself. You are…you're in love with…with," she stammered "…with whom Alex?" she placed great emphasis on the "whom" and gritted her teeth in an effort to control her anger.

"I really…" Alex was at a loss for words.

"It's her, isn't it?" she continued, dominating the conversation. "I told you before Alex, but you wouldn't admit it. Well, you can admit it now. You're in love with Genie Lawrence, aren't you?" Her tone clearly turned the question into an accusation.

"The truth is Constance that I don't know," he said with veracity. He was finally beginning to admit the possibility to himself, but he was certainly not ready to admit it to Constance. "All I do know is that I don't want to hurt you. We've been friends for a long time…"

"Just friends? You mean like companions, chums…pals perhaps?" she shot at him sarcastically. "You are kidding yourself."

Is she correct, he wondered momentarily, am I kidding myself? But after only a second's hesitation, what he said was "You are right. We have, at times," he emphasized the "at times", "been much closer than that, but honestly Constance that was a lifetime ago. It's over."

Constance glared at him with one arched eyebrow adding emphasis to her flashing eyes. Without saying a word she slowly walked to the hall closet and retrieved her black Halston slicker. "I know you think it's over Alex……it isn't. Not really."

He could tell she was trying very hard to maintain her composure but straining muscles caused a slight trembling around her jaw line and her voice had taken on a deep throaty rasp that he knew from experience only occurred when she was extremely angry.

"You might not believe it now, but you and I are in the hands of destiny. You will see. One of these days Alex, we will be together."

With those words said, Constance opened the door and left.

Alex was dumbfounded; not exactly sure what had just taken place. He certainly hadn't wanted to hurt her. He knew she would be angry. She was, after all, used to getting her own way. Did she really love him as much as she professed? He couldn't honestly believe it, and he dismissed her remark about destiny as...well... Constance.

Outside, a light drizzle had begun again but she hardly noticed. Furious, she was unaware of the moisture collecting in her hair until finally a small rivulet ran down the side of her face, over one flushed cheek and landed on her collar bone. It caused a shiver and she instinctively pulled the shiny black collar up around her neck. Head down against the increasing rain she walked to the corner and hailed a cab.

"We will just see about Genevieve Lawrence," she mumbled while adjusting the wet slicker in the back seat of the shiny black cab.

"Miss?" Questioned the driver.

"Oh nothing, nothing," she snapped, embarrassed at having been caught talking to herself. "Mayfair, please driver."

Alexandria

Not more than one step into the General's library Anna screamed in shock, "Mon Dieu! General Walker, no! Stop!"

In his favorite, leather, wing chair the General sat, eyes closed, with the muzzle of his 9MM service revolver pointed fatally against his right temple. He hesitated at the sound of her voice, but did not lower the gun.

"I told you to get out of here," he said in an unusually calm, almost reassuring voice. "You don't want to see this."

"General, you mustn't," she pleaded.

"But you see I must...I really must. I could not stand the...... humiliation. And my family, I can't face what I have done to my family. So go...or stay if you wish. In a moment I won't care one way or another." He sat a little straighter in the chair, in preparation for the final act.

"Wait," Anna begged. "It doesn't have to be this way. I believe I have a solution...for us both."

He opened his eyes and looked at her with curiosity. The gun moved a fraction away from its target.

"Please listen to me for just a moment...," she implored and began speaking as rapidly as she was able to in English. "I told you I read the documents...please give me a moment to tell you why." She could see his hesitation and took it as a sign to proceed. "I know that you...with the assistance of a few selected 'friends' were responsible for kidnapping several Soviet diplomats. What I must know is this. Was Anton Kasarov among that group?"

"Kasarov...Kasarov? Ah yes the young man from the embassy in Cairo." The General had become interested enough to place the loaded pistol down on an end table, though it was still within easy access. "Yes, he is part of our select group. Why? Do you know him?"

"Oui,," said Anna brimming with new found hope. "I certainly do. We were...ah...very close. I have been searching for him for months."

Though interested in the turn of events the General was still skeptical. He found it very unlikely that this headstrong woman could do anything to ameliorate the crisis.

"General, do you know exactly where the men are now?"

"Of course I do. This is still my operation." He was actually offended at her question.

"Then why not rescue them?" The derisive look he shot at her was unmistakable. "I know...I know," she went on, ignoring his contempt. "...the plan was to use them as pawns. You envisioned trading them to the Soviets. Or should I say a private group of Soviet patriots.... In any case from what I read there was to be an exchange. For the return of their countrymen the Soviets promised to provide men to play act the role of Middle Eastern mercenaries. Men who would go into Beirut...how do you say it...go in shooting...and bring out the remaining American hostages.

"Your Soviet friends, they would be heroes in their country for rescuing their diplomats and you...well...there is no telling the rewards you would reap for the return of the long-held American hostages.... Isn't that the gist of the plan...have I gotten it straight?"

"Yes, that is pretty much the idea" was all he could say.

"It is not going to happen. You realize that, don't you? Too many people have been killed already...for this grand scheme of yours." Looking at this man and thinking of Roger and Richard and even the American Ambassador, she became enraged. "Do you even realize how many innocent lives are gone?" She shouted close to tears, almost losing what little control she had managed to acquire.

"Finch." She heard him mumble, but his head was down and the words were unclear.

"What?"

"Nothing," he was rationalizing, "nothing for you to be concerned with." The General had known all along that the nasty little man had gone too far. Yet, he was the commander and he hadn't done a thing to stop him. Whatever had happened… everything that had happened…was his fault, was his responsibility.

"General! It has to stop here, but perhaps…if you are willing… …perhaps some good can come of it."

She had finally managed to arouse his curiosity.

"What exactly do you propose?"

"As I said a moment ago, rescue them. You simply cannot have the Americans. You realize that, don't you?"

He nodded.

"So 'rescue' the Russians."

He looked at her with a glimmer of understanding.

"It should be easy. You know where they are. Your men are holding them, so there will be no resistance…well perhaps some feigned resistance…you understand. If you can make it appear to be a small American military operation, under your command, of course, so much the better. Just think of it…You will be a hero. People will think of you as the American General who cleverly located several missing Soviet Diplomats. And who, in a gesture of good will and international cooperation, rescued these men and returned them safely to their homeland."

He couldn't help but smile slightly. It was a very clever plan, but for one flaw. A bright French reporter would always know the truth. Could he trust her enough to put his life in her hands? Did he have any other choice?

And of course, he could not forget about Finch or his mercenary the elusive Eagle. Considering the options, he was confident that he could deal with them. He would buy them off. After all, they were only in it for the money. As long as they got that, they would be happy. "Yes!" he said aloud and for his own benefit. As crazy as it sounded, the idea had merits. And to save his career; to save face in front of his family...to be a hero in their eyes...in the eyes of his country...he would pay any price.

"And what about you Mademoiselle? Why would you do this? Why would you get involved? And how do I know that you can be trusted? If we form this alliance...how do I know you will keep your end of the bargain?"

"It is quite simple General. The man I mentioned...Anton Kasarov...I want him back. I want him returned safely...I want him alive, and if you are dead," she added, "...well, who knows what will happen. If these operatives you have hired hear that you have committed suicide they will not simply release their captives and walk away. Without you, neither Anton, nor any of the others for that matter, would stand a chance of coming home. If it takes turning you into a hero to bring him back," she added reluctantly, "then that is what I am willing do."

Not sure he was convinced; Anna walked slowly across the room and stood directly in front of him. Perhaps, he could not be moved by her love for Anton, but she knew he would understand ambition.

"And of course General, there is the story. I plan to be there to cover the daring rescue, to get the exclusive on how you found the Soviets and snatched them out from under the noses of their terrorist captors. The story I write General will, to put it in blunt American terms, save your ass. It will make you a genuine hero, not to mention what it will do for my own career." Having made her proposal, Anna waited impatiently for his response.

For several long moments, General Armstrong Walker sat staring out of his library windows. Finally in a hushed, almost inaudible voice he answered. "It might work," was all he said.

Chapter 32

Rhododendrons had long since passed their peak, as had the lilies and lilac, but the lawns were neatly tended and the smell of roses hung heavily in the air. Genie should have found the family gardens behind Channing House beautiful, peaceful and relaxing, but even within the serenity of this very private spot, she was unable to relieve the stress that had plagued her for the past several days.

After not hearing from Anna for some time, she had resorted to calling Phillipe for information. The call had only increased her concern. He hadn't heard anything either and was further upset by the fact that, without telling him, Anna had checked out of her hotel room in Washington. So far, he had been unable to locate her.

Genie was also troubled by the distance that seemed to be growing between her and Alex. The realization that she was actually hurt by the situation annoyed her almost as much Alex's aloof attitude. He definitely seemed to have something on his mind. As much as she hated to admit it, she cared…more than she knew she should.

In addition to all her other concerns, Genie still had the odd sensation that someone was watching her. Though, since she hadn't left the estate for a number of days, she realized the unwarranted apprehension was ridiculous. She was too embarrassed to tell anyone of her suspicions. "No use having them think I'm a basket case," she mumbled as she paced barefoot on the soft carpet of grass surrounding an intricate two foot high miniature maze.

All in all, it had been a disquieting few days, so when Ruth suggested she might enjoy helping with their "tourist business" she jumped at the opportunity. It would take her mind off things for a while, and make her feel like she was at least contributing something. After all they had invited her in and made her feel totally welcome. Beyond that she had grown to love the history of this grand old home and looked forward to sharing the experience with Ruth's "guests".

At the sound of Mrs. Gates, one of the Channing House docents, calling her name, Genie hurriedly slipped back into her sandals and rushed around to the front entrance in time to greet the two o'clock crowd.

On a grassy slope well above Channing House, Finch lay flattened against the ground, binoculars in hand. He had an unobstructed view of the back of the east wing of the home. He had been there since early morning waiting, hoping to catch a glimpse of his prey. When she appeared in the garden his heart began to race, his breathing quickened.

Strawberry gold hair sparkled in early afternoon light. And when she slipped out of her shoes and stepped lithely around the miniature maze he experienced a tightening of his jaw muscles and an ache between his legs that he found hard to control.

The more she moved in and about the maze, the more enraptured he became. It seemed she was almost dancing...a dance that was meant for his eyes only.

Maneuvering to a comfortable position he continued to watch her and was rewarded when she lifted her full flowered skirt hip high revealing firm, smooth, shapely thighs. It took only the sight of her bare limbs for desire to consume him and white hot anger to overwhelm rational thought.

Perspiring heavily he lay back on the cool green grass for a few moments to collect himself. Only then did he turn over and once again pick up the binoculars. She was still there in the garden, but to his dismay she had ended the dance and was slipping back into her shoes. He watched as she hurried around the side of the home toward the front entrance.

Grabbing the binoculars and a canteen of water that was, by now almost empty, Finch hunched himself over and half walked, half ran, to a position in a lightly wooded area on a hill overlooking the front of the estate from which he could get a clear view of the entrance to Channing House.

Out of breath, he hid behind a two hundred year old oak tree and with trembling hand adjusted the right eyepiece. What he saw when he finally focused in on his victim amused him to the point of laughter. "Oh this is going to be too easy," he chuckled when he realized that Genie was busily helping a mixed group of tourists through the first part of their guided visit. She was obviously explaining certain "points of interest" such as the hand carved eleventh century Italian door and the symbolism of the Griffin gargoyles above their heads…he had heard it all before.

Within minutes she disappeared through the door, the entire mob at her heels.

Finch had seen all he needed to see for that day. It was time to leave. He gathered up his things, rid the area of obvious footprints and walked through denser wood to a little used dirt road he had discovered at the far end of the property. He carried his belongings to the secluded location where he had parked his rented Rover.

Without question he would be back. Though he had all the information he needed he would return both Sunday and Monday …just to watch.

Chapter 33

"Listen…listen to me," the General had to shout as loudly as he could to make himself heard over the roar of the whirring helicopter rotor. "When we get there you keep under cover. Do you understand?"

Anna nodded in acknowledgement.

"These men………I said these men," he was yelling even more loudly, "…they don't know we are coming…and they certainly don't know we are 'friendly' so just stay out of the way and keep your head down."

Anna nodded again and looked out through the open hatch at the endless sand passing beneath the old Huey. They had been over the plan time and time again, but no one could have predicted their biggest problem. The General had been unable to get in touch with his operative, whom Anna now knew was named Finch, and had no way of letting the Eagle know that he was coming in to 'rescue' the Soviets. If, upon landing, the Eagle didn't immediately recognize the General they could have a bloody battle on their hands. As they neared the oasis of Jal Abba Anna said a silent prayer.

The sixty-two year old General appeared calm, in control. No one would suspect the sweat pouring down his back was anything more than a reaction to the unrelenting heat. Only he knew differently. It had been twenty five years since he last faced a combat situation…

The wound he suffered as a youngster in World War II had, in the long run, been nothing. It had not even kept him out of active duty in Korea. But years later, in Vietnam as an advisor, he had been inadvertently caught, during one of his many clandestine operations, in a heated battle just north of an area called Nha Trang. That battle had been so vicious, so confused, so unlike anything he experienced in any previous conflict, that for the only time in his military career he honestly believed he was going to die. That battle, not WWII, was the cause of the limp he suffered from today.

At this moment, all those long buried emotions came flooding back. Nervous anticipation, a combination of both thrill and fear, almost overwhelmed him, for his life, his very existence depended upon success. His own personal internal conflict went on in spite of, or perhaps because of, the devil's pact he believed was his only alternative.

Only he and one other knew the ultimate outcome of a failed mission. The General had made certain private 'arrangements'. If things did not go favorably, if it became apparent that his actions would ultimately end in disgrace then, one way or another, he would not return alive. He must emerge from this mission a hero… dead or alive he would have it no other way.

As they flew low over endless dunes the General reflected upon the decisions he had made over the past couple of days.

Forced to conclude that Anna DuLac's plan might actually work it hadn't taken him long to put it into action. To rally together the three helicopters and twenty four men needed for the operation, he had only to make one call. After speaking briefly to his old friend Barker Robinson it was settled.

Robinson had done this kind of thing before…often. He had long been in the business of supplying personnel for certain clandestine activities. The men he provided, all highly trained, were paid well to ask no questions. They followed orders. All they knew or wanted to know was the objective. Motives didn't interest them. They were told they were going into the dessert to 'liberate' some Russians. For some reason, the old man in charge thought he could get the kidnappers to surrender, but if not, if that didn't happen, they were to take the bastards out… do whatever they had to do to save the Ruskies.

The convoy had been in the air for over an hour. Now looking from side to side the General gave the thumbs up sign to the pilots of the other helicopters indicating that they were approaching the target.

London

By the time the last of Ruth's "guests" had finally departed Genie was close to exhaustion and it showed. Dark circles under her eyes betrayed her weariness to the rest of the family and Ruth was particularly concerned that she was overworking her.

"Come sit by me," said Ruth as they approached the patio. "We'll have a nice glass of cold lemonade. That ought to perk you up a bit."

"Thank you this is just what I needed," Genie responded taking a tall cool glass from the serving tray. "I can't imagine why I am so tired, but it certainly feels wonderful to sit down."

"Are you feeling ill, my dear," Ruth said genuinely concerned. "Perhaps Alex ought to have a look at you."

"No, I don't think that will be necessary. Honestly, I am absolutely fine. The only trouble with me is that I haven't gotten much sleep lately."

"Goodness. If you are uncomfortable, perhaps we can put you in another room."

"Oh, no Ruth. The guest room is lovely. Really it's perfect. To tell you the truth I have been a little worried about a friend. You remember me mentioning Anna DuLac, the French reporter who was a friend of Roger Sims?"

Alex and Genie had briefly mentioned Anna to Ruth, but only in the context of her friendship with Roger and Molly. Ruth had no idea Genie had been to Cairo or that Anna was now in the US. So far they had managed to shield the family from all the craziness going on around them. She believed it important to continue to do so.

"Well," she continued, "Anna has been on a trip, an assignment really, for her paper." She hated these deceptions, but was too deeply in to it now to back out. "in the states and I thought I would have heard from her by now. Since I haven't...I am just a little anxious that's all. Too much of the mother hen instinct is certain to cause a little insomnia," she said standing and walking to the edge of the patio. "A direct result of twelve years as a teacher. I am sure that I'll hear from her soon and until then I am just going to have to stop being such a worry wart."

In her heart Genie knew that she wouldn't stop worrying until Anna contacted her, she just couldn't let it show. She wouldn't let her concerns affect anyone else.

With complete surprise Alex's hand suddenly rested on Genie's left shoulder. She nearly jumped out of her skin. Lemonade went flying, soaking her white slacks from knee to ankle.

"Jeez! Alex you nearly scared me to death," Genie said breathlessly, then, looking at the spill, took the napkins he quickly offered and began mopping up. "Brother what a mess."

"I am sorry Gen. It looks like I have really done it this time." He helped her dry off.

"Don't worry about it," she said, "I am surprised to see you here. Ruth said you were staying in town."

"Yes dear," Ruth added as she refilled Genie's glass and assisted in cleaning the spill. "I thought you were working. Didn't you have patients to see this weekend?"

"Thought so," he said while giving his mother a kiss on the cheek, "but as luck would have it Steve offered to take my rounds today in exchange for one day next month. He has a wedding to attend then, so here I am... Disappointed?... Did you two have something up your sleeves?"

"I only wish," Ruth teased and went in to tell Cook there would be one more for dinner.

Alone on the patio, the uncomfortable silence that had recently grown between them was painfully evident. Each had their own idea as to when it began and what had caused it.

Alex was absolutely positive it had everything to do with Constance. Genie, on the other hand, was certain the tension was a direct result of her clandestine trip to Cairo.

They were both right and they were wrong. Ill at ease for both these reason, they refused to acknowledge there was more...but of course there was. Much more. They were simply unwilling yet to admit it to each other or to themselves. And being unable to admit it, they did the next best thing...they ignored it.

Alex broke the ice. "I apologize for making you jump like that. I must say it's a good thing I don't have that effect on my patients."

"You don't have to worry about that Doctor," she smiled. "I'll bet most of your patients find you irresistible." She was trying a little humor, but it was a strain.

"Well then what is it? You are as nervous as a cat."

"Nothing really," Genie said more seriously now. "But have you ever had that feeling...you know...when you are sure someone is watching you?"

"Not exactly," he confessed. "Is that it...you think someone has been watching you. You think Whiting again...?"

"No, no. I know it sounds crazy...Oh don't give it another thought," she tried to dismiss it. "It's just my overactive imagination. I'm sure that as soon as we hear from Anna all my worrying will be a thing of the past. Anyway I am glad you're here."

He wanted to reassure her that there was nothing to be concerned about, but he wasn't so sure. It had been quite a while since any one had heard from Anna and he was becoming a little anxious himself. As a purely instinctive gesture of comfort, he put an arm around her shoulder and drew her near.

She relaxed against him and he could smell the soft sweet fragrance of her perfume.

"I know it's difficult," he said softly, "but I wouldn't worry... not yet. Maybe you should go into town and visit Molly tomorrow. A change of scenery might be just what you need."

Genie felt herself responding to his touch, and couldn't deny she felt guilty at her reaction. Am I being disloyal to Richard, she wondered, finding comfort with this man...is it wrong...is it too soon. But before she had time to ponder it further, before there was an opportunity for their closeness to evolve into more than kindness, the mood was interrupted.

"Hey there you two," said Jackie enthusiastically and then teasingly. "Uh Oh! Am I interrupting something...personal?"

"No! no!" they responded in unison.

"Gen is a little worried about a friend, that's all."

"Yes, Mother mentioned it. Perhaps, if you don't hear something soon you could contact that Inspector fellow. You know the one helping you with Richard's case…what's his name, ah… Whiting. Yes, Whiting he might be able to help you."

Neither Genie nor Alex could tell Jackie that contacting the Inspector was the last thing they could do. They certainly couldn't confide their suspicions about how deeply Whiting actually was involved in Richard's death. The only thing Alex could say was, "That's a good idea. Maybe we will get in touch with him later."

With the issue seemingly resolved, Jackie informed them that supper was about to be served.

High on a hill above the manor Finch watched. His view of the patio was not as clear as yesterday's garden vista had been. The gardens were open and he had found a perfect vantage point from which to carry out his obsessive observations, but the patio was somewhat obstructed by trees and small shrubs. Never the less, with binoculars in hand, he fixated as best he could on the object of his obsession.

Through the glass Genie Lawrence appeared almost close enough to touch. He imagined soft skin and silken strands of hair gliding slowly beneath his hands. He knew at that moment that he must possess her and that unfortunately, like most women she needed to be punished. She had hurt him, always escaping, always just beyond his grasp. And she had kept things from him…caused all kinds of interruptions in his well thought out plans. If left alone, she might even lead to the one thing he would never accept… failure, that could never be allowed to happen. The photographs, he mused, he had to get those fucking photographs. It would all be so easy this time. His plan was fool proof and by Wednesday he would have her. Like all the women he had ever needed or desired, Genie Lawrence would, in the long run give him whatever he wanted. "It is all so simple," he said aloud. "You're mine."

As he watched from his distant perch, Genie was joined by a man. "You again," Finch mumbled angrily at the sight of Alex. "Well don't get your hopes up Doc. Genie Lawrence belongs to me."

Breathing heavily Finch rolled over onto his back in the soft grass and let the warm summer sun soak in. The patio was empty now but he lingered, dreaming of having her in his arms, planning the details of their rendezvous.

Chapter 34

Hot, dirty, hungry and incredibly thirsty, Anton sat with his back against the rough wall wondering when the next drink of water would come, wondering if it would come at all.

Since the departure of their leader days ago, the men left in charge of the hostages had not been particularly concerned for their well-being. Meals were served erratically and could no longer be counted upon as a means to calculate the passage of time. Water and basic toiletry requirements were also handled sporadically. And the increased grumbling he overheard among the men caused him to worry that even these most basic needs might be terminated.

It was actually with some relief that Anton recognized the sounds of engines in the distance. Perhaps with the return of the rebel leader, Anton and his comrades would not die of thirst after all.

Though disoriented by the everpresent darkness of his blindfold Anton was not immune to a sudden sensation of more imminent danger. The roar of the engines that only moments ago sounded like distant thunder was now almost on top of him. Guards, who were expected to keep constant vigil, could be heard running helter-skelter through the compound.

Without warning an explosion of gunfire erupted around him. Using his knees, he struggled to push the blindfold off his face. Finally, able to open his eyes he saw men, bullets and dust flying everywhere. Rolling into the nearest corner for cover, he tucked himself into a tight ball in an effort to avoid being blown to bits.

Two other captives who shared the space with him had done the same thing. All they could do for protection was try their best to cover their heads.

In the ensuing melee, the terrorists seemed to have completely forgotten Anton and the others. Those who weren't returning rapid fire were busy looking for an escape route. But to their dismay, they were surrounded and forced to confront their unknown enemy as best they could.

The blasting gunfire and deafening concussion of small explosives continued nonstop for only ten minutes, but it seemed to Anton to go on for hours. Two mercenaries lay dead in the center of the room and he still didn't have a clue who was doing the fighting. For all he knew there could be a rival group of thugs out there just waiting to take over the imprisonment of him and his comrades.

And there was nothing he could do to help; no way could he take advantage of the confusion and escape. He was still very much a prisoner of his shackles. The battle raged around him and he cursed his impotence until he noticed that, attached to the belt of one of the dead guards were the keys to his chains.

Laying on his stomach flat against the blood soaked dirt floor the exhausted, disheveled Russian ignored the bullets that shattered down around him and rolled across the room until he lay parallel to the ravaged body. With considerable effort he managed to unhook the keys and free himself.

Keeping his head low, he crawled across the room and freed two other prisoners. On hands and knees, without looking back, the three men scurried out of the shack through a gaping hole that had recently appeared in one wall. In the midst of the confusion no one saw them make a dash between the rusted hulks of two dilapidated Jeeps and take cover behind the oasis' ancient stone well.

Secluded behind the relative safety of the well Anton and the other Soviets took the time to evaluate their situation. From where they were hiding they were unable to tell who had attacked and could only hope they would be able to devise a plan to rescue the other two hostages they had been forced to leave behind.

Gunfire grew louder as the battle drew near. Then suddenly... as quickly as it had begun the fighting diminished. A few sporadic shots were heard...then silence. Anton cautiously poked his head over the edge of the stone cistern, but through dust and smoke that hung in the air, could see almost nothing.

As it cleared he began to comprehend what had happened and was completely astonished. On the ground the bodies of the terrorists were scattered about like rag dolls. Not one had lived through the ordeal. What amazed him even more, however, was the fact that the perpetrators of the surprise attack were all Americans.

Americans, he thought shaking his head. It took him a few moments to decide whether or not to make his presence known.

As it happened the General wasn't given the opportunity to allow the Eagle's terrorist impostors to 'surrender'. Without their leader present, they did not realize that there was no real threat. As soon as the first of three helicopters approached Jal Abba gunfire broke out and the confrontation had begun.

Seeing the lead helicopter in the midst of a fight the General ordered his pilot to back off and land on the far side of the Eagle's stronghold.

He could hear the helicopter return fire before it too backed off. All three Hueys pulled away until they were able to put down safely. The men they carried disembarked with enough weaponry to sustain any type of engagement. They surrounded the building on three sides, but the Eagle's men were fierce fighters and though heavily outnumbered managed to inflict several casualties among Baxter Robinson's mercenaries, before they themselves were all finally killed.

When it was over Robinson reported to the General that four of his men were dead and two seriously wounded, but the job had been done. Two of the hostage Soviet diplomats had been found huddled together in a small windowless room at the back of the building and his men were searching for the others as they spoke.

Off in the distance on a dune high above the town of Jal Abba, the Eagle watched emotionlessly while his men were blown apart. In his jeep, he had been on his way back to the maggot-ridden little oasis when three helicopters had flown low over his head. Guessing what was about to happen he instinctively pulled to a stop.

When it was over he, cursed Finch and swore revenge for the money he was out, the time he had wasted. In reality they were empty threats. In his business one had to be a pragmatist... Things don't always go as planned, it happened. It had happened before and it would probably happen again. Casually, callously turning his jeep around the Eagle drove back across the desert.

Anna slowly raised her head. When the fighting began she had taken cover as best she could in the back of the helicopter. It wasn't supposed to be this way. The General had been sure he could talk to the Eagle, explain that they were on the same side, that he would still get paid. She didn't know what had gone wrong, but as soon as they neared the town bullets began flying.

With her heart in her throat she managed to get her camera focused for a few shots of the fighting before she came to the sickening realization that Robinson's men were indiscriminately killing everyone. The story she and the General had planned for coverage of the phony rescue included random action pictures which she would use to accompany her article. They had even anticipated having to stage certain shots, and suspected there might be a minor skirmish but this senseless violence was insane. It had gone far beyond the simple mission she had expected.

It was deadly quiet when she finally judged it safe enough to leave the aircraft. What she saw when she emerged took her breath away. There were bodies everywhere. Robinson's men were casually walking about kicking the corpses and looting them of their possessions.

Several yards away in the shadow of a demolished building the General stood talking to Robinson and two men she recognized as Russians. Her heart raced. Anton, she thought, he has to be here. Trying her best to put the carnage out of her mind she hurried to join them.

They were tired, dirty and very thin, but appeared to be relatively intact. Speaking rapidly in both Russian and English the two freed men were overwhelming the General and Robinson with words and gestures of gratitude. An hour ago they had been praying for death and now they were free. Quite unexpectedly, they would soon be reunited with their families and friends.

When Anna finally reached them the first words out of her mouth were of Anton, but all the men could do was shake their heads.

They hadn't seen any of the other hostages in days.

"But how can that be," shouted Anna, in frustration. "They have to be here."

"They were," said one of the Soviets softly. "We could hear the other men in an adjacent room, but we weren't allowed to communicate. Since that fellow they called Eagle took off a few days ago... "

"What!" the General broke in. "What do you mean...he's gone?"

Until this point the General had assumed they would find the Eagle's body among those Robinson's men were gathering together in a makeshift morgue.

"Yes," the Russian continued. "He left a few days ago...it is hard to tell exactly how long he's been gone. I am not even certain what month it is."

Anna and the General looked at each other both, wondering if Eagle's escape would prove a fatal blow to their effort.

Anna couldn't believe it. She had come this far it wasn't possible she would lose Anton now, but he wasn't here and her only consolation appeared to be that his body wasn't among the dead.

Leaving the small group that had gathered around the General and Robinson she found her way into the dusty shell of a building that, until only a short time ago, had housed the Russian hostages.

Inside the building shadows played tricks causing her to turn quickly to her right thinking she spotted movement. It was nothing, some loose boards slipping to the floor causing dust motes to hang in the sun beamed air. Walking from room to tiny room she shuddered to think of Anton spending months in this hovel.

Still sequestered behind the old well, it didn't take Anton and the two other Soviets long to make their decision. If they were to have any hope at all of getting out of this place, they would have to turn themselves over to the Americans. To stay hidden in this God forsaken oasis of Jal Abba would certainly mean death.

Anton took off his shirt, which had at one time been white, and raised it above his head in the universal sign of surrender. Crossing fingers that the Americans wouldn't think them Hezbollah terrorists and shoot them on the spot, the three ragged survivors stepped from behind the relative safety of the well, and proceeded toward the group.

The General was the first to spot the men coming his way. They were a rag-tag lot carrying a white 'flag'. He knew immediately who they were and cautioned Robinson to control his men. The last thing he needed was the inadvertent slaughter of Soviet Diplomats.

"Anna," he called. No response. "Mademoiselle DuLac... I think you had better get out here."

Shielding her eyes against the brilliant sunlight Anna appeared in the doorway. She couldn't imagine what he wanted but for the first time since she had known him, the General had a smile on his face. He nodded his head in the direction of the center of town and her eyes followed his lead.

She knew him immediately. Silhouetted against the pale earth and sky she recognized his shoulders first and his gait. There had always been something distinguishing about his walk and as he came across the courtyard it was unmistakable. He was painfully thin and as he got closer she could see his beautiful blond hair matted with sweat and grime. But even the scruffy full beard could not disguise that wonderful face. Her heart at once skipped a beat and then began pounding at a furious rate.

She wanted to run to him but restrained herself, thinking it better to approach cautiously. After all she couldn't know what shape he was in and the sight of a wild woman running in his direction might be more trauma than relief. As difficult as it was she started slowly toward the three men.

As they neared the American soldiers Anton realized he was

probably in worse physical condition than he had imagined for his mind began playing the worst kind of tricks.

One of the men, dressed in desert fatigues, had begun walking toward them. But in his weakened state he imagined he recognized the approaching figure. In his mind he was thinking 'Anna', but of course that was impossible. He rubbed his eyes furiously with one grimy hand. But the image did not change and in his confusion he came to a dead stop. Anton couldn't move until he came to grips with reality and saw the young soldier for who he was.

Anna stopped for a moment also. She wasn't certain why Anton was no longer coming toward her, so she too came to a halt. It was obvious that he didn't recognize her, that he was confused, and it was no wonder. Here she stood in the middle of the sand, covered with dust and wearing army camouflage clothing.

The "young soldier" was about fifty yards away, Anton guessed, he too was just standing…waiting. And then the soldier did something completely unexpected…he took off his hat.

To Anton's complete shock…surprise…amazement out from under the fatigue cap was a mass of curly dark hair. Without the brim to cover her face he could see that he hadn't been crazy at all. Staring back at him from across the desert courtyard was the most beautiful sight in the world. He had absolutely no idea how or why she was here but that hardly mattered now. The woman he had spent countless hours dreaming of was walking, quickly toward him. Even in his weakened state, he found strength enough rush to her arms.

When Anna removed her cap, she saw immediately that Anton knew her. That spark of recognition was all she needed to get her moving. Even the heavy protective desert boots she wore couldn't slow her down as she hurried to embrace the one man in the world with whom she could share her love.

When they came together under the searing desert sun there were no words. For several long moments they just held each other. When Anton's, still strong, arms encircled her, almost smothering her, Anna felt...for the first time since that horrible morning she woke to find him missing...completely at peace. She held him, still not quite believing he was real, until he pulled back slightly and with tender blue eyes looked directly into her soul.

"I love you" was all he could say before tears flooded his eyes and choked his voice.

It was all Anna needed to hear. It was all she could reply. "I love you too," she whispered and she too was overcome with tears of relief and overwhelming joy.

Chapter 35

It was unusual for Alex to remain at Channing House on Sunday evenings, but as Genie planned to visit Molly Monday morning he offered to stay and drive her into town. And he hoped the extra time together might give them an opportunity to talk. It seemed that recently they hadn't had any time alone.

In the brightly sunlit bedroom Genie ran a brush through her hair and, upon surveying her reflection in the antique glass, applied a bit of lipstick before going downstairs. She was getting used to formal breakfasts served promptly at eight and wondered if she would fall back into the old doughnut grabbing, coffee gulping routine, when she returned to New York. New York! She had to think about it. As much as she wanted to, she realized she simply couldn't hide away here forever. The time was coming when she would be forced to reenter the real world. And now that they were at a roadblock in the investigation of Richard's death there wasn't any excuse to stay in England. Face it lady, she thought staring at the face in the mirror, as soon as you hear from Anna you really must get back home......the idea actually made her nervous.

On lovely summer mornings, Ruth preferred to have breakfast served outside. A warm gentle breeze slightly ruffled the pink cloth on which sat sweet rolls, crumpets, marmalade and a generous selection of fruit.

Though in a hurry to get to Mayfair, having been elected to

open the gallery, Jackie took the time to pour tea. "I understand you are going to see Molly today," she said to Genie. "How is she doing these days?" She only knew Molly as a neighbor of Alex's, but was concerned.

"Much better," Genie replied. "I believe she is considering finding a job. The last time I spoke with her she said that she knew it was time to get on with her life."

"And you, Genie, how do you feel ah! About getting on with your life?"

"Jackie!" Alex exclaimed, aghast by his sister's blunt question. "I am surprised at you."

"I am sorry. That didn't come out quite as it should have. I didn't mean to be rude. I just meant......"

Genie interrupted. "That's perfectly alright. I know what you meant. Actually I have been thinking about it myself. I know I'll have to return to New York sometime soon. I have a lot to take care of before the new school year begins."

Alex was disappointed to hear that she had already begun to think about the States. For some reason he hadn't thought of her as actually 'leaving'.

"Gen," he was about to ask her to be more specific about what she considered 'soon' when Hollings interrupted.

"There is a telephone call for Ms. Lawrence, ma'am," he announced to Ruth. "Long distance."

Genie and Alex looked at each other, both hoping it was a call from Anna.

In his hotel room Finch lay back down on the bed to ponder the situation. Unable, for days now, to contact the General, he had used not only their private secured line, but had taken the chance to make a direct call to his home.

Having spoken to the General's wife he could not tell if she was being purposefully vague or genuinely sincere when she said that he was out of the country for a few days.

It bothered him. Why would he leave the country? It disturbed Finch to be out of touch, unless, of course, it suited his own purposes. Until yesterday it had. Now an uneasy knot settled in the pit of his stomach. Something was going on. His instincts rarely failed him. He had better get in touch with the crazy old coot soon.

Until he spoke to the old man he would proceed with his plan. Soon he would have both the photographs and the woman, though the General didn't need to know his plans for her.

Once he turned the evidence over to the General he would collect his money and be out of it. The General could deal with the Eagle directly. He was on his own; free to put his planned 'trade' into action without fear of any surprise witnesses or incriminating evidence surfacing to spoil the fun.

Finch was tiring of the game and glad it would soon be over. Hell if it weren't for the woman it wouldn't be any fun at all.

Though Finch usually relieved stress through work, fantasizing about Genie Lawrence definitely helped relieve his mounting frustration. He experienced intense gratification from his 'occupation'. And though most of what he did remained a secret, to all but the few people who hired him, a plan well-conceived and well executed could satisfy him for weeks. A shrink he had been forced to meet with during one of his many terms in prison told him he was a master of sublimation. Not sure exactly what she meant, he took it as a compliment.

It had been at least half an hour since Genie followed Hollings to the phone. When she returned, ashen faced and a little dazed, to the patio Jackie had, fortunately, left for work and Ruth was busy tending the operation of Channing House.

Alex was alone anxiously pacing the patio perimeter when he saw her emerge through open French doors.

"It's over," she said quietly.

"What?"

"It's over...just like that. It's over." Genie absolutely didn't know whether to laugh or cry.

Alex was stunned. Not sure he understood, he took her by the hand and led her to a chair. She appeared completely drained. To help her he needed answers.

"Come here," he said gently. "Sit down and tell me what is going on." He poured her tea though from the look of her, he wished he had some brandy to add to the cup.

"That was Anna," she began.

"Is she alright?"

"Yes she is fine. More than fine actually. She is wonderful."

Alex was extremely curious, but let her proceed at her own pace.

Then everything began to spill out at once "She found the General, she found Anton, she knows why Richard was killed... and Roger..." Genie was babbling, making very little sense.

"Calm down. Here drink this," he said handing her a cup. "Now take it slowly, one step at a time."

Genie sipped the hot amber liquid and took several deep breaths. "Oh, Alex," she said. "It is so complicated, so totally bizarre; I don't know where to begin. I need a little time to sort it all out."

He reached out and put an arm around her shoulder. "I know," he said, though he didn't really. "Just take your time. Is there anything I can do?" It was a somewhat rhetorical question. At least one to which he didn't expect an answer and he was surprised when she suddenly seemed to have a plan in mind.

"Yes Alex there is," she said immediately more composed. "Can we go to Molly's...now?"

He nodded affirmatively.

"Will you have time, when we get there, to stay for a while? I think it will be much easier to explain it all to both of you at once."

"Of course I'll stay," he said not adding that he was dying for answers, that she couldn't get rid of him now if she tried.

An hour later Alex, Molly and Genie were huddled around the table in Molly's bright kitchen.

"I know it really is unbelievable," Genie almost whispered. "I don't know how to react yet either, but Anna was anxious for us to know everything...the whole story...before it appears in the papers tonight. And you should know that the wire services picked it up. Unfortunately she thinks most of the major TV networks will also air the story this evening.

"You're certain that neither Roger nor Richard will be mentioned." Molly was concerned about what her children might hear.

"She promised me that," Genie assured her. "But this is really difficult. Let me explain it to you the way she explained it to me. At least let me try." She began with Egypt......

"............Anna recognized the photograph of General Walker when we were in Cairo and against Phillipe's wishes went to Washington to confront him. And confront him she did with more than he ever wanted to know. It seems that the whole thing began with him. It's all the result of a scheme he has been planning for years. He's obsessed," she said as she stood up.

Jumpy as a cat she just couldn't explain it all sitting down.

"Obsessed?" questioned Molly.

"Well, I would call it that. He believes that he has been unjustly passed over for recognition, that he should be Chairman of the Joint Chiefs of Staff or something. He is a man who has seen younger men, men who once served under him rise to outrank him and I guess it has made him a little nuts. Hell," she emphasized. "A lot nuts. Anyway, he got it into his head that if he could be the one to return the American hostages from Beirut to the US he would be assured of his place in history, of his just rewards so to speak."

"What does that have to do with......?" Alex began.

"I am coming to that," interrupted Genie.

"Apparently he devised a plan to kidnap several Soviet diplomats and use them as bargaining chips. He convinced a small group of Russian friends, or I suppose I should say colleagues, to use their influence in the Middle East to get the Americans into Russian hands either diplomatically or, if necessary, by force. Once the Russians had them he would then trade the Soviet diplomats he was holding for the Americans. And as you can imagine after recovering the Americans he would become an instant hero."

"But why would the Russians go along with such a crazy scheme?" asked Molly.

"Think about it. If they didn't go along with it...well who knows how much information could be forced out of those men."

"He would do that?" asked Molly shocked.

Both Alex and Genie just shook their heads at her naiveté.

"I suppose that was a stupid question," she confessed.

"And if they did go along with the General's plan," Genie continued, "they too would be heroes. Imagine TASS headlines 'Soviet Patriot Group Returns Missing Diplomats to the Motherland'. Heroes are instantly created in two countries. It was an easy choice. Everybody wins."

"Except Roger and Richard," said Molly sarcastically.

"Except Roger and Richard," she agreed.

"What went wrong?"

She looked at Molly. "Roger," she said bluntly. "Roger is what went wrong, and Richard and Anna and those damn photographs.

"When Roger was in Cairo a few months ago he attended a party at the home of the American Ambassador, Ian Stanley, and inadvertently took some photographs of the General and the Ambassador 'helping' one of the Soviet diplomats at the party into a limousine. That man was Anna's friend Anton Kasarov. After that night she never heard from him again." Genie stopped for a breath.

"You know," she began again. "I don't believe Roger knew what he had until much later, until he read about the missing Soviets and realized what he had actually gotten on film, but someone did. Someone obviously saw him taking the pictures and knew how damaging they could be."

"So the General killed Roger for the photographs, but how?" asked Molly.

"He didn't actually do it himself. According to Anna there is a middle man. A man she believes is called Finch, though she only overheard the name in passing. The General is very secretive about him. She is convinced that he is the one behind most of the actual operations.

"From what she could tell me, it was he who set up the kidnappings and hired a bunch of mercenaries to keep the Soviets under wraps."

For a moment Genie's throat seemed to close a bit choking off her air, making it difficult to proceed. She instinctively gulped down lukewarm tea to compensate. In a slightly raspy voice she added, "and she is certain it is Finch who killed Roger...caused his accident, and murdered Richard." She paused, "He probably even killed Ian Stanley."

"Ian Stanley?" Alex looked up. For some reason he was more surprised at this fact than anything else. "It's hard to believe the American Ambassador would get involved with something like this."

"Blackmail," said Genie pointedly. "It seems his wife has a drinking problem, and when she drinks she becomes...ah...indiscreet."

"But why have him murdered," Alex added.

"Who knows? They probably thought he would talk, maybe let something slip. I really didn't ask."

"Finch," Molly said softly. Her months of suspicion now confirmed. She was finally able to put a name to her husband's killer. Sitting very quietly for the past few moments she was trying to take it all in. "How could he?" she asked. "How could he convince the police it was an accident. I mean I always thought something was suspicious...didn't they. Is it that easy to 'create' an accident?"

"He didn't have to be too clever," remarked Genie. "After all, he hired Whiting."

"Oh damn!" sighed Molly. "I'd forgotten all about him."

"Finch hired Whiting to cover things up, pick up the pieces, and make certain clues disappear. In short to make it look like an accident. He also tried to slow down the investigation of Richard's murder, steer us in the wrong direction so he could eventually close it out as just another unsolved homicide. And, of course," she added. "To try and get those damn pictures. They were a very real threat. Finch apparently promised the General that the photographs would never become a problem, that they and anybody who had seen them would simply disappear. God," she sighed, "I wonder if Richard knew how important, how dangerous, they were."

"I am sure he did," commented Alex thoughtfully. "After all he had the foresight to mail them down to Dartmoor. Obviously he believed they were too dangerous to keep in the hotel."

"But we've all seen……," stammered Molly in shock.

Suddenly concerned Alex jumped to his feet. "She's right you know. What about this Finch? We could still be in danger. Especially you Gen. Hell, this mad man can only guess that we may have seen Roger's pictures, but you! He must know you've seen them."

"Don't worry," she tried to allay their fears. "Alex, really Anna promised me that it's over. Finch and Whiting aren't a problem anymore. It is all part of the deal."

"Deal," they questioned in unison.

"Anna made a deal with the General."

Genie knew this was going to be as hard for Molly to accept as it had been for her. Before she could continue she needed a break and so, she suspected, did the others. "Would you mind…," she said. "Can we stop for a few minutes. I…I just need a moment."

Without waiting for a consensus she walked over to the open back door. Stepping out into the beautiful little sunlit garden she realized the incredibility of the story she was telling. It was all too insane. A bad movie, someone else's life. Even as she spoke the words, relaying Anna's chronicle as accurately as she could, she struggled to make it her own. Struggled to personalize the events, accept them as part of her life.

Alex came up behind her and gently put an arm around her shoulder. "Lovely isn't it," he said reassuringly. "We don't get enough of these perfect summer days here."

She leaned against his shoulder and allowed tight muscles to ease. "I hope it truly is over Alex," she said softly. "I want to believe Anna, but this deal of hers…I don't know."

"Shh!" he said comfortingly. "You'll tell us about that in a while. Right now all you need to do is breath the air, smell the flowers, walk barefoot in the grass…unwind."

She smiled at his attempts to help her relax. "Doctor's orders?" she asked with a slight smile.

"Doctor's orders."

A short time later Molly joined them in her garden and sitting cross-legged by the small fishpond, dangled her fingers in cool water. Expecting food, three golden coi splashed around her hand. "I am worried about the boys," she confessed. "Really worried. How can we be sure they'll be safe?"

Genie sat on the grass next to Molly. "I think we can trust Anna," she said. "I know you don't know her, but she was very careful when I met her in Cairo. So careful, in fact, that it almost drove me crazy."

"This Finch sounds like a bit of a wild man. Does she know where he is now?" Alex tried not to show his own concern, but he wasn't nearly as inclined to believe Anna's promises as Genie seemed to be.

"I am not sure. But she says he is only in this for the money, greed, nothing more. The General is just going to pay him off and get rid of him. Anna assures me that as soon as he gets his money he will simply vanish."

There, she had said it and Molly's reaction was predictable. It perfectly mirrored her own response to what Anna had told her a few hours earlier.

"Pay him off." Molly was astounded. "What do you mean pay him off? He murdered my husband for God's sake. He murdered Richard." She was clearly furious. "We just can't let him get away with it."

"I know, I know… When Anna told me…," said Genie. "But I just don't know what to do. I've been struggling with this all day. I wasn't even sure how to tell you. Damn, it's so frustrating."

"What about Anna," suggested Alex. "Perhaps she could get more information about Finch from this General Walker."

Genie shook her head.

"Why not?" Molly didn't yet fully understand.

"It is part of the deal she made with him, with the General."

"You mentioned it earlier. Can you tell us about it?"

"I'll try," she said. "When Anna finally confronted him with everything she knew and showed him the pictures… she threatened to expose him."

"She should expose him," said Molly bitterly.

Without responding Genie continued speaking. "He put a gun to his head."

"You're kidding." Alex couldn't quite believe it.

"No, and think of it, if he had killed himself Anton and the others would be dead now and we wouldn't know any more than we did yesterday. And if the men holding Anton found out that the General was dead…realized there was no way they would be paid. Well… It doesn't take much imagination to know what they would do."

"Hence the deal," said Alex who already guessed Anna's intentions.

"Right. Anna made her own particular bargain with the Devil. The General's plan was blown apart but she was able to convince him to go ahead and supposedly 'rescue' his own hostages, the diplomats, and then, as "a gesture of American good will", turn them over to the Soviets. Anna promised to write a cover story that would prove to the world the General's deeds were nothing short of heroic."

"And the American hostages?" questioned Alex amazed.

"My question as well," added Molly

"Hopefully, if everything works out as planned, the Americans will be located next month in a neutral location selected by those 'Russian colleagues' the General has been working with."

"That seems a bit problematic...I mean really dicey," Alex continued.

"You're telling me," said Genie. "Of course only the few of us know about that part of this colossal, convoluted, cluster fuck. Excuse the...you know...French," she sighed, "but I don't know what else to call it."

"Agreed," said the others in unison.

"I guess we will have to wait until this evening to see how well Anna's cover story holds up. She was reluctant to discuss much about the actual rescue mission, but believe it or not Anna and Anton are together as we speak."

For the past several minutes Molly had been only half listening. She was obsessed with the idea of bringing Finch to justice. "How can we let them get away with this? Whiting is practically under our noses and that man Finch... there must be a way."

"We don't even know what he looks like," reminded Genie.

"All those pictures. They must be able to give us a clue."

"I don't know what to tell you Molly. There just isn't any evidence. The most incriminating of the pictures only show a blurry image of the General 'helping' an 'inebriated' Soviet Diplomat into a limousine. Without any corroboration...,"

"But, what about Anna?" Molly pointed desperately.

"She has done everything she can. She made it very clear that she and Anton will both claim he and the others were indeed kidnapped by the Hezbollah. In fact the other hostages actually believe the Hezbollah were responsible."

Genie was exhausted. By now afternoon sun streaked across the lawn on which Genie sat, legs outstretched, hoping some alien pod creature would invade her body and get her off the hook. For some reason she felt responsible for the fact that Finch and Whiting were going to literally 'get away with murder.' Had she let Richard down again, wasn't there anything she could do to change things?

"Look you two," Alex began. "I know these aren't the answers you hoped for, but at least it is something. At least you know what happened and perhaps when the initial story fades a bit...well maybe then something can be done to bring Finch and Whiting to justice." He was grasping at straws and he knew it, but the two women sitting on the grass in front of him were absolutely miserable and he was at a loss as to how to comfort them. He certainly couldn't remind them that in the real world the bad guys often win. All he could do was try to give them a little hope and help them get on with their lives.

When the story finally broke that evening, as Anna promised, there was no mention of Roger or Richard or photographs or even Ian Stanley. No connection was made between the General and the American hostages. In fact the American hostages in Beirut were mentioned in only the most reflective way, with concern and prayers that they too would soon be free. No one spoke of Finch or Whiting, but to the surprise of all three there seemed to be some concern about the escape of an international mercenary who called himself "the Eagle". Genie silently wondered why Anna had failed to disclose that little piece of information.

The cover story appeared very credible. As far as anyone would know a young French investigative journalist had stumbled upon the story of her career. She had given the world a firsthand account of the daring rescue of five missing Soviet diplomats. And an intimate portrait of the "brilliant" American General who had accomplished the spectacular mission.

In the eyes of the world, General Armstrong Walker had indeed become a hero.

Chapter 36

The boy sat on his mother's lap, one great big tear rolling down his left cheek. Alex reached out and took his hand. "My goodness," he said. "Such a sad face. And here I thought you would be happy to learn that you're all better. I guess that tear means you are going to miss me."

The four year old child perked up a little trying to fully understand his doctor. "Better?" he said pointing to the still bandaged hand.

"Almost," said Alex winking at the boy's mother while handing her a tube of Vitamin E ointment. "You let your Mum rub this special cream onto your hand every day and before you know it that hand of yours will be practically as good as new."

"No more gaffs?" asked the boy. The prospect of additional painful skin grafts had been the source of the tear.

"Not for you young man. I am afraid we are done with you," he said with a broad smile. "Unless of course you change your mind," he teased.

"No thank you Dr. Tempptin, it's all better," he said it quite seriously and slid down from the security of his mother's lap.

As the child and his mother left the office the boy turned and waved. For an instant his bright golden red hair reminded him of Genie.

Genie...he couldn't get her out of his mind and realized, of course, that wasn't good. After all, though she hadn't said anything yet, he knew she would probably be leaving any time now.

She had her own life to attend to, and though they were all still reeling from Anna's phone call and all the news she had generated, there honestly wasn't any reason for her to stay on.

If only they had a little more time then maybe...but it wasn't going to happen and he had to accept the fact that it simply was not meant to be. We'll remain friends, he thought, we will stay in touch and perhaps next summer she can come for a visit, or I could go over there..."Stop kidding yourself, old man," he scolded aloud. "She's going back to her own life and that is that. She is a nice woman, a wonderful woman really, but that's the extent of it. Some things just don't work out."

"Doctor?" inquired his nurse, peeking her head into the examining room, "Is everything quite alright?"

"Oh! Yes, of course," he responded flustered. He hadn't realized how loudly he had been lecturing himself. "Thank you. Would you please send in the next patient?"

Channing House

"So now what?" Genie questioned the reflection in the mirror. "Now what are you going to do?" Frustrated she fussed with hair that had suddenly gotten much too long and in desperation pinned it to the top of her head, tucking one errant strand behind her ear.

Until only moments ago she had been preoccupied with the morning news. She had already gotten a taste of what to expect on last night's evening newscasts, but she hadn't come close to anticipating the amount of media attention Anna's story would continue to generate. The papers, radio, TV had all reported various versions of Anna's report. And this morning Genie had turned to every station and read every paper she could find.

It was big news and obviously wasn't about to go away anytime soon. Everyone was jockeying to interview General Walker and Anna and even Anton, and was surveying every possible angle for more 'in-depth' information. But true to her word Anna never mentioned a thing about Roger or Richard.

And the General...well...he wasn't about to ruin his one opportunity for heroic acclaim.

And if Finch and Whiting were never held accountable for their crimes she would learn to live with it. She would have to; there was nothing else she could do.

Listening to a local anchorman praising the efforts of the 'American General' it amazed her. She could not comprehend the fact that Anna's plan seemed to be working perfectly.

So... why was she so depressed? Was it because Richard's murderer would go free, that was part of it, but not all. No...that realization infuriated her, but depressed? "Give it up," she scolded herself. "Admit it. It's Alex. You're going to miss him."

But, she had a life...in New York and, she had to get back to it. If only, she thought...then she thought...Well maybe. "Sure," she said to the twin in the mirror. "I'll come back next year. Once everything dies down. Maybe even for Christmas vacation."

It was just a pipe dream. "Get with it lady. How do you know he would even want you to visit? Sure, you started to get close, but the timing...damn! It's just wrong. You're only now coming to terms with Richard's death," she continued the dialogue. "Anyway, Alex has a life too you know."

Reality easily won the argument. Knowing what she had to do she sighed deeply, picked up the phone and called Thomas Cook Travel for flight information to New York.

Half an hour later she stood at the front entrance to Channing House anticipating the arrival of the first group of guests.

"I am so sorry you have decided to leave us, Genie, you know you are welcome to stay as long as you like." Ruth was genuinely going to miss her new American friend.

"Thank you Ruth. You have really been wonderful to me, but it is time. I honestly think I am ready to face New York...the apartment and our friends again. As much as I would like to, I simply cannot hide out forever you know."

Estimating the number of visitors expected in the next few moments Genie thumbed through a handful of brochures, while continuing her conversation. "I would like to visit Richard's Aunt Sarah again before I leave," she explained, "and I've made plans to see her over the weekend. My flight home is scheduled to leave next Monday."

"We are all going to miss you dear," said Ruth giving Genie a warm hug. "Especially Alex," she added with just the slightest sly smile crossing her face.

"I am going to miss you all too," said Genie somewhat embarrassed by Ruth's observation. Thankfully, the timely arrival of the first group of camera-laden tourists distracted them from any further awkward moments.

Somehow he missed the story when it first broke Monday evening. Only now after watching reports for the second time this morning could Finch begin to comprehend what had happened. "That God damned bastard," he shouted. "He double-crossed me." In one vicious swipe with his sterling silver weapon he slashed out in anger slicing the back of a blue velvet armchair.

Enraged as he was he had the presence of mind to recognize the stir this little tantrum would cause...luxury hotels aren't often vandalized...except perhaps by the occasional Rock star...and he arranged the furniture so that the ruined area would probably be overlooked by housekeeping. It was purely a small act of self-preservation. He couldn't give a damn about the mess.

Within minutes of this one reckless act he was once again in control, flipping frantically from station to station searching, in vain, for additional information. When it became clear that no more could be learned from the local networks Finch demanded the concierge send copies of every available newspaper to his room immediately.

Once again, in a storm of rage, he paced his spacious quarters. "Walker won't get away with this. Neither will his pretty French reporter. If they think they can dump me...change the whole plan after all the work I've done......no way old man." He seethed with the conviction that the General had manipulated this change in the operation purposely to cut him out of the deal. "And that Lawrence bitch. She's in on it too. Oh yeah! You can just bet she is. You can just bet it was her and those damn photographs that led that little French number to the General in the first place. Well those two broads don't know what they have gotten themselves into... at least not yet they don't."

His world was spinning. It had been years since anyone had the nerve, the serious misfortune, to cross him. But he would deal with it..."They can count on it."

He tried again to reach the General. No longer bothering with discretionary code names and covert telephone numbers, he was able to get through to the General's Alexandria home with no problem...but one. The person who answered was obviously military staff and would only state that the General could not be reached.

"I want you to listen to me very carefully," Finch said biting his tongue to control his temper. "It is absolutely imperative that the General get in touch with me at the earliest possible moment. Do you understand? Urgent." He then gave the Sergeant his name and telephone number and reemphasized the urgency of the message.

The arrival of a stack of morning papers did nothing to abate Finch's anger. Although they went into more detail than the networks, he didn't learn anything that would help him understand what had really happened. The one thing he did learn, the one piece of information that had barely been mentioned over the air was that somehow the Eagle had managed to escape. That was a bit of luck. He expected to hear from him as soon as safety permitted. But, in all other respects the basic story was the same. Anna DuLac reported the spectacular rescue of five missing Soviet diplomats. No mention of Russians attempting to secure the Americans in Beirut, no mention of any murders...neither Roger Sims' nor Richard McBride's, or for that matter Ian Stanley's connection to the operation. And though he searched and searched he could also find no mention of his name and no mention of any damn photographs. "At least General, you had the good sense to keep me out of it. Though don't expect that one act of discretion to buy you a reprieve. Not a chance. You and your bitch friends will pay for this one."

The idea of exacting revenge had a uniquely calming effect on Finch. He became focused, structured, he found direction. It was so simple. The General and the DuLac woman were out of reach... for now. His first target remained the same, Genevieve Lawrence. It was difficult to remember now that he 'loved' her. She had betrayed him in so many ways and like the others would have to be punished. And it would be easy really; she was practically in the palm of his hand.

His "John Talbot" identification tucked securely into his wallet, Finch stood patiently with the rest of the three o'clock group waiting to enter Channing House. He was calm now. He had put the events of the morning into perspective...he had a plan.

Herdlike, he shuffled with the others, up enormous stone steps and accepted a brochure from an elderly docent, while Genie escorted them through large double oak doors.

"To your left," said the small, silver haired woman, "is the first of two libraries in this part of the manor. It was here in 1606 that King..."

Having heard this all before Finch stopped listening. Eyes trained on the pretty redhead he watched every move she made for an opportunity to speak to her. Perhaps when the group moved on up the long winding staircase he could get her attention long enough to convince her to remain behind and chat.

But, as they reached the bottom of the staircase Genie took over as guide leading the group. Irked at yet another missed opportunity, Finch lagged behind, remaining close enough to the others so as not to be conspicuous. After several minutes of endless explanations...the uses of this room, the decor in that, they reached the grandeur of the main dining hall. Sixty feet in length, it held a broad mahogany table that spanned fully two thirds of the room. For, almost the entire distance, additional sideboards and serving tables provided working surfaces that would dwarf even the most generous modern home. It was easily the most impressive room in the home. Ornate 15th century tapestries hung on stone walls creating an almost medieval atmosphere while massive mirrors reflected the glow of afternoon sunlight.

The twenty or so visitors were free to wander about the area for a few moments before proceeding to the kitchen facilities. The tour would end in the kitchen with tea and a brief question and answer session. Finch realized he had to make his move.

While everyone roamed about inspecting, at close hand, the tapestries and other items of interest, Genie waited patiently near the doorway to the adjacent pantry.

"Excuse me aren't you Miss Lawrence," Finch approached humbly, wire rimmed glasses perched on his nose, Michelin guide tucked under his arm.

Startled, she looked up, "Yes," she said.

"Genie Lawrence," he repeated for effect and began his charade. "I thought it was you." Smiling broadly and extending his hand he continued. "My name is Talbot and I, er, ah,...I was a friend of Richard McBride."

"You were a friend of Richard's?" she asked, stunned.

"Yes. We worked together at the Times." For emphasis he showed her his identification and press pass, though it was unnecessary. In her heart Genie wanted to believe him and it never occurred to her to doubt. "I just wanted to tell you how very sorry we all were at the news of his unfortunate 'accident'."

"Thank you so much, Mr..."

"Talbot."

Now that she looked at him more closely, Genie had the odd sensation that, in fact, she had seen him before. "Thank you Mr. Talbot that is very kind of you. Tell me," she asked. "Have we ever met? I am sorry that I don't remember it but, you do look familiar."

The unexpected question threw him for a moment. He counted on the fact that she would not connect him with his role in Cairo.

"Perhaps," he responded. "At an office party or someone's Christmas bash."

"I am sure that's probably it," Genie concluded. "But how on earth did you know I was here?"

"Through the paper. Word gets around you know. Someone, I can't remember the name right now, mentioned that you were still in London, but meeting here, like this. Well…this is just a happy coincidence…serendipity you might say."

"How is everyone?" She was surprisingly anxious for news from New York.

"Well I can tell you everyone was quite shocked by Richard's death. We all miss him terribly, but more to the point, how are you doing?"

An overwhelming urge to disclose everything about the photographs, the General, Anna…the entire story caught in her throat. She couldn't do it, she realized in time. After all he was with the paper and if she revealed anything it would be all over the place in no time. Too many other people would be hurt, she thought and bit her tongue.

"Actually, I am doing much better. In fact, I am planning to return to New York in about a week."

"I know that won't be easy," a facade of sympathy masked his intentions. He took the next step. "I wonder, Miss Lawrence, would you have lunch with me tomorrow?"

"That sounds lovely Mr. Talbot. Any other time I would be happy to but this week is so…"

She was slipping away, but he had anticipated possible rejection.

"I happen to have some wonderful pictures with me," he lied. "And, believe it or not, Richard is in several of them."

Her eyes became alight with interest. Finch knew he had selected exactly the right bait and prepared to set the hook. "They were taken on an assignment we were on together. That Richard, he could certainly liven up a place."

Genie was caught. She had no recollection of the assignment Talbot spoke of, but it didn't matter. A chance to see candid pictures of Richard at work was impossible to turn down.

"You are very persuasive Mr. Talbot. Thank you I would really enjoy having lunch with you."

"Good. It's set then. Shall we meet at Cheshire's at say 1:00 o'clock?"

That sounds wonderful," she said. Noting that most of the group had gathered around the doorway she smiled politely and excused herself.

Chapter 37

Finch arrived at Cheshire's early and selected a booth that would allow him an unobstructed view of the double, leaded glass, entrance doors. A booth that would also give him and Genie complete privacy for their 'luncheon'.

All his planning, the endless hours of preparation were about to pay off. Even the secluded suite he had hastily rented was there... waiting.

Indulging himself at the Ritz had been a splendid idea at the time, but of course it required that he find other accommodations for his guest. Finch soon came to realize that the inconvenience was actually a blessing in disguise. If he had been languishing in one of the less desirable hotels he often frequented, he may have been tempted to bring his prey directly to his room. And though those establishments were less than diligent with their clientele, the possibility of causing any 'unusual disturbances' could have proved embarrassing. All in all, he felt particularly comfortable with the new arrangements he had made.

It was several minutes past one o'clock when Genie finally found a suitable parking space not far from the pub, and managed to squeeze Ruth's Rover snugly against the curb.

From the moment she awoke little things had gone wrong. First, she had run out of toothpaste, then she had been unable to connect with Alex about dinner this evening, and now, she was late for this lunch date. What else, she groaned, a decidedly uneasy feeling knotted in the pit of her stomach.

Her instincts screamed that something about Mr. Talbot wasn't right, but logically she couldn't think of any reason why she should listen to them.

And, she had to admit that she was more than just curious to see photographs of Richard. She was driven to see them.

Richard was gone. She felt compelled to know every little detail she had missed when they were together and pictures of him on assignment were a rare treat.

Dismissing her anxieties as simply nervous anticipation, she rushed across the street to the quaint old building which she recognized immediately as Cheshire's from the green cat's eyes and wide grin painted on an old wooden sign hanging over the door.

Finch looked at his watch again and, as was his habit when under stress, nervously fingered the silver pen resting securely within the pocket of his lightweight jacket. Where the hell is she, he thought. Perspiration began to collect in the hairline at the back of his neck. He took a large swallow of ale, appropriately Old John Courage, and waited.

His renewed patience was soon rewarded when Genie stepped into the darkened atmosphere of the pub. Her eyes had not yet adjusted to the dimly lit surroundings so he stood and waved to attract her attention. Unknowingly, he also caught the attention of the waitress who promptly appeared at his table.

The attentive service was definitely not what he wanted at the time and his dismissal of the harried woman was ruder than he had intended. After all, he would need her services again when Genie was ready to order.

"Miss Lawrence," he effused charm as she approached his booth, "I am so glad you are able to join me. Please have a seat."

"Thank you Mr. Talbot," she said removing her trench-coat and smoothing the wrinkles out of the raw silk slacks and pale peach silk blouse she had on beneath the coat. The misty rain made her hair unmanageable. She had pulled it back and tied it into a pony tail with a long pastel watercolor print scarf.

With her hair pulled away from her face and the pastel colors floating about her head Genie's bright aqua eyes appeared enormous. Finch had never seen eyes that color. He found himself momentarily mesmerized. He came close to forgetting his mission...almost remembered again that once he believed he loved her. If she hadn't spoken, hadn't broken the spell, he might have been lost.

"Mr. Talbot," Genie said for the second time, he seemed to be in a daze, "how long have you known Richard?"

"Richard, ah yes," that brought him back to his senses, "poor boy, such a shame."

"How long did you know him?" Genie repeated anxious for any information.

As he didn't know anything about him at all, except that he had whacked the jerk in the park, Finch realized that he had to do some fast talking. Change the subject. Maybe he could actually get some useful information before he had his fun. She sure is a pretty little bitch, he thought almost remorsefully. Too bad she had to stick her nose in where it didn't belong. She cost me...and it's gonna cost her.

"Here let me order you a drink...and lunch we really should order lunch," he said and waved again to the disgruntled waitress.

Genie wasn't particularly hungry. All she really wanted was information, bits of Richard's life even gossip would do. But she had to be polite. Part of the Genevieve Lawrence package. She was invited to lunch...so...lunch she would have.

"Now," said Finch after he had ordered the Plowman's special for both of them and, hoping to dull her senses a bit, strong ale for Genie, "tell me how you are doing?"

Oh great, she thought, taking a small sip of the strong malty brew, how am I going to turn the conversation from me to Richard. After a few more sips from her mug she felt a little bolder and prepared to take the bull by the horns. She wanted to know about Richard, that's why she was here and if Mr. Talbot just wanted to use Richard as an excuse to hit on her well he would be very disappointed.

"Mr. Talbot, I appreciate your concern, really, and I am doing much better, but you said yesterday that you worked with Richard. Maybe you could tell me a little about that."

Finch proceeded to invent nonexistent scenarios from "days together at the Times" that were just ambiguous enough to keep her interested. It was a game that he was very good at, but one he knew couldn't continue much longer. As soon as they finished their meal and he had gotten as much strong drink into her as he could, he would lure her to his room.

Genie was disappointed. John Talbot wasn't giving her the kind of intimate details she had hoped to hear. She should have realized from the start that he couldn't have known Richard very well. After all she knew most of his really close friends. All he could tell her about the man she loved, she already knew...what it was like to work in New York. And beyond that he made her uncomfortable. She couldn't put her finger on the problem, he was certainly charming enough...very polite in an odd, boring, nondescript sort of way, but there was something... Genie was ready to leave. She absolutely could not eat another bite of cheese or bread and the ale ...it had already gone to her head. She wouldn't have another sip.

"Would you care for anything else?' Finch asked considerately.

Genie shook her head.

"Miss Lawrence, I am very sorry. It seems I have gotten you here under false pretenses."

She looked at him in surprise.

"What I mean is," Finch feigned humility, "I don't think I have the kind of anecdotes about Richard that you had hoped to hear. I didn't know the more personal side of his life. Unfortunately we only spent time together at work."

Could he read her mind? She shifted uncomfortably. "It is perfectly understandable Mr. Talbot. And it really was very considerate of you to go out of your way like this. I don't know what I expected. I hoped for too much I guess. It isn't your fault at all. Believe me I appreciate the things you have been able to tell me." She was glad this meeting was finally coming to an end. Her head was fuzzy. She needed fresh air and a good long walk before she could attempt the drive back to Channing House.

"One thing Miss Lawrence," Finch set the trap, "let me make this up to you. My rooms are just around the corner."

Genie's eyes widened.

Finch saw this and worked quickly to ease her mind. "Oh no, my dear girl," he chuckled. "What I mean is, if you will walk over there with me I would love to give you the photographs I have of Richard. I believe you would get quite a kick out of them."

Now she was really confused. This Talbot character made her uneasy, but he was trying so hard to be friendly. And she would love to have those pictures of Richard. But her head hurt and she was becoming cranky. Definitely too much ale, she thought. No... She should just clear her head...take a couple of aspirin... And get going.

"I'm sorry Mr. Talbot. I really must be going."

"Are you sure?" he tried not to sound desperate. "I am only a short distance from......"

"Oh! What the hell," she said, suddenly feeling like a total idiot and realizing how rudely she had been behaving. "It is a very generous offer and I would love to have those photographs Mr. Talbot," she said with as much of a smile as she could manage under the circumstances, "It is just the ale," she confessed. "I've had a bit more than I am used to.

Chapter 38

To Constance it seemed like a lifetime since she had seen Alex. The explosive scene that erupted between the two of them, in his town-house the other night, had angered and frustrated her and instinctively she knew to keep a low profile. Alex had made it clear that any feelings he once had for her were, done, over, finished. Well that's what he thinks, mused Constance on the drive to Channing House, we'll just see. She was one very determined woman.

She knew Alex well enough to be pretty certain that the eye of the storm had passed. As long as she remained cool, let him do his thing, she could remain close enough keep an eye on him.

She learned from Jackie that her nemesis would be returning to the states in less than a week and she wanted to be around to pick up the pieces of Alex's poor shattered spirit. "A little contrition is the order of the day," she chuckled to herself. "Alex never could stay angry with me for very long." As much as it went against the grain, she would play the role of penitent best friend...until she could manipulate him into wanting more.

Constance had already begun the game by coaxing Jackie into a working business dinner at the house. It was time to get into Alex's good graces again. Of course, Jackie knew exactly what was going on. They had been best friends for years...she was on to every one of Constance's tricks. "I don't think it is going to work this time," she had warned. "Genie is different. This time even he doesn't realize how much he cares."

"Don't worry love. Our Miss Lawrence is winging her way back

to the 'Big Apple' in a few days and I plan to take it from there."
She was nothing if not confident.

"Hmm...I don't know," was all Jackie had said and for some
reason that bothered her more than anything else. She had learned
to trust her best friend's instincts, at least where Alex was
concerned.

When she arrived she found Channing House absolutely silent.
No one was at home, not even the ever faithful Hollings.
Constance had been let in by a new girl, she thought her name was
Sylvia, but she too seemed to have disappeared, leaving her to
entertain herself until the rest of the family showed up. She poked
about the library a bit and finally decided to brew a pot of tea in
the kitchen.

Constance couldn't remember when the place had ever been so
empty.

The harsh ringing of the telephone startled her. In the rest of
the house one only heard muted bells and the calls were usually
picked up by one of the staff on the second ring, but not today.

Obviously Sylvia was still in training so Constance, being
'practically a member of the family', waited until the fourth, then
picked up the receiver just before the answering machine clicked
on.

"Channing House."

"Constance?" Genie would recognize that voice anywhere.

"Yes, may I help you?" She too knew the voice of her rival, but
would never give the slightest hint of recognition.

"Constance, its Genie Lawrence. May I speak to Ruth please?"

"I am sorry Genie, but no one seems to be home at the
moment. I believe Ruth is in the gift shop. I am sure she will return
shortly. May I have her ring you?" Her chilly response was cool
but courteous.

"No, I am calling from a public phone, in a pub called

Cheshire's. Please give her my apologies and explain that I may be delayed. I will probably miss dinner and they shouldn't wait for me."

"I'll let her know. I am sorry I'll miss you. I understand you are returning to New York in a few days."

"Yes, Monday evening. I had hoped to see your gallery, Jackie raves about it, but I am afraid it will have to wait until another time."

"Certainly," she said, "some other time." Of course she was thinking, yes! You're gone! Terrific!

"And Constance, one more thing. Please tell Alex that I'll see him later."

"Sure," she said. Oh! Sure, she thought.

They had walked only a few feet when Finch stopped at a news stand and picked up an afternoon paper. It was a calculated move of observation and reaction. "Quite a story about that American General," he began, "have you been following it?"

Genie's heart skipped a beat. She should have expected that a reporter like Talbot would be interested in the story, but still, it took her by surprise. "I, ah...yes I've read about it." She tried to be brief and make light of it but, Finch, having his own agenda, pursued the matter.

"You know," he said pointedly as they continued to walk through a light drizzle, "I can't help but believe there is more to this thing than meets the eye."

Genie's eyes widened. "Oh?"

"Yes, he said, "I am certain that we haven't heard the last of this story." He looked her straight in the eyes, glared for just an instant, and then smiled as brightly as a child.

A cold shiver ran through her. Her grandmother used to say

when that happened someone was walking on your grave. Great, she thought. Then, dismissing the morbid old saying she turned her attention again to Talbot. Where had she seen him? She knew those eyes, but where...well it would come to her. For now, she just had to keep her cool, but that disquieting feeling had once again settled in the pit of her stomach. Maybe she should forget the pictures.

"Ah! Here we are," said Finch, suddenly turning right into a quiet little alley. The mews opened up into a tiny courtyard surrounded by six ancient Tudor row houses. Finch led Genie to the third house on the left. She noticed in the window of the ground floor apartment a neatly printed "rooms to let" sign with the number 6 crossed out and 4 hand written in its place.

"This is charming," she said gamely attempting to ignore her nagging doubts, "Have you lived here long."

"No, not very," he admitted and turned his key in the cheerful red door.

Though she didn't realize it as she passed through the darkened, hallway and up two flights of incredibly narrow stairs, the unimaginable terror into which Genie was about to become trapped had already begun. It had masked itself in the morning's anxiety. It had been the source of the gnawing uneasiness she ignored in the pub and it had grown ever so slightly during their walk to 'Talbot's' rooms.

As she stood before one of two doors on the third floor of the quiet old rooming house she almost turned to leave. But she didn't. Again logic prevailed over instinct and she waited for the little man in the dull grey suit to unlock the newly painted door.

The landlord had described Finch's rooms to him as a two room suite. In actuality it was one large dormer room divided by an oriental screen into a sitting area and a 'bedroom'. However, unlike the rooms on the first and second floors, he did have his own bathroom. Tiny as it was it would more than meet his needs. After all he wouldn't be here long. Just long enough to enjoy his 'guest', to exact the revenge he so richly deserved, to experience a little pleasure......to make her pay.

The first thing Genie noticed when Finch stepped back and let her enter was the starkness of the interior. Other than the few items of furniture provided by the landlord, there was absolutely no sign of habitation. Not shirt or jacket carelessly tossed about, not a TV or radio, no shoes or comb, not even a stray pad or pencil. He says he is a reporter, she thought quizzically, granted he said he has not lived here long, but... Her immediate reaction, that tiny spark of foreboding should have moved her to dash out while she had the opportunity, but that would have seemed foolish. She could take care of herself.

Once inside, she tried to make herself as comfortable as possible in an ancient, straight backed, cane chair. Finch came in behind her and she did not notice him lock the door when it closed.

"Please excuse my humble abode," he pleaded. "As I said earlier I've only just found this place." That, at least, was the truth. "As a matter of fact most of my belongings are still at the hotel."

Genie only nodded. She really didn't care what kind of life style he led. By this time she only wanted to get the pictures of Richard and get out.

"May I get you something to drink Miss Lawrence?"

"Yes please, glass of water," said Genie, "and I would love a couple of aspirin, if you have any? That ale seems to have gone straight to my head."

"Oh dear, I don't have a glass in the place. Perhaps I can offer you an ice cold can of ginger ale. Sorry no aspirin either, I'm afraid."

"That's ok. The ginger ale would be great though, thanks,"

Genie said shaking her head at his unusual behavior. He retrieved two cool cans of the sparkling beverage from a small fridge tucked tightly next to a small sink. She heard him pop the top on both cans and when he handed one to her she immediately took several quick gulps. The lunchtime brew had not only contributed to a headache, but had made her very thirsty as well, and she found herself briskly consuming half the can.

Finch handed her an envelope he said contained the photographs he wanted her to see.

When she emptied the contents of the package she was so stunned at what lay scattered across her lap that she actually let the remainder of the soda slip from her hand and spill across the floor.

Finch didn't move. He stood above her looking down with a menacing grin masking his more violent intentions.

"Surprise!" was all he said while he gave her time to compre-hend the situation.

Genie rifled through the photographs in complete shock. She recognized them all too well. They were copies of Roger's photographs. Pictures of that party in Cairo, pictures of the General and Anton...they were all there. And there was more... clippings of Anna's story from every newspaper in London.

She looked up at him and something clicked. "Cairo," she said, "that's where I saw you."

He only nodded.

"I don't understand. Who...who..." she shook her head, every-thing was becoming a little fuzzy.

"Think about it," he said, "who do you think I am."

But she couldn't think. Everything was blurry; her head suddenly felt as if it were full of cotton and her mouth was very dry. No, she couldn't think at all. She tried to stand, but her legs were like rubber and in the effort all the photos and clippings spilled from her lap. They seemed to drift in a slow motion stream of black and white from her lap to the floor. As she watched them fall slowly one after another all the events of the past weeks suddenly flooded her mind and she could hear with absolute clarity the story Anna had related to her only days ago.

With the little strength she had left she managed to raise her head and look one last time into his feral eyes. "Finch," she said in the instant before darkness engulfed her.

Chapter 39

If he had known Genie wasn't going to be there Alex would never have driven all the way to Channing House for dinner. To add to his disappointment, Constance was back in the picture. It was all he could do to be civil to the woman. Though, for now, she was acting with unusual restraint. Maybe he had gotten through to her after all.

"Did Genie say what time she would be here, Mother?" Alex attempted to make the inquiry sound casual.

Ruth could read her son very well. The slightly anxious quality to his voice betrayed his true feelings, perhaps no one else noticed, but a mother knows these things. She wished he would open up and admit that he cared.

"No dear, but I am sure she won't be too late."

Alex was actually contemplating skipping the evening meal and driving back into town when Hollings, who was thankfully back on duty, announced, "Dinner is served, Madam." He spoke directly to Ruth who made a fuss of gathering her chicks together in the dining room.

Much to Alex's dismay Constance, after all these years considered one of the brood, seated herself at his elbow. Realizing that he was in no mood for conversation she wisely implemented her new tactic of non aggression and simply sat quietly by his side.

Alex, honestly amazed at her restrained demeanor, remained on guard for the fall of the other shoe. But dinner was surprisingly uneventful and he began to believe that he and Constance might actually be able to come to terms with their stormy past.

As they finished their entrees and prepared for dessert, Hollings unexpectedly reentered the room. "There is a call for you, Doctor." He still found it hard to call the man he had known since childhood, doctor. He would probably never be able to address him completely as Doctor Templeton, though he used the appellation with pride when speaking to non family members about how brilliantly 'his young man' had turned out. "Would you like to take it in here?" he asked.

"No, thank you Hollings, I'll pick it up in the hall," he responded with relief. Assuming the call to be from Genie he wanted a little privacy.

"Hello Gen," he found himself almost out of breath when he grabbed the phone and was stunned to hear a man with a decidedly New York accent on the other end of the line.

"Hello is this Channing House?" the nasal voice inquired.

"Yes," responded Alex, "May I help you."

"Oh, hi" he said, but it sounded like "Aw hoi" to Alex who had to strain to catch what the fellow was saying. "My name is Ira Fishman I would like to speak to Genevieve Lawrence please."

"Mr. Fishman, I am afraid Miss Lawrence is not available at the moment. Perhaps I can take a message for her."

"That would be great. My wife and I are friends of hers...I used to work with Richard McBride you see and......" Ira found all this explaining necessary, but a bit uncomfortable," and she sent us a letter saying she was coming home...and we just thought...well...if there was anything we could do to make it easier...you get the picture."

"Yes, I understand. That is very kind of you and I will certainly let her know that you rang. Would you like her to call you?"

"Yes please...tell her any time is OK."

Ira was about to hang up when Alex continued… "By the way you may be interested to know that Miss Lawrence is spending the day with a colleague of yours."

"Oh really," Ira responded curiously.

"Yes, she had lunch and apparently dinner with your John Talbot. It seems he had some photos of Mr. McBride which he thought she might like to have."

"My John Talbot?" he questioned, "I can't say I've heard of him."

Alex was quite surprised, "Are you sure? He told Genie that he and McBride worked together at the paper."

"No," said Ira, "there is no John Talbot that I know of. Are you sure you've got the name right?"

"Yes, quite sure." An awful feeling of dread centered in the hollow of Alex's stomach and extended to damp clammy palms.

Ira too became concerned, but unaware of the circumstances came to a totally different conclusion. "You don't think some joker is trying to hit on her… do you?"

Alex wished Ira were right, but he was afraid the implications were much more serious. If this John Talbot is an imposter then whom had Genie met this afternoon and where was she now? Unfortunately, he was confident that she wouldn't spend this much time with someone who was just trying to make advances.

It was too soon to have her friends in the states become concerned and they were too far away to be of any real assistance. Reluctantly, Alex went along with Ira's supposition. "She is quite lovely. You are probably right. It is very likely that she attracted the eye of someone who would like to get to know her better," Alex prayed he hadn't aroused any suspicions, "When she returns I'll warn her about this Mr. Talbot."

"Thanks, that makes me feel much better. Tell her to take care of herself. Judy and I will be waiting for her call."

Trying to concentrate, Alex stood by the phone in a daze, receiver still in his hand. Is it really possible there is no John Talbot? His heart knew the answer. Something was terribly wrong and in the back of his mind an idea too awful to contemplate began to take root. No, it couldn't be...yet... The idea wouldn't quit. The more he thought about it, the more it became a possibility until finally he convinced himself of the truth of it. He didn't know how he knew, but he would bet his life on it.........Genie was with Finch. Those disquieting feelings she had had of being followed. She had been right all along. He had probably been after the photographs, and Genie, from the very start. "Damn," he groaned and dialed Molly's number.

When Alex reentered the dining room Ruth could see he was terribly on edge.

After the disturbing conversation with Fishman, the call to Molly only made things worse. Though she had expected to hear from Genie that afternoon, Molly hadn't spoken to her all day. For the time being, Alex decided to keep his suspicions about Finch to himself, but he was unable to hide from his family the fact that something was very wrong. From his wrinkled brow and scowling eyes, Jackie and Constance, as well as Ruth, could see the man's distress.

"Alex?" Ruth questioned. "What on earth?"

"Mother," he responded not able to give her an answer, "Where is Sylvia? Has she left for the day?"

"I am afraid so dear. Why? What is it? Can I help?"

"No, I don't think so. I need to ask her about the call she took from Genie this afternoon. You know the note she left."

Constance inadvertently swallowed down a large gulp of hot tea which caused her to eyes to tear up, almost, but not quite, ruining her mascara.

After her own 'little conversation' with Genie that afternoon she had left a simple "Don't wait dinner......Genie" note tacked to the message center in the kitchen. It was short, to the point, unsigned and calculated to appear slightly rude. She had hoped they would believe Sylvia had intercepted the call and that the "slightly rude" tone of the note was a product of American breeding (or lack of it). It was only a small deception; one which Constance calculated would begin to tarnish the glow on 'perfect' Genie's halo. But, if Alex actually spoke to the witless maid, he would find out that Constance had taken the call herself and the terseness of the message would look spiteful.

Thank God she isn't here, she thought, and decided on a wait and see tactic for the time being. Maybe his little American friend has found herself a beau, Constance mused. Maybe that's why Alex looks so distressed. Not that John Talbot character, she chuckled to herself. This could be very interesting.

Alex was beside himself. He had to find her, but where to start. "Mother, did Sylvia mention where Genie was having lunch?'

"No dear, actually I didn't speak with her. Hollings brought me the note this afternoon. He found it after she had gone for the day. Silly girl, when will she learn to relay all messages personally? I'll speak to her about that in the morning.

"Mother," he said wondering how he could express the urgency of the situation, without revealing the whole story, "think carefully. When she borrowed the Rover did she mention where she might be going?"

"No Alex, I'm sorry she didn't say a thing except that she was having lunch with that Mr. Talbot. Alex, what is this all about?"

Out of desperation, he decided to use Ira's misdirected concern. "The phone call I just received was from a friend of Genie's in the US. He says that there is no John Talbot at the paper. He never heard McBride mention the name and we are both afraid that some unscrupulous character might be trying to take advantage of her."

"But why would someone do that?"

Constance wanted to hear this one too.

"Who knows Mother," Alex snapped. Anger and frustration were getting the better of him. "It is possible that a reporter from one of those tabloids might be after a story, or a con man might think she will receive money from McBride's estate. There are all sorts of sleazy people out there. All we know is that this bloke isn't whom he says he is and, well…I just want to find her before anything happens. You can understand that can't you?"

Ruth couldn't remember when she had seen her son this upset. She truly believed he was exaggerating the situation, that Genie would probably return at any moment. She tried to explain this to him but nothing she could say seemed to allay his concerns.

"Perhaps I can ring Sylvia. You must have her number."

During the few moments Ruth took to find her newest employee's personal information file Alex paced about like a caged animal.

"Alex, calm down," said Jackie not fully understanding his impatience, "Mother is right. Genie will probably show up any moment wondering what all the fuss is about.

"You're right," he said trying his best to hide the depth of his fear. "I am most likely overreacting."

Now Constance didn't know what to do. She knew exactly where Genie had gone that afternoon, but should she tell them. How could she tell them without incriminating herself? And no matter, if the idiot had gone and gotten herself into trouble it was no concern of hers. Was it? But look at Alex, she thought, the more worried he is about her, the more emotionally involved he gets. Maybe if he does find her, sees that nothing is wrong, sees that she is just having a lovely dinner with some fellow who is infatuated with her…well then maybe that will put an end to it.

"Damn, Sylvia why aren't you home?" Alex hadn't hung up until the tenth ring. Now he didn't know where to turn. "Mother, I know I was going to stay the evening, but I think I'll run along back to town. He didn't mention that he planned on driving all over the city until he found something...anything that might lead him to Genie. It was a long shot, impossible really, but he couldn't think of any other option. And he couldn't stay here doing nothing. "Ring if you hear from her."

Ruth and Jackie both protested his sudden decision to leave, but Alex was adamant. He had to keep busy and he had another idea. If he and Molly did some brainstorming they might come up with a plan. And Molly was the only one he could confide in, it was time she knew his suspicions about Finch. Coat in hand he gave his mother a kiss on the cheek and headed for the door.

"Alex!" Constance had made a decision. "Have you ever heard of a place called 'Cheshire's'?"

"What?" What on earth can she want now, he thought. "I'm not sure I think there used to be a pub over in Battersea. Why?"

"Well I just remembered...,"

Alex was immediately skeptical, "Remembered?"

"Yes, this afternoon. I came by early and while I was waiting for Jackie I made myself some tea..."

Get on with it, he thought impatiently.

"...and Sylvia asked me how to spell Cheshire's. I told her I wasn't certain and she just said something like 'oh well it isn't important'. But it was right after she answered a call and I thought ...well maybe," She tried her best to play the innocent, "maybe that was the call from Genie." There...she had said it she braced for the reaction.

Alex stopped in his tracts. "Are you sure? You are absolutely certain she said Cheshire's?"

"Yes, I am quite certain." She was shocked. He was almost bursting with delight. She had expected fury. After all she had waited until the last possible moment to give him the information.

She thought he would bite her head off for not telling him this sooner, but instead he grabbed her and gave her a big kiss on the cheek. It certainly wasn't like him and for some reason she regretted his lack of anger. Anger, at least, she could deal with.

"Cheshire's, that's wonderful, thank you." At least now, thank God, he had a place to start. He was so relieved he only briefly wondered at the coincidental timing of Constance's amazing flash of memory. But it wasn't important...she wasn't important... finding Genie was.

Chapter 40

Weird surrealistic images danced to discordant tunes under painfully brilliant flashes of day-glow colored lights. A maze of exotic shapes floated lazily, surrounding her, holding her captive without bonds. No matter how she tried she couldn't seem to escape her dream. She gave up and slipped back into darkness.

Much later, she found herself groping through heavy gray green mist to an unknown surface, to the promise of fresh air and sunlight. Slowly, she emerged from her drug induced unconsciousness. Heavy eyelids struggled to open, and when they at last fluttered apart, she gasped, stunned by an overwhelming sense of disorientation.

All too quickly reality began to return. She was laying flat on an ancient brass bed, while above her loomed the shadowed figure of a man. A groan escaped her lips and she closed her eyes against the truth. Opening them again, she attempted to sit up and comprehended, for the first time, that ropes bound her hands and feet to the bed. Her head cleared and she realized, with terror, that the madman standing above her had removed all but her white lace panties strapping her almost naked to the upright bars in the head and foot boards of the old brass bed.

"What have you done?" she whispered, not wanting to hear the answer, "what do you want?"

"Nothing yet my dear," Finch chuckled answering both questions with a single response. Seating himself on the edge of the bed he lightly teased Genie's left breast with the tip of one long, effeminate, index finger. Betrayed by her body's own responses, Genie's pink nipples began to harden in response to his touch. Delighted by this control, Finch continued to toy with his captive, carelessly drawing circles around the excited areola. Then sliding his hand down over her flat stomach seductively, coming to a stop at the top of her bikini line, he whispered, "I haven't done anything…yet," he repeated, emphasizing the last word.

Genie knew exactly what he meant. Until this point she had remained perfectly still. Terrified that he would kill her on the spot, but understanding that he had "plans" gave her courage. She reasoned she had at least some time. Struggling vainly against the ties she shouted angry insults at him. "You crazy bastard! What do you think you are doing? You will never get away with this. Of course, protesting got her nowhere. If anything, Finch seemed even more pleased with himself.

"But I have, you see, I have gotten away with this, this and much, much more." He leered at her, got up off the bed and began to walk away. Then suddenly spinning to face her he dropped his full weight on top of her body and with his mouth almost touching her ear licked the tip of her earlobe and whispered "You're mine."

"Never!" Genie shouted and wriggled as best she could beneath his heavy body.

Finch laughed out loud as he left her and went around the tattered oriental screen to the 'sitting room'.

Never in his life had Alex driven with such speed or determination. Every instinct he possessed screamed at him that Genie was in serious trouble and all he could think of was to get to Cheshire's a quickly as possible. As he pushed the accelerator to the floor, he kept an eye in the rear view window for a constable. He didn't give a damn about a ticket, he just didn't want to be slowed down.

Fortunately, at this time of night London traffic had abated considerably and he was able to bob and weave his sleek green Jaguar throughout the narrow streets with little difficulty. Within the hour he had turned on to Battersea Bridge Road and pulled up in front of the pub.

Alex hadn't even come to a complete stop when he noticed his Mother's Rover parked directly across the street. He dashed across to have a look. Not knowing what to expect, but imagining blood stains or other signs of desperate struggle, he was relieved to see nothing amiss. Thank God, he sighed and ran back across the street, hoping against hope, that Genie would still be inside drinking and eating with the fellow who calls himself Talbot. It was a crazy, impossible dream; of course, it had been hours since her 'lunch date'.

As soon as he entered the quiet, smoke filled room he knew she wasn't there. The place was almost empty; he could see everyone at a glance. Genie wasn't among them.

"Excuse me," he said stepping up to the bar.

"Yes sir," said the portly man in a long white apron. "What'll you av mate."

"A pint of Guinness," Alex said thinking he would get more information if he were a paying patron.

When the bartender sat the pint in front of him Alex asked, "I am wondering if you can answer a question for me?"

"I'll giv'er a go."

"I am looking for a friend of mine. I was supposed to meet her here you see and I am terribly late. I wonder if you may have seen her. An attractive woman with red hair and freckles. She may have been in here this afternoon at about one o'clock."

"Sorry mate, but I just came on duty an hour ago. Sounds like a pretty one though, ope you find er."

Alex gulped down some Guinness and fished around in his

pocket for change. Perhaps Molly has heard from her by now, he thought, and searched the walls for a phone.

As he stood to make his way to the phone he had spotted in the back of the pub someone caught his arm. "Hey luv," started a short middle aged waitress who looked like she was probably a permanent fixture in the place. "Did I 'ear you ask old Mike there about a pretty girl with ginger 'air?"

"Yes, yes, you did," Alex said hopefully. "Have you seen her?"

"You know I believe I did. Though I can't say much for the company she was keepin'."

Alex's eyes widened and the waitress continued talking. "They were in 'ere about one, when I came on. Well, the bloke she was with was the really nasty sort. You know, pushy an' rude like. You might 'ave guessed it too, 'im bein American an' all."

Alex's heart began to beat faster. Finch, he thought, he was sure of it. "Do you know what time they left, where they went?"

"Where they went? Now 'ow would I know where they went?"

"Please," he said, "this is really important. Can you tell me anything?"

"Well," she said trying to remember, "they left about three. I remember because I finally got a break, and when I stepped outside for a breath I saw them walking down the street that way." She pointed to the right. "Can't for the life o' me figure what a pretty young thing like 'er sees in a little mouse like that."

Alex's mind raced. As he contemplated his next move he slipped her a five pound note. "Thanks," he said, "you've been more help than you know."

"Why are you doing this?" Genie cried, "You still haven't told me what you want."

Finch came back around the screen. "Yes, I have," he said menacingly. "I want you."

"But why? You don't even know me."

He bent down close to her face and she reeled from his hot, foul breath.

"Ah! But I do. I know you very well. I know you came to London with your boyfriend. The late, lamented Richard McBride. I know you spent time with his dotty Aunt Sarah down in the moors. I know your favorite perfume is Opium, I know you like to dance barefoot in the grass, and now I know you have a lovely little diamond shaped birthmark on your right hip." He reached down, sliding his hand roughly under her pants, poking at her birthmark.

Tears, resulting more from humiliation and rage than pain, welled in her eyes, and she turned her head hoping he wouldn't see the effect he was having.

"You murdered Richard!" was all she could say and this time the tears flowed in earnest. This time she didn't care.

He nodded his head. "You cost me plenty and now, my sweet Genie, you are going to pay."

Finch stood, eyes gleaming, and continued to stare at his beautiful captive. He would have some fun, he thought. Yes, before the night was over he'd have some fun. Instinctively his fingers fondled the sterling silver weapon that rested, as always, in the breast pocket of his white dress shirt.

"God!" she sighed. "I don't know...I really don't know what you mean."

Finch disappeared for a moment and returned, his hands full of photographs and clippings. "This," he said. "This is what I mean." Slowly he dropped the pictures, one by one, onto Genie's bare stomach. They landed haphazardly on and around her and she struggled to lift her head.

"These?" she questioned. "But it's all over. Your friend the

General," she added with biting sarcasm, "he is the one who changed things. He is the one who went in and rescued the Russians. And exactly why do you think he did that, do you suppose?"

Finch grew agitated. "For the hell of it. To cut a better deal with someone else. You and your little French friend perhaps."

He was crazy, Genie realized. Didn't he know his part in the General's plan would never be revealed? "Please," she tried to explain, "you've read the papers...listened to the TV. He never mentioned you at all. No one will ever know. I can't even prove you killed Richard. You could leave right now and no one would ever know anything."

"That's not the point," he shouted. "Of course no one will ever know. I'll see to that. But he betrayed me and," he said with cold deliberation, "the bastard never paid me. I worked for months on the crazy old man's scheme. Worked out all the details, made all the arrangements, and the fool sells me out. Well, he won't get away with it. Neither will that little French number he's hooked up with...neither will you." With that he dropped the rest of the photographs onto the bed and walked away.

"Damn," she thought. "How am I going to make him understand that the General is going to pay him? That the General didn't turn on him, that he wasn't betrayed."

Though it seemed an eternity it was only a short time later and Finch was back. What she saw when he returned from behind the old screen frightened her almost to the point of panic. Though she had been determined she would not show fear, instinct overwhelmed her and a long, low moan escaped her lips......and she began to struggle, struggle like hell. She pulled and twisted against the ropes until her wrists and ankles were raw to the point of bleeding.

And all the while Finch just stood there...smiling. Now completely naked, he hovered above her like a vulture, gingerly tossing a long, sharp silver blade from his left hand to his right, right to left, left to right and back again. Slowly terrorizing his victim to the point of exhaustion…and silence.

It was useless. Alex looked up the street and down and didn't know where to begin. Hell, he didn't even know what this Finch character looked like. How could he ask around, ask if anyone had seen him if he didn't even know what he looked like?

He needed a photograph, something…but what, where? Then it hit him that he didn't know what Finch looked like, but he knew someone who did. He raced back up the street to his car and jumped in, furious at the wasted moments.

He knew that time was growing short, he could feel it.

"Look," Genie said desperately, "you don't have to do this. Please," she begged, "the General will pay you, I know he will. He planned to all along…he just couldn't find you." She was breathing heavily and sweat glistened off her pale skin.

But Finch didn't listen.

Genie could not block the horror, the revulsion she felt as this crazed man flashed the glistening knife closer and closer to her exposed breasts. The heat of his naked thighs suddenly touching hers nauseated her, forcing her to bite hard on her lower lip or be sick.

Silent tears ran down her cheeks and she tried desperately to think of something to say, some way to make him stop. But she knew it was impossible, so with absolute certainty that her situation was hopeless, she closed her eyes and waited for the inevitable.

Finch had her exactly where he wanted her. He had planned for this moment with the precision of a priest readying a sacrificial ritual. With blade in hand he jabbed at the photographs still scattered on the bed, slicing them to shreds, tossing them to the floor. "Open your eyes," he ordered. "I don't want you to miss any of this."

Genie refused. What the hell, she thought, he'll kill me anyway. Her eyes remained closed until she felt the sharp stinging in her abdomen. In shocked surprise her eyes grew wide and she looked down to see a small pool of blood collecting below her navel. It ran sluggishly down her hip, staining the faded yellow bed covers bright orange. "Agh!!" she cried. "Please......don't."

"I thought that might get your attention. Don't worry, my dear, it's only a tiny nick. Amazing how those things bleed though, isn't it. Here let me make it all better." In a mocking gesture of concern, Finch patted the small cut dry with the corner of a protruding sheet, but he was unable to clean away the spilt blood. "This is a bit of a mess," he continued. "Let me get you a damp towel."

Genie was beside herself. Why doesn't he just do it and get it over with? "Please," she cried again, "don't you understand? You will get your money. Just call the General if you don't believe me... just call him." The last words were almost silent. It was obvious he wasn't listening.

Almost tenderly Finch wiped away the blood that had fallen on Genie's hip and stomach, but the warm water started blood flowing again and he was forced to find a drier cloth. When he returned, small crimson droplets had fallen onto the discarded pictures on the floor by the bed. Finch bent to pick them up and something caught his eye. There was a look about the blood on the photographs that stirred something deep within his soul. The revelation hit him like a man who has just found religion. Something had been missing and now he knew what it was. Now he understood how to make his ritual complete.

Like a man possessed he jumped up and searched frantically

through the suite. It wasn't there. "Back at the hotel," he mumbled to himself. "Damn," he swore. "No, it doesn't matter. I'm in control. I'll simply go get it."

Genie lay in silent, stunned amazement. What the hell was he doing? Though she didn't really care, for the moment, at least, he was distracted, for the moment he was leaving her alone.

He dressed quickly and returned to the bed. "Don't worry, my love, I'll be back in no time and then we will have our fun, won't we." He was speaking more to himself than to Genie and she didn't bother to answer. "Just let me put this around your mouth," he said, tying a ragged old cotton scarf between her open lips and around to the base of her skull. "Not that it matters really. There isn't anyone else in the building but us. And if you think the neighbors...well, an occasional scream in this neighborhood doesn't cause much of a stir these days. But better safe than sorry, right?" He pulled tightly on the ends of the scarf insuring against any possibility of it slipping. "There you go, all safe and sound. Now I am off, but don't worry I won't be long." He disappeared once again behind the screen, but in seconds his ratlike face reappeared to leer down at her. "Oh!" he said. "In case you are wondering, I've decided that what our little adventure here needs is to be accurately chronicled. We need our own private pictures." With that he was gone.

Chapter 41

Alex burst into Whiting's office like a madman, the desk Sergeant right behind him. "We need to speak now," he demanded.

The startled Inspector looked up and barely had time to say a word before the Sergeant had grabbed hold of Alex's arm and was in the process of ejecting him. "Sorry, sir, I'm afraid this bloke dashed right passed me. Shall I lock 'im up?"

"No, no, Sergeant," Whiting said recognizing Alex, "I will take care of this. You may leave. I'll call you if I need you. Now, Dr. Templeton, isn't it?" He attempted to shake hands. "What can I do for you at this hour?"

Alex was in no mood for ingratiating pleasantries. This bastard had been part of it from the beginning and he wasn't about to let him off the hook. "Forget it, Inspector," he said forcefully. "Sit down and listen."

"Now just one moment, Doctor," Whiting responded defensively. "This is my office, you know. You are the one who had better sit down and tell me exactly why it is that you are here."

Alex got right to the point. "I need a picture of your pal Finch and I need it now."

Whiting turned a bit green but managed to play his part. "Finch, Finch... I am sure I don't know whom you are talking about."

"Oh, don't you, Inspector? You can drop the charade. It's just you and I in this office of yours so you can drop your little act. I know all about it."

Whiting stood silently, not certain how much Templeton actually knew or how much he was guessing.

"I believe you had b...better tell me what you think you know, Doctor, before I am forced to call my officer."

"I know about your involvement with Roger Sims' death, with the coverup in the McBride case. I know about your connection to that US general, with that Finch character..."

Whiting sat heavily into his chair.

"...all of it, Inspector...everything."

Inspector Whiting looked straight at Alex with defeat, resignation, utter sadness clouding his eyes. "What is it?" he asked, "Wh...What do you want?"

"Let me say this first," Alex began. "Right now, only a few people have any idea of your involvement in this matter and they ......well, I can assure you they won't say anything. As far as the rest of the world knows, none of this ever happened and if you help me...no one will ever have to know a thing. Do you understand?"

Whiting shook his head. "What you want is," he repeated almost in a daze, "Finch...a...p.p.picture."

"Yes, a photograph, a sketch, anything."

"But..." Whiting was about to ask the inevitable 'why?' when Alex pressed on.

"He has Genie," Alex blurted. "God only knows what he will do to her."

In astonishment Whiting stood and came around to the front of his desk. "What do you mean h...he has Gen...Miss Lawrence?" he said, leaning heavily against the furniture. "Has her where?"

His stomach churned, he was sick with comprehension, he knew exactly what Finch was capable of. "You had better tell me, Doctor, precisely what is going on."

Alex related to Whiting the entire story. The Inspector listened intently, then removed a key from his wallet and unlocked his bottom desk drawer. "Here," he said handing Alex a manila folder, "Top page. I'm afraid it's the best I can do."

Alex opened the folder and removed the top sheet of paper. It was a Xerox copy of a very old mug shot. The man in the picture was thin, almost gaunt, with small beady eyes, and sported a Van Dyke style goatee.

"He has much less hair now," offered Whiting, "and he is clean shaven. At least he was the last time I saw him."

"Thank you," said Alex and turned to leave.

"Just a moment," added Whiting, "I am going with you. I can't get the department involved just yet...y...y...you understand...but two of us looking for that madman stand a much better chance of finding him."

Alex just nodded. He would take all the help he could get.

......Silence...Genie couldn't hear a thing but to make sure, she called his name. "Finch." Because of the gag a muffled "...iinnch ..." was all she could manage. Still there was nothing. She was alone.

Her first instinct was to shake the bed as wildly as she could, but after several seconds with no results other than her own exhaustion, she ceased. This is getting me nowhere, she thought, Oh, Alex, where are you? It surprised her a little to realize that when she needed someone so desperately she thought of him first... Where are you?

She tried over and over to loosen the ropes by wriggling them, but nothing seemed to work. There was no way to reach the knots with her fingers, and her wrists were becoming so swollen that the bindings were actually becoming tighter.

Frustrated, she yanked again against the bed. "Agghh!!"

To her surprise, that last furious tug against the bars had done something and she craned her neck backward to get a better look at the headboard. It was ancient, yes, but not so different, really, than the one she and Richard had in New York. And the one problem they were always complaining about was that the pieces, the brass tubing and the little brass knobs that held it all together, were always coming loose.

By this time her arms had been tied up and behind her head for hours, and they ached terribly. But she couldn't give up. An idea had begun to formulate and, giving it one last try, she tugged again against the unyielding metal. As she had hoped...prayed they would do, the upright posts to which her ropes were secured moved, almost imperceptibly, but they did move.

Excitement and determination dulled the ache in her tired arms. Carefully, she twisted her right hand so that she was able to grasp the bar itself. Holding it as tightly as she possibly could, she tried to give it a turn. Nothing. She tried again. Still nothing, damn...damn...damn, she thought, wishing she could scream. She tried again, and this time the bar turned slightly.

She managed to force it about a quarter turn then had to stop and readjust her hand on the bar. After she had followed this procedure three or four times she realized that it was becoming quite easy to twist the vertical bar.

She became a fanatic: turn the bar, adjust her hand, turn, adjust, turn, adjust. Soon, she found she was getting nowhere. The bar was now spinning freely but she couldn't pull it out. She stopped and took a deep breath. This has to work, she thought, realizing with some sense of panic that Finch must have been gone for at least fifteen minutes and she probably didn't have much time. With renewed determination she began again turn, adjust, turn, adjust...

Then suddenly with no fanfare, none of the attendant drama that should have accompanied such a momentous occasion, she heard a slight chink...thunk and out from under the bed rolled a tiny brass ball. Oh! God! Thank you! Genie frantically shook the bar with all her strength until quite unexpectedly the bar separated from the bottom crosspiece.

With the bottom loose it was relatively easy to unscrew it from the top member. And there she was, her arm free but still stubbornly tied to the brass bar. It actually took a moment for the muscles in her arm to respond to her command, but when they finally did she reached over clumsily, bar and all, and untied her left hand.

She then untied her right hand and yanked the gag off her face. Mmm" was all that escaped as she massaged aching muscles. There was no time. She reached down and undid both feet, then swung her legs to the side of the bed. Her first attempt to stand proved unsuccessful as wobbly legs collapsed beneath her. She grabbed the bedpost and pulled herself up.

Half expecting Finch to pop up like some demented 'jack in the box', Genie cautiously peeked around the screen. There was no need. The room was still empty and there, piled in the corner, were her clothes. Ignoring bra and pantyhose she grabbed only the essentials, slacks, shirt, shoes, coat and was dressed and out the door in thirty seconds.

He looked at his watch. It had taken more than half an hour to get back to the hotel and retrieve his camera, precious time lost, but no matter he was here now. A few more minutes and the fun would begin. Finch tipped the driver generously. No time to cause a stir from a disgruntled cabby, he thought.

Unprotected from the steady drizzle, Finch tucked the camera under his coat and hurried up the steps to the front door. He stopped for a moment to listen. There was nothing. Only the sound of rain falling into puddles in the street broke the deathly silence of the night. Standing beneath the porch light he fumbled urgently for his key.

Cautiously Genie made her way down a dark staircase to the second floor hallway. One small overhead light bulb dimly lit the empty corridor. Certain that Finch would reappear at every turn, she stealthily crept past two unoccupied rooms to the next flight of stairs. It was all she could do to control her urge to run at breakneck speed through the hallway down the second flight of stairs toward the front door and freedom. But illuminated only by the porch light flooding through stained glass, the next flight was even more dimly lit than the first. As difficult as it was, she proceeded with careful restraint. This was not the time to lose her footing, an all too probable occurrence on the narrow old stairway.

Even taking care, she descended the stairs quickly and within a few seconds had reached the bottom step. Standing there in the absolute stillness she listened.

Nothing...silence. Then, without warning, in the darkness of the first floor parlor... something...movement, a slight noise.

But, no... Whatever she imagined had been a product of this nightmare, it was quiet. Thank God, she sighed, and turned again to the front door and escape.

The instant her hand grasped the knob, the shadow appeared. Finch...a rainbow apparition through the stained glass, stood just on the other side of the door... almost close enough to touch.

Instinctively she jumped back. Her hand recoiled from the knob as if burned by hot coal. In her panic she froze, standing there like stone while merely inches away, he inserted his key into the lock.

Finch could have sworn he heard something, but when he opened the door everything appeared the same. The darkened hallway, the dimly lit staircase, all was as he had left it. He closed the door and proceeded up the stairs to his rooms.

Alex and Inspector Whiting parked in front of Cheshire's. Not much of a lead, it seemed the only place to begin. As he expected, the waitress confirmed Finch's picture, though it took her a moment to imagine him older and with no beard. With Finch's identity established, each man took a copy of the mug shot and began asking everyone in the neighborhood if they had seen either him or Genie.

Alex made the first important discovery when he spoke with the owner of a Greek deli who was able to point them in the right direction. According to the man's wife, they were headed north toward the Thames. They were walking. Alex took one side of the street, Whiting the other, and they knocked on every door .

Unfortunately, other than the first couple, no one remembered a thing. It appeared they had vanished into thin air.

Because he was a professional, and supposedly objective, Whiting had a much more profound understanding of how hopeless their task was becoming. The lateness of the hour and the increasing rain had driven most pedestrians off the streets. Shops and businesses had almost all closed and those that remained open had already been questioned by one of the two men.

Whiting feared the worst. Though he couldn't convince Alex, he didn't see much point in continuing the investigation. Finally he said, "I don't think you should get your hopes up. I know this man. He is vengeful and mean. He thinks he has been crossed…he just won't let go of that."

"What are you saying? Do you really think he has hurt her?"

Alex was angry, frustrated at his inability to find her. "If anything happens to her..." he threatened and hated himself for sounding like a petulant child.

"Look, Doctor, I don't know what he will do. I just know that he...he has his own...p...p...perspective on things. He can be very violent. You should be prepared... That's all I can say, just be prepared."

Alex didn't like the tone of Whiting's implications. "So what do we do now?" He realized their door to door search was getting them nowhere.

"I don't know," admitted Whiting. "Just keep looking, I guess. Here you take this," he gave Alex his whistle, "and continue down in that direction." The Inspector pointed toward the river. "There are several small side streets, alleys really, with rooming houses and a few small inns. Do some looking about and give me a whistle if you find anything. I'm going to make a phone call...I've an idea I want to check out. But remember, give me a shout if you suspect anything... anything at all. I know Finch... B...b...believe me, he is dangerous."

The Inspector headed back up the street. Alex stuck the whistle in his pocket. Standing in the rain, dampness soaking through his corduroy blazer, he could almost feel her presence. She was nearby, he knew it. But where... "Where are you?" he said softly.

Unable to stop shaking, Genie waited in the darkness, crouched behind a chair in the isolated front parlor, until Finch had climbed the first set of stairs and was starting up the second flight to his room.

When she was certain he was out of sight she quietly crept out around the chair and back into the hallway. She looked up terrified she would see him standing on the landing waiting for her to come out from her hiding spot. But he had gone on up to the third floor.

There was no time. She grabbed the doorknob and turned... the door wouldn't budge. She turned it again and pulled. In her haste she had overlooked the small knob that opened the lock. Trembling hands faltered over the lock. "Come on...come on," she mumbled. But her hands were shaking so badly that it took three tries before she succeeded in releasing the latch. As she opened the door there was a thunderous roar from above.

"G...E...N...I...E!" Finch's violent, angry voice screamed her name. She almost stopped, but fear, the adrenalin pumping through her veins, kept her moving. The door flew open in her hands and she was out. Running for all she was worth, she jumped down the three stairs to the sidewalk, slipped on wet pavement, picked herself up, and made an instant decision to dash around to the back of the building.

Hoping to find some safety in the dark shadows behind the row of homes, she splashed through puddles that had collected on the cracked and broken footpath along the side of the old house.

Behind the houses were small plots of ground, some of which had been turned into gardens, and ancient wooden garages, most of them unused. She ducked into one of these decrepit shelters and found a dark corner in which to hide. At least for the moment, at least until she caught her breath.

She cursed the falling rain. Splattering against the tin roofs of the rickety structures it caused a din so loud that it was impossible to hear Finch's approaching footsteps. But for now, it didn't matter. If she couldn't catch her breath she wouldn't be able to go on anyway, she had to take the chance.

Curled into a ball in the corner of the long abandoned structure, hidden behind the rusted hulk of an unidentifiable automobile, her eyes darted around the area for any sign of her pursuer.

She realized with dismay that if he did find her here, there was no way out; she would be trapped.

After some moments the rain began to abate, then thankfully came to a stop. A heavy mist still hung in the air, forming halos around the few street lamps she could see from her cramped sanctuary.

She was contemplating the wisdom of a quick exit when quite surprisingly, directly behind, on the other side of the garage wall, she heard his footsteps. Nearly silent, catlike creeping came closer and closer to the door. There was nothing she could do. He was too close, the walls were too thin.

If she moved even a muscle he would hear her. Praying that he would pass her by, she huddled tightly into the shadowed corner.

It was no surprise when he came around to the front of the garage, Genie had predicted his appearance by the way the fog swirled before him. Still it was a shock to actually see him there, silhouetted against the street lamp. He appeared to be looking directly into her eyes. She held her breath, convinced she would be betrayed by the sound of her own heartbeat.

When Finch had approached his room earlier, he had known before he entered that she was gone. He didn't need the physical evidence; the open door, the missing clothes, to perceive the awful truth. He could sense it. Almost before he reached the top of the stairs he could feel the emptiness. It struck him like an icy knife, slicing into his chest. How long had she been gone?

After his initial, almost involuntary reaction to her betrayal, he was actually paralyzed by rage, unable to move...... until he heard the front door open and knew...he would catch her.

Chasing her through the rain, he was surprised at how quickly she could run. But though he lost sight of her after she rounded the side of the building, he could clearly hear her footsteps as they splashed against the wet ground.

By the time he reached the back of the buildings himself, there was silence. He too remained still, looking, listening. She had holed up somewhere... but she was close...he could feel her.

Genie's choices were severely limited and she had to make a decision quickly. To remain hidden and pray he wouldn't find her, or to make a surprise dash, blowing right by him and hope she could outrace the bastard back to the main street. She almost opted for the foot race, not because she actually believed she could win, but because she could no longer stand being trapped like a helpless animal. If he was going to get her she wouldn't make it easy.

Unknowingly, Finch made the decision for her. Though he was only a few yards away from her and looked directly at her, shadow and light played their own games. He didn't see her. After what seemed like an eternity Finch moved on, ever so cautiously, to explore the remaining empty sheds.

Genie waited a few more moments until she could stand it no longer. Slowly she stood on cramped legs. "Here we go," she whispered to no one in particular and inched her way out of her hiding place.

It was difficult to see through the mist. She was disoriented and realized that even if she did make a break for the street she couldn't be certain which way to run. There would be no second chance. She had to think.

Still hidden in the shadows she looked around and saw no signs of Finch, though she was almost certain she could hear light footsteps coming from the right. Ahead of her and to the left the sound of a ship's horn caught her ear. The river...that was it, not perfect, but her best option.

There were several streets...there must be someone, she thought...between her and Battersea bridge a few blocks away. If there was any help to be found, it would be there. She broke from her cover and sprinted across the back alley toward safety.

Where is she, Finch fumed silently, she couldn't have gone far. Having quietly searched through all the old garages behind the row houses on his block and for two adjacent blocks, he found no sign of her. Certain he must have missed something, Finch furtively retraced his steps, moving back in the direction from which he came, and though he didn't know it heading directly back toward Genie.

Shortly, he found himself back where he had started. Standing directly under his third floor bedroom window, he once again heard her footsteps. She was close...did she know how close...he smiled. Finch listened for a moment longer to be sure, but easily guessed what she was thinking, where she was going...it wouldn't do her any good. No longer concerned with quiet pursuit he took off after her at full speed.

Chapter 42

Alex stood alone in the middle of the dark quiet, rain soaked street. He had spent precious time diligently knocking on doors, up one side of the street and down the other until there was no one else to question. At a loss as to his next move, he looked about for Whiting, but the inspector was nowhere to be seen.

It was no good. He had to admit he wouldn't find Genie this way. The only thing he could think to do now was phone Molly. It was a desperately weak plan of attack but he simply didn't know where else to turn. Maybe she has heard from her, he thought, though he didn't really believe it. So, with no other ideas coming to mind he reluctantly walked back toward Cheshire's.

The sound of his own footsteps rang through the mist. He was moving too slowly, he realized, almost sluggishly, he quickened his pace.

When Alex first heard the other racing steps he thought them a quirk of heavily humid atmospheric conditions. He thought them an echo of his own scurrying steps.

Instinctively he stopped. He looked around, but could see nothing ...no movement at all. Then in the distance, to his right... to his left, he couldn't be sure, the steps continued. His heart quickened...Genie.

Trying to guess direction, Alex listened a moment longer and to his surprise heard a second, heavier, set of steps running, quickly, steadily following the same path as the first.

Within seconds he realized what was happening and calling,

Genie's name as loudly as he could, took off in pursuit of the echoes.

It was becoming more and more difficult to catch her breath. She had been running as hard and fast as she could for several minutes now, but there seemed to be no help anywhere. And Finch was gaining on her. As the steady drumbeat of his footsteps became steadily louder, it was obvious he closing the distance between them.

Ahead she saw lights. Please, she begged, give me the strength to reach them. Please, she thought again, let there be someone... anyone... Genie kept going, but she was slowing down.

Suddenly she could see, only a few yards in the distance, the corners of Hester and Battersea roads and knew she was nearing the busy bridge over the Thames.

But when she rounded the last corner reaching the intersection only minutes before Finch, her heart sank. It was deserted. Neither a car nor pedestrian in sight. The only activity at all seemed to be across the bridge on the other side of the river. Too far she sighed trying to catch her breath.

From the sound of his steps she realized Finch would be upon her at any moment and frantically began banging on closed shop doors. It was useless, no one answered. The store fronts were barred or chained so she couldn't even break in and hide.

Playing for time, she ducked into a small space between two buildings. Not even wide enough for a proper footpath, she knew she couldn't remain there for long. If Finch noticed her she couldn't possibly get away, but she just had to rest and this small shadowed alley was the only place available.

Less than a minute later Finch appeared at the intersection. He didn't see her hidden in the shadows, though she had a clear view of him and of his silver blade as it glistened under the street lamp.

g...e...n...i...e...

From somewhere in the distance Genie thought she heard her name. Oh Lord, I am going crazy, she thought.

g...e...n...i...e...

But...no...she heard it again. She was certain of it this time. It was Alex. He was near.

Taking a deep breath she opened her mouth, ready to scream for all she was worth...then stopped. Finch...He was only twenty feet away. If she screamed now she would be dead before Alex could do anything to help her.

Finch heard the call too, but only laughed confident that he would find his prey long before the doctor could do a thing.

"I know you are here," he called. "You might as well come out. Your boyfriend won't be able to help you now." Finch looked around, eyeing the dark corners, trying to decide into which crack his prey had secreted herself.

She didn't move a muscle. Please Alex, she prayed, I'm here. Please come this way.

Alex called her name as he ran in the direction of the elusive footsteps, there was no answer, but he kept going. She was out there and he had to reach her...before...

Then, unexpectedly, the drum beat stopped...there was nothing. Alex called her name again, still no response. A wave of nausea swept through him, slowed him for only an instant, then he raced even more quickly in the direction of the now silent footsteps.

Finch was directly across the street peering into alleys, behind parked cars, into stairwells...looking.

Genie knew it would not be long before he found her. Her only hope she realized, was to try to dash across the bridge to the other side where she could see an open restaurant and people milling about. But could she out run this mad man? It was at least a quarter mile down the street and across the concrete and steel span. Not that far, but her legs...they felt like rubber. And if she did manage to reach the other side? Would he then catch her...kill her anyway...Even in front of witnesses.

Finch was crossing the street.

No more time to think...just go.

Genie crouched down and crept out behind a large black Daimler parked along the sidewalk a few feet away. She stayed as low as she could and made her way behind other parked vehicles inching closer and closer to the bridge......where, to her dismay, she could see there would be no cover at all.

Finch heard something and stopped in the middle of the empty street. "Genie? You might as well come out. Come on we'll just talk. You know...I've been thinking about what you said," he shouted into the night air, "You are right, I should take the money the General owes me and disappear. What do you think?"

She wasn't fooled. Staying as low as possible she snuck quietly, closer to the bridge.

"Genie" This time his voice was soft. So soft she could barely hear it, but when she did it was right behind her.

Slowly she looked over her shoulder. Finch stood not ten feet behind her, smiling, holding his knife in front of him like an offering.

He took a step closer and she bolted. Running as swiftly as she could on weary legs she was across the street in seconds. She could hear him panting behind her and with every step the sound of his breathing drew closer.

One third of the way across the bridge Genie thought she might actually make it.

…"NO!"… His hand landed heavily upon her shoulder, grabbing her and pulling them together…crashing to a halt.

"NO," she cried again as he grasped her firmly around the waist.

The scuffle on the bridge caught the attention of passersby at the far end, but from that distance it looked, for the entire world like a lovers' quarrel. No one paid much attention to the encounter.

"I think you ought to come with me," he said forcefully holding the razor like blade precariously close to her face.

Genie knew that if she yelled now she would be cut off mid scream. She forced herself to calm down and pretend to go along with his plan. As long as she was alive there was a chance…Please God, she whispered……help.

"What's that?," he asked sarcastically, "Praying for help are we…well I am afraid it won't…"

"FINCH!"

Finch, startled by the sound of his name, took his eyes off his captive to look back toward the dark streets.

"Templeton," he smirked, not surprised by the sight of the doctor blocking his way. "I can't say I haven't expected you to turn up. Though I don't know exactly what you hope to accomplish."

"Let her go Finch…it's over. You know that."

"No it isn't over doctor. This beautiful bitch here cost me too much to let it go now. She has to pay, surely you realize that."

"Look, you can have your money. You know the General will give it to you," Alex walked slowly toward Genie and Finch as he spoke.

"It is more than the money now Doc…Surely you understand that. I loved her and she betrayed me…she ran from me."

Alex could see he was deluded. He no longer tried to approach Finch rationally. "Then let her go," he pleaded, "She's not worth it. Let her go, get your money and disappear. Start over again…"

"Hold it," Finch screamed, "Don't come any closer or I'll slice her throat." He moved the knife in a threatening gesture that caused Alex to stop dead in his tracks.

"No," Alex shouted, "Don't. Think about it, if you kill her here. That's it. You will be caught…everything for you, will be over."

Finch did think about it but his response was not what Alex had hoped for. "You are right about one thing doctor. It wouldn't be any fun to kill her here…no fun at all." He grabbed her arm and forced her ahead of him. "Come on…you and I are going for a little walk.…Back up doctor, unless you want to see her blood running all over the tarmac."

She was terrified. She realized once they were off the bridge, out of plain sight anything could happen. She made up her mind.

When they were as close to Alex as they were going to get in their exit from the bridge, Genie took a chance and kicked back as hard as she could and caught Finch in the shin just below the right knee. It wasn't the part of his anatomy she had been hoping for, but it proved good enough.

In astonishment and anger he threw her harshly against a concrete abutment giving Alex one fleeting opportunity for attack.

It took Alex completely by surprise when Genie kicked out against Finch. One moment the knife was dangerously close to piercing an artery, the next Finch had flung her against the rail. Alex used Genie's quick thinking to its full advantage.

With Genie out of Finch's arms Alex instinctively rushed against the armed assailant. He hardly noticed the glint of silver as it sliced through the air and ripped into the shoulder of his jacket.

The knife caught nothing but thick corduroy, Finch pulled back and attempted another slash...this time the target was Alex's throat.

Alex felt the sting just under his ear, a nick, a warning. He had to dislodge the knife.

Finch could not believe the turn of events. He had let nothing unsettle him. Even the arrival of the eminent doctor could be dealt with. He just had to get himself and Genie off the bridge and he would take care of both of them. But when she kicked him, hard, with the heel of her shoe a searing pain shot through his leg surprising him and knocking him off balance.

His mistake had been one of emotion. Throwing her off him, throwing her into the concrete rail had been stupid. He had let go of his cover, tossed away his bargaining chip and given that stupid doctor the opening he needed. Now he was fighting for his very existence and for one of the few times in his life not certain how it would turn out.

In a fit of rage, Finch lifted his silver blade high above his head and prepared to strike.

In a futile attempt to cushion the coming blow, Genie held both arms out in front of her body. As she smashed against the concrete and stone wall, she heard a sickening crack and watched in shock as her arm bent slightly at a peculiar angle. She sank to the pavement cradling the broken limb and fighting to ward off nausea that threatened to drag her into unconsciousness.

Before her, Alex and Finch wrestled on the ground, stood, attacked and wrestled again. She couldn't tell who had the upper hand and she could do nothing to help. What frightened her most was the blood she noticed pouring from a cut on Alex's neck. To her, it looked more than superficial, but she took heart in the fact that it hadn't seemed to hamper his ability to defend himself.

She tried to stand, but couldn't. Not only couldn't she help, she couldn't even escape. It was all up to Alex now, and for some reason she felt comforted and assured by that fact.

After struggling for a few minutes both men found themselves grappling with each other dangerously close to the railing. Alex could feel sharp edged concrete dig into his back as Finch pushed him farther and farther over the edge.

Close to losing his balance, he heard shouting from people running in the direction of the melee. He wondered if anyone would get there before he went careening into the river.

As he raised his knife one last time, Finch knew he had the upper hand. He would slash this man to pieces, grab the woman and end it all. The knife was poised, ready for the end when he heard the nearing of the intruders. Damn, would he never have his revenge?

Looking up from the bug he had pinned beneath him he saw two men hurrying to interfere. He realized there was no time to complete his task and only one way to escape.

Suddenly Alex felt himself being pulled from the rail to a standing position. Finch, now himself against the rail, was holding him as a shield against two officers he could see rushing toward them.

His adrenalin pumping, Alex did not let Finch have his way and though he had already been struck twice by the deadly blade that now hung above his head, he continued his struggle to subdue the frenzied attacker.

Without warning, in the midst of their ongoing tussle a shot rang out cracking through the misty night with the same surprise as a clap of winter thunder.

His face frozen in shock, Finch was knocked backward with unexpected force and before Alex could grab him he pitched headlong into the black swirling waters below.

A soft, almost imperceptible splash made by his body as it hit the river was an ironically silent ending to the bloody battle and violent events that had just taken place.

Inspector Whiting followed his two officers onto the bridge. Upon seeing the blood on Templeton's face as he bent over an obviously distraught Genie Lawrence, he sent one officer to call for an ambulance while the other searched the river for signs of Finch's body.

"Dr. Templeton."

"Yes," said Alex distractedly as he tried to comfort Genie. "What is it?"

"Can I be of any assistance?"

"No Inspector. I think you have helped quite enough thank you. Can I assume that it was your bullet that dispatched Mr. Finch?"

"But you know we don't carry weapons Doctor," he responded sarcastically. "Let's just say I was doing my job. As I saw it, he had the advantage. As I saw it, you were about to go into the drink yourself."

"And it certainly doesn't hurt your position that he won't be around to be prosecuted...does it Inspector." Alex's tone was unmistakable.

"I was just doing my job Doctor," said the Inspector again, and then joined his officer in the search beneath the bridge.

Alex knelt beside Genie and tried to make her as comfortable as possible until the ambulance arrived.

He had checked her over as best he could under the circumstances and other than the broken arm she seemed to be unharmed. In the few minutes they had to themselves Genie had managed to tell him most of what had happened that day. Alex was astonished ...she appeared to be dealing with everything quite calmly. Perhaps, in a few days she might benefit from speaking to one of the hospital counselors, but for now she was holding up quite well.

"Thank God you are alright," he said holding her close. "Well almost alright," he added gently supporting her damaged arm. "Gen, I don't know what I would have done if anything had happened to you," he said tenderly. Damn it, he at last, admitted to himself, I love her.

Genie looked into his soft hazel eyes and saw love. It warmed and comforted her, and somehow eased the physical pain of her badly broken arm. "Alex, I wouldn't be here if you hadn't found me. That man, that horrid man, he wouldn't let go. The harder I tried to escape the more he chased me down. He was crazy, he really was..." She couldn't stop the tears from rolling down her cheeks. "Thank you Alex," she said softly, and though she couldn't say it just yet, in her heart she knew she loved him.

Chapter 43

It was early but Genie couldn't sleep. She pulled the cool crisp sheets of her hospital bed snugly up around her neck. Not even the awkward cast on her left arm could dampen her spirits. She felt more comfortable, more secure...more loved than she had in a very long time. It was finally over and she was ready... no anxious... to get on with her life.

The door opened quietly and Alex peeked in. "Hi there," he said almost whispering. "I can't believe you are awake." He walked over and, handing her a bouquet of freshly cut daisies, sat gingerly on the edge of the bed. "How are you feeling?"

"Achy, still a bit dazed, but so, so relieved," she replied brightly. "All in all I am really quite good. And how are you?" Though partially hidden by the collar of his lab coat, she couldn't miss the large bandage on his neck.

"I'm good," he said touching his neck. "This is really nothing."

She was skeptical, but didn't pursue it. "You are certainly early."

"Rounds...and flowers," he added sheepishly.

"I think I'll actually be getting out of here later today," she added.

"That is terrific." His arms tenderly encircled her shoulder and he gave the top of her head a gentle kiss.

"You know," she said. "Being forced to lay here like this has really given me time to think......to put everything into perspective, and the only conclusion I can come to is that I'm finally ready." As much as she tried, she couldn't help the sly smile that crept across her face.

"Ready?" he replied hopefully.

"Yes... ready. I loved Richard very much, you know that, but now that everything is resolved. Now that Finch is gone, now that we know what happened, why Richard was murdered, I can begin to accept him as part of my past. Put him into a nice warm place in my heart, in my memory where he won't be forgotten, but where he won't prevent me from moving on either." She reached out and took hold of Alex's bruised hands, "I know that some people will think I'm crazy or maybe even cold hearted, but I can't let them live my life. After...everything...well... I am an entirely different person than I was just a few weeks ago. And for this Genie Lawrence...it's time," she said gently, "time to begin again."

Alex's arms were around Genie when they were interrupted by a, not entirely unexpected, visitor. Dr. Steven Maxwell, Alex's friend and colleague, had come to give Genie a final check up before her official release.

"Well Steve," Alex asked anxiously, "how is our patient?'

"I would say that she is almost perfect. In fact if you will get your amorous old body out of here I will be able to give her, her walking papers."

"Consider me gone," he said blowing a kiss to Genie. "I'll pick you up later. Noon OK?"

She looked at Steve Maxwell who nodded in approval. "Perfect," she said. "Now get out of here and let the doctor do his job."

Steve checked Genie's pulse, pressure, heart and lungs, all the usual things, and pronounced her fit to travel.

"Do you have any complaints?" he asked. "Is the cast giving you trouble?" he inquired, checking the plaster monster that extended from just below her left elbow to the back and palm of her left hand.

"No," said Genie. "I'm great, a little tired, achy and a bit nauseous from the cracked rib, but all things considered I'm surprisingly OK."

"I think you are too," Steve agreed. "I am not surprised that you are feeling run down. Alex told me about all you have been through. But just to be on the safe side, I'll run a standard panel. I'll send a technician around to take a little blood. You should still be out of here by the time Alex gets back. All I can recommend after that is a quiet afternoon and good night's sleep."

Alex pushed open the door to Genie's room and was startled to see her bed empty. Probably in the day room he thought and walked down the hall toward the waiting area. But she was nowhere to be found. Looking around he saw Steve coming out of a nearby room.

"Steve," he called, "Have you seen Genie?"

"Alex, hello" the doctor replied. "Hey old man I thought you knew. She checked herself out of here awhile ago Molly Sims collected her at about nine."

"No, I had no idea. I guess we've gotten our signals crossed."

"Listen, if you have a minute I would like to talk to you. How about a cup of tea before you leave......my treat," said Steve directing Alex toward the waiting area?

Fifteen minutes later Alex raced out of the hospital and jumped into his car. "Oh Genie," he mumbled as he started the engine. He knew exactly where to find her.

Chapter 44

"Are you certain?" asked Aunt Sarah. The two women were sitting at the kitchen table in Sarah's cozy cottage, thick stone walls shielding them from the heat of the midsummer afternoon.

"Yes," replied Genie. "I found out this morning. That's why I had to come to see you. I didn't mean to just dump myself on you like this, but you are Richard's only relative......and he loved you very much. And Sarah," she said softly, "Your opinion means a great deal."

"Well, my dear I am very glad that you came to me. I want you to feel free to stay here for as long as you like. I rather enjoy your company you know." She patted Genie's hand and then gave her a little wink.

"I expect you could use something cool." Sarah said and began to putter around the kitchen.

Pans clattered, china rattled and drawers squeaked as Sarah prepared an elaborate citrus concoction she called lemonade, but which was in fact more a multi-fruitade.

Genie chuckled at the production. Sarah loved fussing over her and she had to admit that it felt wonderful to be pampered.

"Have you said anything to that young man of yours?"

"Alex," Genie replied surprised. "No I haven't, not yet. I wanted to talk to you first. And, by the way, what makes you think of him as my young man," she smiled.

"Oh, I saw the way he looked at you when you two were here together. I had a feeling that he would give you the time you needed to come to terms with our poor Richard's death, and then well…But of course, my dear! I had no idea at the time the utter madness that was going on. My goodness," Sarah handed Genie a tall frosty glass, "I should have realized that night when your room was turned topsy turvy…well that just isn't ordinary behavior is it."

Genie walked over to the window and looked wistfully into the lovely little garden.

"None of us had any idea at that time what was going on and I was so hurt and so determined to find the answers…for Richard that I wasn't ready to accept Alex's attention as anything more than friendship."

"And now," asked Sarah.

"I thought I was, at least until this morning. Oh Sarah, what a mess, I am so confused."

"I know you are my dear," Sarah put her arm comfortingly around Genie's waist, "but I truly believe that once you discuss this with Alex, once you trust him enough to confide in him, everything will work out swimmingly."

"You honestly believe that?"

"I think you can count on it."

"Sarah you are wonderful, you always know just what to say." Genie turned and gave the older woman a big hug.

"Now luv," said Sarah as she bustled about the kitchen. "I must dash. I hate to, but I have an appointment in Exeter that I just can't put off. Will you be alright alone for a couple of hours?"

"Of course, Sarah, don't think a thing about it. After all I am the one who barged in on you," Genie chided.

"Well then just make yourself at home and I will be back as soon as I can."

Sarah picked up her gigantic black purse and scurried out the back door only to return ten seconds later to deposit the bright orange apron she had almost worn into town. "Well ta ta again," she said in a fluster as she rushed toward the car.

Pouring another glass of 'lemonade', Genie went out to the garden and sat in a patch of sunlight by Sarah's small man-made fish pond. Gold, black and white mottled coi glistened in the sunlight and splashed the water uproariously when she tossed in crumbs of bread. This is the life she thought as she lay back lazily on a soft carpet of grass.

"Ugh, maybe this isn't the life after all," she mumbled to herself. After a few minutes she had become decidedly uncomfortable. The afternoon heat seemed to smother her, her cast was beginning to itch and small unnamed creatures were crawling over her toes. "Yuk!" she exclaimed as she stood and with her one good arm vigorously brushed off her clothes.

Back in the confines of the cool cottage Sarah's couch looked soft and inviting. Genie kicked off her shoes and snuggled into the feather cushions. She propped her heavy, cast laden arm on a pillow and quickly fell into a light sleep.

"g e n i e"

......The voice came softly through her dreams wiping away any hope of sweet delirium. That voice, that nightmarish voice, would it plague her life forever.

"g e n i e"

...There it was again. Slowly her eyes opened...... She could not comprehend what she was seeing. Standing above her wielding a razor like blade was a viciously glaring Finch.

Her heart was pounding, her mind raced. A dream, she thought, it must be a dream...he is dead. "But...You're dead," she hoarsely whispered as the knife sliced through the air toward her face. Instinctively she raised her arm in protection; the blade glanced off the cast slicing a chunk of plaster so violently that it flew across the room.

Finch raised his arm again, preparing for a second thrust, when another voice interrupted.

"F I N C H… DROP IT." The voice shouted in anger.

Finch turned and grabbing a confused Genie with vice like control, faced Inspector Whiting. The Inspector stood, gun in hand, blocking the doorway.

"It's done," he said. "Let her go."

"Like hell it is, you foolish prig." Finch now had Genie firmly in his control. The knife was pressed expertly against her throat and had already caused a slight scratch. A drop of blood spilled onto Genie's collar causing a small red stain.

"Let us through that door or I'll kill her now, right here where we stand." Finch threatened.

Genie was terrified. She tried desperately not to move though she was sure he could feel her trembling.

"Don't you realize that we've failed, that it's over?" Whiting implored.

"It isn't over for me… not yet." Finch slowly dragged Genie toward the door.

"No, I guess it's not," said Whiting, his voice was sad…resigned. "I had hoped that night on the bridge, that there was an end to it but, when you stumbled wet and bleeding into my flat I knew I was wrong, dead wrong you might say. I wish I had killed you on the bridge…or sooner," he sighed. "It was my fault. I should have been stronger. I shouldn't have given in to your threats, the blackmail."

"We all have our little weaknesses, don't we Inspector," Finch remarked sarcastically.

"I should have understood, "Whiting continued without regard to Finch's remarks, "When exactly was it that the plan died for you, that the mission was no longer important...no longer driving you. When did she become your obsession?"

For a few moments there was complete silence as the two men faced each other for the final time. "I suspect," Whiting continued, "it happened long before your chum Walker......"

At the mention of the General, Finch's demeanor subtly changed. He pulled Genie slightly closer, held her a bit more firmly. Whiting immediately stopped his questioning. "I can't let you do this Finch, you know it. I can't let you kill her."

Finch and Genie were now quite close to the door. The two men stood only three feet apart glaring into each other's eyes.

"Unless you want her blood on your hands you'll back away from the door." Finch's voice was icy cold, emotionless.

All along, Whiting had known that someday it would come to this. When he harbored Finch after the incident on the bridge, he knew how it would have to end. Yet even after everything he had done Whiting still thought of himself as a policeman, an inspector......an officer of the law, and he was having a great deal of difficulty with the idea of simply raising his gun and killing Finch where he stood...killing him in cold blood.

No, he thought, he would not succumb to Finch again. As he stood there looking into Finch's fierce bloodshot eyes he was sure he could see the devil himself. Ultimately, he had no choice. The man was as purely evil as anyone he had ever known. He resolved then that he must shoot him like he would any mad dog.

Whiting looked at Genie, almost as if asking her permission and with resigned determination began to pull the trigger.

Finch stiffened. He knew Whiting had reached his limit and he was ready for the end. He didn't even mind dying. For his last act, his final curtain he would kill the bitch...and he would die fulfilled, that was all that really mattered.

Genie felt the cold steel of the blade pressing harder against her throat. Tears streamed down her cheeks as Whiting looked into her eyes.

Then...quite suddenly...the blade was gone. During that fleeting second, that momentary instant Whiting had allowed himself to glance at Genie, Finch, with the speed of a snake, struck him down.

As Whiting looked into Genie's pleading eyes, Finch sliced like a surgeon at the hand that held the gun. He struck Whiting's wrist, almost completely severing it from his arm.

Blood shot across the short distance between the two men heavily splattering both Finch and Genie. Whiting gasped in surprise and pain. The gun dropped from his ruined hand and he bent to cradle his agonizing wound.

When Whiting instinctively crouched down in front of him, Finch struck the final, fatal blow. He brought the knife blade down hard against the back of Whiting's neck and with his expertise as an assassin sliced from side to side, killing him instantly.

During Whiting's brief final moments of conscious thought he realized with pride that he hadn't been afraid, he hadn't stuttered at all.

Genie heard someone scream in horror as she wrenched herself free from Finch's grip. Who was that she thought, as she clumsily tried to back away from the bloody scene. She couldn't yet comprehend that it was her own voice she had heard crying out.

Finch looked up from the heap on the floor and saw Genie awkwardly backing away across the room. He smiled ever so slightly and slowly, deliberately began to stalk his prey.

The cast, which had earlier been Genie's salvation suddenly, became a terrible hindrance. It threw her slightly off balance and in her panic to get away caused her to stumble into a small table. In a useless attempt to slow her attacker, she kicked the table so that it lay between her and Finch.

Finch moved slowly closer. He was in no hurry and actually enjoyed toying with the terrified woman.

Neither Finch nor Genie realized that beneath her terror lay a spark of anger that was beginning to find its way to the surface. "How dare you...," she mumbled inaudibly. "How dare you do this to me," she finally screamed as she grabbed for a brass floor lamp and awkwardly pushed so it fell toward him. Continuing her awkward retreat around the room, her thoughts focused on the possibility of reaching the kitchen and trying to escape through the back door. She felt certain that, even with the heavy cast, she could out distance him. At least for a little while......at least it was a chance.

Finch sensed her plan and immediately stalked her from the opposite direction. He effectively blocked her only exit to freedom. "A futile effort...did you really think you could escape me this time?"

Genie was trapped. Her back was pressed up against the fireplace; the hearthstones were cold against her bare feet. "You bastard...," she yelled as her hand reached up to the mantle. With tears beginning to cloud her eyes Genie tossed two brass candle sticks, a porcelain figurine and a small copper tea kettle as hard as she could at the advancing menace.

Finch could reach Genie easily from where he stood, but instead slashed the knife almost playfully in front of her face. She instinctively pulled back bumping her head hard against the edge of the mantle. Genie knew that the next time Finch struck out, the blade would not miss. Her breath was coming in short gasps. She saw him raise his arm; saw the unmistakable look in his eyes and tried one last time to get away. Summoning all her nerve she ducked under the swinging arm and attempted to jump over the only piece of furniture blocking her way to the front door, Sarah's couch. Adrenalin gave her the edge she needed and she awkwardly cleared the small couch .

For one brief moment Genie thought she had made it, but as she touched down on the other side, her foot caught, and she fell heavily face down on top of the Inspector's inert body.

A loud "Ugh!" escaped her lips as she fell. For a moment, she didn't move. She could feel Finch standing over her.........and she remembered. Where is it? she thought, wildly searching around Whiting's body.

Finch ignored her apparent struggle. Lost in visions of slicing her pretty throat, he leaned forward and grabbed a handful of red curls twisting them through his fingers.

Just as Genie felt her head being yanked back, her hand touched it. She grasped in desperation at the cold steel object.

Tears stung her eyes as she was roughly turned onto her back. The knife blade caught, in the late afternoon sunlight, glowed like fire over her head. In the same second that Finch readied to kill his prey, Genie raised her hand and, with Whiting's gun, fired blindly into the shadowy figure towering above...

Alex pulled into Sarah's driveway and was relieved to see Molly's borrowed car parked in front of the cottage. After his discussion with Steve this morning, he was certain he would find Genie here. Thank God he had guessed correctly, he needed to see her, to talk to her, to convince her that he would always love her...no matter what.

Walking toward the front of the house Alex noticed two other vehicles parked nearby. He recognized Whiting's car at once, but the other? Something wasn't right. There was no reason for Whiting to be here.

As he neared the ominously silent cottage, he saw the door ajar. An odd foreboding and something he could only describe as instinct warned him to approach the door with caution.

The sight that assailed his eyes, as they adjusted to the dim interior of Sarah's home, was so horrifying that he involuntarily stepped backward, back out into the daylight, into reality. To alleviate mounting nausea he took two deep breaths. Quickly, he forced himself back into the cottage. There was blood everywhere. Furniture was strewn about like so many match sticks, and there directly in front of him were three bodies.

His stomach knotted when he recognized Finch.

"Gen…Genie," he called frantically. "Please let her be alright… Genie?" Alex was desperately afraid as he climbed over Finch to get to her.

Crouched in a fetal position between the couch and the mutilated body of Inspector Whiting, his gun was still in her hand.

"Gen," he whispered. There was absolutely no movement. "Oh my God Genie please," he said softly. He grabbed her hand. She was as cold as ice……but she was alive.

Alex carefully lifted her head and looked into her eyes. There was nothing, no sign of recognition, no fear, and no emotion at all. He sat there for a few moments quietly holding her, smoothing her hair, soothing her. After a short while, he just wanted to get her out of there, to get out of there himself. He firmly lifted her into his arms and carried her out into the warm afternoon sun.

"Alex," she said suddenly, as he carried her from the house. He looked into her eyes again and this time saw tears. He breathed a sigh of relief and hugged her tightly, praying that she would be alright.

It was only a few minutes later when the old Daimler rumbled slowly up the drive. Sarah was pleased to see Alex with Genie sitting on a bench in the front yard. Just the tonic that girl needs, she thought.

She had barely gotten out of the car when Alex came rushing toward her.

"Hello dear boy," she began in her usual chipper manner, then quickly noticed his distress. "My goodness Alex what is it? You look white as Marley's ghost."

"Sarah, I am so glad you are home. I am afraid there has been… trouble. I need to take Genie into town…a clinic…any place where I can give her a thorough check-up." He realized he was rambling. "And we must get in touch with the authorities."

"Alex, calm down. Authorities? What, what is going on? Has she been hurt…what is it?" Sarah was totally bewildered.

"I'm sorry Sarah I know you are confused believe me, so am I, but if you will just take us into town I will explain as much as I know on the way."

"Of course…of course. We'll take her straightway to my friend Dora's. She is the local vet. Don't worry. She knows more about fixing people than anyone else around here. You two will know what to do." Sarah patted Alex's hand. "I'll just go fetch a sweater for her I wouldn't want her to catch a chill." Sarah began to walk toward the house, Alex caught her arm.

"Sarah stop. Don't go in there."

"Oh?" She was stunned.

"Please don't go into the house." Alex was adamant.

"For heaven's sake why not?"

"Trust me you don't want to go in there, not now."

"Alright Alex," Sarah said calmly. "Let's take her into town.

Chapter 45

Channing House   December, 1990

Soft glowing candle light created the illusion...the long winding staircase appeared to go on forever. Seated on a riser, just one step above a landing, halfway up the wide staircase, Genie hovered above the milling guests, quietly surveying the scene below. Content, for the moment, to be alone with her thoughts she watched clandestinely while friends and family joyfully shared eggnog and Christmas cheer. Shifting awkwardly on her lofty perch she gazed down at her ever expanding girth and smiled radiantly. With gentle hands she unconsciously soothed the restless child within. Once again, she offered up a silent prayer that she... that they...were both still alive.

It was difficult for her to believe that six months after that impossible, horrible summer she was still here, in England, difficult for her to comprehend that the nightmare had finally begun to fade. The pain of that final fateful day in July had begun to ease and she could put into perspective the irony of the miracle with which the day had begun.....................

......for Richard's baby was truly a miracle. Though, when she first heard the news she was, to put it mildly...ambivalent.

She remembered Steve Maxwell's words exactly. He returned to her hospital room that summer morning with the results of her final blood test. "It looks like you and Alex are about to be parents," he announced with glee...not realizing how wrong he was.

"Excuse me," Genie said stunned, "What did you say?"

"I said," he continued smiling like the cat who caught the canary, "You are pregnant...just a few weeks but it is definite"

Genie had been so astonished that she could only manage to think. She certainly wasn't prepared to explain to him the numerous reasons why Alex could not possibly be the father, not the least of which was that, although they had become very close, they were not 'that' together.

She just said, "thank you," as politely as she could without appearing completely incoherent and hoped he would soon leave. She needed to be alone.

Fortunately, he took the hint and didn't pursue the point.

"Now what?" she sighed when he left the room, "Now what am I going to do?"

Just when Genie had made up her mind about Alex, just when she thought she had a handle on her future...this. Richard's baby. She didn't know whether to laugh or cry. And she had no idea how Alex would take the news, or if she would even tell him.

In only a short while Genie realized she did know one person who could help. She knew one person who would be thrilled.

Going to Dartmoor...visiting Aunt Sarah had been exactly the right decision. At least it began that way.

Perched safely on the steps at Channing House, amid the warmly festive Christmas atmosphere, Genie shuddered involuntarily as she remembered the events of that day...

The image of Finch leering above her with that wicked smile, wielding his silver blade... When she first opened her eyes she thought him an apparition, her own, delirious invention. Still, she reacted to the sight instinctively shielding herself behind plaster armor.

She only vaguely remembered the scene that followed. Impressions, fleeting images of Whiting, the knife, blood...there was blood everywhere. The counselor she had been seeing told her it was quite possible she would never fully recall all the events of that afternoon. She considered that a blessing.

The one thing she clearly remembered, though, the one event she would never forget was shooting Finch. That last final, desperate act to save her life, to save the life of her unborn child would live with her always. She sometimes wondered if, after all she had gone through, she would have fought so hard had she not also been protecting the life of her baby.

Thinking back to that day and the bizarre kaleidoscopic images that flashed through her mind, it continued to amaze her that she had no recollection of Alex's arrival.

Later, when they had time to talk he told her that he was only there because Steve, thinking him the father of the baby, had inadvertently congratulated him on the news. So much for breaking it to him gently.

Fortunately, he put two and two together and guessed where she had gone.

Genie had absolutely no memory of him finding her in the cottage.

She did have one fleeting impression of being carried in his arms and an overwhelming sensation of relief and abiding comfort. But that might have been much later when they and Aunt Sarah had settled into the Grange.

And did she actually remember, or had she been told, that from the moment he found her Alex refused to leave her side... remaining awake all night while she slept fitfully in his arms.

All that had been months ago, and though it had taken her some time to let go of the fear, to feel secure enough to be left alone she and Alex had finally gotten on with their lives. She and Alex had finally become lovers.

Now that she remembered...

......One evening in late August Genie was, for the first time, alone at Channing House. It was an unusual event. Generally someone in the family tried to stay at home and keep her company. After considerable discussion she was finally able to convince them that she was perfectly capable of staying by herself. It was a test really; she wanted to prove to them, to herself, that she could do it, that she no longer needed a baby sitter.

To her surprise she found she didn't mind being alone at all. She actually relished it and decided to take full advantage of the opportunity. She would read a book, take a bubble bath, take a nap...whatever she wished she could do with no interruptions...or so she thought.

Wrapped in a lush raspberry terry-cloth bathrobe, she had just stepped out of warm bubbles when there was a soft knock on the door. After nearly jumping out of her skin, "just stop this," she scolded herself. "Who is it?" Tying the long belt in a loose loop around her waist she answered the door.

"Alex, may I come in."

"Alex?" she was genuinely surprised, "I thought were staying in town tonight."

"I was," he confessed, "but I couldn't help thinking of you alone here and...well," he stammered, "I... hell I worry about you."

And she loved him for it, though she refused to let him believe she wasn't absolutely independent. "I appreciate it Alex, I really do, but honestly...I am perfectly fine."

"Well then perhaps a perfectly fine woman wouldn't mind this." From the hallway he wheeled in a tea cart with "champagne" which, considering her condition, was actually sparkling cider, and a uniquely 'creative' selection of hors d'oeuvres he had fashioned in the kitchen.

"I think we should toast to your good health, and to the health of that little one," he said handing her a glass and gently placing his hand on her only slightly protruding stomach.

Genie couldn't decide if it was the gentle way he caressed her stomach or the tender look in his eyes, but she knew then exactly what she wanted. It had been too long in coming and she could no longer wait. Taking him by the hand she led him to the soft down covered bed.

Alex wasn't surprised. Physical expression of their love was inevitable, but it was up to Genie to make the first move.

They sat there silently looking into each other's eyes. He slowly loosened her robe and slipped it from her shoulders.

Though she didn't move a muscle, she began to tremble slightly. There was an excitement growing that she could not control. She was pregnant, yet felt like a virgin.

Alex placed his hands on her soft, freckled shoulders and leaning close he carefully pulled her to him until their lips met in a long loving kiss.

The smell of his cologne, the touch of his hands on her breasts, the soft secure way he kissed her made Genie weak. She threw her arms around him and lying back pulled him lovingly down on top of her.

Later, snuggled against Alex's firm body she slept, without nightmares, for the first time in weeks......

Her sweet reverie was suddenly interrupted by outrageous laughter from below. She would know that voice anywhere. Constance. Dressed in an absolutely stunning midnight blue sequined number, cut to her waist in the front, with absolutely no back Constance would always be Constance.

Genie could only chuckle, all must be right with the world, she thought, for even they had managed a sort of tenuous peace.

Of course, Constance had been overjoyed at the idea of Genie being pregnant with Richard's baby. She was certain that the turn of events would spell the end of the Alex-Genie relationship. But, after one last futile attempt to gain Alex's affection, she had finally moved on. These days an art director at the Tate was taking up most of her time.

"Enough of this," Genie scolded herself, "time to join the party," though raising her cumbersome body from her seat on the stairs was not easy.

"Hi there, need a lift?" said Alex coming up the stairs. He could not believe how beautiful she looked. "Pregnancy suits you," he joked. "We'll have to do this again sometime."

"Oh please," she said, "Can't you do it next time."

"Here," he said handing her a crystal cup, "Have some nogless eggnog. It's good for the tyke."

Genie could not believe how lucky she was. Alex loved her, she knew that, but more than that, he loved the baby. From the way he fussed and carried on no one in the world would believe that it wasn't actually his child.

"Mind if I share your perch," he said sitting on the step just below her, "Peter just called Jackie. It looks like he will be here for Christmas." A slight frown crossed his face.

"Do you think they will get back together?" She had only met Jackie's ex-husband once, but even then she got the distinct impression that he was still in love with Alex's sister.

"I don't know. I think it's up to Jackie. I guess we will just have to wait and see."

Genie could see he was concerned...brotherly tradition. She changed the subject. "Shall we mingle," she asked attempting once again to attain a standing position.

"Sure, in a moment. First I have something I want to ask you."

"Oh," she responded curiously. They had already decided to put off any permanent planning until after the baby arrived so she couldn't imagine what he had in mind.

"Gen, I've been thinking. Why don't we bring this little munchkin into a real family? I know we talked about this and decided to wait until...well later. But Gen, I love you, I love you both," he said gently touching her abdomen. "I don't want to wait." For a moment he faltered, but resolutely continued.

"Genevieve Lawrence," he said so seriously that he sounded almost imperious, "will you marry me?"

Before she could answer, Alex took her left hand and on her third finger placed a glorious teal green emerald ring. Surrounded by diamonds the beautiful clear, dark, blue green stone radiated in the candle light with the same blue green sparkle he saw in Genie's eyes.

Tears streaked her smiling face. She looked into Alex's soft hazel eyes and knew she would never know fear or loneliness again. "Yes," she said softly, "Yes I will marry you."

Epilogue

Alexandria, Va.   *December, 1990*

A thick blanket of new snow covered the ground. Peering out through leaded glass windows the General didn't really notice the heavy flakes floating lazily to the ground. Forecasters were predicting a blizzard, but his mind was elsewhere. He was reflecting, with considerable remorse, upon his failure to rescue the son of his long dead companion from the tyranny of the Hezbollah. It was his only regret. Regret he would soon put right. Admittedly, the mission had not gone according to plan, but the outcome had been most successful. And yet, he could not forgive himself this one failure.

Here, in his private domain, the world was warm and should have been comforting and forgiving, but until he finally accomplished that most important missing piece of his mission, his heart would never truly be at peace.

Birch logs crackled on the hearth radiating light and heat and security. "Brandy," he said to his guest. Slowly he turned away from the window to face the dark skinned man standing by the mantle. "It takes away the chill."

"No," said the other brusquely. "Perhaps later. Right now I do not feel the need."

"Have a seat then," ordered the General seating himself in his favorite old brown leather wing chair. "Let's get on with it. Tell me, have you heard anything?"

The Eagle shook his head solemnly, "No, General, and I don't think we will. The 'unfortunate demise' of Mr. Finch seems to have put an end to it."

"But you will continue to watch Templeton and the Lawrence woman, will you not."

"For as long as you like General, after all you are paying me... very well......"

"Thanks again to the untimely death of Finch," the General interrupted.

"Yes, thanks to Finch." He felt no remorse at Finch's death. Concerned only with the moment at hand, the Eagle was now working directly for the General. It was as good as working for anyone else. His services went to the highest bidder, for the present that meant the General. "As I was saying. I think you will have nothing to fear from them."

"I hope not, but if anything...well leaks. You will know what to do...correct?"

"Of course," the Eagle commented with masked sarcasm.

"And the others. That DuLac woman, and Kasarov."

"Ah, you mean Mr. and Mrs. Kasarov. No, you have no worries there either. Right now they are living in France, in Lyons I believe, but my sources tell me that they will be returning to Moscow any time now. It seems big changes are afoot and he is needed on the home front. And Ms. DuLac, excuse me Mrs. Kasarov, will be right there to cover the story. No, you don't need to worry; she is not interested in old news."

"Good, good," mumbled the General mindlessly fingering one new medal prominently displayed among the many other decorations he carried on his left chest.

"Is that it?" asked the Eagle

The General touched the multicolored striped ribbon and laughed out loud. "Can you believe it," he said, "I'm a god damn hero."

"Only in America could a man receive a medal for rescuing his own hostages." The Eagle was openly cynical.

"I don't know about that my friend, but I must say I love the irony of it. Of course, the Pentagon was never absolutely certain how I found the Russians and I guess they decided it was far easier to give me this medal than to try to explain that they didn't know what the hell was going on." He laughed again. "I know it didn't go exactly as I planned, but in the end...we all came out ahead. Eh?" After a bit of thought he amended his first statement. "Well maybe not all of us..." In his mind he reflected upon the reason he had summoned this ruthless mercenary to Washington.

The Eagle decided the time had come for that brandy. After holding the paper thin crystal snifter between his palms long enough for the potent drink to emit a tantalizing aroma, he took one large swallow nearly emptying the glass. "So General," he began, "Shall we get to the heart of the matter. Exactly why is it you wished to see me. Certainly not for surveillance reports."

"No, you are right. There is something else I wish to discuss with you." A spark of excitement shone in the old man's steel grey eyes. And for an instant, behind the pompous military facade, the Eagle saw strength worthy of his respect.

"Here," he said, "I want to give you something." The General stood and walked across the room to his hidden wall safe. From behind the Wyeth painting he extracted a plain manila envelope which he offered to the Eagle.

His hand had not yet released the document when, quite unexpectedly, mid transaction, he was struck with an overwhelming sense of déjà vu. So strong was the image of Finch, of a meeting just like this one that had taken place, what was it...years ago that he actually had to stop and catch his halting breath.

"General?" The Eagle wasn't exactly concerned, in any emotional sense, but he did think the old bastard might actually keel over and die right there in front of him. "General," he said again. "Can I get you anything? Are you..."

The General waved a hand to indicate he was alright, sputtered a little and took a large swallow from his glass.

Sitting back in his chair he breathed deeply then slowly lit one of a dozen, cherished, hand rolled Cuban cigars.

The Eagle waited patiently for the General's cue. No more was said about the incident. Both men acted as if nothing unusual had occurred. "This envelope is for you," said the General, again in full control. "Read it carefully."

The Eagle looked him straight in the eyes.

"You see," said the old man, thinking once again of the, still missing American hostages. Still determined to find the son of his long lost friend. "Rumor has it that our Russian friends have gone back on their bargain. They are no longer in touch with the Hezbollah. They were to have arranged for release of the Americans months ago, but there has been no word. I suspect they have washed their hands of the matter. Have you heard the same stories?"

The Eagle simply nodded.

"You know that my greatest concern has always been for our own people. I am willing to pay you quite handsomely to go back into the desert and reopen trade negotiations."

"And what will our bargaining chips be this time General?" The Eagle knew they couldn't go around kidnapping more diplomats.

"I have access certain weapons," said the General. "It is all right here," he added, "if you're interested that is."

The Eagle did not hesitate to reach for the envelope which he immediately opened and began to read. Slowly, so he would miss not one detail, he took in its contents. Then with a wry smile he shook the old man's hand confirming that they were back in business.

Acknowledgements

I would like to thank my wonderful friends in the MBYC book club for reading and supporting a much unpolished manuscript. Special thanks to Nikki Greene, Natalie Marinak, Mable Steepe, Barbara Hoey and Terry Smith for their patient editing and proofreading. Thanks also to everyone at BookbookBiz and to cover artist, Kib Prestridge.